WARNING

This book contains sexually explicit scenes and adult language. It may be considered offensive to some readers. This book is for sale to adults ONLY.

* * * * * * * * * * * * * * * *

Please store your files wisely where they cannot be accessed by underage readers.

ISBN-13: 978-1773501727
ISBN-10: 1773501720

Other books by Shyla Starr:

<u>Tenacious Billionaire BWWM Romance Series</u>

Adalia is too proud to accept help from the billionaire playboy, Trent Dawson. How long can she maintain her resolve? The bank is at her heels to repossess her business. To make matters worse, Adalia finds suspicious evidence of Trent's philandering ways. She must determine whether to trust Trent with the fate of her business and her heart.

<u>Elusive Billionaire Romance Series</u>

Billionaire Hendrick is trying to repair his company's image by putting in some volunteer work, building a school and hospital for the impoverished children in Africa. There, he meets a beautiful African American volunteer, Jocelyn. They hit it off right away but does she belong in his world?

<u>Lonely Billionaire Romance Series</u>

Tricia was hired to care for billionaire John's wife, who is dying. An unlikely romance emerges after his wife, Rebecca, gives John permission to pursue his happiness after she is gone.

<u>Ardent Billionaire Romance Series</u>

Deirdre doesn't know what to make of the gorgeous man that seems to be interested in her. His name is Parker Walters and he seems friendly enough. There is just something off about him. Why is he trying the hide the fact that he is the heir to his father's billion dollar software empire?

Fervent Billionaire BWWM Romance Series

Alexandra had never been with a white man before. She had seen William at the café before but she always kept her distance. It was unfortunate that their first chance meeting happened when she dropped her breakfast and spilled coffee all over his expensive business suit.

Audacious Billionaire BWWM Romance Series

Chante is torn between staying close to a man beyond her league, and fleeing from him to spare herself from a hopeless position. But she finds she is propelled into a place where she needs to confront her doubts and cast her fate aside to follow the dictates of her heart. Damned if she does and miserable is she doesn't, how will Chante face the events that will lead her to a place of pure happiness or to the pits of a broken heart?

Get the latest update on new releases from the author at:

https://shylastarr.com/newsletter/

This book contains all the stories of the "Persuasive Billionaire BWWM Romance Series"

1 - Love Invested

Stacey is trying to keep a handle on her life the best that she can. She is on the verge of losing her job and her apartment, while taking care of her sick grandmother. Her life takes an unexpected turn when she meets Charlie, who works for the construction company that is attempting to persuade her to move out of her home.

2 - Love Divested

After discovering that Charlie has a fiancée, Stacey's world has turned upside down. She cannot help but feel as if she is in over her head. Struggling with her job, her bills and her family, will Stacey be able to figure out how she can get her life straightened out?

3 - Love Reinstated

Stacey decides that she has to put Charlie behind her and move on with her life. As Stacey dates Tony and is pulled into his world, she slowly realizes that although she likes him, it might not be enough to brush aside her feelings for Charlie. Leaving everything behind, she lets herself get lost in the money and privacy that Tony brings to her.

4 - Love Confirmed

Stacey can't believe the turn of events in her life. After losing her grandmother and running away to Tony's private island, she was content to stick her head in the sand and forget her past. But a proposal from Charlie changes everything.

5 - Love Divine

Stacey must ensure she relaxes in order to keep her baby safe. But life is never that easy. Her new husband's father is bent on sabotaging their fledgling investment firm. To make things worse, her brother-in-law isn't content with just being in the background. Stacey finds herself wishing she could have the brothers patch things up.

Persuasive Billionaire BWWM Romance Series

Books One to Five

By Shyla Starr

Table of Contents

Book One – Love Invested

Chapter One

"THEY'RE ASKING for the eggs to be cooked again."

"What? Those are fine!"

"What do you want me to do about it, Brad? The customer is complaining. Just make them again, alright? He wants the eggs overcooked, apparently."

Brad took the plate from Stacey's hand and returned to his grill, grumbling loudly. Stacey wiped the sweat from her brow and turned around, getting ready to head back out onto the floor of *Papa's Grill and Diner*.

It was the middle of the day in mid-summer, which made the sweltering kitchen unbearable. Stacey was glad to leave the kitchen even if it meant dealing with a couple of jerk customers.

Back in the dining area, she looked around. She had only one couple in her section. They were older, with their shoulders hunched over and beady eyes pointed toward the kitchen. The woman hadn't touched her sandwich, probably waiting for the man to get his eggs back before digging in.

There was only one other waitress, Maria, working, and she was in the corner, texting on her phone. Their place wasn't exactly the hot spot of the city to eat during the best of times. During mid-day, it was more like a graveyard.

The woman motioned for Stacey to come over. She clenched her jaw, exhaled slowly and got ready for whatever ridiculous request the woman was going to make. This couple had been a hassle from the moment they were seated.

"How can I help you?" she asked, plastering a smile on her face.

The woman scowled, "Where are my husband's eggs?"

"They're making him a fresh batch right now."

"Tell them to hurry up!" the woman snapped.

The husband sat there silently, playing with the edge of his napkin. But he nodded at Stacey as if to tell her he better get his eggs soon.

Stacey scurried back into the kitchen. It was mind-numbing if she let it get to her. How long had she been working here now? Four years? It was supposed to be a pit stop before she moved onto bigger and better things. She had been there, scraping by, instead of returning to college or working on making something more of herself.

No use in thinking about that now.

Brad handed her a plate of freshly cooked eggs. She walked back to the table and placed it in front of the man and his wife.

The man wrinkled his nose and said, "This will do, I suppose."

Stacey clasped her hands together and inquired as politely as she could muster, "Would you like more coffee?"

They grunted, and she gave them a fresh pot, making sure not to add it their bill. She was sure they would want something for free out of the egg fiasco. By the time the couple left, Stacey was ready for a break.

In the break room, she slipped off her shoes and rubbed her feet, wincing. Her shoes were cheap, and it showed after standing in them for more than a couple of hours. Her feet were killing her.

She checked her phone next. There was a voicemail from her sister. It was a rare event that her sister reached out to her and she was filled with dread listening to the message.

"Stacey, hey. It's your sister, Allison," she added for clarification as if Stacey wouldn't know her own sister's name. "Listen, call me when you can? I have a question to ask you. Well, more of a favor? But I need to talk to you first. Thanks, bye."

Stacey sighed as the message ended. Her sister wanting a favor never led to anything good. *If she wants money, she can forget it.* There was no cash to give Allison. There were barely any funds for Stacey.

A small TV in the break room played the news. The image was grainy but she could just make out the weatherman talking about rain later on in the evening.

Great. She made a mental note to make sure the roof didn't leak all over everything when she got home from work. Last time it stormed, Stacey had to set out buckets to catch the drips.

She closed her eyes just for a moment. If she left them closed for too long, she would fall asleep on the spot. It felt as if there was always something to do. She finished one thing, and another task popped up in its place. Maybe that was how it would always be.

"Wake up, sleepyhead."

Stacey opened her eyes to see Amanda stepping into the break room.

"You work today?" Stacey asked, surprised, wondering why they needed another waitress working during such a slow day.

"Nah, I left my wallet here last night in my locker. I was so tired after closing, it just slipped my mind." Amanda walked over to her locker and glanced back at Stacey. "You okay?"

"Yeah, just tired."

"Looks dead here. I'd be tired too," Amanda remarked as she opened up her locker.

"Yeah, it's pretty boring."

Amanda paused in front of her open locker, grabbed her wallet, and tucked it into her purse. When she turned back around, she had a strange look on her face. Stacey sat up straighter.

"What?"

Amanda hesitated and then sat down on the wooden bench. Stacey could see the purple circles under Amanda's eyes. Although they both worked full time at the restaurant, Amanda also attended college. She was probably just as tired as Stacey.

"I heard something. Probably just a rumor. I don't know. I wasn't going to tell anyone but—"

But I know how much you need this job was the unfinished thought there.

"What is it?"

Amanda lowered her voice, "Heard at a class yesterday this place might close down."

"Who was talking about that in your class?" Stacey scoffed. "Especially about our little place."

"Well, I mentioned that I work here. I was in my accounting class, and we were doing a project. This kid in my group said that I should look for other work because this place is going to shut down. Especially with all those investment groups coming in here trying to revive the area."

Stacey scowled. Her neighborhood, which was predominantly black, had indeed been crawling with rich white men in suits lately. All of them wanted to knock down and rebuild her section of town. They wanted to make it new and fresh again. They wanted it to appeal to the elite, which naturally meant getting rid of anyone who was low income.

"Thanks for the heads up, Amanda, but one kid in a college class saying we're going to close doesn't mean we are going to."

"Maybe. But this place is always dead. How long do you think we can stay open like this?" She stood up. "Don't tell anyone I told you, okay? I'll see you later."

Stacey watched her go, suddenly feeling wide awake. Even though she had sounded confident to Amanda that they weren't going to close, the girl had a point. Business had been awful lately. How long would they really be able to stay open?

Maybe it was time to find another job. The only reason Stacey had stuck around there for so long was how flexible the hours were. Few places would accommodate Stacey like that. But if this place was going to close, she may have to put some applications out.

She sighed and rubbed her forehead, fending off a headache. Just another worry to add to her long list.

Chapter Two

Stacey closed the front door of her apartment softly. She crept into the living room. The TV was on, showing the weather report. Apparently, Stacey wasn't going to be able to escape from bad weather news today. The rain was rolling in. She was glad that she had beaten it in time.

"That you, Stacey?" came a voice from one of the other rooms.

Stacey headed down the cramped hallway and stopped in front of one of the doors. She pushed it open a little and peered inside. Her grandmother, Tina, was sitting up in her bed with a magazine in her lap. Her lamp was on next to her, giving her just enough light to read by. Her eyes looked a little glassy, and her fingers were curled around one of the magazine pages. Her mind had been slowly deteriorating for a couple of years now. Stacey wondered how long Tina had been staring at the same page.

"Hey, I figured you'd be asleep."

"Couldn't sleep. Joints ache. It's going to rain, isn't it?"

"Yeah, it is."

Stacey came into the room and sat down at the edge of the bed. The room smelled like mothballs mixed with perfume. There was no point in telling her that she had left the TV on. Tina would have probably forgotten she was even out in the living room at one point.

"How was your day, doll?"

"It was okay. How are you feeling? Were you okay here by yourself?" Stacey asked.

Tina smiled and replied, "Just fine, dear. Although I wouldn't mind some warm milk."

"Let me get you some," Stacey said as she got up.

She was almost at the door when Tina spoke, "Oh, someone came to the door today."

"You answered?" she asked with a sigh. "You know you should be resting, not answering doors."

"Well, he wouldn't go away."

"What did he say?"

Tina's face scrunched up as she tried to remember. Stacey watched with a stab of pain in her chest. It was so hard watching her grandmother like this. It was even harder leaving her alone during the day while she worked. She could barely afford doctors and medicine, so there was no way she could pay for a nurse or an assisted-living facility.

"I don't know, dear. What were we talking about?"

"You wanted warm milk."

"Ah, yes. That would be lovely," Tina replied and smiled at her.

Stacey returned the smile and went back to the living room. She turned off the TV and continued to the front door. There was a small table beside it where she had tossed her keys and hadn't noticed the envelope. It had her name typed on it.

Stacey didn't even have to open it to know what it was going to be. She picked it up and debated just throwing it out without reading it. But that could come back and bite her in the ass.

As she warmed up the milk, she opened up the letter and scanned it quickly. It was the same old shit. They were trying to vacate everyone from the building so they could knock it down. They probably wanted to build some high rise or something in its place.

This time, they were offering money. But it wasn't enough. Sure, they could take the money and could go. But between Stacey's debts, taking care of her grandmother, and then trying to find a place that was cheap enough for them to live, this money ultimately didn't help. There was no other place in the city that Stacey could afford that wasn't in a seedy neighborhood or by some noisy factory.

A headache she had been fending off all day came back with a vengeance. The panic that she tried to fight off at the same time also threatened to return. Where would they go? She didn't want to live in the slums. She didn't want to put her grandmother in danger. On top of that, if the restaurant did close, she would be out of a job.

"When it rains, it pours," Stacey mumbled and shoved the letter back into the envelope.

She took the warm milk to Tina who was still on the same page of the magazine. She put it next to her on the night table and adjusted her pillows.

"Need anything else?"

"Oh, someone came to the door for you today," Tina repeated.

"Did they?"

"Yes. They were from that business group. The construction group."

Stacey pretended as if this was new information for her. "What did they want?"

"Just about the area. About improving it," Tina said, settling in with her milk.

Stacey doubted they would have told her grandmother anything. It was common knowledge, even among the people working in the company that hovered around there, that her grandmother was forgetful and not well. At least they had the decency not to harasses her.

"Well, thanks for letting me know."

Tina smiled and looked back down at her magazine. Stacey studied her for a few seconds and then slipped out of the room quietly. Sometimes, Tina forgot that anyone was there and would be startled by Stacey speaking. Best to leave her alone.

Back in the kitchen, she made herself a sandwich and sat down at the tiny dining room table. Then she remembered it might rain. Leaving the sandwich, she pulled buckets out of the closet and put them down where the roof sometimes leaked when it rained. With that finished, she was finally able to eat.

The rain started when she was halfway through her meal. It was a mean summer storm that rolled through hard. The lights flickered at one point, and Stacey wondered idly if they were going to lose power. She finished her sandwich, washed the plate, and sat down in the living room.

She could hear Tina snoring. Warm milk always helped her sleep, and once that woman was dozing, there wasn't much that could wake her. Stacey listened to the rain pounding against the roof. There was a soft dripping noise from the kitchen which meant the roof was leaking a little.

Not for the first time, Stacey tried to talk her way through the scenario of accepting the money and vacating the apartment complex. Surely, there had to be some place to move that was decent and affordable.

If the restaurant closed down, maybe she could work part-time at another restaurant at night and find a better job during the day. She had very little experience outside of waiting tables. But it wouldn't hurt to try to find an office job. Someplace that would give her work from nine to five so she could get extra hours during the evenings.

Right before Stacey fell asleep on the couch, she remembered she forgot to call her sister back. But she

was too tired. Her sister would have to wait until the
morning.

Chapter Three

After Stacey got out of the shower the next morning, she stopped in front of the floor-length mirror. She had originally bought it when she had been determined to lose weight, thinking it would have been a great way to see the changes in her body.

Now, as she stared at herself, she found nothing had changed. While she normally wore her black curly hair in braids or Bantu knots for work, she liked to keep it natural. Her body weight was also unchanged. The old *compliment* she always got reared its head.

"You're pretty for a plus-sized girl."

As if she wasn't pretty enough for a regular-sized woman. Just plus-sized. She groaned a little and considered getting rid of that damned mirror. She was dressing for work but wasn't looking forward to the double shift today. *Must get some coffee.*

Stacey yawned and went to check on Tina while she made her cheap coffee. Tina was still fast asleep and could stay like that for hours. Stacey moved the magazine from the bed and watched her sleep.

Her parents had died when she was young. They were killed in a car accident on the way back from a party. Stacey's grandparents had taken both her and Allison in. The elderly couple had done what they could to care for the girls. When her grandfather died from cancer two years ago, and Tina also grew ill, Stacey knew that she would take care of her as long as she could.

Now, watching her sleep, she felt guilty again at leaving her at home. Was Stacey doing a good job taking care of her grandmother? Barely scraping by, living in this shitty apartment—surely, there had to be more she could do to improve things.

Stacey blinked back tears. Growing emotional right now before work did her no favors. She would figure something out. She was a fighter, just like Tina.

She closed the front door behind her and locked it. Then she headed down the hallway. As she got close to the stairs, one of the apartment doors opened. Leon, a younger boy who had dropped out of high school a month ago, slouched in the doorway.

"Good morning," Stacey said.

"Hey. Those pricks were here again yesterday."

"Yeah, I heard."

He shook his head and then said, "They offered us money this time."

"Well, they really want us out of here. Prime real estate we're sitting on here."

"Mom says we should hold out for more money." He frowned. "Where're we gonna go, though? You even said it yourself. This place is the best we can get without ending up in the ghetto."

"Well, we'll figure it out, Leon," Stacey said trying to sound positive.

Leon narrowed his eyes at her as if he didn't believe her and shrugged. "I guess."

He slunk back into the apartment and closed the door without another word. Stacey felt bad about brushing him off, but she didn't know what else she could say. The last thing she wanted to do was tell him that he should be worried, and have his mom freaking out on her. Holding out for more money was a good idea, but it still didn't help them figure out where they were going to go.

She went down three flights of stairs. The elevator had been broken for two months now. Stacey doubted that it was going to be fixed at this point. It was just another thing the owners could use to try to get them to move out.

She reached the lobby, for lack of a better word, of the apartment complex. An old desk sat in one corner, left over from the days where there apparently used to be a security guard. There had never been one the entire time Stacey lived in the complex. Yet the desk remained as if to remind everyone that the place used to be nicer than its current state.

The tiles were cracked in places and in need of repair, but Stacey didn't notice them anymore. The mailboxes were against the other side of the wall. She had forgotten to check the mail last night and wanted to grab it before she left for the day.

Yet she hesitated. Leaning against the mailboxes was a man, and he had his phone out. It wasn't one of the old flip phones she normally saw around here but a smartphone with a giant screen. It looked more like a tablet than a phone. Expensive.

Her eyes scanned the figure in front of her. He was decked out in a suit that looked as if it was perfectly tailored to his body. There wasn't an inch of fabric that wasn't fitted to his movements. His tie was neat and looked expensive. His hair was slicked back, and he had fine stubble along his jawline.

Even though the man was undeniably handsome, there was no way that Stacey didn't know where he was from. From his suit to his phone to the casual way he was leaning against the mailboxes—*her* mailbox, she realized—it was clear that he was part of the construction company trying to make her and everyone else vacate the property.

Stacey cleared her throat. The man didn't look up. Irritation swept through her. She didn't bother to clear her throat this time.

"You're in my way," she announced loudly.

This finally got the man's attention. He looked up from his stupidly large phone, and he gave her an embarrassed smile.

"Sorry, miss." He moved to the side, allowing her access to her mailbox.

Stacey opened it up and slipped out two letters. She glanced at them and knew they were about overdue bills. The man was staring at her as if she was some sort of exhibit. It angered her.

"What? Don't have poor people in your company?"

The man's eyes widened slightly in surprise. *Take that*, Stacey thought vindictively. She was just in the mood to tell off anyone working for that construction company.

"My company?" he finally replied.

"Yeah, Lexington & Albert Construction. A subsidiary of Albert Investment Corp."

"You've done your homework."

"I try to when a company sweeps in here trying to kick us out of our homes," Stacey said, slamming the small mailbox door shut.

"Ah, well, that's not exactly it—"

"Please," she said, holding her hand up as if to ward him off. "Not this morning. I don't need to hear this bullshit speech yet again while I'm on the way to work."

A strange look flickered over the man's face. It looked almost as if he was amused. Of course, he was. What else could be more hilarious than watching the tenants of this small apartment complex struggle under the mighty foot of this construction company? It just irritated her more.

"You know, you and all your other companies that are circling around this area might think it is going to be great to rebuild here. But you have no idea what it will be like for us," she continued, pointing to herself and the stairs, "to find a place that is as decent as this."

"Decent?" the man scoffed. "No offense, miss, but I've seen what this place looks like. We're offering everyone here a fair sum to vacate."

"And go where? The slums? The ghetto? The only other place we can all afford is at the far end of the city, and you know what that's like." Stacey caught herself and shook her head. "Never mind. You probably don't. You're kicking us out to a section of the city that will eat us alive. All we have going for us are these shitty apartments. No, you're right. They aren't much. They're busted up, broken and tarnished. But they're ours. They keep us as safe as they can and keep us going. Think about that the next time you come down here to bother us."

She breezed past him without another word. Their shoulders brushed against each other as she walked by him. An electric shock fired through her all the way down to her toes. Stacey paused for just a moment to process what she had just felt. She shook it off, opened the front door of the apartment complex, and went out onto the street, slamming the door behind her.

"Two coffees. Need anything else?" Stacey asked the elderly couple that had just sat down.

"No, not yet. Thank you, dear," the woman replied.

Stacey smiled and nodded, leaving them alone. She was on autopilot today. The restaurant was busier than usual for lunch, which was a welcome distraction from her own feelings. She couldn't help but regret how she had spoken to that man in the lobby. It wasn't that she worried about hurting his feelings. She was worried that he was going to go back to his boss and complain that the people in the apartment complex were openly hostile. What if it made things worse?

Stacey had let her irritation and emotions get the better of her. She had to keep them in check next time. Lashing out at some low-ranking company official wasn't going to fix anything.

In the kitchen, Amanda was yawning and pouring herself a cup of coffee. Amanda's fingers shook slightly, but noticeably.

"Girl, how much caffeine are you drinking?" Stacey asked her.

"Way too much," Amanda quipped, looking down at her hands. "I'm studying for a major biology test as well as putting all my work hours in."

Stacey leaned over and plucked the cup out of Amanda's hands.

"Hey, give that back!" Amanda protested.

Stacey shook her head. "Cutting you off. You're going to give yourself a heart attack. You're too young for that."

"Fine, fine." Amanda yielded and then leaned forward. "Maria called in sick today."

Stacey groaned, "Really?"

"Yeah. Just you and me until closing." She patted Stacey on the back. "You might want to keep that cup of coffee for yourself."

Stacey watched her go and looked down at the coffee. Gingerly, she took a sip and cringed. It was bitter and had been on the burner for too long. She dumped it out and began to make a new pot. She was surprised the elderly couple she had just served wasn't complaining.

"Stacey, hey. There you are."

She turned around to see her boss poking his head into the kitchen.

"William! Hi. Good morning."

"When the customers are settled in, will you come see me?"

"Sure," Stacey replied.

William, the owner of *Papa's Grill and Diner,* nodded and ducked out of the kitchen. A lump formed in Stacey's throat. She couldn't remember the last time he had wanted to speak to her directly. Whatever it was, she knew it wasn't going to be good.

The next few hours dragged by. Even though they were a bit busy for once, Stacey dwelled on whatever William wanted to discuss. By the time her break rolled around, her stomach was a knot of tightly wound anxiety.

She paused for a moment outside his office door, listening to hear if anyone else was in there, but there was just silence. She knocked twice and heard him tell her to come in, to which she obliged. The office, like the rest of the restaurant, had a theme that wasn't quite as identifiable as other places. It was as if William had tried to create a family friendly place with a western theme, but a few years ago thought that adding a few art-deco modifications would be a good idea. Now, the place looked like a fevered dream of the worst sort.

His office had the same sort of feel. Behind his desk was a giant cowboy hat on the wall. Yet the desk itself was modern-looking. There was hay in the corner that should have been swapped out two weeks ago. The paintings on the wall were sleek and full of silver lines and dark shapes.

"Close the door and have a seat," William said to her.

Stacey closed the door which only increased her anxiety, and sat down across from him. William was a very thin man who looked more like an accountant than a restaurant owner. His glasses were taped in the middle and rested on the edge of his nose. He was balding but tried to cover it up with a terrible comb-over. His suits were always a size too big for him. Even today, the cuffs of his shirt seemed to swallow up his hands. For a moment, Stacey pictured the man from this morning and how well his own suit fit compared to William's.

"I won't take up too much of your break."

"Oh, that's alright. Everything okay?" Stacey asked nervously, fiddling with a ring on her finger.

William pursed his lips and then leaned forward a little, "I wanted to tell you first. You've been here the longest, and it only seemed fair."

"You're closing, aren't you?" she blurted out.

William looked surprised and pushed his glasses higher up his nose. He blinked twice. Stacey waited for him to confirm what she already knew had to be true.

"Yes," he finally said.

It felt as if someone had punched her in the stomach. More bad luck upon bad luck. Her shoulders slouched forward, and she closed her eyes for a couple of seconds.

William continued, "I'm selling. You've noticed, I'm sure, how we haven't been doing too well. I'm bleeding money here, Stacey. I thought this place would be bigger than what it is. Ten years ago, who knows," He shook his head. "A decade is a good run. Especially for a family-owned restaurant."

"Who's buying this place?"

"Griffins."

"The restaurant chain? The ones that have an arcade where parents can shove their kids during meals?"

"Yes. They're knocking this place down—"

"And rebuilding," Stacey finished with a sigh. "Makes sense."

William took off his glasses and rubbed his eyes. "I know it's hard. You've been here the longest. I wish things would have turned out differently."

"How long do I have?"

"A month. We close in thirty days."

"A month," Stacey repeated. "Longer than I thought."

"I know once word gets out, everyone will quit. I'll give you as many hours as you want, Stacey, to cover for how short staffed we will be. I'll give you a recommendation letter for future jobs. I know it won't be easy," he said as he cleared his throat. "I know that Tina is ill, and this job gave you the flexibility to be with her when you could. I'm sorry."

"Well, thanks for letting me know first. It means a lot." She stood up quickly, suddenly desperate to get out of that small, strange office.

William nodded and said something, but she didn't hear him. She turned around and left with a wave, anxious to leave. Then she marched down to the bathroom in the break room and closed the door behind her tightly.

She fumbled for the light switch and stared at herself in the mirror. She wasn't sure exactly how she was feeling right now. Crappy, obviously. Panicked, certainly. Anxious, without a doubt. It felt as if the walls were closing in on her, and escape was impossible.

They were going to lose their home and end up in the slums or worse. Stacey was going to be out of a job at the end of the month if she didn't find something quickly. Her head throbbed with the promise of another headache. It was just one bad thing after another.

Amanda had told her, hadn't she? Just yesterday. Stacey had been so quick to blow her off, but she had been right. This entire section of town was going to be renovated. It was going to leave Stacey floundering, it would leave her in the dust.

Chapter Four

By the time work was done that night, Stacey would have given anything to sink into a hot bath until the water turned cold. But the bus was delayed in traffic due to a two-car accident on the road. She didn't get home until close to midnight.

The apartment complex was as quiet as a mouse by the time she reached it. There were only a few lights on. She climbed up the stairs to her home and looked around. The TV was off at least, which meant she hadn't been paying for that all day. Stacey slipped her shoes off with a sigh and went to check on Tina.

She was fast asleep, snoring a little. Stacey watched her sleep for a couple of minutes. She tried to digest what it would be like moving Tina to a new place and finding a different job. There were changes ahead—yet were any of them going to be positive?

Stacey went to her own room. It was small and could barely fit her bed, a dresser, and that mirror she detested. She changed into her pajamas and curled up in bed.

She had been anxious and thought she would be up all night with worry. But exhaustion won out, and she fell asleep in a few minutes. She had forgotten to brush her teeth.

<<◇>>

"There you go," Stacey said to her grandmother. "Do you want to read your magazine?"

"Not yet. I think I'll relax here for a few minutes."

"Terrific, I'll relax with you."

She sat down next to Tina and stared out at the area in front of them. Stacey had the day off, thankfully, and she wanted to spend it with Tina. There was a small yard at the back of the apartment complex that served as a garden or play area for the residents. Tina liked to sit in the sun and admire the view. It wasn't much of a view, Stacey secretly thought, but it made Tina happy and that was all she cared about in the end.

There was a breeze today which helped ward off the heat. They were under a tree which offered shade as well. Stacey had brought a book, but she wasn't sure if she would be able to focus on it today. Tina closed her eyes and hummed.

There was a sprawl of garden in front of them. A few of the residents tended to it although it looked badly in need of watering. Once they got the notices to vacate, the garden had fallen by the wayside, like so many other things it seemed. Two of the younger kids from the complex were climbing a tree on the other side of the park.

"Nice, isn't it?" Tina asked.

"Yeah. Very pretty," Stacey replied.

"What's bothering you?"

The question surprised Stacey. She had thought she had been masking her inner turmoil well enough to hide it from her grandmother. Tina seemed to sense this and smiled at her a little.

"Stacey, I have known you since you were just a little thing. I can tell when things are bothering you."

She was on the fence about how much to share with her grandmother. She didn't want to worry her. It was also easy to confuse her with too many details or things to remember. Sometimes, they would be mid-conversation and Tina would forget what they were discussing.

She didn't get a chance to reply. Tina spoke up again.

"Is it the man who came to the door yesterday?"

Stacey was surprised that she still remembered. "Yes."

"They want us out of here, don't they?" When Stacey nodded, Tina clicked her tongue against the roof of her mouth. "We'll figure it out."

"Yeah, we will."

Tina wrinkled her nose a little. "They want to rebuild the city, don't they?"

"Yeah. Make this area better for the rich folk."

"It's because we have the ocean over there," she replied, gesturing over to the west. "This area has too much potential. I assumed it would be sooner or later that we would get the interest of profit-seeking companies."

Stacey hadn't been to the ocean in ages. Even though they were so close to it, she had no interest in trying to find a bathing suit she felt okay in. Last time she had gone to the shore was back in high school where her boyfriend at the time had made such a cruel remark about her weight that sometimes it still bothered her.

"Yeah, you're right."

Tina opened her magazine and looked down at it. Stacey could see that her grandmother had lost interest in the conversation. She didn't want to press it further. She opened her own book, but the words seemed to float in front of her eyes without making sense.

It was then that a cry came out from the tree across the garden. Stacey looked up. One of the kids who had been playing was at the bottom of the tree, shouting up. A panicked voice was shouting back.

"Can you stay here alone for a second?" Stacey asked Tina, who nodded.

She hurried over to see what the fuss was about. As she got closer, she saw that the two kids were Zack and Kevin. They were brothers who lived on the second floor with their mom. She worked long hours, so she probably wasn't home.

"Hey, Zack," Stacey said to the first boy. "What's wrong?"

"Kevin is stuck," he said, pointing with his thin finger up to the tree.

"What?"

"Help me!" Kevin wailed as if he was going to fall to his death at any moment.

Stacey went to the base of the tree and peered up. High above her, she could see Kevin. He was clinging to one of the branches. He was awfully high up, way higher than he should have been. She sighed inwardly.

"You're going to be okay, so don't panic. Just hang on, alright?"

Kevin wailed in reply. Stacey turned to look back at Zack.

"Why did he climb so high?"

"He said Mom was at work and couldn't yell at us, so he wanted to see if he could reach the top. But now he's stuck." Zack turned to face Stacey. "You have to help get him down! Mom will kill us if he falls and breaks his leg or something stupid."

"We'll figure something out," Stacey said and looked back up the tree.

Kevin was sniffling loudly. Zack was shouting encouraging remarks to try to convince him to climb down on his own. Staring up at Kevin, Stacey tried to think of a way she could get him down safely. There was no way she could climb up there. She'd end up flat on her ass on the ground.

"Trouble?" A voice came from behind.

Stacey turned around. To her chagrin, it was the man she had lectured in the lobby the other day. He was wearing a different suit and looked the same as before, dapper. He slipped his phone into the pocket of his suit jacket.

Before Stacey could stop Zack, he was bounding up to the man and was telling him about Kevin being stuck up in the tree. The man went over to assess the situation. Kevin cried back in reply.

"I'll get him," the man said abruptly. "It's a manageable climb. The kid is just afraid to come back down."

"He could break his leg if he fell from that distance," Stacey said pointedly.

The man flashed her a grin. "Well, he won't fall then, will he?" He turned to look at Zack. "You said his name is Kevin?"

"Yes, sir."

"Kevin?" he called up the tree as he shrugged out of his suit jacket. "My name is Charlie. I'm coming up to get you, okay?"

Kevin made a little whimpering noise in response. Charlie's jacket hit the ground, and Stacey cringed. She was sure that jacket alone was hundreds if not thousands of dollars yet Charlie barely noticed as it fell onto a pile of dirt.

Before she could caution him, he began to scale the tree. For some reason, she had expected his climbing to be dismal, but he managed with ease. In what felt like a matter of moments he was halfway up the tree.

"Be careful," Stacey called up. The last thing she needed was the two of them toppling down to the ground.

She could hear Charlie talking to Kevin in a low voice. He was trying to soothe the boy. Next to her, Zack bounced nervously on the balls of his feet.

There was a shifting noise, and for one awful second, she swore the entire branch was going to crack underneath their weight. But Charlie was shimmying down the tree now, holding Kevin tightly with one arm.

Climbing down took longer than going up. After ten minutes, they landed safely on the ground. Charlie released Kevin, and Zack promptly went over and pushed his brother.

"Idiot! Mom would have flipped out!"

Stacey separated the two boys before they could start fighting. "Stop it, you two. Go inside. Wait for your mother to get home, okay? No more climbing trees for either of you." She hesitated for a moment. "And don't forget to thank Mr. Charlie for saving your miserable necks."

The boys mumbled their thanks. Both looked embarrassed for their stupidity. With an extra thank you from Kevin, they took off across the garden back toward the apartment. Stacey could see Tina flipping through her magazine from where she stood. She turned back to Charlie.

"Thank you for your help. I'm so sorry, but your shirt is dirty," she pointed out.

He had been wearing a white dress shirt underneath his suit jacket. There were dirt smears from the tree along the sleeves. He tried to brush them off, but they didn't budge.

"I'll clean it later," Charlie said with a shrug.

Stacey bent over and picked up his suit jacket. She thrust it toward him, trying to avoid his gaze. He took it from her and slipped into it. She wondered why he would wear it when it was so warm out today.

"Good thing I happened by," he said as he finished adjusting his jacket. "Kid would've been stuck up there for a while."

"We would have figured something out," Stacey said, automatically defensive.

Charlie grinned at her. It was a lop-sided grin, one that looked as if he was in on a private joke. Even if he did help her out with Kevin, he still worked for Lexington & Albert.

"Why are you hanging around here, anyway?" she asked.

"Business."

"Business," she repeated coldly.

"I don't think I caught your name?"

"That's because I didn't tell it to you."

Charlie grinned again. Her chest tightened at the sight of it, and she looked away from him over to her grandmother. It infuriated her that she found him attractive and charming.

"I need to get going," she said, determined not to look at him again. "Thank you again for helping Kevin."

As she turned around, eager to escape the way he made her feel, Charlie said, "It's Stacey, right?"

She turned back in surprise, "How did you know that?"

"The boy told me. Up in the tree. He said you were going to help him and he was glad you were around."

Stacey shrugged. She didn't know what to say in reply. Anything else could possibly drag out the conversation, and she wanted to put some distance between her and this fellow with his fancy suit and inviting grin.

"See you around, Stacey," he called after her.

She scowled but kept on walking.

Chapter Five

By the time Stacey made it to work the next day, the other employees had been told that the restaurant was closing at the end of the month. Three people quit on the spot, leaving them just as short-staffed as William had predicted. Her five-hour shift quickly turned into a ten-hour one.

She was by herself until Amanda came into work that evening. When Stacey saw her, she dashed over and gripped her arm.

"Please tell me you aren't quitting just yet. I swear, if you do, William will have me work every day, all day until we close."

"I'm not leaving," she promised. "I'm on this sinking ship with you."

Stacey sighed in relief, "Great. At least someone is sticking around."

"I have a job lined up at the end of the month already. My friend's dad needs someone to work as a receptionist in his real estate office."

"That's great. I'm glad you have somewhere to go."

"What about you? Any ideas?"

"No. Not yet, anyway."

"I'll let you know if I hear of anything you'd be a good fit for." She put her hair up in a ponytail. "I should head out there."

Stacey trailed after her, lost in thought. She needed to start looking for work, but how, when she was pulling double shifts? It would be a disaster to find herself unemployed at the end of the month. She was so preoccupied about her work situation that she didn't notice until she went over to take a new table's drink order that her customers included Charlie.

He was sitting at the table along with two other men. One of the men looked ancient. His face was lined with wrinkles, and he was hunched over in the booth, staring at the menu. The other man was younger and was sitting very stiffly. He had red hair that was askew from the wind outside. He flattened it down when he saw Stacey approach. Then there was Charlie who had sat alone on the other side of the booth.

His hair wasn't slicked back and his clothes were a bit more casual than the last two times she had seen him. When he saw her, he smiled brightly as if they were old friends. She hoped that he would pretend he didn't know her.

Stacey's heart raced unexpectedly. Why should she care that Charlie was there, in her restaurant? He was nothing to her. She decided to be professional and simply asked the party what they wanted to drink. Charlie ordered water while the other two men ordered tea.

She left quickly, hoping they wouldn't notice her blushing. She had no idea why she should be embarrassed. Despite her best efforts to avoid eye contact, she glanced back at the booth on the way to the kitchen.

Charlie was watching her go. Under the table, he wiggled his fingers at her to say hello. She felt her face flush even deeper and turned away. What was that guy's deal, anyway? She had made it clear from their first meeting that she thought he was a slime ball. Even if he was good looking, that was no excuse.

She almost ran into Amanda who was on the way out of the kitchen. *Good looking?* Since when had she even looked at Charlie close enough to think that he was good looking? He was probably some low-level grunt at that construction company, determined to kick everyone out of their homes. It didn't matter what he looked like. He was the enemy.

When she returned to serve the drinks, she avoided looking at Charlie completely. Stacey could feel his eyes on her as she took their food orders. Her hands were sweaty, and she almost dropped her pen.

It felt like they took ages to eat their meals once it arrived. Every time she stopped by to check on them, she wanted to hide her face. She couldn't pinpoint why she felt so weird around him but was relieved when Charlie and his companions left.

By that time, the so-called dinner rush had calmed down. Amanda had two tables in her section. Stacey heard the front door of the restaurant open. The hostess had quit this morning so Amanda and Stacey had been taking turns seating people but it wasn't as if there were a lot of customers, anyway.

She looked up to see who had come in when her mouth went dry. Charlie had come back inside and was sauntering up to her.

"Forget something?"

"Nope."

"What do you want then?" She crossed her arms as if to ward him off.

Charlie didn't seem to notice. "I was wondering if you'd go out with me."

Stacey stared at him, certain she hadn't heard him correctly. "What?"

"You and me," he gestured between the two of them, "on a date."

"Why would I want to go on a date with you?"

Charlie ran his fingers through his brown hair and smiled. "Right, you don't like me, is that it?"

"You work for the company that is trying to kick us out of our homes."

Something flickered across his eyes. It was only a second. Stacey wasn't even sure if it had really been there or if she had imagined it. But then his easy-going smile returned, and he shoved his hands into his pockets.

"Gonna blame a man for what his work is doing? I have bills to pay too. Wouldn't you do it if it meant you could make rent that month?"

Stacey hesitated. He had a point, but she still didn't want to admit it. He waited for her to reply, seemingly unbothered that it was taking her a few seconds to think it through. She inwardly groaned. Despite the racial difference, he was good looking, and she had been thinking about him lately, hadn't she? But how would that work out? They were worlds apart in many other things.

But it had been ages since she had been on a date. The last time she went on a date, the guy told her that they couldn't go anywhere public because he didn't want to be seen with a *'girl like her'*. Stacey didn't bother to ask if that meant her weight or her skin color because she left promptly afterward.

"Fine," she conceded.

"Great. What's your phone number? Does tomorrow night work for you?"

"No. I'm working a double."

"No problem." He handed her his phone—that giant smartphone again. "Put your number in there."

Stacey held the phone gingerly as if she was afraid she was going to drop it. The contact screen stared back at her. She supposed it was touch screen, but she had never had a phone like this in her life.

"I don't wanna hold this thing," she admitted. "Is this even a phone? Looks like you have a computer strapped to your ear."

Charlie laughed. The sound of his chuckle made her skin break out in goosebumps. He took the phone from

her, and she gave him her number verbally instead.
Then he slipped his phone into his pocket.

"I'll text you."

"Call me. I have to pay for texting."

"Alright. I'll call you then. We'll figure out a time.'
Goodnight, Stacey."

He nodded his head at her and turned around. She
watched him leave, feeling slightly shocked by the
sudden turn of events.

"Wow, who was that?" Amanda said, slinking up
next to her. "He had a cute butt."

When Stacey got home that night, she was looking
forward to curling up in bed and sleeping. Not only had
the day been long and her feet ached, but the fact that
she was apparently going on a date with Charlie had left
her with mixed emotions. She was surprised that she
wanted to go on a date with him and was looking
forward to it. Was it wrong of her to see him when he
worked for Lexington & Albert construction?

When she arrived at her apartment and went to
unlock the front door, she saw that the door was already
unlocked. With trepidation, Stacey opened it and looked
inside. She was expecting something terrible to have
happened.

Instead, her sister, Allison, was lying on the couch.
She had a bag of chips on her stomach and was
watching TV. When she saw Stacey, she sat up quickly.

"Finally, you're home."

"What are you doing here?" Stacey asked bluntly.

Allison got to her feet, brushing the crumbs off her t-shirt. Stacey hadn't seen her sister in a long time. They looked like polar opposites. Her skin was a bit lighter than Stacey's, and she was rail thin. Her t-shirt looked as if it wasn't even hers because it was too big on her. Knowing her sister, Stacey thought it was safe to assume that it wasn't Allison's t-shirt but one of her boyfriend's. Her sister's hair had been curled, and the tresses rolled down across her shoulders, framing her heart-shaped face.

"I tried calling you," Allison protested. "You never called me back."

"So, you just show up? That's nice of you to check in personally, but I'm fine. We're both fine," she said, meaning Tina.

"I need a favor."

"Of course, you do," Stacey mumbled as she walked past Allison to get to the kitchen.

Her sister trailed after her. The last person that Stacey wanted to see, to be honest, was her sister. It wasn't that she didn't like her. It was just that in her vast experience whenever Allison appeared, it meant nothing good for Stacey.

She grabbed a soda out of the fridge and turned to look at Allison. She didn't say anything. Instead, she watched Allison squirm under her gaze for a few seconds. Finally, she sighed.

"What's the favor?"

"I need to crash here."

Stacey threw her hands up. "No!"

"What? Come on, Sis."

"Why do you need to crash here? I thought you were dating what's-his-name."

"Steven? Things sorta crashed and burned on that front."

"You mean his wife found out about you," Stacey scoffed.

The look on Allison's face told her that she was right. Stacey shook her head again. Allison began to plead.

"Come on, Stacey. I need a place to sleep. For like a week or two. Just until—"

"Until what? You get a new boyfriend? Another rich guy to pay your way through life?"

"Well, yeah."

"You can't keep doing this, Allison," Stacey said. "This isn't how you should plan your future."

"Save the lecture, seriously. No offense but if I did things your way, I'd be, well, here." She gestured around the kitchen.

"You are here," Stacey pointed out, leaning against the counter.

An embarrassed look crossed her sister's face. She mumbled something that Stacey couldn't hear. Stacey sighed.

"I have no room for you here. I only have two rooms, and they're both in use."

"I know. I'm not asking for a room. I'll sleep on the couch. I'll watch Tina during the day. She won't be alone."

Ah, there it was. The trump card. Her sister had a good point. With Allison there, Tina wouldn't be alone during the day. It would help her out on her days off when she looked for work, too. It would be one less thing to worry about. Allison knew it as well by the victorious look on her face.

Stacey sighed. "Fine. Two weeks."

"Great!" Allison beamed. "I promise I won't be any trouble."

"I'm sure," Stacey replied dryly.

Allison opened the fridge and pulled out a soda of her own. "This is a big help, really."

"Yeah, well, you can help with Tina and do some chores around the apartment. For as long as we have it, anyway."

"That still going on, huh?"

"Yeah." Stacey briefly thought of Charlie and shook her head. "The restaurant is closing down too."

"No shit, really?" Her sister's eyes widened. "That sucks. I'm sorry. You'll find other work though. Have you told—"

"No. I don't want to worry Tina about that yet."

"I saw her earlier. She let me in. She's getting worse, isn't she?"

"Yeah."

Pain flickered across Allison's eyes and she ran her fingers around the rim of her soda can. "That sucks. Where are you guys moving if this place gets knocked down? It's the only decent housing in the area."

"Yeah, things aren't looking that great right now from any side."

Allison sucked in a breath, looking around the kitchen. "Well, we'll figure something out. Somehow."

Stacey nodded and watched as her sister headed back into the living room. She had a strange relationship with Allison. They had been close as little girls, but life eventually lead them separate ways. Now, they rarely saw each other and usually got on each other's nerves after only a day. Allison was content with sleeping with rich men and letting them spend money on her. Stacey thought her sister could do better and should aim higher. The differences in opinion had led to strife between them.

She rubbed the temples of her forehead and went to check in on Tina. Even though Allison said she was sleeping, she still wanted to see for herself. A quick look inside the room showed Tina curled up on one side, fast asleep. The lamp was still on, and Stacey turned it off. Her grandmother stirred slightly and mumbled a name.

"Macy—"

The name was Stacey's mother. The sudden mention of her mother seemed to suck the air from her. She tried not to think of her parents. It only dredged up happier memories, which seemed to hurt her now instead of bringing her pleasure.

She tucked the covers around Tina and left the room, closing the door gently behind her. She stood in the hallway for a few seconds. In her mind, she could see Macy tucking her in at night after reading her a bed time story. Thinking back on losing her parents and grandfather and seeing her grandmother so ill constricted her heart.

She could hear Allison talking to someone on the phone in the living room. Her voice was low and hushed. Normally, Stacey would want to know who her sister was talking to this late. But she was too weary to care. Instead, she turned around and went to her own room.

She changed into her pajamas and crawled into bed. However, unlike the other night where exhaustion had won out over her worries, Stacey found herself just lying there. She stared up at the ceiling. Distantly, she could hear thumping music. It was probably the Robinsons on the first floor. They threw parties sometimes. Everyone went along with it because calling the police did nothing except piss off the Robinsons.

The events of the day replayed in her mind. More specifically, Stacey kept picturing Charlie asking her out. Why in the world had she accepted? It seemed insane to accept a date from someone working at the company that wanted them to vacate. A man like him could get any woman he wanted. Why would he want her? Not only that, but she was terrible with dates. She never knew what to say. She was unsure of herself and felt ugly during most social engagements.

Stacey groaned in her pillow. She had let herself be drawn in by the handsome man in a well-tailored suit. Maybe Charlie wouldn't call. He would realize he had had a serious lapse in judgment and wouldn't want to go out with her in the end.

I have better things to worry about than a date, Stacey reprimanded herself. Losing her job and her apartment were bigger concerns than Charlie taking her out on a date. She was going to hit the pavement hard and fast. She would find a new job and put her feelers out for another place to live.

A cute man wasn't more important than that.

With that in mind, Stacey closed her eyes and willed herself to sleep.

Chapter Six

"We close at four in the morning," the man said, "since the city changed the law about the 2 a.m. close time. That work for you?"

Not really, Stacey thought as she stared at the man. But beggars can't be choosers. She had been hoping to find a place that closed by midnight. That would give her enough time to get home and catch some sleep before she could *hopefully* work a day job. Closing at 4 a.m. would put a fly in that ointment. But Stacey didn't have any job yet.

"Yes, that's fine."

The man nodded and wrote something down. Stacey cast a wary eye around the place. It was a rundown diner with a bar shoved in one corner. It was in a bad part of town. Even the man in front of her, who hadn't bothered to tell Stacey his name, smelled of cigarettes and whiskey and it was only noon.

Stacey had taken the interview, making sure not to turn her back on any opportunity. She had been flitting from one place to the next over the past week, with different restaurants all over town calling her due to her experience. She was confident she would land one of them.

It was the office jobs that were causing problems. Without any prior experience, no one wanted to waste their time in interviewing her. Stacey sent resumes anyway, spending evenings at the library to use their computer. It had required a couple of shift changes with Amanda, so she wasn't stuck at the restaurant until too late.

The man asked her a few more run-of-the-mill questions that Stacey answered. Then he stood up.

"Well, we'll give you a call."

"Thank you for your time."

The man grunted in reply and walked away, not bothering to show her out. Stacey truly hoped it didn't come down to working there. With one last look around the dismal place, she left.

The humid afternoon air smacked her in the face as she left the diner. The heat rolled off the pavement. Stacey hated summer. It was so hot that her clothes stuck to her in a matter of moments. The sun beat down on her relentlessly. Inside the restaurant, the AC didn't work very well, but at least it offered some relief from the sweltering heat. Her own apartment's AC was garbage, too. It felt as if there was no escape from the summer sun.

As she reached the bus shelter and tried to cool off, she glanced at her phone. No call. It had been a week since Charlie had asked her out and her phone had remained silent. Part of her was relieved. That was what she wanted, wasn't it? Yet she felt a tinge of annoyance too. Perhaps she had been banking on that date more than she had led herself to believe. *Best not to think about him,* Stacey reminded herself. She had to get to work now. For whatever reason, Charlie had backed out on their date.

Work was more of the same. *Papa's Grill and Diner* featured daily specials to drum up a little extra money before the place finally closed its doors. Because of the specials, there were more customers than usual. Stacey found herself flitting around from table to table, trying to make sure everything was taken care of properly.

By the time she got home, she was wiped out. Stacey couldn't help but notice that she was feeling like that every night now. Get up, go to work, come home, and sleep. There was very little time for anything else.

This time when she came home, Allison was on the couch. Her feet were propped up on the coffee table. She hastily lowered them when she saw Stacey. Tina was sitting in the armchair near the TV. There was an infomercial playing.

"What are you guys watching?"

Tina replied, "They're selling this gizmo that is supposed to whiten your teeth with one pass."

Stacey rolled her eyes. "Sure."

"We've been making fun of it," Allison chimed up. "You get only three channels, do you know that?"

"We get whatever the little antennae can pick up," Stacey grumbled, sitting down next to her sister.

Allison faintly smelled of crushed roses. Stacey knew the scent well. Her sister wore that perfume whenever she was trying to snag a boyfriend.

"Busy day?" asked Stacey.

If Allison noticed the insult behind Stacey's words, she didn't pay attention. "Yup. Tina and I went to the deli down the street earlier."

"Oh." Stacey was surprised. "How was that?"

"Good. I ran into Jake."

Stacey scowled and didn't reply right away. Jake was Stacey's last serious boyfriend. They had been together for two years before she caught him cheating. She knew he was still in the area but mercifully, she hadn't seen him.

"How is it that I haven't seen him since we broke up but you run into him right off the bat?"

Allison shrugged. "Don't know. Just did. He asked about you."

"Of course, he did."

"So, you never think about getting back together with him?"

The question took Stacey by surprise, and she shook her head. "No way. After what he did to me? No."

"Don't blame you. He looked good though."

Stacey was going to ask why Allison thought that when Tina turned around to look at the two of them.

"Your mother used to want one of these little kits," she said out of nowhere, pointing to the silly teeth whitening kit on the screen.

Allison wrinkled her nose. "Why?"

"Oh, she was a sucker for these things," Tina said in a rare moment of clarity. "Loved buying whatever gimmick rolled through on the television."

"Never pegged Mom as the type," Stacey replied, trying to remember if she had ever seen Macy buying things like this.

Tina turned back to the TV. Whatever train of thought she had was gone already. Allison glanced over at Stacey. That was when Stacey's phone went off in her purse. Surprised, she rummaged through her bag, trying to find it.

Maybe it's a job offer, she thought hopefully. Better than that—maybe a business office was calling her for an interview. A quick glance at the screen showed her that it wasn't a number she knew. She excused herself from the living room and stepped into her bedroom.

"Hello, this is Stacey," she said primly.

"Is it really? Sounds more like a formal little robot."

Charlie. She was taken aback by the sound of his voice on the other line. Smooth and deep, it sent tingles up her spine. Stacey had given up on Charlie, thinking he wasn't going to call her. To be suddenly talking to him made her nervous.

"Hey," was all she finally said and cringed at how lame it sounded.

"Hey," Charlie echoed, and Stacey could tell that he was poking fun at her. "Sorry it took so long for me to call you."

"It's fine," Stacey replied, desperate to sound as if she hadn't thought of him once since she gave him her number. "I've been busy."

"Yeah, I had something come up and had to leave town for a week."

"Everything okay?"

"Yeah, yeah," Charlie said quickly, brushing her question off, "but I'd still like to see you if you're interested."

"I am, sure," Stacey said before she could stop herself.

"Great. When are you free?"

"I'm free this Thursday. I'm supposed to be done work at seven. Is that too late?"

"No, that's perfect. I can pick you up at eight."

"Okay." It struck her that he knew where she lived because of where he worked, but she pushed the thought out of her mind.

"Wonderful. Looking forward to seeing you, Stacey. Have a good night."

She was going to ask where they were going and what they were doing but Charlie had already hung up. She huffed, staring at the phone. He could have asked, at the very least, what she wanted to do or given some indication what he had planned.

Part of her wanted to call him back and tell him to forget it. Yet all she could do was sit down at the edge of her bed. What was it about Charlie that made her still want to see him?

A knock at the door made Stacey shove her phone under her pillow as if it was a dirty magazine. Allison stuck her head inside.

"Everything alright?"

"Yeah. I think I can handle a phone call," Stacey snapped, on edge. If Allison knew she had a date this week, she would never hear the end of it.

"Geez, calm down."

"Sorry, long day. That was Amanda from work. She wanted to go out for a drink on Thursday. You'll be home?"

"Yeah, I can be here." Allison turned to go and then stopped. "It's good you're getting out."

"You make me sound like a hermit."

"You are, sorta. You work a lot and come home and sleep." She held up her hands as if to ward off Stacey's protests. "I know why. I get it. Just saying it'd be good to get out, too."

"Thanks."

Allison gave her a small smile and left, closing Stacey's door behind her. She sighed. She didn't want to tell her sister and make a big deal out of the fact she was going on a date. But to her sister, every date was a big deal. Probably because her sister had tons of money on the line when she tried to snag a boyfriend. Stacey just wanted someone who she could share her time and have fun with.

Before Stacey knew it, it was Thursday. She was back home and in front of that dreadful mirror. She had tried on five different outfits and was growing more frustrated by the second. Not only that but she was beginning to psych herself out the longer she fussed with her appearance. The dreaded question of *'why'* was rearing its ugly head.

It was something she had to ponder and have a backup plan ready just in case. Too many times had Stacey seen guys who liked her only because of her size and nothing else, as if she wasn't a person with real emotions and feelings. Strange, she never knew if men were with her because of some kinky *big woman* fetish, or if they genuinely liked her for who she really was deep inside.

In the back of her mind, she was worried she would have a nice time with Charlie and he would expect her to sleep with him on the first date. That also happened sometimes. Guys assumed she was easy to sleep with because she would be so desperate for attention from them.

She pulled off the dress shirt she had been trying on. It didn't help things that she had no idea where they were going. On top of that, she wanted to meet Charlie outside the apartment. Both Allison and Tina were home. If Charlie knocked, she would have to fend off questions from her sister.

Finally, she settled on a navy-blue dress with a simple necklace. She grabbed her purse, slipped into her high heels and slunk into the living room. Allison was with Tina in the kitchen.

"Alright, see you later!" Stacey yelled quickly and was out the door before her sister could see her outfit or ask any questions.

Even though night had fallen, it was muggy outside. Stacey waited outside the building. In the back of her mind, she was worried that he wouldn't show up. Her anxiety was getting the better of her. She felt like a high-school girl waiting for her boyfriend to show and take her out.

But right on time, a car pulled up to the curb. Charlie got out. Stacey exhaled. At least he showed up. He looked surprised at seeing her on the street.

"Hey, I could have knocked."

"Then you'd have to meet my family," Stacey said bluntly, "so this is fine."

"What, you think they'd scare me off?"

"No, I think you'd scare them off," she retorted.

Charlie smiled at her and opened the passenger door of the car. It was a nice car, nicer than anything else she had seen in this area. It was sleek and perfectly clean which was a far cry from the cars that normally cruise around her neighborhood.

As she slid into the car, she looked at Charlie out of the corner of her eye. He was wearing a white button-up shirt. The sleeves were rolled back a little because of the heat. Something about the white shirt and the way it looked on him made her heart skip a beat. His hair wasn't slicked back, and it gave him an almost boyish charm. She could smell his cologne as she sat down.

He got in the driver's seat. "You look beautiful," he said to her.

Stacey instantly let her nerves get the better of her, and before she could stop herself, she was rambling. "Well, I wasn't sure where we were going, if it was somewhere formal or not. So, I tried to find something in the middle, if that makes sense, so no matter where we go, it'd be okay." She cut herself off before she could say anything embarrassing. She wished she could just smack herself when she rambled on like that.

But Charlie didn't seem to notice. Instead, he laughed a little. "I should have told you, shouldn't I? It's a place on the beach. But you're dressed perfectly. Promise."

Stacey smiled weakly at him, still trying to quell her nerves. Now she was worried about finding things to talk about. They would have to fill the silence in the car ride as well as dinner. That was a lot of talking. Why the hell was she so nervous? She had told this guy off in the lobby and by the tree without a problem. Now they were on a date, and she was stumbling over herself like a schoolgirl.

But Stacey didn't need to worry. Charlie seemed to sense her nervousness and took charge of the conversation. He spoke a little about where they were going to eat and then about the beach. When he started telling her how he had been at last year's summer festival, the ice broke. The summer festival at the beach was always crowded and a bit of a mess. Almost the entire city turned out for it at some point. People got drunk and rowdy. College kids would make trips out of it since they were on break. Everyone had a story about the summer festival.

By the time they arrived at the restaurant, the nervousness Stacey felt subsided. Charlie had her laughing most of the drive, and her anxiety had mostly left her. When she realized where they were eating, however, it threatened to return.

There were numerous places to dine at the beach. When Charlie had said they were going there, Stacey assumed it was at one of the middle-of-the-road eateries near the end of the beach. Now she realized he was taking her to one of the finest seafood establishments in the area.

He got out of the car and walked around to open the door. In the few seconds Stacey had to spare, she told herself to stop panicking. It was a nice place, so what? She could handle a nice place. She wasn't going to freak out.

"Have you been here before?" Charlie asked innocently as he helped her out of the car.

Stacey was distracted by his fingers gently resting on her wrist. Her skin broke out into goosebumps at the smallest touch from him. His cologne was making her head feel light. The ocean spilled out in front of them. It glittered under the moonlight. She could smell the salt from the water. There was a breeze rolling in that cooled off the summer heat.

"Stacey?"

"Sorry," she said, snapping back to the present, "No, I haven't been here. Did you really think I'd have been here?"

"Figured a beautiful woman like you would have been taken to all the best places."

Stacey chuckled as they walked toward the restaurant, "Yeah, sure. The finest delis with the best five-dollar dinner deals in town."

Charlie laughed at this. Making him laugh made her more confident. The comfortable feeling was starting to come back. Nice place or not, Stacey was at the very least with someone she liked being around. It surprised her that she enjoyed his company and he enjoyed hers.

Inside the restaurant, she was stunned into silence by how beautiful everything looked. Low lighting and the open atmosphere of the place created a relaxed feeling. The floor to ceiling windows projected the image that she was really on the beach. She assumed they'd be sitting in one of the booths near the back but instead Charlie whispered something to the host.

"This way," he said to her and gently rested his hand on her back as they walked. "We're going to sit on the balcony if that's okay."

Stacey mumbled a reply. She was still soaking in her surroundings, still wondering how she ended up on this date. Unlike the tacky joints she had seen on the beach, which seemed to love hanging fake crabs from the walls and having a Hawaiian print thrown everywhere, this place was subtle. There was no ocean theme shoved in her face. There was a small fountain in the middle of the room they passed by. Pearls rested at the bottom of the pool of water.

Around them, people were well-dressed, wearing outfits costing thousands of dollars. They were dining on food priced more than whatever Stacey made in a month as a waitress. The host opened a set of doors near the back, and they were escorted outside.

They had a fantastic view of the ocean and the diverse crowds enjoying the beach. Someone was having a picnic date. A group of kids were playing in the surf. A live band from a restaurant next door played soft music.

"Wow," Stacey breathed, "this is amazing."

"I prefer eating outside here. I like being this close to the ocean."

"You come here often?" she asked.

"Often enough. Do you drink wine?"

"Yes, but you should order it. I don't know much about wine."

Charlie turned to the host and rattled off the name of something she had never heard before. She was definitely out of her comfort zone. Stacey wasn't even sure she could see her comfort zone from where she was. Sitting in a place like this—a place she had walked by many times, envious of the people who could come here—watching someone as handsome as Charlie order wine—was an experience she never thought she would have.

Charlie turned to look out at the ocean. Stacey admired his jawline and the stubble that peppered his face. He must have felt her staring because he turned back to look at her. His eyes were a deep brown, like dark chocolate. She looked down at the menu, embarrassed that he caught her staring.

"What do you recommend here?" she asked him. "I don't know the first thing about seafood."

She felt stupid for asking him for help in ordering. It was just a restaurant after all. But Stacey wanted to find the most delicious thing on the menu. She might not get another chance to come here again. The fact she even got to come here once was enough for her. She'd rather ask for help than miss out on a delicious opportunity.

But if Charlie thought it was stupid she was asking for help, he didn't show it. Like in the car, the conversation flowed smoothly. Before she knew it, the food had arrived, and they both ate and spoke with ease. There were no awkward silences in the conversation.

Stacey didn't feel as if she were stumbling over her words or having to hide details about herself.

Charlie mentioned a brother in passing but hadn't gone into any detail about him. In fact, where Stacey had spoken about her family and her living situation, Charlie hadn't really shared specifics about his. She hadn't pushed it, assuming there had been a reason for that.

The only dark cloud over the entire date was the fact that Charlie worked for the company that wanted her out of the apartment complex. She was careful to avoid it. She didn't want to bring it up, not now. It would ruin the night.

When dinner was finished, Charlie suggested walking along the beach. She agreed, eager to feel the sand in between her toes. The balcony led directly to it so after they finished, they walked down.

"Would you be offended if I took off my shoes?" she asked him.

"No, that's a good idea, actually," Charlie replied, and before she said anything else, he slipped off his shoes and socks too.

They walked along the water, allowing the waves to lap around their ankles. Stacey felt so happy that she swore she could fly up in the air if she tried hard enough. The entire night so far had felt like a fairy tale. Being swept up and taken to a nice place to eat and now walking along the beach like this felt like something she would have dreamed up late at night when she couldn't sleep.

"Been ages since I've been here," Stacey said with a little sigh. "Can't even remember the last time."

"Probably the summer festival," Charlie joked.

She smiled. "Might have been, actually."

"I was here a month ago."

"Day trip?"

"Sort of." Something crossed his face. "Wasn't enjoyable. Not compared to tonight."

A shiver snaked down Stacey's back. She felt a blush creep up her face and looked away from Charlie.

"It's getting late. I have a meeting in the morning so I should probably get you back home," he said, looking at his watch.

Stacey couldn't help but feel disappointed. Secretly, she wished the date could last for hours. She was having such a lovely time. Instead, she nodded, and they turned back toward the car.

They were almost off the beach when Charlie suddenly stopped. Stacey looked back at him curiously. He was looking up at the moon and then looked down at her. He took a step toward her. Stacey froze. He brushed a lock of her hair away from her face. The slightest touch of his fingers against her skin made each nerve feel alive and aware of how close he was to her now.

"This would be a lovely place to kiss you," Charlie said very softly, his eyes flicking to hers, "unless that would be overstepping."

Stacey's throat had gone dry. He was so close to her that she could kiss him easily. He was waiting for her to give him permission. All she could do was nod. It was enough. Charlie gently tilted her face up to his and brought his lips softly against hers. Stacey closed her eyes and returned the kiss.

It had been a long time since she had kissed a man. She couldn't remember ever kissing a man like this on a first date. Normally, she was so guarded that the date would end with a chaste kiss on the cheek and a promise to see each other soon. After a string of bad luck, Stacey hadn't ever thought she'd be kissed like this. She could hear the ocean next to them. The moonlight poured across the beach, revealing the soft waves forever making their journey up the beach before fading away in the white sand. Charlie's lips pressed against hers. It made her head spin as she closed her eyes for the kiss.

He pulled away from her after a minute or so. Stacey felt breathless as if she had just run a mile. Her heart thumped hard in her chest. Charlie gave her a little smile. His eyes crinkled when he smiled, she realized.

"Been wanting to do that all night," he murmured.

Then his hand grabbed hers. They walked back to the car together in a comfortable silence. Stacey held onto his hand the entire walk. She could feel how warm he was. During the long drive to her home, her lips tingled from his kiss.

When Charlie pulled up to the curb, he looked at her. "Want me to walk you up to the apartment?"

"Ah, no, I'm okay. My grandmother might still be awake, and I wouldn't want to startle her," Stacey said.

Charlie nodded. "I had a lovely time tonight, Stacey. I'll give you a call, okay?"

"Thank you for everything," she said, half hoping that he would kiss her again.

But he didn't. Stacey got out of the car and walked into the apartment complex. Through the grimy window, she watched him drive away into the night. Part of her was relieved that Tina and Allison were upstairs. She knew that if she had let Charlie walk her to the door, there was a big chance that she would fall into bed with him.

Trying to keep a smile off her face, she walked upstairs.

Chapter Seven

"Have a good night?" Allison asked her without looking up from her phone when Stacey opened the front door.

"Yeah, I had a nice time," she replied, trying to keep her voice neutral.

"That's good," her sister replied in a monotone voice as she typed away on her phone.

Stacey took off her shoes and asked, "How were things here?"

"Fine. Tina is asleep. I've been flirting with this friend of Steven's, and I think he is going to want to see me tomorrow."

"Gosh, I'm so happy for you," Stacey deadpanned.

Allison finally looked up and rolled her eyes. "No lecture, please. Also, you wore that to hang out with Amanda? Trying to get laid or something?"

"Why are you so crass all the time?"

She shrugged. "Is it crass or is it just the truth?"

"Crass. Anyway, I'm tired and going to bed. Good luck with your flirting."

Allison arched a brow. "Definitely trying to get laid then. No luck. Well, next time, Sis."

Stacey ignored her and walked to her room. She was glad she hadn't told Allison about the date. In her room, she stripped off her dress and hopped in the shower. She smelled like the beach and wanted to get the sand off her feet.

In the shower, Stacey made the water as hot as she could tolerate and stood underneath the spray. It pounded against her skin. She closed her eyes and let it wash over her.

Her mind drifted back to Charlie. She couldn't believe how hard she had fallen for him on the first date. She had wanted more than just a simple kiss. Stacey had wanted his hands on her body and his lips across her skin. Just thinking about him like that made her body ache.

Surely, he had enjoyed himself too. She hated to think that she wasn't going to hear from him again. She had felt a true connection with him. Their conversations had gone well. Dinner had been lovely. The walk on the beach had been perfect.

Stacey finished her shower and dried off. She changed into pajamas and curled up in bed. This time, she had trouble falling asleep because she couldn't stop thinking of Charlie taking her in the worst way, or the best way.

The weekend was a blur of work and sleep. Stacey managed to fit in a couple more interviews as well.

They were all for restaurants. She had had no luck in finding an interview for an office job yet.

During the long hours of working at the practically empty restaurant, Stacey had more time than she would have liked to think about Charlie. She hadn't heard from him since their dinner and was trying not to think negatively about it. Didn't everyone wait a few days to reach out after a date now? Stacey knew she sorely lacked information on what the dating scene was like but was too embarrassed to ask anyone for advice.

Stacey had ended up with Monday off after a last-minute schedule shift with Maria. Allison had already made plans to take Tina out for the day, leaving Stacey home alone for the first time in what seemed like ages.

"Are you sure you want to take her out?" Stacey asked her sister as they got ready to leave.

"Yes. Will you calm down? We're just going to the beach."

"You aren't—you aren't meeting some guys there are you?"

Allison scowled, and Stacey knew she had gone a little too far. Her sister was a lot of things, but she had never done anything to disrespect their grandmother.

"Really, Stacey? You're going to be a bitch right now?"

"No, sorry. I'm sorry. I'm glad you're spending time with her. Maybe I should—"

"You're not coming with us," Allison said shortly, still irritated with her. "I don't know. Do something fun. We'll be back tonight."

With that, she turned away to help Tina down the stairs. Stacey watched them go and sat down on the couch. Time seemed to stretch out in front of her. It made the most sense to go to the library and send more resumes to different places. She probably would have been able to go with Allison and her grandmother if she hadn't suggested her sister had an ulterior motive for the outing.

Stacey sighed and went to grab her things. Going to the library and applying for work on her day off wasn't her idea of fun. But what else was she going to do? If she sat around and watched TV, she'd be dwelling on how she could be doing something productive.

There was a knock on the door. *Allison probably forgot her keys,* Stacey thought as she went to open the door. She opened it without checking through the peephole. So, when she saw Charlie there, she blinked in surprise.

"Hey. Sorry for popping by like this. I wasn't sure if you'd be home or not. Are you busy?"

Stacey was still thrown off by Charlie appearing at her door. He was dressed for work, in a suit and tie, reminding her yet again of just what he did for a living. Even so, her heart thumped against her chest at seeing him.

"No. I ended up having the day off. Are you, uh, are you here because of the apartment situation?"

Charlie shook his head, "Not exactly. I was here for work and thought I'd come by and see you."

Stacey smiled, "Want to come in? My sister and grandmother went to the beach."

She moved aside to allow Charlie to enter. He looked around the living room. For a few moments, Stacey tensed. She realized that someone who could afford to eat where they had for dinner the other night probably thought her place looked like a shit hole. But if Charlie thought it was a dismal little place, it didn't reflect on his face.

Instead he turned to look at her. "You didn't go with them?"

"I sorta pissed off my sister," she replied, feeling bashful. "I wasn't exactly invited. Do you want anything to drink?"

"Water is fine," he said and followed her into the kitchen. "Can't imagine you pissing anyone off."

"My sister and I have a messy sort of relationship. You said you have a brother, right? Do you two get along?" She handed him a bottle of water, secretly glad that Allison had bought some the other day. She doubted Charlie had meant tap water when he had asked.

Her hunch about his sibling was correct when he replied with, "No. Not really."

"That's rough."

"What can you do, right?"

"Is he older?"

"No, younger. Maybe that's why we don't get along. Older siblings are always in charge of things. The younger ones get to run around wild and free."

Stacey thought of Allison and found herself nodding her head in agreement. "Yeah, and you never know when they are going to get serious and grow up."

"Well, if she is anything like you, then I'm sure she will figure things out."

Silence fell between them. She hadn't missed the fact that she was home alone with Charlie. He had to have noticed that as well? But he was working. He wouldn't act on anything he was feeling during his workday, would he?

Stacey crossed her arms self-consciously. "You said you were here for work?"

"Yeah. Talking to a couple of people."

"People who want to take the deal?" she pressed and then shook her head. "Sorry. I shouldn't ask about your work."

Charlie took a step toward her. "I've wanted to call you and see if you would go out again. But, you know, I get it. With everything going on, I mean. If you don't want to see me anymore."

She should tell him that she shouldn't. It was wrong, wasn't it, to date a man working so hard to evict all these families from their homes? But already her mind was attempting to justify it. It wasn't like he owned the company or oversaw the project. Everyone had to pay their bills. Everyone had to scrape by. Wouldn't she do the same in his position?

"I want to see you again," she heard herself say. "I'm glad you're here."

A smile broke out across Charlie's face. He seemed relieved at the fact that Stacey wanted to see him again. Before she could stop herself, she crossed the short distance between them and pressed her lips against his.

Charlie's hands snaked up her back as he returned the kiss. His fingers went to her hair, sending shivers down her back. Her own hands wrapped around his waist. Any fears or concerns she had about making the first move faded. With Charlie, it felt natural to be wrapping her arms around him. It felt right to have his lips on hers. Had it only been a weekend since she had seen him? Somehow, the distance felt a lot longer. It felt as if she had been walking ages to get to him.

The kisses grew deeper. Every nerve in Stacey's body felt awake and alive, yearning for more from Charlie. His fingers trailed down her neck, and his lips followed. She could feel her heart beating hard as he pressed himself against her.

"Come with me," she whispered and laced her fingers through his.

Chapter Eight

Stacey led him to her bedroom. Everything felt as if they were moving in slow motion. She swore she was in a dream as she turned around to face him. His lips found hers again.

There was no other conversation. None was needed. They were home alone and in her room. They both knew exactly what they wanted from each other. All the insecurities that Stacey usually felt when she was going to have sex with a guy faded to the background. Her mind was buzzing with an energy focused solely on Charlie, to touch him.

They teased each other as they took their clothes off, tossing them in a heap. Soon, they were both on her bed, very naked. He dragged his lips across her neck. She trailed her fingers across his back as he brought his lips back down on hers. She could feel how stiff he was against her thighs. The only thing separating them was his boxers. Everything else had been stripped away.

Charlie brought his lips to her nipples and flicked his tongue across them. Stacey closed her eyes and marveled at how that small touch could make pleasure radiate through her body.

He played with her breasts, squeezing them and sucking on her nipples before moving down lower. He left kisses along her belly and down her thighs as he opened her legs. Before Stacey could say anything, Charlie's tongue ran down her pussy.

She gasped in surprise. It had been so long since anyone had done that. Jake had always whined if she had asked to the point where she had stopped asking. But there was no hesitation on Charlie's end. His tongue probed her wetness gently, sending shivers throughout Stacey's body.

His tongue found her clit, and he flicked his tongue against it. She arched her hips slightly and her toes curled in delight. Charlie took this as a sign to keep going. He began to alternate between licking her clit and running his tongue down the length of her wetness.

The pleasure was overwhelming. Stacey had her eyes squeezed shut as Charlie brought her close to climax. She couldn't stop herself. As he brought his lips to her clit, she lost it. Her hips buckled, and her orgasm rolled through her. Her moans filled the air as Charlie worked his tongue into her pussy, letting her orgasm take her over.

As she lay there, breathless, Charlie brought himself up from between her thighs. He kissed her passionately. She could taste herself on his mouth, and it brought a thrill to her. Her hands fumbled with his boxers. She wanted them off. She wanted his cock inside of her, and she wanted it now.

With his boxers thrown to the floor, she pressed herself against him. Charlie's fingers were in her hair as he began to enter her. He was thick, and it took a little wiggling around on Stacey's part to get his cock fully inside of her.

Once he was in, however, he let out a soft moan. Something about hearing Charlie utter those noises made Stacey crazy. She dug her nails into his back and began to move her hips against him.

Charlie took the hint. He began to move inside of her. At first, he went slowly. There was a grin on his face as he watched her wiggle underneath him, wanting more.

"Don't tease me," she whispered.

"Why?" he replied quietly, leaning down to kiss her. "You don't like being teased?"

"No, not by you." She smiled against his skin as he moved deeper inside of her.

Charlie laughed in her ear—it was low and throaty, filled with desire, "Maybe that's why I want to tease you."

Their lips found each other again, and this time he began to move harder. His thrusts became more urgent as they clung to each other. Stacey could hear Charlie moaning, and she timed her own hip thrusts to go against his movements.

The only thing she could focus on was how his cock felt inside of her. She was breathless. Their bodies were slick with sweat as they fucked. Every noise Charlie made turned her on more. Each kiss they had was enough to drive her wild. The sensation of being filled by him was more than she could take.

When she came again, so did Charlie. They came together, holding each other as if they were each other's life raft.

As their orgasms subsided, Charlie rolled off her. Together, they lay there, trying to catch their breath. After climaxing two times, Stacey felt exhausted. She had never had an orgasm with Jake. He had always finished quickly and then fell asleep. She didn't know her body could respond with someone like it just had with Charlie.

Sleepily, she turned to look at him. He looked at her and smiled.

"Probably shouldn't have done that while I was working," he joked.

Stacey smiled. "Ah, well. Live a little."

He leaned over to her. His lips grazed hers. Stacey responded by pressing her lips against his. They kissed like this for a few minutes until he pressed his forehead against hers.

"I should go. But I'll call you."

"Okay," she said, smiling a little. "Thanks for stopping by."

"Thanks for having me," he replied.

Stacey watched him dress. She admired the way his body looked. It was clear he worked out religiously. His muscles looked amazing even in the low light of her room. His fingers deftly did up the buttons on his dress shirt. He ran his fingers through his hair, trying to flatten it from where Stacey had mussed it up.

She watched him from her bed, still lying there naked. Her limbs felt as if they weighed a thousand pounds each. Even her eyelids were heavy. When Charlie finished getting dressed, he leaned over and gave her one last kiss.

"I'll see myself out," he laughed gently.

Stacey murmured something in reply. She heard him leave the room as she curled up on her side, lazily dragging her blanket over her naked body. The front door closed. Before she could think of anything else, she fell asleep, feeling content for the first time in ages.

Chapter Nine

"Where are you going?" Stacey asked Allison who had been hogging the bathroom for over an hour.

Currently, her sister was leaning over the counter. She had a mascara brush in her hand and was opening and closing her mouth like a fish as she tried to apply it. She stopped what she was doing and looked over at Stacey.

"I have a date tonight." Allison's tone was frosty.

Stacey sighed. "Are you still upset about my remark from the other day?"

"The one where you implied I was only spending time with our grandmother because I had some ulterior motive to pick up a man?"

"I said I was sorry."

It was true. When Stacey got home late from work last night, Allison was still awake. For once, her sister had her nose in a book although the cover looked as if it was one of those cheesy pulp novels that she loved so much for some reason. She hadn't looked up when Stacey had gotten home.

Stacey had apologized there on the spot. She didn't want to be in the cramped apartment with her sister and not be on speaking terms. Allison was family, after all, frustrating or not. She had grunted in reply which hadn't exactly left Stacey feeling confident. Allison could hold a grudge over both big and little things.

Clearly, she wasn't over it yet. She had turned back to the mirror and finished applying the mascara. Stacey looked her over. She was wearing a sleek black dress that had a hint of glitter on the hem and sleeves. It brought out the darkness of her skin and accentuated her hips. She looked beautiful. Whatever man she had snagged for this date would no doubt be sucked in.

Allison picked up a tube of lipstick. From here, Stacey could see it was a dark red.

"Good shade," she remarked.

Allison didn't bother to look over at her. "Of course, it is. Brings out my eyes."

"Well, good luck with your date. Can you tell me where you're going at least? In case something happens."

"What could happen? You think I have shitty judgment or something?"

"No, Allison. You're my sister. Just want to make sure you are safe. It has nothing to do with your dating options or anything," Stacey replied, feeling tired from dealing with Allison.

Her sister paused and then replied, "That banquet downtown. Hodge's Benefit."

Stacey's eyes widened, "You're going to *that*?"

Even though Allison was still irritated with her, the chance to gloat was too much for her to resist. She put down the lipstick and looked over at her. A small smile crossed her face.

"That guy I mentioned I was texting? The friend of my ex? Well, he invited me to it."

"That's one of the biggest events of the entire year."

"I know," Allison replied primly.

Stacey couldn't believe it. Hodge's Banquet was where the richest of the rich went once a year. The event was technically created to raise money for a charity to help with education, but over the years, the focus shifted less on the charity and more toward the event itself so the rich could showboat.

It always garnered massive media attention in the city. Celebrities had begun to attend as well over the years. Tickets were almost impossible to get. If Allison was going, then whomever she was dating must be a big shot.

"Who is this guy, anyway?"

"His name is Jacob Benson. Works in oil."

"Never heard of him. Not like that matters. I don't know anyone with more than twenty dollars at one time," Stacey joked.

Allison looked serious for a moment and said, "Listen, I know you think what I do is sort of silly. Snagging rich guys and—"

"Living off them?"

"I'll let that slide," Allison replied dryly, "only because I'm in a good mood. But Jacob is a high roller. I mean, he has billions to his name. He's single too. Do you get what I'm saying?"

"You're going to try to succeed where all other women have failed and try to snag a marriage out of him?" Stacey shook her head, "Won't ever work."

"And why not?"

"That guy probably already knows that you have that in mind. If he is worth billions of dollars, then he has seen every sort of woman try to win his heart. He's probably going into this date knowing you want to marry him. I wouldn't get your hopes up."

The words seemed to go in one ear and out another with her sister because she had turned back to the mirror, clearly tuning Stacey out.

"We'll see," she finally said, looking up at her.

"Well, have a good time."

Stacey left her sister alone in the bathroom. Tina was coming down the hallway.

"Allison still here?" she asked her.

"Yeah, she's getting ready."

Tina clicked her tongue against the roof of her mouth. "Wasting her time, that girl. Never understood why she is constantly trying to marry rich."

"Well, just let her do her thing. We aren't going to change her mind now, are we? Would you like something to drink?" Stacey asked her grandmother, lacing her arm through hers.

"Hot milk would be lovely."

"Come on then."

She led Tina to the small dining room table and then went to heat up some milk for her. Allison appeared a few minutes later. She really did look stunning. With a pang in her chest, Stacey looked away. She hated comparing herself to her sister, but how could she not? Where Allison was thin and currently looked as if she had stepped out of the pages of a glossy magazine, Stacey felt plain and gross standing there.

"You look beautiful," Tina spoke first, getting up to give Allison a big hug, "And I hope you have a wonderful time."

"Thanks. I'm sure I will," she said with a bright smile. "He's sending a car for me so I should head downstairs."

Stacey bit her tongue. She wanted to ask what sort of billionaire couldn't pick up his date himself but she knew it would only piss her sister off more. Allison turned to look at her, awaiting a compliment.

"You look gorgeous. If he isn't smart enough to fall head over heels for you, then you don't need him," Stacey said automatically.

Allison beamed. This was how it had always been, she thought somewhat bitterly. Her sister got the dates with the gorgeous guys. As a teenager, it was the popular kids in school. Stacey could recall plenty of times where Allison had come down the stairs dressed to the nines for a date. Stacey would prattle off compliments to her and watch her leave. She had always secretly been upset.

Now, it still stung. Not only because Allison was going off to the biggest event of the year looking so beautiful, but also because since Stacey had slept with Charlie, she hadn't heard from him.

As she watched her sister leave, she couldn't help but wonder if she had made a serious mistake with Charlie. Allison constantly tried to snag a rich husband. Coming from a poor background, she craved the sort of life they had dreamed about as little girls. Stacey didn't agree with how her sister was doing things, but she always seemed to know how to handle men.

On the opposite side of that, Stacey felt as if she bumbled her way through relationships. Her last serious relationship, with Jake, had blown up in her face. She had been confident in that one. Sure, he hadn't been perfect, but she had been willing to overlook that to be with him. She had a long trail of broken relationships behind her. Jake had merely been the only one that felt like it might really stick.

Now she had jumped into bed with Charlie because she felt so connected to him. It had been a passion that felt almost impossible to fend off. As she watched Allison close the front door behind her, heading off into the night, Stacey wondered what Charlie was doing at this very moment. No doubt her sister would have handled it better than she had. Her sister seemed to understand men. She had an innate ability to wrap them around her finger and get what she wanted. Stacey just seemed to bungle it up at every chance.

"Dear?" Tina's voice snapped her out of her thoughts.

Stacey shook her head. "Sorry. Warm milk. I forgot."

She went back to the kitchen, vowing to try not to think of Allison or Charlie that night.

Chapter Ten

"I accepted it," Stacey said to Amanda the next day at the restaurant, "It's a nicer place than here, and it's something, at least."

Amanda nodded, pouring herself what was probably her fourth cup of coffee. "Sounds good. You said they close at midnight? I haven't actually ever been there."

That morning, Stacey had gotten a job offer at a diner down the street from where she currently worked. It was a fifties-themed place that seemed to bring in steady clients. When she interviewed there last week, they actually had a lunch rush. She couldn't recall the last time she had handled a rush of any sort. They closed at midnight, which meant she could still swing a second day job. She was starting to lose hope at ever finding an office job.

"Yup. So, I have that covered at least."

"What about the apartment situation?"

"Still bad. They're offering us money to vacate. Most of us are banding together, but I think a couple of people are planning on taking the money to go and risk finding a new place to live."

"That area you live in is the last place in this entire city that is affordable and not in a shitty section of the city. If my parents weren't helping me out with college, I'd probably move."

"Where would you go?" Stacey asked curiously.

Amanda took a sip of her coffee. "No idea. Guess we are both stuck here, right?"

"Guess so."

"Well, I'm sure you'll figure it out. Even after this place closes down, we'll keep in touch. I'll keep my ear to the ground for anything about a solid place to move into."

"Thanks," Stacey replied and meant it.

Amanda headed out to deal with the couple of customers they had. For the thousandth time that day, Stacey peeked out of the kitchen to see if Charlie was there. It was silly and made her feel like a schoolgirl. He had shown up there once. If he was avoiding her, would he show up there again?

There was no change inside the diner. Stacey slumped against the wall and tried not to berate herself. Why had she gotten so hung up on this guy so quickly? It was so stupid of her. Better to forget the entire thing.

William stuck his head in. "I have the paper here. I was going to throw it out but wanted to see if you'd like a look first?"

"Yeah, sure," Stacey mumbled, "I'll take it."

She took it from him, thinking she could give it to Tina that night to read. William shot her a quick smile and walked away. He had a little jaunt in his step lately.

Of course, he did. He was finally going to turn a profit on this place by selling it.

Stacey went to the break room and shoved the newspaper in her purse. She yawned. She had stayed up too late last night, waiting for Allison to get home. She had fallen asleep before she heard her sister come in. By the time she got up for work, however, Allison was fast asleep on the couch in some baggy t-shirt and sweatpants.

At least I have another job waiting, she told herself firmly. That was one goal accomplished. She just had to figure out how she was going to afford everything plus moving.

Stacey told herself to stop dwelling and get to work. She would take things as they came and forget about Charlie as much as she could.

When she got home that evening, Tina was watching TV. She had a pair of knitting needles in her lap which looked as if they hadn't been touched at all. Stacey could hear Allison in the kitchen heating something up in the microwave.

"Hello, dear. How was your day?"

"It was good." For a moment, she considered telling her grandmother about her new job but realized she would then have to explain that her current place of employment was closing.

"That you, Stacey?" Allison called from the kitchen.

"Yup. Hey, how did it go last night?" she asked as she walked over to her.

Her sister looked over her shoulder. "You wouldn't believe it even if I tried to explain it. It was crazy. It was filled with the most gorgeous people I have ever seen in my life! Honestly, I felt a little out of my element. My dress wasn't designer or anything, but I made it work, you know? My charm saw me through."

"Right," Stacey said slowly, "I meant how was Jacob? Did you two get along? Were you nervous?"

"I'm never nervous," Allison boasted.

Stacey stopped herself from rolling her eyes. While she was glad her sister apparently had a nice time, she could tell this was going to make her even more insufferable than normal.

"But no, he was nice. I'm convinced he's hooked on me. He is definitely going to want to see me again. I had his friends eating out of the palm of my hand. And look!" She turned around and stuck her hand out toward Stacey.

On her wrist dangled a tennis bracelet. It was brimming with diamonds. Allison studied Stacey's face very carefully. Even though Stacey knew she should be happy for her sister, she couldn't help but want to snatch the item off her wrist. Why keep such a trinket? If they pawned that thing, they wouldn't have to worry about money for ages.

"Pretty," was all she could muster up the strength to say.

Allison seemed disappointed by this and yanked her arm away. "Jacob gave this to me. Do you know how much this thing probably cost him?"

"Enough for us to pay rent somewhere nice for probably six months in advance," Stacey retorted.

Allison scowled. "Don't."

"Don't what?"

"Don't lecture me. I knew I shouldn't have shown you."

"Yet you still did," Stacey said, feeling the irritation swoop over her swiftly. "You still showed me a bracelet that could fix almost all of our problems."

"No, *your* problems," Allison snapped back. "Your problems, not mine, Stacey. It isn't my fault you're broke."

"Are you fucking serious right now? You're staying with me *because you have no place to live.* Because you technically never have anywhere to live. You flit around from one rich guy to the other, unable to lock any of them down to get the money you want!"

Allison spun around as the microwave beeped. The frozen dinner stunk up the kitchen, which only seemed to remind her of the situation. She wrinkled her nose.

"Oh, excuse me, Stacey. Sorry that I am trying to get out of my shitty situation. All you do is work at some dead-end job without ever trying to better yourself or move onto something new!"

"Better myself? That's rich coming from you! How exactly do you better yourself? Spread your legs wider each time?"

Allison's face blushed. It spread across her features. Stacey was furious as well. She wished she could slap her sister but instead just took a step back. It had been a long time since the two of them fought, mostly because they avoided seeing each other for this very reason.

"You're just jealous," Allison hissed through clenched teeth. "That's all it has ever been with you."

"What the fuck would I be jealous about? At least I have a place to live."

"You're jealous because I have confidence and people flock to me. You never had that, Stacey. You were always in the background, seething with jealousy over what I brought to the table."

Stacey shook her head although she couldn't think of anything to say back. To be honest, it was the truth. She had always been jealous of her sister. Her sister had always gotten the attention and the boys. Stacey had always felt fat and ugly compared to her.

Even if it did hit close to home, there was no way she was going to let her sister know that. Allison had crossed her arms. The pinkish hue that had spread out across her face contrasted with her dark skin. Even now she looked pretty. Stacey was sure she looked like a mess compared to her sister.

"I was nice enough to let you stay here when your boyfriend decided to stay with his *wife,* and this is how you treat me?"

"So what, you going to kick me out?" Allison stuck her chin out as if daring her. "I have nowhere to go."

"That isn't my problem," Stacey said, raising her voice again. "It isn't my fault—"

"Girls! Enough!"

They both looked over to see that Tina had wandered into the kitchen. Her face, normally serene, looked taut and irritated at the sight of the two sisters fighting. Instantly, Stacey felt ashamed. She didn't want to fight with Allison and stress out her grandmother.

"Enough of this," Tina repeated, "I can hear you out in the living room. This bickering doesn't suit either one of you." She looked at Allison. "Is this true? You have nowhere to go?"

Allison looked embarrassed at having her lie exposed. She looked down at the floor and mumbled something.

Tina shook her head, "Nowhere to live. You should be treating your sister with more respect than that if she is letting you stay here, Allison. As for you," she looked over at Stacey, "you shouldn't speak to your sister like that. Neither of you should be treating each other so disrespectfully. In this house, we only love each other, do you understand me?"

"Yes," the two women said in unison as if they were little girls being chastised.

"I'm going to bed. No more fighting, understand?"

The girls agreed again and watched Tina go. Stacey waited until she heard the bedroom door close before she exhaled. Allison yanked her frozen dinner out of the microwave violently, still clearly simmering with irritation over the fight.

Stacey trailed after her. She wanted to say something but didn't know what. Somehow, they always ended up fighting like this. She wasn't sure if they'd ever smooth things over. Both had their pride. Stacey would never admit she was jealous of Allison, and she would never tell her sister what she really thought about their relationship.

Trying to find a topic of conversation, Stacey pulled out the newspaper that William had given to her earlier and plopped it on the table.

"If you want something to read," she said with a small shrug.

Allison's eyes lit up, "Hey, I wonder if any photos of me are in here?"

Of course, Stacey thought, the mere idea that Allison could find a photo of herself in the paper was enough to let her forget their fight. Instead of making a catty remark, she just sat down.

"You should look."

Allison was already opening the paper. The front page was about the event. There was a photo of two men heading into the banquet hall. From where she stood, Stacey couldn't make out their faces. Allison looked disinterested and opened the paper up, eager to find more of the story.

After a few minutes, her sister found the full-page coverage of the event. Her eyes scanned the images, but she pouted.

"Jacob is in here but not me."

"Let me see," Stacey said, curious to see the billionaire that her own sister was seeing.

She slid the paper over to her and Stacey studied the man. The newspaper photo was grainy, so it was hard to make him out. He was turned to the left speaking to someone and had a champagne flute in his hand. From there, he looked very dignified, but it was impossible to make out other details.

"He's probably talking to me too," Allison whined, "but they cropped me out because I'm a nobody."

"Sorry about that," Stacey said although she didn't see why Allison was so upset—she still got to go, didn't she?

She closed the newspaper, and for the first time, Stacey saw the image of the front page. For a few seconds, she just stared at it. Her sister must have noticed because she stopped eating.

"Nice looking, huh?"

Stacey didn't reply.

Oblivious, Allison kept going. "I wouldn't find him too attractive though. Maybe at first glance, I was like 'oh wow, cute,' but not after."

Stacey found her voice. "After what?"

Her sister beamed again. She always looked pleased to be the first one to break some gossip to her first. In this case, Stacey's chest tightened even more as she waited to hear what Allison had to say.

"That guy is the owner of the company trying to kick us all out. He's like, a total billionaire. Charlie Albert. He owns the investment and construction company that is trying to rebuild this section of the city." She tapped his face in the picture with her index finger. "I wanted to tell him off, but you know. It wouldn't have been classy at an event like that."

For a few seconds, Stacey felt as if she couldn't breathe. All she could do was stare at Charlie's photo in the newspaper. The caption underneath the photo backed up what her sister had just told her.

Charlie didn't just work at Lexington and Albert Construction. He owned the company. He owned all of it. He was a billionaire, and he was the *bad guy* trying to take over the complex, trying to take their home.

Chapter Eleven

"Are you okay?" Allison asked, peering closely at Stacey. "You look like you're going to barf."

"I just—just don't feel well all of a sudden," Stacey replied lamely.

Her sister leaned across the table and put the back of her hand against Stacey's forehead and frowned. "You feel clammy. You should get to bed before you get sick or something. I don't want to catch anything."

Stacey couldn't even be annoyed by her sister thinking only of herself again. Instead, she merely nodded and stood up. She felt extremely dizzy as the newspaper stared back up at her. Charlie, posing with what was probably another billionaire, hadn't magically vanished or changed to someone else. It was really him.

"I'm gonna take this," Stacey said and crumpled it in her hands before Allison even answered. "Goodnight."

"Yeah, take it. I'm not in it, so I don't care. Listen, get some sleep, okay?"

Stacey mumbled something and headed toward her room. She felt cold all over as if she had been dunked in a tank of ice water or something. She managed to get inside her room and shut the door before the feeling overwhelmed her again. She leaned against the door and looked at the newspaper.

Charlie was the owner of the company that was responsible for trying to kick everyone out. She had been trying to justify dating him when she thought he just worked there. *He owned it*. He owned the company that wanted them out! He wanted to knock this place down and rebuild it for more of his rich friends.

Why hadn't she noticed this before? How stupid was she that she dated—no, fucked—the man who was a billionaire owner of a company that was causing her nothing but strife? Standing there, Stacey couldn't help but feel like an idiot. She opened the newspaper and scanned the article.

For the most part, it was only about the banquet. It detailed the history of the event and how popular it was. Near the end of the article was a small blurb about the sort of business people who turn up. Charlie was mentioned as a *dashing bachelor worth billions with his construction, media, and other ventures through his investment firm.*

Furiously, Stacey crumpled up the newspaper and threw it at the wall. It bounced pitifully and landed on the floor. It wasn't as if she could even corner Charlie and demand to know why he hadn't told her. She hadn't heard from him since they slept together. Now she knew why. He was probably one of those guys that liked the chase. He probably got a kick out of fucking someone he was trying to kick out of their own home.

Tears sprung to her eyes. Stacey had been so sure that this time was different. Everything with Charlie had felt natural. But it had all been a lie. Someone like that was fantastic with people. He probably had her pegged from the start. She had fallen right for it. Now all she had was the relief that she hadn't told anyone about the date or the fact she had sex with him. Her shame would remain her own.

Stacey curled up in bed and tried to push Charlie out of her mind. Yet it seemed impossible. Her night was spent in a fretful mood.

Even though Stacey had strived to forget Charlie, it proved to be impossible. The more she swore she wouldn't think about him, the more he seemed to pop up into her mind.

She should have been expecting it then when Charlie showed up to the restaurant a few days after she had discovered the truth. It was almost as if Stacey had summoned him by mere thought. One second, the restaurant had a few families coming in for dinner. The next, Charlie stood in the doorway as if conjured up by will.

Stacey had been taking drink orders from a table when she saw him out of the corner of her eye. Her throat went dry. As usual, she and Amanda had been splitting the hostess duties since William wasn't going to hire a new one.

Quickly, she scribbled down the drink orders and ran off to the kitchen. Amanda was back there, flirting with Brad. She had always had a crush on the gruff cook but had put off trying to score with him because they worked together. As Stacey watched Amanda lean over to him and twirl her hair, she assumed that was now out the window.

"Amanda!"

She looked up and shot Brad a smile before walking over to her. "One of my tables complaining?"

"No, but they will be if you keep holding up our one cook," Stacey said pointedly.

Amanda looked a little embarrassed but brushed it off. "What is it?"

"Remember that guy you thought had a cute butt? The one talking to me before?"

"Yes. Why, is he here?"

"Yeah, but I need you to seat him for me. Please? In your section. Please!" she pleaded.

"Sure, sure, relax. Is he bothering you? Want me to deal with him?"

The idea of Amanda 'dealing' with anyone was comical, but Stacey was too panicked to even laugh.

Instead, she shook her head. "No, no, I just don't want to talk to him."

"Alright, I'll handle it."

Stacey watched her leave and leaned against the wall. Brad had turned his attention back to his actual job of cooking. Each second Amanda spent out there felt like hours to Stacey. How long did it take to seat him?

After a minute that felt like an hour, Amanda stuck her head into the kitchen. "Hey, he wants to see you. I tried to tell him you went on break but he called my bluff."

"What did you say?"

"I said you didn't want to see him."

Stacey went over to her, flustered. "You said what?"

"I said you didn't want to see him. Don't look at me like that! You don't!"

"I'm working right now. I can't talk to him."

Amanda shrugged. "Well, he's waiting for you. I can tell him to sit down and eat. I don't think he's going to leave."

"I'll just take my break now," Stacey grumbled. "Thanks, Amanda."

She didn't want to talk to Charlie. What was there to say? Whatever he had come to tell her, she wasn't interested. Steeling herself, she went out to the dining area. He was waiting by the front door still. He had his phone out and was typing away. *Probably about the city. How to knock it down. Closing a deal worth millions.* The thought fueled her toward him. He must have sensed her because he looked up.

Stacey faltered only a little at the sight of him. He was so gorgeous just standing there. She could recall the way his skin had felt against hers and how he sounded when he was moaning in pleasure. The thought threatened to make her blush, so she fixed her gaze above his head, so she didn't have to look directly at him.

"Hey, sorry to bother you while you're working," he said and then frowned. "Uh, your friend? She said that you didn't want to see me."

"Why are you here?" Stacey snapped and crossed her arms as if to ward him off.

Charlie's confusion was clear on his face for a few seconds before he cleared his throat. "I'm sorry I didn't get back to you sooner. If you're upset about that, I completely understand—"

"Let's talk outside, okay?" Stacey said, not wanting to tell him off in front of the entire restaurant.

He followed her outside. She walked to the side of the building. It was littered with cigarette butts. Maria snuck out there throughout the day for smoke breaks and never bothered to clean up. If it bothered Charlie, it didn't show on his face.

He kept on with what he had been saying before. "I'm sorry it took me so long to get back to you. I had to go out of town again and just got back. No excuse, I know. I should have called—"

"Stop. Just stop, please. Charlie, I have no interest in seeing you again."

He looked surprised and blinked a couple of times. He probably wasn't used to getting dumped. Why would he be? He probably swept people off their feet at the mere mention of his money.

"Why?"

"I saw the paper the other day. With you on the cover. I know who you are."

"Shit, Stacey, let me explain."

"No." She held up her hand. "No, I don't want to hear it. You know I can't see you anymore, right? Not only did you lie about who you were but you own the company that is trying to fuck me over royally."

"That isn't true. If you could let me explain—"

"Explain what? Explain it to me then. Explain to me how the only place I am going to be able to afford is the ghetto. Moving my grandmother into the slums all because people like you think it's nothing to knock down sections of town and rebuild it for the rich and famous. You can't explain to me what I already know, Charlie."

"We're just improving it, Stacey. It's a solid piece of the city. It just needs improving."

"And by 'improving' you mean making sure everyone that isn't worth a lot of money ships out, right?"

Charlie was shaking his head. "No. That isn't true. We are offering money for your complex to vacate.—"

"Yeah, great. So now I have some money to move into the slums. I'm paying more to live there, by the way, than I am here. So, I'm paying more for a worse area. What a great trade off."

Charlie spoke again, but she barely heard it. It sounded like a sales pitch. He was on autopilot, she realized. Of course, he was. Hadn't he been pitching this to plenty of people already? Anyone who had the same concerns that she had may have spoken to Charlie already. The human side of him that had endeared Stacey had faded and was replaced by the businessman.

"I don't care," she said bluntly.

He fell silent. Not for the first time tonight, he looked surprised. No one probably spoke to him this way.

"Why did you waste my time?" Stacey asked him. "Asking me out and sleeping with me. You lied about who you were. You knew it wasn't going to work out. You knew I would eventually find out who you were."

Charlie took a step toward her. Even though she wanted to take a step back, Stacey felt rooted to the spot. He looked genuinely upset now. When he looked at her with those puppy dog eyes, part of her wanted to lean forward and press her lips against his. *Get your shit together*, she told herself roughly.

"I wanted to tell you. I just didn't know how to bring it up."

"What about as soon as we met? When I told you off in the lobby, you should have said something then. Or when you helped Kevin out of the tree. You didn't tell me then either."

"I know. I didn't think that I would like you so much, Stacey. I didn't think I'd feel so connected to you. I was afraid that once you knew who I was and what I was doing, I'd lose you," Charlie said, pleading with her.

He reached out for her arm but she took a step away from him, trying to put more space in between them. Stacey was worried that if he managed to touch her, she would crumble. Some part of her felt weak to his words. He was right, wasn't he? She wouldn't have wanted to see him again if she had known who he was. Things would have been different.

But as soon as she thought it, she pushed the thought out of her mind. It was still wrong. Charlie should have been honest with her.

"You should have told me upfront. I don't know what would have happened. But now I know for sure I can't see you again," she said, hoping she sounded confident in her choice.

"You're telling me you would have gone out with me if you knew who I was? You know you wouldn't have. I've—" His voice caught for a moment before he cleared it. "I've never had someone not know who I am before. And I wanted to see you."

Her resolve was weakening a little. Stacey could feel it. It was those damned puppy dog eyes and the tone of his voice. She stared at him for a few seconds. *He's a billionaire. He lives in a different world than you do. He wants to take away your home. How can you tell yourself that this is okay?*

Her inner dialogue was right, and Stacey knew it. As Charlie stared at her, she knew that she owed it to herself not to make any snap judgments. It would be so easy to forgive him and run back into his arms. He was there, living and breathing in front of her, wanting her forgiveness. When was the last time that had happened in her life?

Even so, he was still the tyrant trying to evict her. He had lied about who he was. No matter his reasons, the lie was still wrong.

"I can't. I'm sorry, Charlie," she finally whispered.

He looked crestfallen. For a couple of seconds, it looked as if all the air had been let out of him. His shoulders slouched forward. But it was only for a couple of seconds. Then Charlie straightened himself up. His poker face came back. His expression was unreadable.

"I understand, Stacey. Have a good night."

He turned around and walked away. For a moment, Stacey wanted to call out to him. For some reason, she was the one who was feeling shitty. Why? She had done the right thing. The look in his eyes came back to her, and she felt a wave of sadness wash over her.

Stacey stood there and watched Charlie cut across the parking lot toward his car. He didn't look back.

Chapter Twelve

"I need a favor."

"No."

Allison sighed and rolled her eyes. "Stacey, you don't even know what it is yet."

Stacey glanced up from the puny sandwich she was making for dinner. Her sister was leaning against the wall in the kitchen. Her arms were crossed. She had just painted her nails, and they glittered underneath the low light. Her features were tight, signaling to Stacey that whatever her favor was, she wasn't going to like it.

"Tell me so I can say no."

"Jacob is having this party on his yacht. He invited me."

"Okay—" Stacey said, not following.

"Well, he told me to invite any family or friends I wanted."

"You have no friends," she pointed out.

It was a bit harsh but was ultimately still the truth. Her sister had always been more concerned with snagging up the boys than making friends. She also tended to sleep with men who had girlfriends. It wasn't exactly shocking that Allison struggled to make friends.

"Well, he said family, too."

Stacey was about to finish making her sandwich when Allison's words made her freeze. She looked over her shoulder.

"Are you kidding me?"

"No," Allison replied quickly and hurried over to her side. "Come with me. Please. I don't want Jacob to think that I don't have anyone to bring. I want to look like I at least have a good relationship with my sister." She meant it as a joke but it came out harsh, and Stacey winced.

"Some high-end party? On a yacht? That isn't my scene at all. Besides, I probably have to work."

"No, it's this Saturday, and you don't. I checked," she remarked, pointing to Stacey's schedule she had stuck up on the fridge.

"I have nothing to wear. I have nothing to do there."

Allison gripped her arm. "Please. Seriously, I'm begging you. I'll sell the stupid tennis bracelet if you want me to."

This took Stacey by surprise, "What?"

"The bracelet." She shook her wrist in Stacey's face as if to jar her memory. "You said we'd get a lot of money, right? Well, if you come with me to this, I'll sell it."

She narrowed her eyes, "Why? You love that thing."

"Right, but if I snag Jacob, I'll have so many tennis bracelets that I won't need this one. Let me wear it to the yacht party, and then we can sell it, alright? But I need you to come with me. I need to have someone with me at the party. Jacob will think I'm weird if I don't take him up on his invite."

Stacey stared at the tennis bracelet, thinking about just how much money they could get with it. It would be worth it. Even if Jacob had given Allison subpar diamonds, the money would still be more than she currently had.

"Fine."

Allison's face lit up. "Amazing!" She threw her arms around Stacey and gave her a hug.

When the hug ended, her sister added, "Also, I think that asshole is going to be there. We could totally spit in his drink or something."

"Are we five?" Stacey asked before frowning. "Wait, which asshole?"

"That Charlie Albert guy," Allison replied as she grabbed a bag of chips out of the pantry. "He's going to be there. I figured we could do something. I don't know, stick a *kick me* sign on his back or something."

"Seriously, are we five?" She shook her head, still trying to digest the thought of seeing Charlie again.

"Well, what else do you want to do? Throw him off the boat?" Her sister paused as if it were a viable option, then shrugged. "Well, whatever. I'll help you plan an outfit, alright?"

She left the kitchen, humming a song to herself. Stacey watched her go and looked back down at her sandwich. She wasn't hungry anymore. She had been telling herself that she would be okay if she never saw Charlie again. Now, through her sister's schemes, she was going to see him again. On top of that, she was going to be completely out of her element.

"Great," she said aloud to no one.

<<◇>>

"I'm so excited. Aren't you excited?"

"You've asked me this about fifty times in the last hour," Stacey grumbled.

Allison ignored her. They were in the car that Jacob had sent to pick them up. Yet Stacey couldn't help but be irritated that once again this guy hadn't come by to meet her sister directly. Was Allison being treated like Charlie had treated her? These billionaires apparently were fond of dating people far beneath their income level. It was probably some sort of game to them.

Not for the first time that night Stacey had found it funny that both she and her sister had ended up with a billionaire. While it wasn't shocking for Allison to be dating one, the fact that Stacey had also fallen into dating one was.

She still hadn't told Allison about it. She could almost hear the fight in her head play out. Her sister would simply ignore the fact that Stacey hadn't known who Charlie was. She would flip her shit over the fact that Stacey had been seeing the man responsible for their issues. She would then accuse her of *copying* off her lifestyle after judging her for it. It gave Stacey a headache just thinking about it.

To make matters worse, the money offered to vacate had been increased a couple of days ago. Stacey was sure this was directly related to what had happened with Charlie. The only thing she couldn't figure out was how he had meant it. Had he wanted to offer more money as an insult to them, knowing that it meant people would surely vacate? Or had he thought it would patch things up between them?

"Hello? Earth to Stacey!"

"Sorry," she said, snapping back to the present, "just not looking forward to this."

Allison rolled her eyes and leaned back in her seat. She was wearing a dress that Stacey had never seen before. She wasn't sure where her sister had gotten it. Stacey had dug out her nicest dress from the back of her closet. The last time she had worn it was when Jake had taken her out to dinner on their first anniversary. They had gone to a fondue place which had been way out of their budget. They had saved up for ages to go.

It had been strange slipping the dress back on. Stacey couldn't help but wonder how out of place she was going to feel. There were going to be rich people wearing designer clothes. While her own dress was nice, there was no way that it was going to be as lovely as the other outfits there.

If her sister was thinking the same thing, she didn't show it. That had always been yet another thing Stacey had been envious of. Allison never let anything shake her confidence. She could be attending a party in a garbage bag and would make it work.

"You aren't nervous?" Stacey couldn't stop herself from asking.

"Why would I be?"

"This isn't really our scene, is it? We are going to stick out like sore thumbs."

"How? We're invited by Jacob. Everyone will be too busy sucking up to him to give a shit about us," her sister said dismissively.

"Yeah, I guess so," Stacey responded unconvinced.

The car pulled up to the harbor in what felt like a couple of seconds. Stacey wished the drive had been longer, so she had more time to get emotionally ready. Who was she kidding? She wasn't going to feel ready no matter how long she had.

She moved to open the door, and Allison smacked her hand. "They'll get it."

Sure enough, the driver got out of the car and opened the door for Allison. She slinked out of the car with a smile plastered on her face. Then the driver went to the other side and opened the door for Stacey.

She stepped out into the summer air. Thankfully, it was cool tonight. The wind blew off the ocean and tempered the heat. It could have been enjoyable if she weren't so nervous.

The yacht was directly in front of them. She had never been on a boat of any size before. Seeing the sleek and massive yacht in front of them made Stacey feel very small. There was a group of people in front, waiting to be allowed on. Allison gripped her arm tightly and pulled her forward through the crowd.

They drew no attention. No one glanced their way. Everyone else seemed to know one another. No one cared about two no-names cutting through the crowd. Stacey was on high alert. She kept expecting to see Charlie appear at any moment. But there was no sign of him. She felt a mixture of both relief and disappointment.

"There you are!" Allison exclaimed, pitching her voice an octave higher.

Jacob came into view. He was taller than he looked in his photo and very skinny. He had long slim fingers that were holding a cigarette. His eyes were clear blue and his skin was so pale that he looked almost transparent.

He looked better in the grainy newspaper photo, Stacey thought as she slapped a phony smile on her face. She shook his hand, which felt clammy to the touch as if she was shaking hands with a dead trout rather than a man. *This* was the guy that Allison was trying so hard to woo? There was nothing remarkable about him. Stacey was sure that if he didn't have his money, no one would look twice at him.

"You made it. Wonderful," he said in a slight accent that Stacey couldn't pinpoint. "They're about to let us on board."

"Is this your yacht?" Stacey asked, trying to grasp for a topic of conversation.

"No, but it belongs to a close friend. Tony Lang owns it. You'll meet him soon enough."

"Great," Stacey said with an enthusiasm she wasn't feeling.

They boarded the yacht after a few minutes of waiting. Instantly, people fanned out across the deck. A live band was setting up on the bow. The doors to the interior were open, welcoming people inside. Stacey couldn't imagine what the cost of such a vessel was.

"I prefer the stern, actually," Jacob said as he looked around. "Less crowded."

Allison slipped her arm around his and beamed. "Then we'll go there. Lead the way."

Jacob took the hint and escorted her toward the rear of the yacht.

Seeing her sister so agreeable was cringe worthy. This was the same woman who used to throw a tantrum if Stacey sat on the right side of Tina's car instead of the left. Seeing her have no issue with following Jacob around was strange.

She trailed after them, quickly feeling as if she was turning invisible. With her eyes scanning the deck for Charlie, she tried to engage in conversation with Jacob and Allison. Yet Jacob seemed to never shut up. It became clear that his favorite topic of conversation was himself.

By the time they got to the stern, where a full bar had been set up, Stacey had decided she would try to get off the yacht before it launched. Allison had barely paid attention to her. She knew that her sister had wanted her along to look as if she was close with her family but now that Stacey had met Jacob, she doubted he cared. He had probably offered just to appear nice.

She was ready to turn around and head out when a handsome looking Asian man approached them.

"Tony!" Jacob said with more emotion than anything else he had said so far.

The two men shook each other's hands. Stacey assumed this was the owner of the yacht. As she stood next to her sister, she studied Tony. He was handsome. Next to Jacob, he looked like a male model. His skin was a lovely tanned shade that made Jacob look even more watery and sickly just standing next to him. His dark brown eyes looked almost black which fit well with his jet- black hair.

When he turned to look at Stacey and Allison, he had no accent at all when he introduced himself.

"I'm Allison. Jacob's date," her sister said, sticking out her hand to Tony. "This is my sister, Stacey."

"Lovely to meet you both," Tony replied, shaking her sister's hand.

Stacey held out her own to be polite. Instead of shaking it, however, Tony brought it up to his mouth and kissed the top of her hand very gently. Stacey was so startled that she yanked her hand away. She could feel a blush threaten to rise. If Tony noticed it, he was nice enough not to say anything.

"Well, if you will excuse me, I have to greet the other guests," he said, shooting one last smile at Stacey before heading off back into the crowd.

"He's nice," she said casually.

Allison shot her a knowing look, but all Jacob said was, "Yes. Actually—" and he launched into a boring diatribe about meeting Tony.

Stacey couldn't bother to pay attention. Especially because her heart felt as if it had stopped beating. Across from their small group was Charlie. He was by the railings and was looking directly at her. He had a drink in his hand and a strange look on his face. *Had he seen Tony kiss my hand? Or is he just surprised to see me here?* She convinced herself it didn't matter.

Seeing him was harder than she had expected. Even though the yacht was massive, it suddenly felt very small. She wanted to get out of there. Allison was draped over Jacob as he kept talking away. Two other people had appeared and were pretending to be interested as well.

Stacey took this as her cue to bail. With Charlie still staring at her, she turned around and began to weave her way through the crowd. She'd splurge and take a taxi home. She had shown up. That was enough to get the bracelet, right? She'd fight with Allison about that later.

Stacey finally got to where the ramp was to get off the yacht, but the plank was being pulled up. She shoved her way through a cluster of people and got the attention of a crewman.

"Sorry, I need to get off the boat."

"Sorry, ma'am. We're setting off in a few minutes."

"What? Are you sure you can't let me off this thing?"

The man looked at her apologetically. "I'm sorry, ma'am."

He walked away. Stacey stood there, staring at the dock. Sure enough, she could feel the engine come to life underneath her feet. There was a slight hum to the yacht that hadn't been there before. They were setting off, and she was stuck in a confined space with Charlie.

Chapter Thirteen

Stacey had been half expecting Charlie to appear at her side as soon as the yacht left the dock. But he was like a mirage. The crowd apparently swallowed him up, leaving Stacey alone.

She grabbed a flute of champagne from a passing waiter and found herself staring out at the water. It was strange to be there, on the deck of the ship. Life had been chaotic lately. Losing her job, worrying about an apartment, accidentally dating a billionaire—and now' there she was, looking out at the ocean as she stood on a yacht.

The champagne was probably the nicest she had ever tasted before. She took another sip and glanced around the deck. No sign of Charlie. Perhaps she had a case of wishful thinking. She hated to admit it to herself, but maybe it would have been nice, to have Charlie seeking her out, chasing after her. It would have been a nice change of pace, to have her ego stroked.

"There you are!"

Her sister appeared at her side. Stacey was slightly surprised to see her. She was convinced that Allison had forgotten all about her.

"Hey. Just admiring the view." She decided to omit the fact she had been trying to get off the yacht.

"We're going in to eat with Tony in the saloon. Come on."

Stacey didn't get to protest. Allison had a firm grip when she wanted to. She pulled Stacey away from the railing and toward the saloon. She had been expecting something quaint and cozy. That was quickly proven wrong when they stepped inside.

The room looked as if it belonged to a penthouse. The floor had been cleared, and tables had been set up so guests could dine. There were servers everywhere, delivering plates brimming with food and refilling drinks. Everything was in varying shades of white. Art in golden frames hung on the walls. If it weren't for everything being bolted down, Stacey never would have guessed she was on a boat.

Allison dragged her toward one of the tables near the middle. Stacey automatically dug her heels into the carpet. Sitting at the table was Charlie.

"Oh look, that prick is here," her sister hissed quietly.

Stacey made a non-committal noise as she was shoved into a seat across from him at the end of the table. She stared down at her plate, wanting to avoid his gaze. Allison sat down on the other side of her, next to Jacob. Tony sat down next to Charlie with a beautiful woman that must have been either his wife or his date.

Jacob instantly dominated the conversation. Allison appeared to be hanging onto his every word. Stacey supposed this was why her sister was so good at snagging rich men. She was a great actress. Stacey could barely pretend to be interested.

At one point in the middle of a dull story, Charlie's eyes caught hers.

"The lion was right there," Jacob was droning on, "right by our jeep! He could have killed us, you know. We could have died right there on the spot if it decided to ravage us for a meal!"

Charlie smirked a little at her as if to say *this guy*. Stacey returned the smile, silently agreeing with him. Then, as if remembering they had broken up, she looked away, trying to wipe the smile off her face. What was she doing?

The meal they were served was delicious. Normally, she would have loved nothing more than eating such an amazing lobster. The presentation on the plate was gorgeous. But with Charlie being so close to her, she couldn't help but feel distracted.

He looked so handsome tonight. Glancing at him when she thought that he wasn't looking, Stacey could feel the longing in her chest. No matter how many times she told herself it was wrong, she couldn't help but want to reach out and grab him.

By the time dinner finished, Stacey couldn't have told anyone who asked what was discussed and if she had even engaged in conversation. As they wrapped up their meal, Tony turned to Charlie.

"You're awfully quiet tonight," he said to him. "Everything okay on your end?"

"Ah, yes. I have just a bit of a headache tonight. You know that I am prone to them." Charlie replied smoothly.

Tony went to open his mouth to reply when Jacob chimed up, "Have you tried peppermint tea? Might I suggest—"

Stacey tuned him out and stopped herself from rolling her eyes. Instead, she shot her sister a look. Allison gave her a small shrug as if to say *what do you want me to do with him?*

"Have you two seen the rest of the ship?" Tony asked, swiftly cutting Jacob's speech off.

"No, we haven't. Jacob, why don't you show me the rest?" Allison cooed.

Jacob looked placated at this after being interrupted. He nodded, and they both stood up from the table. Allison looked over at Stacey. Great. Either she went to be bored by Jacob or she was stuck there with Charlie. Which was the lesser of two evils?

She was saved from making any choice, however.

"I'm sure Tony·or Charlie could show you around, sweet sister."

Sweet sister? Had Allison completely lost her mind? She couldn't recall any point in time that they had ever referred to each other like that. Jacob was smiling down at Allison though, so she supposed it was for his benefit. Gross.

"Uh, yeah, Sis. Sounds good."

"I'd be more than happy to show your sister around," Tony offered.

Tony's date looked a bit miffed at this. Stacey couldn't blame her. While she knew that this was his yacht, and he was just being kind, she was sure this beautiful woman wanted to spend time with him and not show another woman around. The woman said something in another language to Tony who replied in kind. Stacey couldn't understand any of it.

Charlie, possibly sensing the tension, came forward, "I'll show her. You have this entire party to tend to. I've been on here before." He smiled brightly.

"Ah, thanks so much," Tony replied. "I'll be seeing you around then? Nice speaking with you, Stacey."

They turned around and walked off. Stacey watched them leave and stood up from the table. At one point, Tony glanced behind him at the two of them. Stacey wiggled her fingers at him in a wave.

"Well, the stairs are this way."

"You're not actually going to show me around, are you?"

Charlie looked surprised. "You don't want to see the rest of the yacht?"

"I don't want to see it with you." She crossed her arms defensively.

"Well, no one else is going to show you around," he countered.

It was true. It wasn't as if she knew anyone else there. Allison had sauntered off with Jacob trying to woo him. Tony, while nice and admittedly lovely to look at, was off with his own date. Was she going to pass up seeing the rest of this place? She would never be near a yacht like this again in her life. She'd be kicking herself in six months when she remembered turning down seeing it because of Charlie.

"Fine. But conversation remains strictly about the yacht."

"Fine," he said, his features hardening slightly.

She followed him as he went to a door at the back of the saloon. Stacey hadn't noticed it before. It was carefully designed to look like part of the wall. The only way anyone could tell that it was different was because of the keypad next to it. Charlie pressed a few buttons, and the door clicked open.

"You know the code?"

"Tony and I go way back. I helped him out a while ago with some dealings in China."

"Kicking people out of their homes over there too?"

Charlie ignored her. She knew that he had heard her by the way he pressed his lips together. But all he did was open the door. A staircase was at their feet. It was narrow and steep, and Stacey balked at the idea of walking down it in her heels.

"Those look like stairs of death."

"These are the back steps to the cabins. The front staircase isn't much better."

"Why can't we use that one?"

"Everyone is using that one. We have this one all to ourselves. Listen, I'll go first. That way, in case you fall, you can snap my neck, and all your problems will be solved," he deadpanned.

Stacey wasn't sure if he was serious or joking. It was impossible to tell with his tone that dry. In any case, Charlie stepped down the staircase first. Stacey followed, moving so slowly down the steps that she was sure she heard him snicker at one point.

By the time he got to the bottom, she was only halfway down. He stuck his hands in his pockets and began to whistle. Had he always been this frustrating? Stacey got to the bottom of the stairs where they were now in a narrow hallway.

"Everything is so cramped."

"It's a boat."

"A massive one, so I assumed everything would be more normal sized."

"Hallways are narrow because the rooms are indeed massive. This back staircase leads us to the crew quarters, laundry room, a storage chamber, and a couple of cabins."

"And the front?"

"Access to the engine room and the master staterooms. Too crowded there right now. Tony really outdid himself there, so everyone wants to see them first."

"Great," she mumbled, feeling just how alone they were back there.

Everyone was either up front, upstairs, or on the deck. As she followed Charlie through the crew quarters and one of the smaller cabins, she couldn't help but feel nervous being this close to him.

While she had made it clear that she hadn't wanted to discuss anything but the yacht with him, being this close to him was affecting her. They were alone back there. Stacey could smell his cologne. She could recall how it felt when he had kissed her.

"This cabin is my favorite," he said, snapping her out of her memories.

Charlie pushed the door open, and they stepped inside. It was the smallest out of the other cabins that Stacey had seen so far but had the most décor. Everything had a soft pinkish hue to it. The carpet and the bed were in pastel shades of pink. The lamps on the night tables looked like giant seashells. There were more seashells painted along the wall.

"Sort of cheesy," she remarked. "None of the other rooms had this décor. Like, seashells? We're on a boat."

Charlie grinned, "Totally cheesy which is why I like it so much. Kinda campy, right? For a boat?"

She couldn't help but laugh. "You really like that? A boat having a beach theme?"

"Of course, I do," he said, running his hands over one of the seashell lamps. "Tony hates this room. But his late mother decorated it, and he leaves it like this in her memory. He changed the rest of the cabins except this one."

"Why does he hate it?"

"Because it's a corny seashell-themed room on a yacht. Way too on the nose for him."

"But you like it because of that very reason? Just to clarify."

"Yeah, exactly. It's cheesy. Sometimes cheesy can be a good thing. Tony said way back in the day having nautical themes on boats like this were the regular thing to do. But eventually, it fell out of fashion. People thought it was too corny. If I had a yacht, I'd have it all done up in a nautical theme. Too funny to pass up."

"I thought for sure you'd have a yacht," Stacey said.

"Nah. Not yet, anyway. The upkeep is crazy on a boat like this. If I got one, it'd be a smaller one."

"With a nautical theme."

Charlie grinned. "Definitely."

Stacey couldn't help but return the smile. Even though she had been so nervous only moments ago, the tension seemed to have faded. Now she felt exposed. They were close together in this cramped cabin. Stacey was feeling light-headed being this close to him.

Charlie seemed to sense it as well. He looked away from her and leaned against the wall of the cabin.

Stacey tried to find something to talk about, "You know, you can't even feel the engine. You would think we could feel the hum of the engine or something down here in the cabin," she rambled. "Something to indicate that you're out at sea. You know? It's sort of amazing, and I—"

She didn't get to finish her thought. Charlie took two swift steps closer and kissed her. His hands were against her cheeks as he cradled her face. Stacey was so shocked that her mind went completely blank for the first couple of seconds. Before she could stop herself, she was returning the kiss.

Then she remembered why she had broken things off with him and why it wouldn't work. With all the strength she could muster, she pushed away from him.

"We can't," Stacey whispered.

"Why not? I know you feel this. Why try to hide it? I even tried to make it right. I tried to offer more money."

"Charlie, I can't be bought!" She ran her fingers through her hair, feeling frustrated. "Why can't you see that? Offering more money isn't what I want. I want to stay where I live. I want to be there with my grandmother and my idiot sister and have enough money to take care of things and not live in the ghetto."

Charlie grabbed her hand. "Then I'll fix it."

"You can't. You can't, Charlie. We're too different, anyway."

"No, I'm going to fix it," he repeated, stubborn as ever.

Stacey was about to tell him yet again that he wasn't going to be able to fix this problem with more money. But his lips were on hers again. Just briefly. He ended the kiss after a couple of seconds and looked her in the eyes.

"I'm going to figure it out, okay?"

Stacey couldn't reply. Her throat had gone dry. She wanted to kiss him again, so very badly, that her entire body was aching. Part of her could picture tossing him down on the bed and taking him right there on the spot.

But she couldn't. As much as she wanted to, she couldn't. Charlie took her silence as a sign to go. He nodded once as if to himself and then left, leaving her alone in the cabin.

At that moment, with Charlie's lips still feeling as if they were pressed against hers, Stacey had never felt more alone.

Chapter Fourteen

"You didn't like him?"

"Oh, come on Allison," Stacey replied. "There is no way that you found Jacob at all interesting."

It was the day after the party. Stacey had just come home from a shorter shift than usual at the restaurant. Allison had her feet propped up on the coffee table and was painting her toenails a pale purple. Next to her was Tina, who was watching TV silently.

"You're right. I didn't. But so what?"

"You have to have some sort of connection with that guy."

"No, I don't. Besides, what about you?"

"What?" Stacey asked.

"Tony said Charlie showed you around the yacht. Why did you run off with the guy fucking us over?"

Stacey felt put on the spot. Her sister's glare was questioning yet her tone was slightly hostile. Part of her wanted to just admit the entire thing there and then. But she balked under the sudden gaze of her grandmother.

"You met the man in charge of the apartment deal?" Tina asked.

"Yeah, he was on the yacht last night," Allison replied. "So, come on, Stacey. What was he like?"

"Fine. He wasn't, uh, very interesting. Sort of droned on. Like Jacob. Guess that's just a billionaire thing," she said, standing up.

"Well, they all love talking about themselves. It's in their nature."

Stacey excused herself and headed off to the kitchen. Sure, Jacob talked about himself absolutely non-stop, but Charlie wasn't like that. She kept telling herself that she wasn't going to have to see him again but how could she be so sure? And what had he meant by saying he was going to fix things?

She grabbed a soda out of the fridge and opened it as Allison came into the kitchen. She was walking funny, trying not to smudge her freshly painted toenails.

"So, what's next for you and Jacob?" Stacey asked.

"Not sure. Just waiting for him to call me, I guess. He's going to Europe next week. Maybe he'll invite me."

"Yeah, maybe," Stacey said, unconvinced that Jacob was interested in her sister in any way other than a fling.

"Hand me a soda?"

"Here," she said, shoving her own can toward Allison. "I need to stop drinking this junk anyway."

There was a knock on the door. "I'll get it," said Stacey as she headed over to open it.

Charlie stood there. He was dressed plainly, in just a black t-shirt and a pair of jeans. She had never seen him dressed like that before. The sight of him made her mouth go dry. She glanced behind her. Tina was oblivious, still watching TV. Allison would be trailing into the living room in any second.

Stacey stepped out into the apartment hallway and closed the door behind her. "What are you doing here?"

"I need you to sign something. All the tenants are signing it."

"What?" she asked as he handed her paperwork.

"You can take some time to go over it. I don't need it back right away."

"What is it, Charlie?" Stacey repeated.

"My company is pulling out of the city expansion. This is just a formal notice that we aren't going to be asking anyone to vacate anymore."

Her head spun. She thought that he was poking fun at her. Surely, he had to be. Stacey was speechless and could only stare at him.

Charlie cleared his throat and avoided her gaze as he spoke, "So you'll want to review it before signing. Someone will be by in a few days to pick it up. Everyone else has had theirs delivered."

"Wait. Wait, I'm sorry." She held a hand up. "What happened? I mean, what about that big speech you gave? About how this was what this city needed?"

"I still do think that. But the city needs it for everyone. We're shifting our focus. Improving public buildings with the assistance of the local government. Improving the parks, things like that. Your landlord will be instructed to start making repairs here as well."

"This is crazy. I don't even—" She pressed her hand to her forehead as if that would stop how fast her head was racing. "I don't know what to say."

Charlie lowered his voice, "Stacey, I promised I'd fix everything. This is how I'm fixing them. I couldn't ask you to leave your home. But I also couldn't save just your apartment complex, right? I could just hear you in my head telling me that sure, I helped you, but what about everyone else?"

"True. That is exactly what I would say," Stacey admitted, "but from the business side of things—how did you do this? How did you manage to swing this?"

"I work quickly and talk even faster." Charlie shrugged as if it was normal to restructure a plan like this so swiftly. "You're right. I did care more about rich people coming in and buying up high rises. But I didn't want to be like that. I didn't want to be like—"

"Like Jacob?" she asked helpfully.

Charlie laughed. His laugh was contagious, and she couldn't help but laugh as well. The situation was too strange not to be funny. A billionaire had just changed his business plan and saved her from having to move out of her apartment complex. It sounded like something out of a movie.

"Why did you do it?" she asked after she had caught her breath from laughing.

"You mean you don't know?" He brushed her cheek gently with his thumb, tilting her chin to look up at him.

Stacey held her breath. She wanted to lean forward and feel him on her lips, but she held off. If Allison or her grandmother were to open the door right now, there would be no explaining something like this. Even so, it was tempting.

"For you, Stacey. I wanted to see if you'd give me another chance if I made this right."

"For me?" She breathed, their lips only an inch away, hovering close, but not touching.

"That's right," Charlie whispered, "for you. If you give me another chance, I'd love to start over. Try us again, do it the right way, with no lies."

Stacey couldn't believe what was happening. What incredible influence Charlie must have to change everything so quickly. She couldn't imagine having so much power and so much respect that he could change a major business plan so fast.

It dawned on her then just who Charlie was. He was a billionaire. He could buy her whole city block if he wanted to, and still be a billionaire.

Yet he wanted *her*. Stacey had told him that they were too different, that their socio-economic backgrounds were worlds apart for a relationship to work. She had made it clear she couldn't be with the man who was trying to evict her and her neighbors from their apartment complex. And Charlie hadn't left. Instead, he had changed everything with the hope for another shot with her.

"I'll have you," she whispered.

Charlie's lips finally found hers. This kiss sent goosebumps up and down her arms. It was a short kiss—neither one of them wanted to get caught making out in the hallway. But before they parted, Charlie spoke.

"When are you free next? Let me take you to dinner."

"I'm free Wednesday night."

"So far away." He ran his thumb over her lips. "Guess I'll just have to wait then."

He pulled away from her. Stacey watched him leave. He went down the stairs and disappeared from her view in a matter of seconds. Her heart raced so quickly that she felt dizzy for a couple of seconds. She looked down at the papers in her hand. *We aren't going to have to leave,* she thought to herself with a thrill.

The door opened, and Allison stuck her head out. "What in hell are you doing out here?"

Stacey turned around to face her sister who was looking at her perplexed. She held the papers out to her.

"I think everything just got fixed," was all she said.

<<◇>>

Wednesday morning, Stacey woke up with a light heart. Today she was going to see Charlie. He was going to pick her up at six. She couldn't wait. All she had to do was get through a short shift at work and be home in time to get ready.

She was still on the fence about telling her sister about him. She had come close the last couple of days but had been holding back for some reason. It wasn't as big of a deal now since they were going to be staying in the apartment complex.

Word had spread around the city like wildfire. The fact that a large company had made such a sudden change was big news. Residents were pleased they could stay in their homes. They were happy they would be seeing improvements to the city that catered to everyone and not just the wealthy. Charlie's face had been splashed on the front page of the newspaper almost daily in the past few days.

So, it would have made sense to tell Allison and Tina what was going on between her and Charlie. Even so, Stacey had been holding back. Besides the fact she knew Allison would still judge her for it, she also wanted to keep it to herself. For some reason, having Charlie to herself made it feel more like a special secret that she could enjoy on the sly, without sharing. Too often in the past, she had introduced Allison to the men she had liked. It had always seemed to jinx things.

No, she had decided that Charlie was going to be her little secret. She had already told Allison she was seeing Amanda later that night. Her sister had barely noticed. She was too upset about Jacob not inviting her to Europe.

"How could this be happening? I thought for sure he had loved spending time with me at that party," Allison bemoaned as Stacey tried not to roll her eyes.

"He loves himself more," she remarked.

Allison ignored her. "I thought I was going to get to go to Europe for sure."

"Maybe he's going there on business and didn't want to invite you. Have you even considered that?"

"Doesn't matter. If he were into me, he would have invited me. We could have sealed the deal in Europe."

"And what? Been his full-time mistress?"

Allison scowled. "Don't start."

"I'm just saying that you should aim higher instead of trying to snag a billionaire."

"God, not this again, please. Not now. I have to rethink this."

Stacey poured herself some cereal. Tina was still asleep when Stacey checked up on her earlier. As her sister rambled in the background, Stacey thought of her grandmother. She had been sleeping more than usual lately. Besides raising her voice at the two sisters when they had been bickering before, Tina had been quiet as ever. Stacey was sure it was because her memory was growing worse. Tina probably couldn't keep up with simple conversations.

Now that there was no threat of moving, Stacey decided she would take Tina to the doctor again sooner rather than later. It had been too long since Tina had gone due to money issues. It was time for a check-up.

"Are you even listening?" Allison asked.

"No," Stacey replied, sitting down at the table. "No, sorry, I don't really care. Listen, don't get all huffy with me because that boring twig of a man didn't invite you to Europe." Something struck her—something she had forgotten with everything going on. "Where is the tennis bracelet, by the way? You promised to use it to help with the bills."

"Oh. Yeah—" A funny look crossed her sister's face.

Stacey braced herself, in case Allison's explanation caused her to get upset just as she was about to head out to work. She could feel it in her gut. The cereal suddenly looked unappealing, and she pushed the bowl away.

"What did you do?"

Allison tried to look insulted. "Why is it me?"

"What, did someone steal it?"

"Well, no."

"Then what did you do?" Stacey repeated icily.

"I gave it back to him."

"Why?!"

"I thought it was romantic!" Allison exclaimed as Stacey got up from the table. "I told him I'd be waiting for him and I'd take the bracelet back when he came back for me. I told him to take it and keep it to remind him of me."

"Allison, why not give him something of *yours*, you complete and total fool?" Stacey snapped as she marched to the front door. "What is he going to do with something he gave you not even a week ago?"

"He doesn't want something of mine, Stacey, he wants diamonds and expensive things. It just made sense to give him the bracelet. Listen, when he comes back for me, I'll get it—"

"Save it, alright?"

Stacey stormed out of the apartment, slamming the door loudly behind her. Leon was in the doorway of his mother's apartment, idly texting on his phone.

"Hey, Stacey," he said to her. "Heard the good news?"

"Yes." She forced a smile on her face, trying to mask her irritation at her sister. "Fantastic, isn't it?"

"Sure is. Guess even the rich assholes can come around, huh?"

"You should watch your mouth, Leon," Stacey lectured, partly because of his age and partly because he was insulting Charlie.

"Sure, sure. Have a good day," he said before looking back down at his phone.

Stacey walked past him and headed down the stairs. She was trying not to be angry at Allison, but that was proving to be impossible. She had been so close to having some actual money coming in, and her sister had blown it trying to impress that idiot.

Downstairs, a woman stood in the lobby. It was clear that she had no place in the housing complex. She was wearing a sleek, pure white dress that hugged every curve. Her hands were wrapped around a purse that was just as white. Her heels were black and matched her jet-black hair that was thrown up in a perfectly messy bun that was the style of the day. She had giant sunglasses on that covered half her face. The only bit of color on her was her red lips.

"Hi, are you lost?" Stacey asked, knowing that everything on this woman was designer made and wondering how she had ended up walking in there of all places.

"Yes, I believe so. I'm looking for someone." She had a light accent, but her tone was clipped, making it clear she didn't want to talk to Stacey any longer than necessary.

"Who are you looking for?"

"Charlie Albert. He had business here before he mucked up the deal. Have you seen him?"

Stacey's heart began to beat quickly. "Uh, no. No, not for a few days. Who are you?" It was a bit blunt, but she couldn't help herself. Who was this woman?

The woman lowered her glasses and looked over the frames. Her eyes were a bright green. Her gaze made Stacey feel insignificant.

"I'm Charlie Albert's fiancée, not that it's any business of yours."

-To be continued in Book 2-

Book Two – Love Divested

Chapter One

DOWNSTAIRS IN the lobby, Stacey saw a woman who was, clearly, not a tenant. The stranger looked like she belonged in a fashion magazine.

Trying to be helpful, Stacey asked, "Hi, are you lost?"

The woman looked Stacey up and down before answering. "Yes, I believe so. I'm looking for someone."

"Who are you looking for?"

"Charlie Albert. He had business here before he mucked up the deal. Have you seen him?"

Stacey's heart raced. "Uh, no. No, not for a few days. Who are you?" It was a bit blunt, but she couldn't help herself. Who was this woman?

The woman lowered her glasses and replied, "I'm Charlie Albert's fiancée, not that it's any business of yours."

Stacey thought she misheard the woman. There had to be some sort of mistake. There was no way that this woman was Charlie's fiancée.

"I'm Adele," the woman went on, oblivious to Stacey's inner turmoil. "I wanted to surprise him, you see. I've been overseas. His assistant said he had been here a couple times, so I thought he could be here now."

"Sorry, he hasn't been here since the apartments were dropped from the rebuilding plan." Stacey hoped her voice sounded as if she had no interest in Adele or her claims of being Charlie's fiancée.

Adele wrinkled her nose. "That's a shame. I suppose I'll try him elsewhere then. Now that I'm here, though, I can understand why he would leave as quickly as possible." She laughed.

Stacey wanted to tell this strange, uppity woman that this was her home. She didn't need strangers coming around running their mouths off about how little they thought of it. But she couldn't bring herself to say anything. Instead, she could only stare at Adele, who was looking around the lobby one last time.

"Well, thank you for the help, dear," Adele said and left the apartment complex in her towering high heels without a backward glance.

Stacey just stood there. Her head was spinning as if everything had suddenly been uprooted. Part of her wanted to chase after Adele and ask her just how she could be Charlie's fiancée.

But a sick, swooping feeling was slowly consuming Stacey. She had to talk to Charlie as soon as possible. She fumbled for her phone and brought up his number. The phone rang three times before a man answered.

"Charlie Albert's phone." The man's voice was deep and somehow familiar although it wasn't Charlie.

No one had ever picked up Charlie's cell phone before and it threw Stacey off guard. She stumbled over her words. "Hi, uh, hello. This is Stacey, and, um, I'm Charlie's—" What was she, exactly? His girlfriend? Or just a girl on the side?

"Stacey!" the man exclaimed as if he knew her. "This is Tony."

In her haze, it took her a few seconds to remember who Tony was. The image of him smiling at her on board his yacht floated back to Stacey.

"Right, hi Tony!" She feigned a cheerfulness. "How are you? Your yacht was very lovely."

"Glad you enjoyed it. I enjoyed seeing you on it."

The remark startled her. His tone had been warm and almost flirtatious. That's odd, she thought to herself.

"I'm calling for Charlie," she blurted out and cringed.

She probably sounded incredibly rude. She was blowing off what Tony had just said. But Stacey had no idea what to make of it and couldn't focus on that right now. The image of smug Adele still danced in her memory.

"He's in a meeting. He's running late, actually, because we had a meeting of our own. That's how I have his phone," Tony joked, "but I can pass him a message."

"Yeah, please. Let him know I called and would appreciate a call back."

"Of course. I had no idea you two were so, well, close," Tony replied tactfully.

For one wild second, Stacey wanted to ask Tony about Adele. He would know, wouldn't he? Tony and Charlie seemed to be friends and ran in the same social circles. But she stopped herself before she could do something so silly. No, whatever was going on was something she would ask Charlie directly. She would not go behind his back.

"Thank you! I have to go to work now. Have a nice day!" Her voice was too high-pitched as she tried to hide her emotions. It just made her sound crazy and somewhat desperate.

She ended the call and headed to work, telling herself that she would get to the bottom of it soon enough.

Although Stacey had promised herself not to dwell on Charlie and Adele, it proved to be impossible. The restaurant had one lone customer—an old lady sitting at a booth asking for coffee non-stop as she read a book.

Maria bustled into the kitchen about two hours into her shift and looked over at Stacey. "I quit."

"What? That just leaves me and Amanda."

Maria shrugged. "Not my problem. I'm going to go fucking mental if I stay here a second longer. See you around."

Stacey stared as Maria headed toward the break room. She hadn't ever been exactly close with Maria so she hadn't been expecting a tearful goodbye. But a mumbled 'see you around' was a pretty shitty farewell.

Tears formed in Stacey's eyes. She turned away to face the wall. *What is wrong with me?* She tried to regroup. Normally, someone quitting wouldn't affect her like this.

She left the kitchen, leaving Brad behind playing a game on his phone and found William in his office. She knocked on the door, and he looked up at her.

"You're not quitting too, are you? I was hoping to run with a skeleton crew until we closed, but it's turning more into a ghost crew at this point."

"Nope, I'm here 'til we close," Stacey replied. "I have a job lined up afterward already."

"Amanda mentioned that the other day. Congrats."

Working at another diner didn't seem like something to be congratulated about. Out of the blue, her sister's words from their last fight haunted her. *All you do is work at some dead-end job without ever trying to better yourself or move onto something new.*

"Thanks," Stacey replied without really meaning it. "Figured I'd see if you wanted to alter the schedule."

"I can't give you any more hours. You're already in overtime on my end. I'll pick up some shifts. You know, Stacey, if you are hurting for money, I'd understand if you have to leave early."

She was touched that William was giving her a way out if she wanted to take it. William had always paid everyone more than the minimum wage plus tips for wait staff. She didn't need much, and it had always been enough to scrape by. Business had been so slow lately that the tips barely made a dent in her bills. But she was determined to stay out of loyalty to an employer who had treated her well the last four years.

"I'm making due," she replied.

William looked relieved, "Thanks, Stacey. Don't worry about Maria quitting. I'll take care of it."

"Just wanted to make sure. Thanks," Stacey said and left the office with a wave.

She had been secretly hoping to get Maria's hours. Not only because she wanted the money but because she had been hoping if she threw herself into her job then she could forget about everything else on her mind.

William had reminded her of another thing bothering her—her foolish sister and that damned diamond tennis bracelet. Allison had promised to give her the bracelet after dragging her to the yacht party. Instead, she had given it back to Jacob when he left for Europe in some misguided attempt at being romantic.

That was Allison in a nutshell. She would make promises and deals and never follow through with them.

She'd change things at the last second on any whim. Stacey should have seen it coming. When she thought about how much they could have fetched selling that bracelet, it made her sick. She closed her eyes for a few seconds. Then she went to go check on her lone coffee-guzzling customer.

Charlie didn't call her back until late in the afternoon when she was almost done with her shift. When her phone vibrated in her pocket, she slunk off to the break room to take the call. Amanda had shown up twenty minutes ago, so Stacey finally had help to cover the customers.

"Hey, sorry it took me so long to call you back," Charlie said when she answered.

"It's fine. I need to talk to you about something."

"Can it wait until tonight when I see you? There're a few urgent matters I need to tend to in a few minutes."

Stacey was taken aback. She was just going to confront him over the phone about Adele and had forgotten about their date later in the evening. But in person was probably better where she could watch his reaction.

"Oh, that's what I'm calling about. I have to run an important errand for Tina tonight. Can we meet up for coffee or something instead?" Stacey felt there was no point in prolonging the agony over a dinner.

"Yeah, sure." Charlie's voice sounded disappointed.

She gave him the name of a coffee place near her apartment complex, and he said he would meet her there at six.

The rest of Stacey's shift dragged by. She was incredibly nervous about seeing Charlie. She finished work with twenty minutes to get to the coffee shop. She tried to fix herself up before leaving to see him.

I shouldn't waste my time, she told herself as she reapplied her lipstick. *Why bother primping for him?* Even so, Stacey ran a brush through her hair and set off to see him.

Chapter Two

Charlie was waiting when Stacey arrived. He had chosen a table in the back of the coffee shop. The place served run-of-the-mill coffee, but it was the only nearby place Stacey could afford. Charlie was on his phone and hadn't seen her yet.

She stood there for a few seconds admiring him. He was handsome, and she liked looking at him. He was still dressed in business attire, probably from coming directly from the office. Stacey imagined his days were busy with a thousand different things going on at once. Perhaps, in another life, it could have worked out between them. But they were too different.

Stacey steeled herself and walked over to him, not bothering to buy a coffee. She was going to keep this short by telling him she had met his fiancée and couldn't see him anymore. She sat down across from him.

"Didn't even see you there," Charlie said, smiling. "Sorry again for missing your call earlier. At least Tony got it. Work has been hectic today."

"I can imagine," Stacey replied, trying to sound casual, "especially with Adele flying in."

Charlie stiffened. He was about to reach for his coffee but his hand froze. He was thrown off balance but Stacey found no pleasure in it. She just felt tired.

"Adele is in town?" he finally asked after swallowing a few times.

"Yup, she stopped by the complex, thinking you might be there. She didn't care much for the place though. Made it pretty clear that she thought it was gross."

"Sounds like her," Charlie said with a sigh.

Stacey drummed her fingers against the table, waiting for him to say more. Her gaze must have unnerved him because he leaned forward.

"She isn't my fiancée, Stacey."

"Really?" Her tone was clipped.

He sighed and ran his fingers through his hair, "Let me explain. My father organized the stupid engagement. He thinks it's good for me to be paired with Adele. Her family owns a huge media company overseas. Dad wants to merge with them."

"Don't you control the company though?"

"Yeah, but only because my father is too ill to keep running it," Charlie replied. "I took over the company a few years ago. Dad is constantly going behind my back, still trying to control things. But he's too sick to manage the company properly. Lately, his schemes just keep getting more and more out of control. And my brother, Eric, sides with him on absolutely everything. He's furious he didn't get to run things so anything he can do to fuck things up for me, he jumps right on board."

Stacey held up her hand. "So, you're trying to tell me that your father planned this engagement with Adele behind your back? Do you think I'm stupid? Why would I believe that?"

"You can't honestly believe I'd be seeing you if I were engaged to Adele!" he exclaimed.

"You haven't exactly been up front this entire time, Charlie."

"I know that but I thought—I thought I made things right. After changing my plans about the city."

"You did. You did make things right," Stacey replied, feeling guilty.

He had changed all his plans, hadn't he? He had come to her with a new business plan just so people didn't have to worry about leaving their homes. Stacey knew that he had gone out on a limb for all the residents, for her.

Charlie saw her weakening resolve and kept speaking, "My father really wants me to marry Adele. I've only met her a handful of times. She's in it for the money. I have no interest in being with her, not for a moment and certainly not in marriage."

"But she's going around telling people that you two are engaged. How can I just stand by while another woman does that?"

"I'll make it clear to her that we aren't together. I'll make it right. I'll tell her you and I are together. You can even be there if you want to see it for yourself." Charlie was pleading now. "Let me show you I have nothing to hide, Stacey."

She was wavering and Charlie could feel it. He had those puppy dog eyes again. Staring into them, she could believe that maybe everything would work out after all. He was offering to tell Adele to back off in front of her. Would someone be willing to do that, not to mention change his business plan for her?

"Fine," she heard herself say.

A smile broke across Charlie's face, "Great. I didn't even know Adele was here. She's probably waiting for me at my apartment. Come with me. We can end this now."

He stood up and held out his hand to hers. Stacey hesitated for only a moment before taking it.

Stacey had never been to Charlie's apartment before. It was near the beach in the section of town she had very rarely visited. His apartment was the penthouse of his building which was so close to the beach she could have walked to it every day if she felt like it.

The entrance had a fountain in the center, spilling out bright blue water. The lobby was otherwise silent, with the receptionist typing away at her laptop. The marble flooring was spotless and shined under the low lights. Stacey couldn't help but marvel at the difference

151

between this lobby and the one back home. This one was so big it could have fit more than two of her apartments.

Charlie grabbed Stacey's hand, sensing her nerves, as he slid his keycard into a slot by the elevator.

"Fancy," she joked as an attempt to hide the butterflies in her stomach.

He shot her a smile and together they took the elevator up to the thirtieth floor. The doors opened silently directly to Charlie's penthouse. Stacey's breath caught.

The hallway opened into the living room which had a fantastic view of the ocean. The sun was setting and the fading light spilled across the ocean which glittered like a gem. She was so caught up by the view that she didn't even hear Adele's heels clattering down the hallway.

"You're home! Finally! I've been waiting to surprise you for ages!" Her voice rang out as she came around the corner and stopped at the sight of Stacey.

Charlie pulled Stacey forward, across the threshold of the apartment. Adele's gaze flicked to Stacey as confusion crossed her face.

"What is someone from that God-awful apartment complex doing here?"

"Adele, you should have told me you were coming," Charlie said firmly, pulling Stacey along with him as they walked into his living room. "So I could have told you not to bother."

Adele scoffed, "What's gotten into you?"

"Nothing new," he remarked, pulling out his cell phone. "What hotel would you like to stay at?"

"I'm not staying at any hotel. I'm staying here!" she snapped.

For the first time, Stacey saw hard iron beneath Adele's lovely features. Without the giant sunglasses to hide her face, Adele's face was fully exposed. She was beautiful, skinny, and tall like a model. She was still wearing the outfit from earlier in the day but now her hair was down, cascading over her shoulders. Her hair was sleek and shiny as if she had just stepped off a photo shoot for a shampoo commercial. Her green eyes were gorgeous, lined in perfectly applied eye make-up. Her red painted lips were kissable and plump.

Standing across from such a woman, Stacey felt fat and hideous. She suddenly regretted agreeing to come here. Charlie didn't seem to be in awe of Adele's beauty, however. He just looked irritated.

"No, you're not. Tell my father you're going back home. Give him back that horrible ring too." He gestured to an incredibly large diamond ring that Adele was wearing.

"Who is this?" Adele pointed to Stacey.

"This is my girlfriend," Charlie said.

"What?" Adele went slack-jawed for a brief moment before glaring. "Surely, this is a joke? What are you doing, slumming for fun now?"

Her words were like a slap in the face. It woke Stacey up from the nervous fog that had enveloped her. She took a determined step toward Adele.

"Apparently money can't buy manners or human decency."

Charlie snickered at Stacey's remark, which just seemed to anger Adele more. She turned to look at Charlie.

"You must really want to piss your father off," she snapped. "If you think he's going to be okay with this—" she pointed to Stacey as if she was a stray dog, "instead of me, you are sadly mistaken."

"Dad doesn't call the shots anymore, Adele. Whatever he promised you or told you would happen, isn't going to happen. I'm not marrying you. So, please leave."

Adele looked as if she had been slapped in the face. Then she snatched her purse off the couch. As she turned to leave, she paused and looked back at Stacey.

"This isn't over."

Then she left, storming out of the penthouse, with Stacey watching. Her heart was beating fast. Sure, Charlie had told Adele off, but it didn't seem to matter too much to her.

"That, uh, sort of went well," Stacey remarked once the coast was clear.

Charlie sighed and closed his eyes for a moment. "That woman gives me a headache."

"How long have you known her?" Stacey asked.

"About four years now. Shortly after I was given control of the company, my father threw a birthday party for me. She was there. I could tell right away he had been scheming behind my back because she knew too many private details about me."

"Why does she want to marry you so badly?"

"Money. Her family is loaded but not as loaded as mine. She loves the lifestyle. This isn't the first time I've told her the engagement isn't happening but my father, brother, and Adele don't care what I think or how I feel."

"That sounds insane, sorry," Stacey said, sitting down on the couch, "I mean, all of this is overwhelming."

It was. The more she learned about Charlie, the more she realized just how far out of her league she was. She had thought dealing with Allison's quest to snag a billionaire was silly and over the top. But Charlie had his own family plotting against him to wed some woman who only wanted his riches. He owned a company worth billions of dollars and had probably been around the world more times than she could count.

Meanwhile, Stacey was excited simply to have found another diner job before her current place of employment closed down. She was happy if she found an extra five-dollar bill in her purse.

They came from two different universes and she was suddenly terrified.

Charlie sat down next to her and grabbed her hand, "You alright?"

"Yeah. Well, no. Not really. This is all pretty crazy, Charlie. I don't know. I had thought once you spoke to Adele, I'd feel better but…" she trailed off.

"Maybe this will help," Charlie whispered.

He leaned over and brought his lips to hers. Stacey could feel the electric charge surge over her as soon as they touched. She still wasn't used to that. She had never been around anyone who could simply kiss her and bring her to life like that.

The kiss deepened. It had been a long time since that day they had been alone and Stacey felt it acutely. It was like she had been suppressing an urge this entire time. Now Charlie had stirred it again, and it was clawing to get out.

His hands were on the side of her face, pulling her toward him as he slid his tongue into her mouth. Stacey's own hands were running through his hair. She could feel his heart beating wildly in his chest, matching her own heartbeat.

She pulled him down on top of her on the couch. He was overdressed, Stacey thought as she loosened his clothes. Charlie, sensing what she wanted, slipped out of his suit jacket and tossed it to the floor.

"Here?" he whispered.

"Anywhere," she replied quietly.

Charlie didn't hold back after her urging. He unbuttoned his dress shirt, and it dropped to the floor as Stacey pulled off her own t-shirt. Would she ever grow tired of drinking in the sight of Charlie? He was so toned and perfectly built. She ran her fingers down his chest and pulled him toward her again for another kiss.

Their mouths smashed together as he yanked her pants off. Every nerve of hers was alert, wanting and needing more of him. Soon, they were both naked. As she felt his hot skin press against hers, she sighed and closed her eyes. Even feeling him just like this was almost enough—almost.

He parted her thighs and ran his fingers along her wet pussy. It caused her to shiver. Here they were, too impatient to even go to his room to fuck. The thought thrilled her. She loved that they needed each other this badly.

Charlie slid one finger inside of her and began to move it slowly. Stacey let out a soft moan and tried to move her hips, silently begging him for more. Charlie refused. Instead, his movements were slow and languid. The one finger wasn't enough, and he knew it. But he still dragged every motion out just to torture her. She took hold of his erect member and slid her hand up and down the hot shaft.

Before she could say anything or beg him for more, he shifted so he was on the floor of the living room. He pulled her down with him in his strong arms. Their lips clashed together again. She could feel how quickly his heart was beating underneath her fingertips. He dragged his bottom lips against her lips, grazing them gently.

His fingers found her pussy again. He slid them inside of her and began to pump them quickly, in and out of her wetness. Stacey gasped and writhed underneath him. His lips found her neck, and he darted his tongue against her warm skin. All she could do was hold onto him as he finger-fucked her hard and fast.

She could feel her own orgasm mounting. But just as she thought she was going to topple over the edge, Charlie's fingers slid up her belly. She gasped in surprise and annoyance. But before she could say anything, Charlie was shifting down toward her thighs.

He left butterfly kisses the entire way down and then his tongue flicked across her pussy. Stacey arched her back. Each movement of Charlie's tongue was enough to almost send her to climax—almost. He seemed to gauge just when to stop, to keep her from finishing.

Ultimately, the mixture of his tongue and fingers proved to be too much. Stacey climaxed right on his living room couch. Charlie held onto her thighs. His fingers dug into her skin as he flicked his tongue gently against her clit as she came.

As her orgasm finished, leaving her warm all over, she realized just how much she wanted to taste Charlie. She got to her knees and pushed him to the floor.

He sensed what she was going to do and whispered her name, "Stacey."

She dragged her tongue up his cock as slowly as she could bear it. It throbbed underneath her tongue as she wrapped her lips around the head. Charlie moaned. The sound of his pleasure encouraged her. She rolled her

tongue around the head of his cock and then tried to fit
as much of him as she could into her mouth. Her other
hand cupped his balls, gently moving them around.

Charlie was gasping from the sensation of her
tongue around his hard shaft. Stacey liked the taste of
him—there was a mixture of sweet and salty that filled
her mouth as she sucked.

After a few minutes, Stacey stopped. She wanted to
feel him inside of her. She climbed on top of him and
positioned his cock so he could easily slide inside of
her. Charlie grabbed her hips as she lowered herself
onto him.

She couldn't help it—she let out a loud moan. She
was glad he lived in the penthouse because there was no
way anyone next door wouldn't have heard them.
Stacey began to ride him. Charlie's hands massaged her
breasts, and he pinched her nipples lightly. He rolled
her tits around in his hands as she buried her pussy
around his cock.

Stacey closed her eyes and focused on how
completely wonderful everything felt. She could hear
their skin smacking together. She could feel his cock
pounding inside of her with each thrust. Charlie's hands
slid to her hips and down along her skin.

Before she could climax again, he gripped her waist
tightly and yanked her down on top of him. She was
pressed against Charlie. Their skin was slick with sweat.
Her own heart fluttered in her chest. Charlie held her
hips so that she couldn't move.

Then he began to thrust into her pussy hard and fast. From this position, her clit was grinding against his shaft. The movement of his cock thrusting inside of her and her clit being rubbed was too much.

Stacey let out a loud moan and climaxed. She was pressed against Charlie and couldn't move. She let the orgasm engulf her. Charlie grunted and thrust inside her one last time before he shuddered.

They came together, clutching each other as they rocked. Stacey, having her second orgasm so quickly, felt this one was even more intense than the first. By the time it ended, she was completely out of breath.

Charlie held onto her. He was out of breath as well and had his eyes closed. Stacey looked at him. He opened his eyes and looked at her. Then he brought her in for a kiss. She could taste herself on him mixed with the saltiness of their skin. She liked it.

He pressed his forehead against hers and murmured something. It sounded like her name. They held each other like this, on the floor of his penthouse. They were in no hurry. There was nothing to bother them here. Stacey couldn't have moved even if she wanted to. Like the last time they slept together, her limbs felt heavy. Her eyelids were trying to close as if they wanted to explore dreams.

She let herself stay like this for a while, enjoying Charlie holding her. It had been a long time since she had connected like this sexually with anyone. *Why rush it?*

When Charlie pulled her in for another round, there was no way Stacey was going to refuse, no matter what her silly eyelids wanted.

Chapter Three

"Where were you?" Allison asked when Stacey got home later that night.

"Stayed late to help cover a shift," she lied, thinking swiftly.

Normally, her sister wouldn't have questioned her. But maybe it was because she was still upset about Jacob going off to Europe without her. Maybe Allison found an excuse to be angry with Stacey who was still pissed off that she had given back the tennis bracelet. Stacey wouldn't have put it past her.

"Really?" Allison drawled.

"Where is Tina?"

"In here, dear!" her grandmother called from the kitchen.

"Come here." Allison motioned with her hand.

Stacey went over to her sister and sat down next to her. She wasn't in the mood to fight or get asked a thousand different questions about why she was late.

"Something happened earlier today with Tina."

Stacey blinked. She hadn't been expecting anything to do with her grandmother. She suddenly felt nervous.

"What happened?"

"She forgot where she was for like, a good five minutes. I managed to help her until her memory came back but… Stacey, you can't keep her here. She needs care. Actual care by a nurse or something. It's only a matter of time until she hurts herself or something bad happens when we aren't here."

Stacey opened her mouth to protest. It was a knee-jerk reaction when it came to Tina. But Allison anticipated this and cut her off.

"Listen to me. Just listen to me," she said in a harsh voice. "I'm not trying to play the bitch here. But we must consider other arrangements because she can't stay here, Stacey. I know you want to take care of her but you can't, alright? She needs a doctor and medical attention."

"I can't afford it," Stacey snapped, feeling defensive. "I'm doing what I can, alright? You don't just get to swoop in here and start telling me what to do."

"I'm not swooping in here and telling you what to do. I'm thinking about our grandmother. She's only going to get worse. You and I both know that."

"What do you propose I do? I can't afford a nurse or to send her to a home. I can barely afford to make ends meet now."

"Get another job then. Work two jobs. Didn't you say you wanted to get an office job? Keep looking."

Something about her sister's tone irritated her. Maybe it wasn't just Allison. Even after being with Charlie earlier today, Stacey was still worried she was in over her head with him and his life. On top of that, she had to worry about everything else going on like work and her grandmother. Coming home to find Allison on the couch, telling her that she wasn't doing enough for Tina and needed to get another job, pushed her over the edge.

"I wouldn't have to worry about any of that if you had just kept your promise about the tennis bracelet," Stacey snapped.

Allison's eyes widened in an attempt at looking innocent, "You're still upset about that?"

"It only happened this morning!"

"I said I was sorry! You'll get the bracelet when Jacob comes back."

"If he even wants to see you again," Stacey hissed.

Allison looked irritated, "Don't start with that shit. Don't take it out on me that our grandmother is sick and needs better care."

"So, why don't you help, then? You know, for all the gold digging you do, Tina hasn't seen a penny of it. Must be nice to come in here and tell me what to do when you don't have to put a cent toward fixing problems!"

Allison looked furious but Stacey stood up to march out of the room. She had no interest in whatever her sister had to say to defend herself. As she headed toward her room, Allison delivered one last parting shot.

"You should take a shower, sis, because you smell like sex."

That brought her up short for a moment. She debated turning around but knew it would just feed into what her sister wanted. Instead, Stacey stormed off into her room.

Once she closed the bedroom door, tears sprung to her eyes. Today had been overwhelming to deal with. Too many things had happened. Between fighting with Allison, the loss of the tennis bracelet, and everything going on with Charlie, she wanted to just curl up in a ball.

The worst part of it? Allison was right. Her grandmother did need a nurse and additional medical care. But she just couldn't afford it. She didn't want to shove Tina in some awful place. She wanted the best for her. But Stacey couldn't afford it.

She couldn't sit around and rely on Allison handing over some diamonds she snagged from a rich guy. She had to take matters into her own hands. That included doubling her efforts to find a better paying job rather than settling for another waitress job.

Stacey took a shuddering breath and successfully warded off the flood of tears. No, she wasn't going to cry. Allison would have loved that. If Tina was getting worse, then she needed Allison to stay there to keep an eye on things. As much as she would love to kick her sister to the curb, she needed her.

She heard the shower turn on in the bathroom down the hall. Knowing the coast was clear from her sister, Stacey left her room to grab something quick to eat. Tina was at the dining room table with a sandwich in front of her and an old paperback book next to the plate.

"Hey," Stacey said to Tina, going over to kiss her on the top of her head.

"How was your day, dear?"

"Good, good. Everything is going well," Stacey said swiftly.

Her grandmother nodded although her eyes looked distant, "Well, that's good."

"Maria quit today. She just left. Barely even said goodbye. I know no one is in love with the diner, but I couldn't just quit and not even say goodbye, you know?"

"Yes, yes."

Stacey looked at her grandmother. Tina was still staring at her, but her response and the distant look in her eyes made it clear that she hadn't been following the discussion. That was the case more and more lately. Conversations ended limply because Stacey knew her grandmother couldn't follow them but was too afraid to let her know.

"How's your sandwich?" she asked, changing the subject.

"Hmm, a little dry but it's okay."

"I think I'll have a sandwich too," Stacey replied.

"Stacey..." her grandmother started.

"Yeah?"

Tina looked at her for a few long seconds and then shook her head, "I can't remember."

Stacey forced herself to smile, "That's okay."

Tina looked back down at her food and Stacey fought off the sadness that rose inside of her.

"Anyplace at all, seriously," Stacey said to Amanda the next day.

Amanda yanked her hair up in a ponytail, "I'll text some of my friends. They might know of an office place hiring."

"I just need an interview," Stacey pleaded. "I know I can land the job if they interview me. I'm really good at interviews."

It was true. Where most people got nervous at interviews and proceeded to panic, Stacey had always found herself good at them. Since accepting the job at the 50's diner, she had been offered three other waitressing positions. None of them were better than the job she had.

"You're lucky. I'm dreadful at them. I just sit there like an idiot and sometimes ramble. I never know who they want."

"They just want you to be your best self," Stacey replied.

Amanda rolled her eyes, "That's so corny, Stacey."

She laughed, "Yeah, I guess so."

"I'll put my feelers out. You should ask your other friends, too, just in case."

Stacey watched Amanda leave the break room. There had been an actual lunch rush today when Stacey had come into work. Amanda had been handling it swiftly herself, but Stacey knew back-up was appreciated. Stacey quickly put her things away and headed into the dining room.

At Amanda's suggestion of asking around for an office job, Stacey's mind flicked to Charlie. She didn't want to ask him for any help, even in directing her to a job. The last thing she wanted him to think was that she was seeing him for his money. It felt wrong to even entertain the idea of going to Charlie for help like that.

Even so, he would be the one to know, wouldn't he? If she made it clear she didn't want money from him, then maybe he could help her snag an interview.

She was still mentally debating this as she went over to a patron in one of the booths. Stacey was so caught up in her own thoughts that she didn't realize who it was until the person looked up at her.

It was Adele. Stacey's breath caught. What was it with everyone in her life popping up at her work?

"May I get you something to drink?" Stacey asked primly as if she had no idea who she was.

Adele looked down at the menu and wrinkled her nose, "Coffee. Lots of cream and sugar, please, I suppose. To give it flavor."

Stacey ignored the dig and scribbled it down on her pad. She snuck a glance at Adele, who was staring at the menu. Today, Adele was wearing a light pink blouse that ended perfectly at her wrists, where a bracelet glittering with rubies dangled. The ring around her finger was the engagement ring Stacey had seen yesterday. Adele's hair was up in an elegant bun. Her make-up was flawless, as usual.

Stacey tore her eyes away from Adele. It was pointless to keep comparing their two appearances. Charlie had chosen Stacey, hadn't he? Even if Stacey felt as if she was double Adele's size and was wearing her stupid work uniform, Charlie had still wanted to be with her. At least that's what last night meant, right?

Stacey turned around to get the coffee. She came back a minute later, pouring it out in front of Adele who watched as if pouring coffee was a circus act.

"Do you know what you would like to order?" Stacey asked.

Adele drummed her fingers against the table, "You know, I didn't get it at first. Why Charlie would be interested in you and have no passing interest in me. But I'm starting to understand."

"So, more time on the menu then?" Stacey replied, pretending not to hear Adele.

But that didn't deter Adele from continuing, "Yes, I get it now. At least I think I do. See, Charlie has always seemingly detested the wealth he has. He didn't even want control of the company but the board voted him in after his father had the stroke."

Something must have flickered across Stacey's face because Adele smirked. Her grin looked faintly like a shark's mouth, getting ready to take a bite of its prey.

"Oh, he hadn't told you about the stroke? Yes, his father had a stroke and was basically removed from controlling the company. Sad. So, Charlie was voted in even though Eric wanted it." She shrugged. "This is probably going over your head though."

"I have other tables to tend to, Miss," Stacey said, trying to keep her voice even. "I'll be back in a few minutes."

"Before you go… Stacey, is it? Before you go, Stacey, just remember that you're a passing fancy to Charlie. He always liked to fool around with girls who live so differently than he does. I suppose he finds it interesting. The life he could have had if only, if only. But he will tire of you. He always does. And then he will return to me."

Adele turned back to the menu as Stacey walked away. Her heart was racing. If she hadn't been at work, she would have told Adele off—and then what? As she blindly rounded the corner to the hallway near the kitchen, she felt acutely aware of how out of her depth she truly was.

What was it Adele had said? *Then he will return to me.* Return, as if he had been hers at one point. Charlie hadn't ever said he had been with her—but he hadn't said that he hadn't either.

When Stacey went back onto the main floor, Adele was gone. There was a five-dollar bill thrown onto the table, apparently for the coffee. It was clear she had come just to harass Stacey and nothing more.

Chapter Four

Stacey stepped into Charlie's penthouse, feeling uncomfortable. She was half-expecting Adele to be waiting by the elevator doors, holding a baseball bat firmly in her manicured hands.

Adele wasn't there, of course. It was just Stacey letting her dark mood get the best of her. She knew what she had to do. She was just dreading it.

"That you, Stacey?" Charlie's voice came from the living room.

"Yeah, it's me," she said, forcing herself to walk down the hallway.

To her surprise, Tony was here. He was on the balcony, talking on his phone. She could see just his back, slightly hunched over as he discussed something. Charlie was sitting on the couch with his tablet in his lap. He had a beer on the table next to him. His tie was undone and hanging loosely around his neck. Stacey felt her heart constrict at the sight of him.

"I didn't know Tony was here," she said casually.

Charlie looked over at him, "Yeah, he came by to discuss a few things. Nothing important. He just wants to avoid his girlfriend."

"Why?" she asked, sitting down next to Charlie.

"He wants to break up with her but keeps stalling. Funny how he's so great with business but when it comes to personal relationships, he turns into a little boy."

Stacey's gaze flicked back up to Tony. He had turned around now although he hadn't seen her. He was handsome but in a different way than Charlie. Charlie always looked as if he was in on a joke no one else knew about. He had those puppy dog eyes and a smile that lit up the room. Tony was handsome in a colder way. Even on the yacht, his smile and flirting felt as if it was something he did more out of habit than with meaning.

"How was your day?" Charlie asked her.

She tore her gaze away from Tony and back to him, "Okay. Actually, I need to talk to—"

It was then that Tony came inside. When he saw Stacey, he smiled at her but it didn't reach his eyes.

"Everything okay?" Charlie asked.

"That wasn't Kate, if that is what you were asking."

Stacey guessed that was the name of his girlfriend. She remembered her from the boat, pretty and gorgeous and determined to get his attention.

Tony continued, "Just an issue at the office downtown."

"What's wrong?" Charlie's eyebrows furrowed as if Tony's problem was Charlie's problem as well.

"Had a few people quit, that's all. They wanted a pay raise and it had been turned down. Now we're short staffed."

Stacey's head snapped up at this. Before Charlie could even reply, she asked, "What sort of positions are open?"

Tony looked at her closely for a second or two before replying, "Couple of financial advisors and a receptionist position."

"What about me? For the receptionist position, obviously, not the financial ones," she was rambling again but was determined to get her message across. "You can interview me. I'm not just asking for the job."

Charlie and Tony exchanged glances. Finally, he nodded.

"Sure. Give me your contact information and I'll have someone call you to set it up."

Relief swept through her. "Amazing. Thank you so much," she said and rattled off her phone number to Tony.

He finished typing it into his phone and then nodded at her. "Alright, well, I have to go. Wish me luck." He directed this to Charlie as he left.

Stacey watched him go. As the elevator doors shut, she was aware that she was alone with Charlie now. Her nerves returned hard and fast as Charlie pulled her in for a kiss.

If our lips touch, my nerve will crumble, Stacey thought and turned her head sharply to the side. His lips grazed her cheek.

"Hey, I need to talk to you," she said.

He pulled away from her, "What's wrong?"

"Adele stopped by at work today."

Anger clouded Charlie's features briefly before he ran his fingers through his hair. "Did she really?"

"Yeah. Just to sort of…ward me away from you, I guess."

"I thought I made it perfectly clear to her that whatever she planned with my father doesn't mean anything to me," he grumbled.

Stacey wanted to tell him Adele was confident that whatever he thought didn't matter. But repeating what she had said about Charlie liking girls in *different worlds* stung too much.

Instead, she decided to plow through what she had come to say. "I don't know if this will work, Charlie. You know, between you and me. I want it too. I really do. But having your fiancée threaten me at work because I'm seeing you is a little too much. Not to mention I'd be dealing with whatever your family might throw my way. And maybe, just maybe, it wouldn't affect you too much. No matter what happens, you'd be okay in the end. But I might not. If anyone were to get hurt in this situation, it would be me. And it just isn't healthy for me to keep trying to push these feelings aside. If I'm feeling overwhelmed now, what will it turn into later?"

She had said this all in one burst without pausing to let Charlie speak. But she stopped speaking as if all the words had been emptied out onto a pile on the floor by his feet. He stared at her with a strange expression on his face. Stacey couldn't read it. She wasn't good at breaking up with people. When she had caught Jake cheating on her, it was a declaration. A clean break.

This was different. She was breaking up with Charlie because their worlds were too different. She wasn't sure if she could handle living in his.

Finally, Charlie found his voice, "So…that's it then?"

"Do you understand? I'd rather leave now before the situation is even more over my head. Your family wouldn't want us to be together. I can't have Adele suddenly pop up in places just to threaten me to leave you. I have too many other things going on to worry about a crazed stalker."

Charlie cleared his throat and said softly, "I understand."

She was disarmed by this. She had been expecting anger. Maybe some sort of passionate speech about why they should keep trying. But Charlie just looked resigned. Stacey didn't know what else to say. She got to her feet.

"Bye, Charlie," Stacey said awkwardly.

Charlie didn't respond. She turned away and quickly walked down the hallway toward the elevators. As she reached for the elevator button, she paused. *Is this it?* She had been expecting more. She thought he would come after her, that he would have tried to stop her.

She pressed the button. Tears sprung to her eyes as the elevator arrived to take her down, away from Charlie.

≪◇≫

"Did you hear me?"

"No, sorry. What?"

Allison rolled her eyes, "What is up with you today? You're so out of it."

Stacey looked up from the store window she had been staring into. It was her day off, three days since she broke up with Charlie. There hadn't been a peep from him. Even though she was the one who had broken up with him to save her from more heartache, she couldn't understand how he hadn't reached out at least once.

"Sorry," Stacey said lamely.

Allison had dragged her out to window shop with Tina. Stacey had agreed because she thought it would be good to get out of the house. If she had let herself dwell on her situation, she would have spent the entire day in bed.

But it seemed she wasn't very good at focusing. Her sister stared at her, waiting for her to explain herself.

177

"I have a headache," she said, trying to look convincing.

"Sure," Allison said with a snort and walked away, catching up to Tina, who had wandered further ahead.

Stacey watched her sister. The annoyance she felt being around Allison lately had faded. Her mind was focused on Charlie instead. Even though she felt so sure she was doing the right thing, she couldn't help but wonder if she was making a mistake.

Maybe Stacey should have dealt with his family and Adele head on. Was it wrong of her to have jumped ship so early? She pushed the thoughts out of her mind. There was no point in dwelling on them. She had made her choice. Charlie's life was too chaotic for her. It was filled with drama and uncertainty. Stacey had her own issues to deal with.

She wandered up to where Tina and Allison were looking at a store window. Allison looked over her shoulder. "I don't know why you're so distracted today. Don't you have that interview tomorrow?"

It was true, she did. Tony's local office had called this morning to schedule a meeting. She set it up, but even that made her feel guilty. She had leapt at the chance to get that interview, breaking up with Charlie not five minutes later. Surely that had to look bad.

"Yeah, I do."

"You'll do great," Tina said, heading into the shop.

The two sisters followed their grandmother into the store. It was filled with mostly tourist trinkets. Tina stopped at the snow globes to admire them. Allison glanced over at Stacey.

"So, you gonna tell me?"

"Tell you what?"

"Who you fucked the other day."

"Jesus! Keep your voice down," Stacey snapped. "Why are you so crass?"

"Because it makes you upset," Allison said, laughing.

Stacey turned away from her, pretending to be interested in a row of ugly jewelry boxes. But Allison didn't get the hint and hovered over her shoulder.

"It doesn't matter," Stacey finally relented. "We broke up."

"Oh. Sorry about that, sis. Whatever, he was a jerk to begin with. You sorta suck at picking them." Allison saw the look on her sister's face and quickly added, "No offense."

Stacey didn't reply. Instead, she looked over to make sure Tina was alright. She had picked up another snow globe and was shaking it. There was something slightly glassy in her grandmother's eyes that sent a pain through her heart.

Behind her, however, Allison was determined to keep the conversation going, "Jake was alright at first, I guess. I really thought you two might work out. You know, when I saw him recently at the deli, he said he was single."

Stacey whirled around, "Are you suggesting I get back with him?"

Her sister shrugged.

"How can you suggest that? After what he did to me?"

"Fine, fine, forget I even mentioned him." She held her hands up as if to ward Stacey off, "Listen, if the new guy didn't like how you looked, forget him."

She stared at Allison who seemed oblivious to what she had just said. She crossed her arms.

"Why can't I have been the one to break up with this guy? Why do you assume it was him? And why do you assume it was because of how I look?"

"Well, I just know in the past how guys have treated you. Are you angry that I just assumed you were dumped? I swear, you just look for a reason to be pissed off."

"No, I don't. And I broke up with him."

The two stared at each other as if they were each deciding how much they wanted to bicker in the store. But Stacey was tired and worn out. She didn't feel like fighting with Allison again.

Instead, she turned around and went to check on Tina.

Chapter Five

Tony seemed to own a lot of different businesses like Charlie did. Charlie focused on construction and investing whereas Tony focused more on the media and publicity for celebrities.

The office in the city where Stacey had her interview was one of the media branches. They owned a local news station and had a slew of celebrities that used them for publicity.

As she waited for her interview to start, Stacey tried to quell her nerves. This job was something she knew she could do. The woman who had called her to set up the interview had made it clear that the position entailed tasks such as making copies, scheduling appointments and events, and keeping the front desk running smoothly alongside two other receptionists. Tony was willing to take a chance on her by getting her an interview. Stacey didn't want to blow it.

She still felt as if she was walking around in a fog. She hadn't been expecting to miss Charlie so much. She also hadn't been expecting how much she hoped he would have reached out to her. Why? Stacey asked herself for the millionth time. Even if he had called, what could she say? She couldn't have gone back to him.

Stacey pushed thoughts of Charlie out of her mind and looked around the waiting room. There was no one else in sight. The TV was playing the news. Everything was decorated in bright colors and there were paintings on the walls. It would have been cozy if she hadn't felt so nervous.

In front of her was the desk she would be working behind if she were hired. A woman sat behind the counter, typing rapidly on the computer. Stacey blanched at the idea of being asked about computers. She had never owned one. All she knew how to do she had learned at the library.

After about ten minutes of waiting, one of the side doors opened, and a smartly dressed woman came out. She introduced herself as Ms. Stark and escorted Stacey down the hallway. It was decorated more of the same. She didn't see anyone else. The area was quiet although in the distance she could hear music.

Ms. Stark opened another door. They entered a small meeting room with a table and chairs. Stacey sat down across the other side of the table and tried to wash everything else from her mind.

It was time to show her best self.

Thirty minutes later, Stacey was shown around the rest of the establishment. The job wasn't offered to her then but she couldn't help but feel confident. She doubted they took time to show every person who interviewed a quick tour of the office.

As Stacey was being shown one of the meeting rooms, someone stepped out of the elevator nearby.

It was Tony. Stacey bit her tongue to stop herself from calling out to him. She would hate it to look as if they were chummy.

He was dressed as formally as she had ever seen him. His hair was slicked back, and he was speaking rapidly into his cell phone, in Chinese, or more specifically, Mandarin, as she found out from Tony later. Stacey didn't understand a word. He finished up the call and turned around.

"Stacey?"

For some reason, she felt a blush rise on her face. Ms. Stark started talking in her high-pitched voice to Tony about how Stacey was here for an interview.

"Yes, I know who Stacey is. Are you showing her around?" he asked with a smile.

"Yes, we were just about to—"

"I'll take it from here," he said, gently interrupting Ms. Stark.

The look that the woman gave Stacey was all she needed to know that this was unusual. Ms. Stark nodded and walked off, looking back one last time at the two of them.

Stacey, feeling nervous and slightly uncomfortable, said, "You don't have to do this."

"Of course, I do," he replied, still smiling. "Ms. Stark is a fantastic worker but can be a bit too bubbly."

"Yes, well, that is one way of putting it," Stacey replied lightly.

Tony let out a laugh. There was something comforting about it that she couldn't put her finger on. As he showed her the rest of the company offices, she found herself relaxing. It hardly felt like a job interview now.

"I have an office here, too, although I'm not here often," he said as they walked down the hallway on the second floor.

He stopped at the door at the end of the hallway and unlocked it. They stepped inside. It was a simple office. For some reason, Stacey had been expecting something completely over the top. She had been thinking about his yacht. She had assumed if he owned a yacht, everything would be grand like that.

But his office was clean and simply decorated. Even the view was subpar—just the street and the buildings across from it. There was nothing to set it apart from any other office Stacey had already seen.

"Nothing much. Like I said, I'm not here often. But I try to have an office set up in each of my buildings."

"Where do you spend most of your time?"

"Around. All over. I have offices here and in China so I bounce between the two," Tony replied.

Stacey looked at one of the paintings. It was an ocean spreading out as far as she could see. In the middle rose a dragon.

"You like that? Don't be fooled. I try to fill my office with at least one token Chinese-looking piece of art. People seem to expect it. Do you want some coffee?"

Stacey looked over her shoulder, "Oh, sure. Thanks." She looked back at the painting. "You mean you don't like this?"

"Nah. I think I got it at a garage sale."

"People really expect Chinese things because you're Chinese?" Stacey asked him as he handed her a cup of coffee.

"Of course," he said laughing. "Might as well give them what they want."

"Well, thank you again for allowing me to come in for an interview. I really appreciate it even if I don't get the job."

"Ms. Stark doesn't show people around the office unless she is impressed. I wouldn't be too worried. Although you look worried."

"Do I?"

"Yeah. Worried about the job?"

Worried about everything, Stacey wanted to blurt out but instead said, "Just a lot going on."

Tony nodded. A ring on his thumb flashed. It was gold with a giant emerald in the center. It glimmered under the office lights.

"My dad gave me this," he said, having noticed Stacey looking at it. "When I was little. It used to be too large for me to wear, so I hid it under my pillow every night as a good luck charm."

"Did it bring you good luck?" Stacey asked.

"Not at first," Tony replied and there was something a little sad in his tone that brought her up short.

Silence fell between them. Her brain tried to find something to fill the silence with, but it was Tony who spoke first.

"Anyway, I'm glad that you will be working here. It'll be nice to see a friendly face every day. And at events as well, since I suppose Charlie will be taking you out."

At the mention of Charlie, Stacey balked. She looked away from Tony. Something must have shown on her face because he raised his eyebrows.

Seeing no point in hiding it or wanting to make him think she was keeping secrets, Stacey said, "I broke up with him. A couple of days ago. That day you were at his place actually."

Surprise crossed Tony's eyes followed by something else that she couldn't make out. Then he said, "I didn't know. I'm sorry to have brought it up."

"No, I should have said something." She looked down at her coffee. "I hope you don't think—I wouldn't want you to think that I—I mean, if you decide to offer me the job, I wouldn't want you to have offered it to me because of Charlie. So, it's better you know."

Tony's gaze softened. "I wouldn't offer you a job based solely on him or any connection. I actually broke up with my girlfriend the same day you broke up with Charlie."

"Oh! Charlie mentioned you two…" She made a gesture with her hands as if to signal that Tony and his girlfriend were on the rocks.

He smiled a little, but his eyes told a different story. "She wanted more of me and I couldn't give it to her. I'm not ready to settle down. I didn't want to keep her hanging around thinking I would change my mind. Better to end it. She was upset but it will be better for her in the long run."

"You didn't want to settle down with her?"

"It wasn't anything personal," Tony replied. "I'm just not ready for that and she was."

For the first time since she had met Tony, Stacey saw a real person beneath the business glamor. It was strange but endearing to see someone struggle with regular problems. Unlike when she met Charlie, she knew Tony was a billionaire. She had assumed everything would be perfect in his world. But he looked upset at the mention of his break-up.

It was this sudden vulnerability that spurned Stacey to ask her next question, "What is up with Charlie and Adele?"

At the mention of Adele, Tony's eyebrows shot up. He took a sip of his coffee before giving a proper response.

Finally, he asked, "You met Adele?"

"Three times, technically."

"And you're still standing here. Amazing."

"You don't like her?" Stacey inquired.

"What's to like?" Tony remarked as he turned around to head toward his desk. "You've met her."

"She came to see me at work." Stacey paused for a moment, searching for the right way to word things. "She said that Charlie dates girls like me for fun. That'd it be a passing fancy. He would eventually go back to her."

"I've known Charlie for quite some time and I can tell you he never liked Adele in that way. She's liked him for years. When his father came up with this stupid idea, Adele jumped right on it. She thought she would win him over right away, see? That Charlie would leap at the chance to marry her."

"No such luck?"

"No. He didn't have a good relationship with his father or his brother. So being shoved into some marriage with Adele just rubbed him the wrong way. Even if he did care for her at some point, that has long since died." He paused. "Why? Were you worried he would leave you for her?"

Stacey decided since Tony had confided in her about his own relationship that she could at least do the same. "No. No, it was partly because of Adele. Mostly it was just the fact that I felt in over my head. See, I didn't know who he was when we started dating. So, finding out and then having some woman threatening me—it was just too much. Especially with everything going on like—"

She cut herself off and shook her head. "Geez, sorry. What am I doing just rambling to you like this?"

"I don't mind," Tony said with warmth in his voice. "Really. I talk about business so often. Sometimes I forget there're other things going on in the world as well."

"My grandmother is sick. She probably needs a nurse or to be placed in a home. But money is really tight and my sister is useless for help so—" she said, trailing off with a shrug. "Worrying about that and finding a new job and then all of Charlie's stuff. Maybe I'm selfish but I just had to put myself first."

Tony was studying her. There was something different in his gaze that made her want to look away. But she didn't. Instead, she met his stare. Her heart skipped a beat.

"I'm truly sorry about your grandmother," he finally said in a soft voice. "Struggling with a sick family member—it isn't easy on anyone."

Stacey was going to ask if he was speaking from experience, but his phone rang. He pulled it from his pocket and looked down at the screen.

"I should take this. I'll have Ms. Stark escort you out."

Stacey felt her stomach lurch. She was disappointed the conversation ended so abruptly. The thought came to her quickly and surprised her.

Tony smiled gently at her as his phone kept ringing. "It was lovely talking to you, Stacey."

Chapter Six

Stacey dreamed she was back at her parents' house. The lights were on and the TV was blaring the news. She stood in the kitchen. Everything was how she had left it the day her parents died. The fridge was covered with Allison's drawings and Stacey's tests demonstrating excellence.

She looked down at herself. She was not a child, not any longer. She looked around the kitchen and then slowly moved toward the living room. It felt as if she was walking underwater. Her limbs weighed a thousand pounds each as she tried to move into the living room.

When she finally stepped inside, the TV turned to static. The sudden noise made her wince. She walked over to mute it. Her parents would be furious if they knew she left all the lights on as well as the TV. What was she thinking?

Stacey turned off the TV and turned around. On the couch was Charlie. His sudden appearance startled her, but she felt rooted to the spot. He stood up and languidly walked over to her. He didn't seem to be affected by the quicksand that surrounded Stacey's own limbs.

He dragged one finger down the side of her face and tilted her chin up to meet her eyes. Her heart beat so rapidly she thought she might faint. She wanted to tell him she missed him. She wanted to ask him why he was there, in her childhood home.

But none of that occurred. Around the corner came Adele. She wore a snake around her neck as she glided toward Charlie. Stacey tried to pull Charlie toward her but Adele wrapped her hands around his waist and pulled him away.

Stacey couldn't do anything. All she could do was watch Adele pull him away from her. Her feet refused to move. She wanted to pull him back—tell him she missed him—

Suddenly, Stacey's eyes snapped open. A strange noise filled her head. It took her a few moments to realize it was her phone ringing. She wiped her eyes, trying to erase the dream that clung to her, as she picked up.

By the time she grabbed her phone, it had stopped ringing. The voicemail icon appeared a moment later. Stacey listened to it. The fog of the dream instantly vanished when she heard the message.

I got the job, she thought to herself, replaying the message from Ms. Stark just to make sure she had heard it correctly. She couldn't believe it. The money she would be getting from the job would make things a lot easier on her. She would be able to afford care for Tina and pay the bills with a little extra to spare.

Her head was swimming. Even though she had gone to the interview and was confident she performed well, she hadn't quite expected to land the job.

She sat up in bed. She was working an evening shift at the restaurant tonight and lay down to take a quick nap before getting ready. The dream quickly forgotten, Stacey got out of bed to tell Allison and Tina the good news.

Yet when she walked out into the living room, Allison was sitting on the couch crying into Tina's lap.

"What's going on?"

Allison looked up. Her eyes were rimmed with red and her cheeks puffy. For a brief second, Stacey thought maybe something truly bad had happened.

But then her sister wailed, "Jacob dumped me!"

She broke into fresh tears. Stacey's first thought was that they were never going to get the bracelet back now. Her second was that she was pretty sure her sister didn't care at all about Jacob. He had been boring and clearly only into himself. What her sister was mourning was the loss of yet another chance at landing a man with tons of money.

"Sorry for your loss," Stacey replied, hoping she sounded as if she meant it.

Allison kept crying and shook her head. "I think he met someone in Europe! He called me and said things wouldn't work out. He said we were just too different!"

"Ah, dear," Tina murmured, stroking Allison's hair.

Stacey fought not to roll her eyes. Anytime Allison ended up single, even if she was the one who did the breaking up, she acted as if it was the end of the world.

Stacey, who had been looking forward to sharing her good fortune with Allison and Tina, saw it fade in front of her eyes.

"I didn't realize you cared so much about him," she quipped.

Allison scowled, "Don't be a bitch now."

"Allison!" Tina scolded.

"But it's true! She's just upset because she got dumped, too."

She was trying to goad Stacey into a fight but Stacey was too happy about the job to care. All Stacey said was, "I dumped him," and headed toward the kitchen.

She could hear Tina comforting Allison in the living room. Even with her sister dealing with the break-up and losing the bracelet forever, it couldn't spoil the fact that Stacey had landed the receptionist job.

As she rummaged through the cupboard for something to eat, finally settling on some instant noodles, her sister came in.

"You want some?" Stacey offered, pulling out another pack.

"No." Allison sniffed.

"Alright."

"You don't seem bothered."

"About what?"

"Well, I can't get the bracelet back now."

"Yup," Stacey replied. "Oh well."

Allison narrowed her eyes. "I thought for sure you'd flip your shit."

"I considered that thing lost as soon as you gave it back to him with your lame-ass romantic gesture," Stacey admitted. "Besides, I got the job that I interviewed for. While the money we could have gotten for that bracelet would have been useful, at least I'll have more income."

"Oh. Well, congrats," Allison mumbled.

"Don't worry. I won't let that steal your thunder of another billionaire breaking your heart. You're on a bad run, aren't you?" Stacey said as she filled a pot with water.

"Don't be such a bitch."

"Well, I guess that means you'll be crashing here a bit longer, right?"

Allison at least looked abashed at this, "Uh, yeah, well, I guess."

"It's fine. You can stay," she replied as she put the pot on the stove.

"Thanks. Sorry for, uh, calling you a bitch."

"It's fine. Wouldn't expect things to change suddenly."

She could tell Allison was biting her tongue. She knew her sister well enough to know that she was pissed off Jacob dumped her. She wanted to argue with someone but also needed a place to stay. That meant she couldn't keep digging in like she was. Stacey had to admit she was enjoying this a bit.

"Well, maybe next time will be the one, right? Surely, all these years of effort have to pay off sometime."

Allison frowned and opened her mouth before quickly closing it. Stacey watched her sister leave the kitchen, clearly hoping to find sympathy from Tina instead of her.

<<◇>>

The next week was a complete blur. Stacey began training at Tony's office during the day and covering shifts at the restaurant during the evenings. By the time she got home, she was so exhausted that she fell asleep in a matter of seconds.

Things became even faster-paced as she entered her second week. This was going to be the week that she was released into the office without training wheels. Stacey had been relieved to see herself picking up on things quickly, even the computer. All the hours she had spent on the library's computers had ended up helping her out. She was a fast learner.

Stacey hadn't seen Tony since her interview day. She had been thinking about him, on and off, as she was learning the ropes of her new job. Everyone at the office spoke highly of him, which Stacey knew was unusual. Everyone seemed to genuinely like him, and they appreciated him working in an office that didn't show off his billionaire status.

On the first day of her second week, a summer storm ripped through the city. It had been ages since it had rained this hard and Stacey found herself making sure everything was okay at home before heading out to work.

Allison had been claiming she was too depressed to do anything around the apartment. Stacey decided that once she had figured out the best way to get her grandmother professional care, she would force Allison to get a job. She was sick of letting her sister crash at her home and not do anything because she was too busy sulking in her misery.

The storm started early in the morning. By mid-afternoon, the rain was coming down in thick sheets, blanketing the city. It was shortly after the power flickered on and off the first time that Tony stopped into the office.

Stacey hadn't been expecting him. It wasn't as if she was kept in the loop about when he would be arriving. She had been focused on trying to get her computer to connect to the internet which kept going down due to the storm.

She heard him before she saw him and looked over her computer monitor. Tony was speaking to Ms. Stark in a low voice about something. She was nodding a lot and looked like a bobble head. Stacey had noticed in the short time working there that Ms. Stark always seemed to be overly caffeinated, reminding her of Amanda from the restaurant.

Tony looked up over Ms. Stark's head. His eyes settled on Stacey, who ducked behind the computer screen. She felt embarrassed. She didn't want him to get the impression that she had been staring at him. She was determined to not look at him again and threw herself into work when suddenly the power went out completely.

The office was plunged into total darkness. It was already dark outside, so windows offered no extra light. The rain thumped loudly against the building along with a wind that had come along with the storm. It had been a while since a summer storm this intense had rolled through.

A few people began to mumble about why the generator wasn't coming back on. Of course, an office like this would have a back-up generator. She could hear Ms. Stark asking someone else about why the generator wasn't on.

"Something fascinating on the screen?"

Stacey looked up and was staring directly into Tony's eyes. Her heart skipped a beat, and she shook her head.

"No, just waiting for the power to come back on."

"Generator needs to be reset. I'm going down to check it. Want to come with me?"

"Me?" Stacey asked curiously.

Tony shrugged, "That way you'll know for next time."

"Oh, um, sure," Stacey replied shyly.

As Tony turned around to tell Ms. Stark he was going to reset the generator, Stacey couldn't help but find his excuse lacking. In the back of her mind, she knew that Tony wanted to get her alone. The couple of times he had flirted with her was not lost on her.

There's no way, she thought to herself. There could be no way that he was interested in her like that, no way that Stacey was interested in him like that. She had been sucked into Charlie's life once. She wasn't going to flirt with another billionaire.

"Come on," Tony said to her over his shoulder.

She got to her feet and tried to ignore Ms. Stark, staring at her. No one else noticed, nor cared that she was going down to reset the generator with Tony. They walked through the hallway toward the basement which he unlocked with a key. A dark staircase led downstairs.

"Creepy," Stacey remarked. "Isn't this how horror movies start?"

Tony laughed and pulled out his phone, turning on a flashlight app. Then he led the way down the stairs first. Stacey followed. She was slower than he was because she was in heels, but Tony waited for her every few steps.

The basement was filled with a random assortment of things. The musty smell of old paper and boxes tickled her nose. Dust filled the air, and she fought the urge to sneeze. Tony looked around the room.

"We probably need to clean this place out at some point."

"At least dust it."

There was a sudden boom of thunder that caused Stacey to make a startled noise. Tony was by her side right away as if she was in some sort of real danger. She felt embarrassed by her reaction.

"Are you okay?"

"Yeah, sorry," she said. "Just wasn't expecting it to be so loud."

This close to Tony, Stacey could feel how warm he was. His cologne was different from what Charlie usually wore. It was deeper and spicier. There was something comforting about it.

"This way." He led her to another door at the back of the basement.

Another clap of thunder rumbled out but Stacey didn't jump this time. She refused to let herself look like a baby again. It was just a storm. Tony stopped in front of the door and opened it. The hinges creaked loudly. Stacey half expected some monster to leap out at them.

Instead, it looked as if this was where the breakers for the building were. Tony stepped inside, holding up his phone to illuminate the wall.

"Internet, power, security, all of that comes down here. The generator is here as well. We haven't had to use it in a while so it just needs to be reset. It'll be good for you to know in case Ms. Stark isn't available."

Stacey couldn't imagine a time when Ms. Stark wouldn't be in the office but didn't say that. She nodded but realized it was dark down here and he couldn't see her.

"Okay," she said aloud.

She followed him to the generator as he held his phone up to illuminate it. He opened a panel to expose several buttons inside.

"Would you please turn on your flashlight app too?"

"Well, no. My phone doesn't run apps."

This seemed to startle Tony. He turned his head to look at her. The look on his face was comical only because he was surprised by something so small.

"I just have a flip phone. I don't even have it on me. I keep it in my purse during the day," she explained.

"Wow," he finally said as another boom of thunder sounded out. "Sorry, I just assumed…"

"It's okay. I get it. Almost everyone has a smartphone now."

"Well, come look at this, at least."

The spot in front of the generator panel was a tight fit for the two of them. But Stacey managed to slide into the small space as best as she could. Her side was mushed against Tony's side. The sudden closeness to him made every nerve of her body snap to attention.

"You just have to turn it off all the way. Sometimes this thing is weird and thinks it is off but it isn't. So, pressing this," he said as he pressed a red button, "will power it off completely. Then we wait a full minute."

"Okay," she murmured, suddenly feeling very shy.

As they waited, he tilted his face to look at hers. They were incredibly close. Their noses could touch if she only leaned forward a little.

"Settling in here okay?" Tony asked her softly.

"Yeah. Everyone has been nice. I can't thank you enough for the job."

"You earned it. Apparently, you gave the best interview so you got the job."

"Right, but…" She hesitated before speaking. "I had no previous office experience."

"I was willing to take a chance on you," Tony said gently.

Something in his tone, the warmth perhaps, made Stacey blush. She could hear her heart beating. Being this close to him had Stacey wondering if he could hear it as well. It would be embarrassing if he knew what an odd reaction she was having because he was so near.

"Well, thank you," she finally said.

"How are you holding up? With the break-up?"

Stacey was surprised at the sudden mention of Charlie. Yet his eyes betrayed nothing. In this low lighting, it was impossible to see what Tony was thinking.

"I'm okay. I mean, I'm the one who ended it, so why dwell on the past?" She cleared her throat. "What about you?"

"Ah, well, I'm okay. Like you said, I wanted to end it. So why dwell on it?" he said softly.

Being this close to him, speaking of past relationships, made Stacey forget that she was down here in this basement with Tony. It even made her forget that Tony was like Charlie—rich and well off, part of another world completely. They were just two people who had ended things because of the cards life had dealt them.

Stacey was going to open her mouth to ask something else when suddenly the power flicked on. The sudden burst of light in the basement startled her. She gasped in surprise and closed her eyes for a couple of seconds.

Tony cleared his throat loudly. "Power is back. Well, I'll tell you anyway. After you wait a minute, press this green button and it resets the generator."

He pressed it hastily, and the generator made a beeping noise. The screen flickered and a green light flashed indicating it was ready. Stacey wriggled her way out of the tight space. Her mouth felt dry. The sudden blast of the lights made her feel as if she had been on stage and the spotlight had found her. Whatever the strange spell was that had settled over the two of them, it had quickly dissipated.

"We should go back up now," Tony said, ending the discussion about their recent breakups.

Chapter Seven

"Can you repeat that, dear?" her grandmother asked after Stacey had recounted the story about the power going off at work.

"Which part?"

Tina scrunched up her face as if trying to remember before saying, "What were we talking about?"

"The weather," Stacey said, sighing inwardly.

It wasn't even that she had told her grandmother the story. It was that telling her the story and having her forget it almost immediately made her heart break.

"It's been raining all day," her grandmother said, looking out the window.

"Yeah, it's going to be raining all week, I guess," Stacey replied. "Things may be sort of crazy. But we'll be okay."

Tina turned to look at Stacey and asked, "Whatever happened to those men who wanted us to leave?"

At the mention of Charlie and his company, a stab of guilt bloomed over Stacey's chest and she replied, "They lost interest. So, we don't have to move."

Relief swept across Tina's face, "Oh, good. I would have hated to move somewhere else."

"Me too," Stacey said, turning around to hide her face.

It wasn't easy to forget Charlie. Even though she told herself that she didn't owe Charlie anything and had to put herself first, it was hard to remember that. He had switched around so much to date her. She wasn't sure how to appease the guilt that seemed to lodge itself in her gut when she thought about it for too long.

The front door slammed, signalling that Allison had returned from whatever crazy venture she was up to today. At least she had left the house instead of moping around about that wet-reed Jacob for another day.

"It's raining so fucking much," she heard Allison grumble.

"Language," Tina remarked as she came into the dining room.

"Sorry, sorry," Allison said. "Man, it's cold in here."

Stacey looked over her shoulder. Allison was dressed in a black t-shirt that was a size too small. It clung to her wetly and hugged her curves. Her jeans were also wet, which must have been uncomfortable.

"Dear, you are soaking wet," Tina observed. "Go change out of those things and put on some dry clothes."

"Yeah, I think I will. Thanks."

Stacey, knowing her sister better than anyone, followed her to the hallway. She had shoved some clothes in Tina's chest of drawers and was rummaging through them. Stacey leaned against the doorframe.

"Nice day?"

"I was trying the puppy dog act with Jacob."

"What, soaking wet clothes, staring at him outside his hotel?"

Allison pulled out a fresh t-shirt. "Something like that."

"Any luck?"

"A little. I pretended I was meeting someone else there at the diner across the street. Timed it so we would run into each other."

"Geez, Allison, is it really worth this much effort? The guy is a total tool."

"Yeah, yeah, I know. But the money, Stacey. If I snag him, imagine the wealth. Not just for me. All of us."

Allison moved past her and headed toward the bathroom to change. Stacey watched her sister and shook her head. She still didn't understand how Allison could put so much energy toward these types of men. Surely, she would grow out of it? She would see how silly it was to try to snag someone rich just to pay her way through life.

The bathroom door shut and locked. Whatever Stacey had been thinking, she knew it was pointless to try to bring it up with Allison. Better to choose her battles.

<<◇>>

The storm continued through the next day. When Stacey arrived at the office, she found herself looking for Tony. She felt foolish for doing so. The shared moment in the basement the other day had been nothing. She was losing her head over minor things just to try to forget Charlie.

Even so, when she left work that day to cover a shift at the restaurant, she felt disappointed at not having seen him.

"How is the job?" Amanda asked as Stacey headed into the break room to drop her things off.

"Going well. Exhausted though."

"Well, we close soon. Are you still going to take that job at the 50's diner?" Amanda asked as she let her hair out of her ponytail.

"I think so. The extra money would be nice," Stacey replied although she was also thinking it would be a good distraction from how she was feeling about her love life. "You look cute. What's going on with you?"

"I have a date with Brad," she said, wiggling her eyebrows. "He asked me out the other day. Throwing myself at him for ages finally paid off."

"Congrats to you. That means…"

"Yup, you're stuck with Chester as the cook."

Chester was the part-time cook, a grumpy old man that William called in for favors sometimes. Stacey hadn't worked with him in a long time but always detested it. Last time he had pinched her ass, and she almost clocked him.

"Great. Well, good luck on your date," Stacey said, knowing how long Amanda had been harboring a crush on Brad.

"Thanks," she beamed. "Hey, whatever happened to that cute guy that came by to talk to you that day?"

Was everyone keen on mentioning Charlie in some way to her? Stacey tried not to cringe and gave a noncommittal shrug.

"Nothing came of it."

"Ah, that's a shame." She looked at the time on her phone. "I have to go. Have fun dealing with Chester."

Stacey waved goodbye and headed out to deal with the one family in the restaurant. The restaurant was closing next week. It would be strange saying goodbye to a place where she had spent four years working. This place, always intended to be a stepping-stone to better things, had ended up feeling like a different sort of home to her.

She knew working at the other diner would be a lot of work. Even now, she was flat out exhausted when she got home from working both at the office and here. But Stacey felt if she were to stop for even a minute, thoughts that she had been trying to stifle would surface. She didn't want to dwell on Charlie or wonder why she had been let down at not seeing Tony today.

Even though the office job made life a lot easier money-wise, Stacey was still terrified of suddenly having the rug pulled out from under her. The last thing she wanted was something to go wrong at Tony's office without a backup job. She felt as if she had lucked into this one. At any time, it could be snatched away, leaving Stacey grappling for money again.

Even with Chester, her shift went by at a good pace. Customers dropped in non-stop during the night. Most were William's friends visiting for the last time before the diner closed for good.

Stacey was tired when she got home but she was growing used to being exhausted.

When she opened the door to the apartment, Tina was sitting on the couch. She had her knitting needles in her lap again although it appeared as if no project had been started. The TV was showing the weather. They only got a handful of channels because Stacey didn't want to put money toward paying for a pricier cable package. Tina seemed to always have it on the weather channel.

"Hey. Is it still going to rain?" Stacey asked by way of greeting.

Tina nodded, "Looks like it. More big sweeping summer storms are coming our way."

"It's been a while since we had storms this bad," Stacey said as she took off her shoes. "I guess we should get used to them."

Stacey turned to put her bag on the table near the front door. She checked her phone just in case someone had tried to reach her. There were no messages. She turned around to ask her grandmother if she had eaten, and let out a strangled noise of surprise.

In the few seconds that Stacey had spent turning around and checking her phone, Tina's eyes had rolled into the back of her head. She was convulsing on the couch. In the back of Stacey's mind, she knew that her grandmother was having a seizure. But all she could feel was blind panic at seeing Tina in pain.

She returned to her phone, fumbling to dial 911 as she rushed over to Tina. Her grandmother was about to slide off the couch but Stacey managed to grab her. Her arms were rigid and had gone straight above her head. Her feet had banged against the coffee table and were currently kicking as if Tina was being pulled under a current.

"911, please state your emergency?" A proper female sounding voice came over the line.

Stacey gripped her phone and tried to stop Tina from injuring herself more on the table. "My grandmother is having a seizure. She's never had one before!"

The operator tried to talk Stacey through what to do as an ambulance was dispatched. All she could feel was overwhelming fear churning in her stomach as she watched her grandmother shake and rock back and forth for what felt like an eternity.

By the time the paramedics arrived, the seizure had subsided. Tina was on the floor with her head in Stacey's lap as the EMTs came in to treat her.

The next hour was a blur. Tina was loaded into the ambulance while Stacey followed. Her grandmother looked so tiny and frail, strapped in the gurney. Her skin looked as if it was paper-thin. Stacey gripped her grandmother's bony hand and tried to swallow her tears. She didn't want to sob the entire ride to the hospital. She didn't want to be hysterical in front of the paramedics. The tears threatened to spill while she gripped Tina's hand tighter.

Tina was whisked away to be evaluated once they arrived at the hospital. Stacey found herself alone in the waiting room. The hospital was freezing cold. Even now, she could hear the storm beating against the hospital roof. She sat down in one of the uncomfortable chairs and stared down at the floor.

She knew she should be calling her sister. Allison needed to know that Tina had had a seizure and was in the hospital. Her phone was shoved in her pocket. She tried to call Allison, but there was no answer.

"Voicemail is currently full," the robotic voice told her.

Stacey ended the call. Normally she would have been furious at her sister for not answering her phone and then having a full voicemail box. Yet she felt numb all over. All she could feel was the metallic taste of worry in her mouth.

It had all happened so quickly. Tina had seemed completely fine. How could they have been discussing storms one minute and then the next Tina was in the hospital? The image of Tina thrashing around, arms rigid and legs kicking, came back to Stacey. She closed her eyes.

She tried her sister again but to no avail. She was sure that Allison was busy trying to woo Jacob back into her spider's web. Sitting there, alone in the hospital waiting room, Stacey had never felt so alone.

When her parents died, Stacey and Allison were doing homework together. Even back then, Stacey tried to teach her sister by helping her with studies, but with little luck. The two sisters had been different from birth like the wind and the sea.

Stacey could recall that evening with perfect clarity. She could see Allison rolling her eyes at her. She could smell the cookies that Tina had just baked and was letting cool in the kitchen. They were with their grandmother because their parents had gone out to a party that night. Stacey could recall feeling pleased with herself because she had painted her nails for the first time by herself. It was a shiny pink color—glossy and applied as perfectly as Stacey could manage.

She had kept glancing at her nails as she lectured Allison. She liked the way they contrasted against the darkness of her skin. Allison had been so mad that she hadn't been allowed to paint her nails by herself yet. But their mother knew it would end up all over the kitchen table.

The TV was on in the living room. Tina and Burt, the girls' grandfather, were watching the local news. Burt had always smelled like cigars. It was a comforting scent to Stacey, even now. She remembered the phone suddenly ringing. The noise shattered the peaceful illusion of the night. In Stacey's mind, that phone ringing was when everything changed. It signalled the end of one chapter and the start of a terrible one.

Allison had gotten up to answer the phone. She had recently started using the phone to call friends as often as their parents permitted, much to their grandparents' chagrin. It seemed natural that her sister would think it was for her.

But it was Tina who had gotten to the phone first. She picked it up, waving Allison off. Then she asked for the caller to repeat the message.

Stacey could recall the sudden swoop of her stomach. Her pencil, hovering over her math homework, seemed frozen in the air. She had no reason to suspect anything was wrong, yet there was something off about how her grandmother was speaking. Her tone was pitched up high, too high, and then she placed the phone down to pick up the call in her bedroom.

Burt had followed Tina, leaving the two sisters alone. Allison began badgering her. Stacey had shushed her, which just annoyed Allison.

Then she heard it, the crying from the bedroom. She had never heard her grandmother make that sound before. It was a keening wail that seemed to silence Allison as if she had lost her voice. The two of them stared at the bedroom.

When Burt came out to tell them that their parents were killed, Stacey found that she couldn't look him in the face. Instead, her gaze fell on the TV right behind him. She stared at it, letting the images wash over her as Allison sobbed.

The picture on the television was fuzzy and sometimes would burst into static. Stacey watched it silently.

Chapter Eight

Something snapped Stacey out of her memories. She felt as if she was dragging herself out of a pool filled with tar as she looked up. The waiting room was still empty. The TV shoved in the corner was playing the news. She was freezing cold sitting there in the small waiting room all alone.

The noises that jarred her were from two nurses walking by. They had clearly come from their break and were talking excitedly about something. The words seemed to slide in and out of her brain without registering.

Her fingers were curled around her phone. When Stacey opened her hand, her bones felt stiff. She wasn't sure how long she had been sitting there thinking about Tina and the night her parents died.

She tried calling Allison again, but the result was the same. She put her phone on the seat next to her and went back to staring at the floor. She had been trying for so long not to cry about the situation that she doubted the tears would come even if she wanted the relief the tears would bring.

Her phone vibrated. Without looking, Stacey answered.

"Finally," she said, although nagging Allison was more out of habit than anything else. "You need to get here to the hospital. It's Tina," her voice hitched. "Tina had a seizure or something."

"Stacey?"

A male voice jarred Stacey, and she looked down at her phone screen. She had answered an unknown number.

Tentatively she replied with, "Who is this?"

"Tony. I'm sorry to have called you. It was about work. Ms. Stark gave me your number but…" He paused and trailed off.

It took Stacey a few seconds for her mind to catch up with what Tony was saying. Out of everyone to call her, she hadn't been expecting it to be him.

"Oh, sorry. I didn't even look to see who was calling."

She had hoped that her voice sounded normal. She had tried to make it sound as if she hadn't answered the phone, word vomiting about her grandmother. But her voice ended up a pitch too high. It sounded false even to her own ears.

"Stacey, your grandmother… is she alright?" His tone was gentle and soft as if he was approaching a deer and trying not to scare it.

Maybe it was Tony's voice. Perhaps it was the fact that Stacey hadn't gotten through to Allison to talk about Tina being in the ICU that finally cracked the ice she had been trying to keep around her heart.

But instead of telling Tony everything was fine and she would call him back later, she let out a choked sob. Her tears came fast and furiously as she recalled the events to him.

Tony listened silently. She was sure that he thought she was crazy. What sort of person sobbed like this to their boss? But Stacey couldn't have stopped even if she wanted to.

When she finished, Tony asked, "You can't get in touch with your sister?"

"No. She's probably trying to fuck Jacob or something," she retorted tearfully.

Tony wasn't sure of the extent of Allison and Jacob's relationship and didn't ask. Instead, he said, "Stay there, okay?"

The call ended suddenly. Stacey stared down at the phone, which was now lifeless in her hand. Where else would she go? Out of habit she tried Allison again but got nothing. With little else to do, she did what Tony had asked. She stayed there. It wasn't as if she would leave Tina alone.

After some time, she was tracing a line in the carpet with her foot when she heard someone speak her name. Stacey looked up, hoping for a doctor or someone who would have an update on Tina.

But to her surprise, Tony stood there. She blinked a couple of times to make sure that she hadn't imagined it. But no, he was standing right next to her. He was wearing a regular t-shirt imprinted with a band name she didn't know. He had a pair of baggy jeans on. For once, his hair wasn't slicked back and was slightly messy. He was wet from the rain. In one hand, he was trying to cradle two coffees.

"Tony," Stacey breathed.

"That took longer than I thought. Rain slowed me down."

"What are you doing? Why are you here?" Stacey asked.

"You were alone. Your grandmother is in the hospital. I thought you could do with some company." Tony sat down next to her and handed her one of the cups.

"For me?"

"Of course. Unless you think I'm the sort of fool to carry two coffees around for myself."

Stacey gingerly took one from him. It was still hot. She held it in her hands, cradling it as she looked away from Tony. She hadn't been expecting this random act of kindness, especially from Tony of all people. The gesture touched her.

"It's mocha. I hope that's okay. I wasn't sure how you take it."

"No, this is perfect, thank you," Stacey replied.

Tony offered her a small smile as he took a sip of his own coffee. The two of them sat in silence for a few minutes. Stacey blew on her cup to cool it off as Tony sat next to her. His phone rang but he didn't check it or get up to take the call. Instead, he sent it to voicemail. They sat together in a strangely comfortable silence. Even though her heart was aching, having him with her made things a little better.

"I should try Allison again," Stacey finally mumbled.

"Still can't get hold of her?"

"No."

"Have you tried texting her?"

The question was a simple one but wasn't even something that Stacey had considered. Stacey's phone plan didn't cover texting. She considered it an expense that she didn't need. But that didn't mean her phone couldn't text.

"I'm an idiot. I should have…" she said as she brought up the text screen.

Tony's hand rested on her knee. She looked up at him. Her chest constricted for a moment. His eyes were kind.

"Don't be so hard on yourself."

She nodded, "Right. Yeah. It's just difficult."

She composed a text to Allison which felt as if it took twenty years to write. Since her phone was a simple flip phone, there was no fancy keyboard to type the message. After what felt like hours, she finally hit send.

"That might get her attention," Stacey admitted. "I don't think I have ever sent her a text before."

She waited a few seconds. She hoped that Allison would get her message and call. But her phone was as silent as ever. She took a sip of her coffee. The warmth of the beverage helped, especially since the hospital was so cold. Tony didn't look bothered by the fact he was wet and sitting in a chilly hospital waiting room.

Something struck Stacey, and she turned her head to look at him, "Why were you calling me?"

"I was going to see if you could work Saturday. Some of us are trying to finish up a last-minute media deal, and I needed someone to handle the front desk. But don't worry about that now."

"Oh, well thanks for thinking of me. I'm always trying to earn extra cash," Stacey said.

"I'll keep that in mind if I can get you more hours. I'll let Ms. Stark know before I leave."

"You're leaving?"

"Not for long. I have some business back home to attend to. I'll be gone for a week or two."

Tony's leaving made Stacey feel odd, although she couldn't pinpoint exactly why. Her head was starting to hurt and she didn't dwell on it. She rubbed her temples.

"You must be tired," he said to her.

"I am, but I'm not going anywhere until I know what is going on with my grandmother," Stacey replied.

"Let me try to find you a blanket, at least."

She nodded and yawned. As soon as Tony mentioned being tired, she could feel the exhaustion seeping into her bones.

By the time he returned with a blanket, Stacey was ready to fall asleep. Tony was draping the blanket over her, when a tall, pale thin man came out of the ICU and walked over to them. Stacey stood up, although she didn't know why. It just seemed as if she should be standing when he came into the waiting room.

He introduced himself as the doctor and then told Stacey of Tina's condition.

"We aren't sure what triggered the seizure yet. But she's going to pull through."

Relief swept through Stacey so hard and fast that she thought her legs were going to give out. Tony must have sensed her weakness because he had taken her elbow to steady her.

The doctor continued, "We want to keep her overnight for observation. We aren't sure how this is going to affect her brain."

"Yes, of course. Please. Can I see her?"

"Not yet. But I'll let you know when you can."

Stacey nodded, although she would have liked to see her grandmother immediately. She wanted to see her with her own eyes that Tina was going to pull through. As the doctor left, Stacey realized that Tony was still supporting her. She quickly pulled away.

"I'm glad she's going to be okay," Tony said to her.

"Me too. I'm just worried about her memory. It was already not that great. Now I am definitely going to have to get her proper medical care. What if this had happened when she was by herself?" She felt sick just thinking about it.

"Well, the good thing is that it didn't," Tony said to her. "So don't dwell on that."

Stacey didn't get a chance to reply. She heard someone rushing down the hallway. Her sister appeared as if conjured up by magic. Her hair was plastered to her head from the rain and she looked out of breath. Her eyes were wild and panicked as she looked around.

When she saw Stacey, she bolted over to her and crushed her in a hug. Not being able to recall the last time that she had hugged her sister, Stacey slowly returned it.

"She's going to be okay," Stacey whispered. "The doctor was just here."

"I am so fucking sorry that I didn't get your message," Allison said. "My phone was on silent. I just happened to check it when I went to the bathroom, and I saw you had texted me. I would have come here earlier if I had known."

"I know. It's okay."

The hug ended and Allison glanced at Tony. She frowned, probably wondering why in the world he was there.

Tony smiled. "I called her to ask something, and she thought it was you. I thought I would come by to keep her company in the meantime."

"How nice of you," Allison replied although there was a strange hitch in her voice that Stacey didn't understand.

"He brought coffee," Stacey added.

"Great. Can we see Tina yet?"

"Not yet. They'll let us know. They want to keep her overnight for observation."

Allison shook her head. "This is so fucked up. Can you believe this? Tell me exactly what happened."

Stacey launched into the story again. When she finished, Allison was fiddling with the hem of her skirt. Her sister was obviously with Jacob because she was dressed for a night out on the town.

"That's awful. I told you. I told you she needed to get placed into a nursing home or something," Allison accused.

"I know. But I couldn't afford it. And I was there."

"What if you weren't?" Allison demanded. "She has to be somewhere safe, Stacey. Not at home. We're going to have hospital bills out of the fucking ass to pay now, anyway."

Stacey hadn't thought of that. She had been so concerned with Tina that she hadn't thought of how little insurance would cover for this hospital stay. She could feel a headache threatening to pounce.

Allison kept going, "We have to find her a home to stay in. We can't risk that again. I won't let you."

She didn't have the energy to fight with Allison. She didn't have the energy to point out that money didn't grow on trees and she was doing what she could. Instead, she just gave into exhaustion. Her sister kept lecturing her as if she had done something wrong. She knew Allison was stressed out and upset by the way she was lashing out at Stacey.

But Tony didn't know that. He swiftly stepped in between the two of them.

"That's enough."

"Excuse me?" Allison snapped.

"This isn't Stacey's fault. It isn't anyone's fault. Your grandmother is going to pull through. The best thing you can do right now is work together."

Allison looked at Tony as if she couldn't believe the words coming out of his mouth. Then she looked over at Stacey.

"What is this? Is this the guy you're fucking?"

"Wow, really?" Stacey snapped, feeling an emotion that wasn't just numbness for the first time in hours.

Tony looked alarmed. "No, we aren't like that."

"Then why are you here? What sort of guy swoops on over with coffee like that? She just got out of seeing a guy. Step off."

"Allison!"

Tony looked abashed. "It isn't like that. I know she just got out of a thing with Charlie—"

Allison's gaze snapped back to Stacey. Oh shit, Stacey thought. She suddenly wished Tony had just kept his mouth shut.

"Charlie? You mean that asshole who tried to kick us out of the apartment complex? You were dating him?"

Tony went to speak again but her sister shoved past him. She was looking directly at Stacey now.

"Are you fucking kidding me, Stacey? You were seeing that guy, but kept getting on me for dating Jacob? Are you a hypocrite or just a jerk?"

"Neither," Stacey snapped, coming to life underneath her sister's judgmental gaze. "I had no idea who Charlie was."

"Oh, so that makes it alright? Did you leave as soon as you found out?"

When Stacey didn't reply, Allison threw her hands up in the air.

"Well, that answers that."

"We don't need to discuss this right now. It isn't important. We can talk about it later."

But her sister was shaking her head. "No way. You don't get to weasel your way out of this one."

Stacey was mortified that Allison was pressing this right now under the circumstances. She didn't feel like discussing Charlie in front of Tony. It felt wrong somehow as if she was flinging his kindness back in his face. So, she turned around and walked away, down the hospital hallway. If Allison was determined to fight about this, then Stacey wasn't going to let it happen in the waiting room in front of Tony.

Sure enough, Stacey could hear Allison following her down the hallway. She walked through the waiting room toward the ER and went outside. The rain was still coming down. It was coming down so hard that it slammed off the ground and the nearby cars, each droplet exploding.

They were under an overhang. Stacey stopped at the edge of it and turned around. It had cooled off considerably from the rain. It felt as if summer had been swept away in the storm. Allison crossed her arms. She was shooting daggers from her eyes.

"Just blurt out what you want to say and get over it," Stacey said simply.

"I just can't believe you. I really can't. This entire time you were hooking up with the guy who wanted us out on the streets. Not only that but how many times have you lectured me about my lifestyle? So, it's okay for you to chase rich men but not me?"

"I wasn't chasing him! I didn't even know who he was. I didn't seek it out. I wasn't trying to snag a rich guy to pay my way through life, Allison."

"How can you have stood there and nagged me about what I was doing with Jacob when you were doing the same thing? You always act so fucking holier-than-thou, Stacey. As if the way you live life is the right and proper way and the way I live is disgusting. But this entire time you weren't any better!"

"I am better!" Stacey snapped, finally bubbling over and having enough. "You really want to talk about this now while our grandmother is in the hospital? No, I had no idea who Charlie was. When I did, I wanted to break up with him. He saved our apartment complex just to have a shot with me, and I still broke up with him!"

Allison's eyes widened slightly but she didn't speak.

Stacey went on, "I broke up with him because that lifestyle he had with his family plotting and planning against him, and some woman thinking she was engaged to him—why would I want that? Money would solve all our problems—I know that! But it isn't enough for me to put up with the insanity that comes with that inner circle!"

"We are never going to have enough money, Stacey! Never! No matter how hard we work or how much we try, we aren't ever going to be secure, much less comfortable. I know you just got that new job so you're feeling as if everything is going to be easier now, but look," she gestured at the hospital, "Now Tina is going to need serious medical care and you're broke as hell again."

"So, what? What does that mean? That I'm just supposed to not try? Should I just run off and try to marry a rich guy? That doesn't solve anything either, Allison. Sure, you'll have money. But what else will you have? A guy who you pretended to like and changed yourself to be with. Why would I want that? Why would you want that? You're always selling yourself short. You think if you show someone who you really are, you'll be shot down."

"Now you know what I'm thinking and feeling? I'm so sick of butting heads with you! No matter what I do, it isn't good enough. Ever since Mom and Dad died, you think you know it all when it comes to me. But you aren't my mom. You don't have any control over me or what I do."

"Obviously," Stacey said through clenched teeth, "Since you have no fucking idea what you're doing."

Allison's jaw clenched, too. The two sisters stared at each other. Part of Stacey wished they were little kids again so it would be socially acceptable to tackle Allison to the ground and pull her hair.

"No, you don't get to do that anymore," Allison finally said. "You don't get to tell me how to live my life."

"Then get out."

"What?"

"Get out of the apartment. I don't want you there anymore. I always do this. I always do this shit for you. I let you crash at my place. I tolerate your poor life choices. I keep thinking one day you're going to wake up and realize there is more to life than fucking rich guys and trying to get their money. But you're right, it's your life. So, leave and live it."

Allison looked shocked. Stacey had surprised herself. She had never actually told Allison to leave before. It had always been some strange mutual understanding that her sister would constantly mess up her life and would crash on Stacey's couch.

But why? Why did she tolerate that? Stacey always bowed to whatever Allison wanted. Ever since they were kids, she had done it. But anytime they were together all they did was fight. It was no longer worth it.

Allison's shock quickly turned to anger. Her pretty features twisted, and she scowled. She didn't say anything. Instead, she just turned around and headed back inside the hospital.

Stacey watched her go, feeling empty and unmoored.

Chapter Nine

"This one is nice." Amanda slid the brochure over to Stacey.

Stacey picked it up and looked at it. It was a nursing home on the outskirts of the city. The photo showed a radiant nurse helping an old man out of his wheelchair. Something about the photo was so phony that all Stacey did was drop it back onto the table.

"Let me see it. I'll look it up." Tony took the brochure off the table.

It had been four days since Tina had her seizure. She was still in the hospital for observation. Stacey had spoken to her grandmother for the first time after the first night of observation. It hadn't been uplifting. Tina had been distant and foggy. She had a difficult time remembering recent events. She kept asking Stacey if she was still considering going to college—something she hadn't considered for many years now. When Tina asked for Allison, Stacey tried to keep the bitter tone out of her voice that her sister wasn't there.

In fact, when Stacey finally made it home that first night, Allison's things were gone. Her sister left the hospital an hour before Stacey did. She must have gone by the apartment and cleared everything out. The living room couch was stripped of all blankets and pillows.

Her clothes were yanked out of Tina's dressers. The bathroom was clear of the makeup piles and perfume sets Allison cherished.

It was as if Allison had never been there. Stacey wanted to feel the loss, but she was so stressed and concerned about Tina that Allison's leaving without saying goodbye was the last thing on her mind. She was too drained to think about it.

Now she was sitting at the small dining room table with brochures of nursing homes splayed in front of her. Amanda had come by to help. To her surprise, so had Tony. He had been a constant presence since the first night at the hospital. He would leave for a few hours a day to tend to business and then would return to her place again to check on her.

Normally, Stacey would have protested. She would have told Tony it wasn't necessary to keep coming back to spend time with her. But he was giving her time off from work and offering a shoulder to lean on. With Allison gone, she needed the support more than she could admit to herself. So, she took it without question or protest.

"This place doesn't have a great rating online," Tony said from behind his laptop.

He was looking up reviews of places where Tina could live. Stacey appreciated it. She didn't own a laptop and felt too frenzied to do her own research at the library. Having Tony look it up and tell her up front if the place was solid or not had helped out a lot.

"Forget it," she said.

Amanda took the brochure and threw it in the trash. "Moving on."

"Guys, this is starting to look hopeless," Stacey mumbled, running her hand over her face.

"Only because you're emotional and want the best for your grandmother like anyone would," Amanda pointed out.

Tony nodded. "She's right. You want Tina to go somewhere nice so you're bound to overthink it. You want the best for her, it's only natural."

"I want the best, but can't afford it," she sighed.

Amanda's phone rang. She excused herself and left the dining room. Stacey looked down at the brochures. All of them were blending together. Very gently, Tony's hand covered hers. The touch of his skin sent a flash of warmth through her. Stacey looked up at him, startled.

His smile was kind, "It'll come together. Don't worry."

"It's hard not to worry. I told myself I wouldn't ever send my grandmother off somewhere. I would take care of her myself. And now look—I'm trying to find a place to dump her."

"You're not dumping her. You're doing the right thing, Stacey. I know you want the best for her. And this is the best."

Stacey nodded and mulled his words over in her head. Her gaze settled on the way his hand covered hers. There was something comforting about his touch. Her heart was beating quickly for the first time in a while for a reason other than fear.

She heard Amanda end the phone call and pulled her hand away. She got up from the table.

"I need something to drink. What about you?" she said quickly, hoping the fact she was blushing wasn't evident.

Before Tony could answer, she went to the kitchen to find drinks. She scolded herself for letting herself feel that pull toward Tony. She had bigger things to worry about. Acting like a schoolgirl wouldn't help anything.

"What do you think?" Tony asked her.

Stacey looked around the garden. The sun was poking through the clouds which were threatening yet again with another summer storm. Even though everything looked dreary and dark, the garden was still pretty. There were fresh flowers in a well-maintained garden, as well as trees that were tall and healthy looking. Benches were stationed around the garden for people to read or just enjoy the day. A couple of chess tables were under one of the largest trees. Two men were hunched over, trying to finish the game before the clouds let loose.

"I love it."

It was true. She did love it. Not just the garden, but the entire nursing home. It seemed to be exactly what Stacey wanted for her grandmother. She had been impressed by the rooms and the nurses. She liked the activities they had for the residents. Even the décor was bright and cheery.

"I mean, from start to finish, everything in it is amazing," she went on, "in fact, I want to move here myself."

Tony laughed at her joke. If she had thought three weeks ago that Tony would have been the one to drive her forty minutes away to check this nursing home out, Stacey would have thought she was crazy.

But the drive had been enjoyable. With Tina still in the hospital and her memory seemingly worse than ever, Stacey was on the brink of a serious crying jag when Tony suggested the trip. She had agreed just to get out of the city and look around.

"Of course, she can't stay here."

"Why not?" Tony asked.

"I looked at the prices. I can't afford to put Tina here. If I had known how expensive this place was, I wouldn't have bothered making the trip."

Tony had been checking one of the activity rooms when Stacey had inquired about the cost. It was completely out of her price range. This place was state of the art and one of the best nursing homes in the state.

"I feel bad that I made you waste your time like this."

Tony shook his head, "It wasn't a waste of time."

There was something in his tone of voice that gave her pause. It had been like that a lot recently. There were light touches from him, like his hand on the small of her back guiding her into rooms, or a casual brush against her hands. Every time he did that, Stacey felt herself instantly react. Her heart seemed to thrum and her throat would tighten.

Yet she hadn't entertained the idea of doing anything with Tony. Perhaps if life hadn't been so messy already, she would have thought that he was interested in her. But the odds of two billionaires being interested in her was too comical for her to consider.

"How wasn't it?" she asked as the sky lit up suddenly with the first lightning strike.

Tony reached out for her. His arm entwined with hers as he pulled her toward the nursing home to get her out of the incoming storm.

"You have a better idea of what you're looking for in regard to Tina," he said as they entered one of the activity rooms.

The woman who had been showing them around appeared by Stacey's side. "Glad you guys got in before the storm! So, what do you think?"

"It's perfect but I'm going to have to think about it," Stacey lied swiftly before Tony could mention money.

"Of course. We understand it is a big decision to make." The woman beamed at her as they followed her toward the lobby.

They said goodbye once they reached the front entrance, and Tony held the door open for her. The sky had darkened considerably in the few minutes they had spent inside. It looked as if it was going to crack open at any moment and pour rain down on them.

"The storms this summer are crazy," Stacey remarked.

"I should have brought an umbrella or parked closer. Want me to pull the car up?"

"No, it's okay," she said, feeling too uncomfortable to ask Tony to do that for her. "We can just walk quickly."

They set off across the parking lot. Earlier, when they had arrived at the facility, it was during the peak visiting time. Because of the increased visitors, the parking lot had been filled. Tony had parked way in the back.

As they hurried across toward the car, the clouds decided they had had enough and opened up. One second Stacey was dry as a bone, the next it was almost as if she had dropped herself into a swimming pool. The rain soaked through her clothes, and she gasped in surprise. It was freezing cold.

Next to her, Tony let out a laugh. She couldn't imagine laughing. She was sure his clothes today—which consisted of a simple white dress shirt and a pair of khakis—were probably designer-made. She would have been in tears after getting expensive clothes ruined by rain.

But his laughter softened his features as he pulled her toward the car. Her clothes were completely drenched in a matter of seconds. When they finally arrived at his car, Stacey couldn't help it. She began to laugh as well.

It was the first time she had laughed this hard in ages. The sight of Tony, laughing, soaked to the bone and apparently not bothered by the torrential downpour struck her as humorous for some inane reason. She just stood there, resting against his car, letting the rain belt against her as she laughed.

It was a welcomed reprieve to feel something that hadn't been frustration, pain, or anger. It was as if she had been swimming in those emotions lately. Laughing with Tony over seemingly nothing was freeing.

She looked up at him and their laughs suddenly died. Before Stacey could do anything, Tony was moving toward her. His fingers were tilting her chin up to meet his eyes. Her breath caught.

Then he brought his lips down onto hers. The kiss was soft and probing as if he was expecting her to pull away.

But Stacey didn't pull away. She returned the kiss. The rain pelted against her skin. Goosebumps broke out across her body. She could feel Tony's wet clothes against her. His lips were warm even in this weather.

The kiss deepened. His hands went around her waist. She pulled him against her as she leaned against his car. His hair was messy as she trailed her fingers through it.

Tony moved an inch away from her and breathed, "I've been wanting to do that for quite a while."

She blinked water out of her eyes and tried to hide her smile. She had wanted it as well. She just had never expected him to make the move.

"We should head back now," she finally said, "before we both catch colds."

Tony laced his fingers through hers and said, "Sounds good to me."

Chapter Ten

Stacey looked out the window of Tina's hospital room. For once, it wasn't raining. The sky was hazy, the sun blocked by clouds. It was overcast and muggy outside, a strange mix of summer and storms.

Tina was watching a daytime soap opera from her hospital bed. Her figure looked somehow skinnier and more fragile than when Stacey had seen her yesterday. Her eyes were glassy and her voice muted. They had barely spoken since Stacey's arrival twenty minutes ago.

"It's really warm outside today," Stacey said in an attempt to jumpstart the conversation again.

Tina nodded but didn't reply. Stacey could feel her chest constrict. Whatever the seizure had done to Tina had been intense with little chance she would bounce back from it.

Stacey spoke again, "Allison is gone. Has she come by to see you? I asked her to leave the apartment."

It was something she normally wouldn't have told her grandmother. She had tried to shield her from the fights she had with her sister once Tina's memory started to worsen. But Stacey thought instead of sugar coating the conversations, she would try to be brutally honest.

And it seemed to work. Tina turned her head slightly to look over at Stacey, whose heart lifted.

"Allison never finished her homework. You tell your sister… you tell her what she needs to do."

Then she turned back to the TV. Stacey watched Tina with the hope lessening in her chest. She knew that Tina needed constant medical care in a nursing home. But she couldn't find one that was solid that would also fall into her price range.

The place that she had seen with Tony had been a dream come true. She told herself not to dwell on it any longer. She couldn't put Tina there. Not with hospital bill debt about to be racked up.

She had told Tony that much on the drive home the other day. After they had kissed, it was as if a dam had burst between them. During the car ride, they had swapped stories about growing up. He talked about his grandfather who had suffered a stroke and ultimately passed away when Tony was a teen. It felt as if he understood why she wanted to take care of Tina and not just lock her away somewhere awful and forget about her.

Even with everything going on, she found herself thinking back to the kiss with Tony. It had been a picture-perfect kiss. The sort of kiss Stacey had seen in movies and had never dreamt she would experience herself.

She wanted to kiss him again. She could hear Allison's voice in her head, calling her all sorts of names over the fact she had kissed Tony. But she pushed it out of her mind. Her sister was gone—running back to Jacob or whatever new billionaire she was trying to snag.

"Stacey."

Her grandmother's voice snapped her back to the present. She stood up and went over to Tina's bedside. Stacey grabbed Tina's hand and held it gently. Her skin felt like wrinkled paper, and she looked old. It was as if she had aged twenty years in less than a week.

"Yes?"

"Don't blame yourself. It isn't your fault that I'm here."

A moment of clarity. That was what her grandmother was experiencing. The doctor had told her this would happen sometimes.

"I need to get you better care," Stacey said quickly as if the clock was running against her. "I need to get people to watch over you all the time."

Tina patted her hand, "I know. You always know what to do. Your moral compass… it always pointed North. Strong and true. Just like your mama."

Tears sprung into Stacey's eyes. She could feel a lump in her throat. Stacey blinked past tears but it was impossible. She could feel them fall down her cheeks.

Tina smiled a little and said, "Your sister was here earlier."

"She was?"

"Yes. She said you two fought. You two were always fighting ever since I can remember. You two are so different. But after I'm gone—"

"Don't talk like that," Stacey said, panicked.

"After I am gone," she repeated firmly, "you two need to take care of each other. You must watch out for one another no matter what. You're sisters. No matter what."

"I know. I know you're right. She's just…"

"Different from you," Tina whispered, "I know this. But Allison will find her way someday. You just need to be patient."

Stacey nodded, unable to speak. It was as if all the air had been sucked out of her lungs. To hear Tina talk about after she was gone, put things in dreadful perspective. Her fear of losing her grandmother seemed to wreak havoc within her stomach. For a second, Stacey was worried she was going to be sick.

Then Tina let out a yawn. Her eyelids looked droopy as if she was going to fall asleep on the spot.

"Are you tired from the meds?" Stacey asked.

"That's right," she mumbled.

Stacey didn't get a chance to reply. Tina's eyes closed as she drifted off to sleep. Stacey stood there and watched Tina sleep. Her chest ached. She didn't have anyone else in this world. It was impossible to deny. But she had always considered Tina to be the one solid force in her life.

Losing her parents had been such a brutal stab to her heart. Even now, when she thought about her mom and dad, sometimes the sadness threatened to engulf her. It was her grandparents who had stopped her from completely losing it as a child.

But her grandfather was gone now. All that remained was Tina. To lose her was going to be a terrible thing no matter if it was ten minutes or ten years from now.

After watching her sleep for a few moments, Stacey left the room. The thought of going back to her apartment depressed her. She wasn't used to being completely alone there.

The muggy summer air hit her as she left the hospital. It was still cloudy and looked as if it would rain again at any moment. Yet the air was hot and made her clothes stick to her skin. She checked her phone to see if Tony had called her.

There were no calls from Tony, but there was a missed call from a number she didn't know. When she listened to the voicemail, she heard a message from a woman who worked at the nursing home Stacey had gone to see with Tony.

Confused, she returned the call and leaned against the hospital wall. A proper sounding woman picked up on the third ring and introduced herself as the admissions agent.

"I'm just a little confused," Stacey said after introducing herself, "I didn't fill out any information about sending my grandmother there."

"Are you sure? We received everything this morning including payment in advance for five years."

"What?"

"Everything is set up and paid for through AAC Investments. Is that not correct?"

Stacey clutched her phone tightly as her head swam. For a brief crazy second, she had thought perhaps Tony had set it up. It had made sense, hadn't it? He had been there with her. But the name of the company that had set it up and paid in advance sounded like one of Charlie's companies.

"Can I call you back?" she said quickly and hung up before the woman could reply.

Charlie had known about Tina. She knew that information was swift and rapid in their little, closed circle. If Tony had mentioned it to anyone about her grandmother, Charlie could have heard.

Even so, Stacey ended up dialing Tony's number.

"Stacey! I was just about to call you."

"Hey, sorry to bother you. I have a weird question. Did you tell anyone about my grandmother being in the hospital?"

"Well, yes, I had to let certain people at the office know why you were leaving for a while. Ms. Stark knew."

"What about anyone else?"

"Oh, did Charlie call you? I told him about the nursing home and Tina but only because he was there—"

"I have to go. I'll call you back."

"Wait, Stacey! Did you—"

But Stacey had already hung up. It was Charlie then who had overstepped and given her this gift to woo her back. But there was no way she could take this. She didn't want to have anything to do with him and she thought she made that clear the last time she spoke to him. There was no way she could accept his paying for five years at the nursing home.

She debated calling him and telling him that she couldn't accept it. But Tony had mentioned that Charlie was still in town. Stacey would go to him directly and tell him she couldn't let him pay for her financial conundrum.

When Stacey arrived at Charlie's apartment, she realized belatedly that she wasn't getting past security. She had forgotten how state-of-the-art everything was. So much for cornering him unaware.

Feeling out of place among such luxury, Stacey went to the front desk. She gave her name to the receptionist and asked to see Charlie. The woman looked her up and down as if wondering why someone like Stacey was there. Stacey felt exposed and vulnerable in front of this well-dressed pint-sized woman but kept her gaze level.

After a couple of minutes on the phone, the woman looked up, looking surprised.

"He says you can go up now."

Stacey thanked her and headed toward the elevators. She pressed the penthouse button and felt the elevator lift her up toward Charlie. Now that she was about to see him, she felt incredibly nervous.

She hadn't seen him since she had broken up with him. He hadn't tried to call her or reach out in any way. Stacey should have known that he was planning some major gesture to try to convince her to give him another chance.

The doors to the elevator glided open. Charlie was already waiting for her. The sight of him knocked the breath out of her. She had seemingly forgotten how perfect he was. He had some stubble across his face, but other than that, he was unchanged. His hair was messy. The sleeves of his dress shirt were unfolded and hung around his wrists.

"Stacey," he said, "I have to admit that this is quite a surprise."

Stacey willed herself to step off the elevator. She forced herself to look into his eyes.

"I need to talk to you. About what you did."

He looked confused for a moment. "What I did?"

"With my grandmother."

Charlie still looked lost. She wondered why he was acting as if he didn't know what she was talking about. She sighed.

"Charlie, stop. I know you paid for Tina's nursing home care. But I can't accept your gift. Please call them and change it. Get your money back. I'll figure something out but I can't take your money."

Charlie didn't seem to have the reaction that Stacey expected. All he did was stare at her as if she had three heads. Stacey was going to say more but cut herself off and crossed her arms defensively.

"Stacey, while I am touched that you think I have stepped into this situation to help you out, I'm afraid you're mistaken."

"What?"

He shrugged, "I didn't set up Tina at any nursing home nor put any money toward it. I don't know who did, but it wasn't me. Sorry you came all this way for that."

Stacey could only stare. The rest of her speech died before it could leave her lips. She had been planning on telling him how she couldn't take his money especially since they weren't together, and how they both needed to move on but all she could do was feel extremely embarrassed.

Charlie moved toward her. He was very close to her now. Up that close, she could recall how his lips felt on hers. The thought made her look away from him.

"I have to admit that it is nice seeing you again," he said very softly.

His voice made the hair on the back of her neck stand up. She could feel his breath brush against her cheek gently. It made her head swim to be this close to him again. Stacey was about to topple off that cliff and leaned forward to kiss him in a moment of weakness when a thought hit her out of the blue.

"Tony."

Confusion crossed Charlie's features, "What?"

"Tony. It was Tony who must have paid for it. That's what he was trying to tell me on the phone," Stacey thought aloud. "I have to go. I'm sorry to have bothered you."

Before Charlie could say anything else, she had spun around and was back in the elevator. The last thing she saw as the doors closed was Charlie standing there with an emotion on his face that she couldn't quite pinpoint.

Stacey tried to reach Tony as she headed back home, but he didn't pick up. She felt as if she had some sort of emotional whiplash. From finding out someone had paid for Tina to be at the nursing home, to being that close to Charlie, and finally to realizing that it was Tony who paid.

It had come to her right before she could kiss Charlie. Of course, it had made the most sense. Tony had been there. Even though Charlie was capable of such a huge gesture, Stacey hadn't heard from him since the break-up.

Why had she jumped to thinking it was Charlie instead of Tony? Tony had even tried to talk to her on the phone. He was probably trying to tell her it was him when she had hung up. Yet she had convinced herself that it had been Charlie.

Because she wanted to see him again, a little nagging voice in the back of her head said. As much as Stacey wanted to ignore it, she knew it was the truth. She had completely convinced herself Charlie was the one who had come to the rescue.

She would have kissed him. If her brain hadn't gotten its shit together, she would have leaned forward and kissed him. Would he have been upset if she had? Stacey doubted it. She had a sneaking feeling he would have kissed her anyway.

Stacey stepped off the bus and got inside the dingy apartment lobby just as the skies opened yet again. Leon was in the lobby, checking the mail for his mother. He looked over at her when she entered.

"How is Tina?" he asked—everyone in the complex had seen Tina loaded into the ambulance.

"She's been better."

"There's some guy waiting for you outside your apartment."

"What?" Stacey exclaimed.

Leon shrugged and pulled out a pack of cigarettes from his pocket. She was too distracted to ask when he had started smoking or to lecture him about it.

"He's Asian."

Tony. Stacey said thanks and hurried upstairs. She was glad he was there because she wanted to speak to him about Tina. Although she wished that he would have given her some warning instead of just dropping by.

Tony was leaning against the wall by her front door. He was dressed casually and was looking at something on his phone.

"Hey."

He looked up and smiled. "You ran off on the phone earlier. You didn't speak to Charlie, did you? He must have been awfully confused if you mentioned the nursing home."

"It was you, wasn't it?" Stacey asked, avoiding his question.

"Of course, it was me!" Tony said and took her by the hands, pulling her close. "I saw how much you loved that place. It would be perfect for your grandmother. I took care of the hospital bills too."

Stacey made a noise that was a mix of surprise and dismay. Tony watched her with his eyes lighting up at her reaction. His smile grew.

"Come on. Let's get inside," he said, casting a glance around the tiny hallway.

Stacey nodded, unable to speak. She unlocked the door and Tony followed her. Like every other recent time she entered her apartment, the silence covered her like a blanket. At night, she tossed and turned, thinking about what it would be like to live in that silence forever.

Tony sat down on the couch and patted the seat. Stacey sat next to him and tried to prepare a speech in her head to tell him there was no way she could accept his gift.

But Tony spoke first, "I know you're going to want to refuse my offer. But it isn't a big deal for me. Paying the bills and putting your grandmother in that home is enough reward for me, truly. I don't mind a bit."

Stacey chewed her bottom lip. "That's a lot of money."

"I guess," he shrugged.

She studied his face as the realization came over her. It was a lot of money to her. To Tony, it was probably nothing more than a drop in the bucket. He had billions of dollars. Of course, he didn't think twice about it.

"I don't know what to say."

"You don't have to say anything," Tony replied. "This is what friends do for each other."

Friends. After the kiss, she hadn't been expecting to hear that word. She wasn't sure what they were anymore. Tony's hand moved toward her face and his fingertips ran underneath her chin. The touch made her heart skip a beat. She looked up at him.

"Friends, unless you would like to be more," he whispered.

For the second time that day, Stacey imagined toppling off a cliff. In saying yes to Tony, Charlie would be shelved for good. There would be no dreaming about him, day or night because Stacey would be committed to Tony and only him.

And when she searched his deep dark eyes, Charlie flew from her mind completely. Her lips pressed against Tony's as she answered his question with her touch. Yes, she would have him to herself. He had been there with her through all these dark times. He had come in like a knight in shining armor to support her. Hadn't she felt that connection with him right at the start?

Tony's kisses grew more urgent. His fingers trailed down her back as he pressed himself against her. Stacey could feel herself reacting to his touch. His lips brushed across her neck toward her lips until they locked, his tongue probing her mouth.

"The bedroom?" he whispered in between breaths.

She grabbed his hand and led him to her room. Through her lust, she remembered that her room was a mess. She had even thrown a blanket over her wall-length mirror in a fit of low self-esteem the other night. Tony cast a glance around the room. She couldn't read his expression.

But he didn't say anything. Instead, he pulled her close. Her hair had been thrown up into a ponytail but he yanked it out, his fingers tangling in her hair as he kissed her again.

Their clothes came off quickly, dropping in a heap on the floor. Stacey felt herself blushing in front of him as he pulled her down on the bed with him. He rolled on top of her and fondled her breasts.

Stacey closed her eyes, trying to lose herself in the sensation of him. But her mind kept spinning. It was flitting around to how odd it was to be there in her room with Tony. She had barely noticed her room when she had brought Charlie in there.

At the sudden thought of Charlie, she pushed him completely out of her mind. Tony made her feel things too. She was just nervous.

As if to expel all the negative thoughts haunting her mind, Stacey grabbed Tony and kissed him hard. Their lips crushed together and he let out a soft moan of surprise. She could feel his hard cock against her thigh.

There was no foreplay. Tony parted her thighs and entered her swiftly. Stacey closed her eyes and gasped in pleasure. He rocked inside of her, slowly at first, then more urgently. His tongue flicked across her nipples as he eagerly moved inside her.

"I love your body," he mumbled at one point.

Stacey wrapped her arms around him and tried to match his thrusts. Tony moved harder, bucking his hips hard against hers. He was moaning now and slightly out of breath, giving her small little noises of pleasure as he fucked her.

Tony thrust harder and then let out a shuddering gasp. He was climaxing, Stacey realized. His eyes were closed tightly as he came. Then he rolled off her and lay there.

Stacey blinked. She wasn't sure how she was feeling. She had just been getting worked up when he had finished. She knew it was unfair to compare lovers to other lovers, but yet.

He turned his head to hers and smiled. "That was amazing."

"Yeah, it was great," she lied.

Tony sat up. Stacey watched him, admiring his body. He was fantastically good looking. Today had been a long day. Maybe she should just give him the benefit of the doubt regarding his performance. It seemed unfair to rule him out just because this one time had been less than satisfying.

"I have a meeting to go to, but listen," he said as he picked up his clothes, "There's a birthday party for a friend of mine this weekend. Will you come with me?"

"Yeah, sure."

"Great. I'll call you with the details."

He leaned over and kissed her. Stacey returned the kiss. He smiled at her and said goodbye. She watched him leave and then stared at the ceiling until she heard the front door close.

Stacey tried to pinpoint her feelings. Surely, she was happy that she was seeing Tony now. She had felt that connection with him from that first night on the yacht. He had single-handedly helped her out with Tina and the mounting bills. She always enjoyed herself around him.

And now she was going with him to an event. An event filled with other people way outside her social status. She could feel the anxiety bubbling up inside of her. She would be out of her comfort zone again. She could practically see the elite of the elite staring at her as if she was some poor little thing that Tony had taken pity on.

She sat up and decided to shower. She wasn't going to dwell on this. She would go to the party with Tony and have a nice time. She deserved a nice time with everything else going on.

Chapter Eleven

"Wow, the room has a view of the garden too, Tina," Stacey said, looking out of the window.

Tina was in a wheelchair, having been too tired to walk. The taxi ride from the hospital to the apartment to pack up her things and then to the nursing home had been long. It had also been extremely emotional for Stacey.

But her grandmother hadn't seemed to sense the change that was going on around her. The doctors had warned Stacey that Tina was in the early stages of dementia and that a home was the best environment for her. Even so, Stacey was surprised to see just how much worse Tina had gotten since the seizure. It was as if the seizure, severe as it was, had wiped out the last remaining solid hold her grandmother had on her memory.

"Yes, the garden view was requested," their nurse, Rebecca, said.

Tony. Yet again he had been thinking things through for her. She had told him before how much Tina loved sitting in the garden at the apartment complex. Now she was close to one here as well. It was just more proof of how thoughtful he was.

"It's beautiful," Stacey repeated.

Tina was sitting upright in the wheelchair, looking around curiously. Her eyes were a little foggy. The worst part, Stacey was learning, was the moments of clarity.

There had been a moment of clarity when they were packing up Tina's clothes. Tina was sitting on the bed and was holding onto a sweater. When she looked up at Stacey, she looked almost sad.

"Is Allison coming by?"

"No, don't think so," Stacey had replied, folding a shirt.

She still hadn't heard from her sister. She wasn't sure where she was. She had called and let Allison know the name and address of the facility where Tina was moving but hadn't heard anything back. She wasn't going to refuse to tell Allison what was going on with their grandmother. She just thought that her sister would have gotten back to her.

"She'll come around," Tina said. She had been saying it a lot the last couple of days almost as if it was a chant.

Stacey hadn't replied. She wasn't feeling as confident as her grandmother about her sister's behavior. She couldn't see Allison returning, having some sense knocked into her head.

"Stacey," Tina said, "you'll come visit?"

It was the first time that she had shown awareness to what was going on and where she was going. Stacey put down the shirt she was folding and sat next to Tina.

"Of course. Whenever I can."

"So many changes," Tina said sadly. "All so quickly."

"I know. But we'll get through them together."

Tina brushed a lock of hair away from Stacey's face and spoke again, "Your parents would be proud of you, Stacey."

Stacey could feel the tears threatening again. She didn't want to cry, not now and with everything going on. She forced herself to smile and then kissed Tina on the cheek.

Tina looked around the room and then back at Stacey, "What were we talking about?"

It was one of those moments where Stacey felt the bottom drop out beneath her. The moments where Tina was there one second and then the next second, she was gone, had Stacey crashing back to earth. Her grandmother was sick. It was something she wished she could forget but knew she never could.

"Well, take your time getting settled," Rebecca said, snapping Stacey out of her thoughts. "I can go over some things with you when you're ready.

"Yeah, of course. Thanks."

Rebecca nodded and left them alone. The door was still open. In the hallway, Stacey could see a man in a walker heading slowly toward Tina's room. Even though the place was nice, it smelled slightly of antiseptic with a hint of mothballs. Seeing Tina in her wheelchair in the strange environment was upsetting her more than she had expected.

Stacey sat on the edge of Tina's bed. Her grandmother was fiddling with her wedding ring and looking around the room.

"What do you think?"

"It's very nice but when are we going home, dear? I'm very sleepy."

Stacey took her grandmother's hand and said quietly, "Tina, this is home now. Remember? We discussed it. We've been discussing it for a few days. This is where you are going to live from now on. But don't worry!" She tried to make her voice sound chipper, "I'm going to be here for you. I'll be visiting you every spare moment I can."

Tina's lips parted, but she didn't speak. She looked as if she was trying to recall when they had discussed her moving into a nursing home. After a couple of seconds, she closed her lips and nodded.

"Alright."

Stacey wasn't sure if Tina actually remembered the conversation or not. It was hard to tell if she truly remembered or was lying that she did.

"Now, let's finish unpacking your things." Stacey stood up and forced herself to smile.

<<◇>>

In the parking lot, Stacey sat behind the wheel of her car. Tony was able to negotiate a good deal on the vehicle for her. With her new job and Tina's nursing care taken care of, Stacey was able to afford the additional monthly payments. The new ride would help save her a lot of time with her busy schedule and the distance Stacey needed to travel in order to visit Tina regularly.

The parking lot was almost empty. She was freezing as if her entire body was covered in ice. She stared at the place where Tina now lived.

For the millionth time in the last five minutes, she had to remind herself why this was good for her grandmother. Tina would have people watching her all the time now. There would be activities and more social interaction than Stacey could have provided.

Even so, some part of her—some small, unfair part of her—thought she was being selfish. Hadn't she told herself she would take care of her grandmother no matter what? Now Tina was in a home and Stacey was driving away like a mother who had sent her child off to summer camp.

Stop it, she told herself, *don't do this to yourself*. It accomplished nothing to do this to herself, yet it felt like a scab that Stacey kept picking.

Finally, she left the facility parking lot and headed back into town. There were no calls from Allison. Stacey couldn't believe that she hadn't come by to see Tina. Anger bubbled in her chest. Yes, she had kicked Allison out of the apartment. But that didn't mean Allison had to desert Tina.

As Stacey drove, she tried to push out all thoughts of Allison and Tina so that she wouldn't drive herself absolutely crazy. She was seeing Tony tonight. It was his friend's birthday party.

Stacey was itching to cancel going to the event. She didn't feel like seeing anyone. She wanted to curl up in bed and maybe watch television all night. But she had promised Tony, and the guilt from cancelling would be too much of a burden.

Yesterday he had sent her a dress to wear to the party. It was a beautiful dress of black and red. The fabric was so lovely that Stacey had been almost afraid to touch it. The card had said the dress was for the party and that he was excited to take her to it. She would hate to tell him this late that she had no interest in going. Not after everything he had done for her, for Tina.

By the time Stacey got home, she was ready for a shower. The hot water pounding against her skin lessened her nervousness a bit. After the shower, she stood staring at herself in the mirror.

What did Tony like about her body? When they had sex, he had said he liked it. But Stacey still didn't understand why. The longer she stood and stared at her shape, running her fingers over her breasts and the extra weight on her that she sometimes loathed, she could feel the nervousness return.

The dress fit her very well. Tony had somehow known her size. She had been worried the dress would cling to her in all the wrong places but the red stood out beautifully against her dark skin.

Her phone hummed. It was a text message from Tony.

"Going to be a little late so I've sent a car to pick you up. See you there."

Stacey could feel anxiety roll through her. She had been hoping to relax with Tony on the drive over. Now she was going to ride in the car there by herself and enter the party alone. She felt abandoned and uncomfortable just thinking about it.

Chapter Twelve

Stacey left the apartment and went downstairs to wait outside. For once in many days, the nighttime sky was clear of storms. The car that Tony sent rolled up to the curb right on time. The driver opened the door and Stacey slid into the back seat.

Soft classical music was playing. She closed her eyes and tried to focus on the music as the car took her to the party venue, outside the city limits. There was an entire section with homes so massive, her entire apartment could probably fit into a closet.

As the car stopped in front of a gated community, Stacey peered out the window. The windows in the car were tinted, so luckily she could gawk and no one would see her. Mansions lined the street. Some of them were two or three stories tall. *Imagine having all that space to yourself!* Just the thought of all those bedrooms made Stacey wonder what she would do with so much space.

There was a house at the end of the street that had a circular driveway. It was two stories tall with a balcony overlooking the neighborhood. Limousines and town cars were pulling up in front. Stacey held her breath, checked her hair, and smoothed her dress.

The car pulled up in the circular driveway and the driver got out to open her door. Before she knew it, she was stepping out in front of the house. She looked around the driveway. People in gorgeous clothes were heading to the front door. She didn't see Tony anywhere.

Holding the invitation in her hand that had come with the dress, Stacey went to the front door and handed it to the man who was greeting guests. He nodded and motioned her to enter.

She was in the foyer. If Stacey had been amazed by Charlie's penthouse, then this foyer was that times ten. It had marble floors with a winding staircase to the second floor. A stunning statue of a woman holding a vase graced the entranceway. Stacey stopped in her tracks to admire it. She hoped no one noticed that her jaw had dropped.

A small crowd had formed in the foyer. People were greeting each other like long-lost friends. Others were taking photos to capture the moment. Stacey felt left out and wriggled through the crowd to get through the foyer.

The foyer opened into a large room with different arches leading to other rooms. Ahead of her seemed to be a massive kitchen. To the right was the living room or den with a TV so large that Stacey couldn't believe such a thing was real. To the left was a sitting room of sorts, brimming with people.

Stacey started to panic. No matter where she went, she was going to look like a misfit, having no friends among the guests. It was like the few times Allison dragged her to similar parties. Stacey had always felt unsure of herself in the corner as her sister soaked up the attention.

"There you are."

She turned around to see Tony. Relief hit her hard. The tension in her shoulders lessened at the sight of him. He was dressed in a suit and looked incredibly handsome. He was smiling at her as he grabbed her hand.

"I am so sorry that I couldn't pick you up personally. I thought I was going to be much later than this. But I'm here now and only about five minutes late."

"Yeah, I'm glad you're here. I don't know anyone," Stacey whispered.

"No problem. I'll introduce you around."

And he did. Stacey spent the next hour swept up in talking to people she would have normally never spoken to. It made her a little dizzy to see all those people discussing things she knew very little about.

She was about to tell Tony as much and ask if she could grab a drink and go outside for air when he frowned at something over her head.

"Isn't that your sister?"

Stacey turned around to look at what he was talking about. To her amazement, Allison had just walked into the sitting room. She was dressed in a dark purple dress that brought out her pretty eyes and gripped her hips just right. Her hair was twisted up in a bun that accentuated her heart-shaped face.

On her arm was Jacob. He was as pale as ever with his hair combed back in such a way that it highlighted his receding hairline instead of masking it. Allison looked radiant next to him as if she had scored the most gorgeous guy ever as her escort.

Before Stacey could stop herself, she marched across the room. Allison's eyes fell on her and widened in surprise. Stacey gripped her sister's arm.

"I need to talk to you, please," she said through clenched teeth.

Allison allowed herself to be pulled away from Jacob. Stacey weaved through the crowd until they entered a smaller room near the kitchen. It was filled with paintings and opened to the patio. Luckily no one else was there. It allowed them a little of privacy.

"Where the hell have you been?" Stacey asked.

Her sister crossed her arms and glared. "Does it matter? You kicked me out."

"From the apartment, not from our lives. What about Tina? She left for the care facility earlier today and where were you? Dicking around with Jacob?"

"She's already in a home?"

"I texted you!"

"Oh. Jacob got me a new phone."

She pulled it out of her purse. It was a smartphone like everyone else seemed to have. Stacey shook her head.

"You couldn't have given me the new number?"

"I forgot," Allison said lamely.

Stacey tried not to roll her eyes. She didn't want to fight with her sister at the party, but it was proving difficult.

"Well, Tina went to the home today. You need to go see her."

"I will. I didn't know you had found a place that you could afford. Who are you even here with? I didn't see Charlie."

"I—"

Allison cut her off, smirking, "It's that Asian guy, isn't it? Your boss. You're dating him." She clicked her tongue against the roof of her mouth and shook her head.

Stacey could feel herself blush. "We aren't talking about my love life. We're talking about Tina."

"Fine. I'll drop it for now."

"Thank you."

Allison's smirk left her. "I do want to see her though. I'll give you the new number. Tell me where she is and I'll see her when Jacob can take me."

"Take you?"

"He'll send a car for me."

"Are you living with him?"

"No, no. He put me up in a hotel when I told him of my evil sister kicking me out of our home. Listen, don't start complaining. It's a blessing in disguise. Jacob was over me until I went to him about being kicked out. Now he feels as if he's my savior. It's working out really well."

What could Stacey say? She didn't understand her sister or how she could try to marry Jacob under less-than honest circumstances. Instead she just nodded. It was safer that way.

"Can we go back to the party and hash things out later?" Allison asked, already turning around.

"I guess so," Stacey mumbled.

She wanted to tell Allison more about Tina and maybe even lecture her for a bit longer. But Allison was clearly not interested. They went back to the kitchen to re-join the party and found Jacob had set up shop there, boasting about his recent trip to Europe. Tony was listening to him with a drink in his hand. Allison draped herself over Jacob and looked at him lovingly. She was a good actress.

Stacey went to stand by Tony, who looked at her. "Everything okay?"

"Yeah, it's fine. She's here with Jacob."

He raised his eyebrows. "Such a strange couple."

"Tell me about it," Stacey mumbled over Jacob's voice.

Tony leaned over to her. He was so close, she could feel his breath on her neck. For a second she thought he was going to kiss her.

But instead, he whispered, "Not in regard to your sister. I just mean with Jacob. How much do you know about him?"

"Not much," Stacey admitted.

"He got all his money from his dad. His dad is still in control of the company. They specialize in tea. They sell this crazy gourmet shit to bored rich people. So, Jacob goes around and oversees some of the offices and comes back to bore us all at these events."

"Tea?" she repeated.

"Tea."

"Geez, I figured he was involved in something a bit more interesting."

Tony laughed. His laugh sent shivers up and down her spine.

"No, just tea. But that isn't the weird part. He normally dates supermodels. Females who are way out of his dating pool but ones he can date because of his money. For him to be dating your sister is a bit unusual."

Something about his words made Stacey go on high alert. She looked at Allison and Jacob. He was still going on about something as Allison pretended to cling to his every word.

"Do you think he actually likes her?" she wondered aloud.

"I wouldn't get my hopes up."

"So, if he only dates supermodels, and he's dating my sister… well, we have to be missing something."

"I would assume so. I just don't know what."

"Just another thing to worry about," Stacey sighed.

"Don't. Your sister is a grown woman. If she wants to date Jacob, then let her."

"She only wants money. It isn't as if she really likes him."

Tony looked at her for a beat too long. Stacey wondered if he was suddenly thinking that was why she was dating him. Stacey was just about to tell him that she wasn't like that when she saw a familiar face enter the kitchen.

It was Charlie. Her heart skipped a beat and she could feel her stomach lurch. The sudden sight of him threw her off guard. Tony hadn't noticed. He had turned his attention back to Jacob.

Charlie hadn't seen her. He was stopping to say hello to some guests. She still hadn't met the owner of this house who was celebrating his birthday. The crowd was growing bigger as the night went on. Stacey suddenly felt very warm in the kitchen stuffed with people.

"I'll be right back," Stacey said to Tony.

She moved her way through the crowd and managed to reach the patio. There was a massive pool with a clear dance floor placed on top of it. People were dancing as the pool water changed colors. The music was loud and thumping. It didn't do anything to help Stacey steady her rapidly beating heart.

She cut across the yard toward the garden area. It didn't seem to be as crowded. This barely felt like a birthday party. It felt more like a giant bash. She had been expecting something quaint and light, not the sort of party she used to see on TV shows.

The garden was quieter. There were only a few people milling around. Stacey sat down on the bench and took a deep breath. The kitchen had suddenly felt so small. To see Charlie had proven to be too much.

The events of the day threatened to engulf her. She was thinking about Tina sitting in her new room, alone and without anyone she knew. Stacey should have stayed home and not come here.

"I can't believe it."

Stacey looked up and stifled a groan. In front of her, out of all the people to run into, was Adele. She was dressed in a pink dress that seemed to have been poured on. She looked radiant.

"What are you doing here?" Adele demanded. "Did you sneak in? I'll call security on you, you know."

"I didn't sneak in," Stacey snapped. "I'm here with someone."

"Of course, you are. Things go wrong with Charlie, and you just happen to find someone else you can latch onto. Some other poor unsuspecting man to mooch off."

Stacey closed her eyes. Maybe Adele was just an annoying mirage who would vanish once she opened her eyes again. She counted to three. Adele was still standing there with her hands on her hips.

"No luck," Stacey mumbled.

"What? Listen, whatever idea you have about coming here to try to win Charlie back, you can forget it."

Adele spun on her high heels and stormed off toward the house. Stacey watched her go. Was Adele here with Charlie? There was no way, she decided. Charlie had made it clear as day that he wasn't interested in Adele. That was some comfort at least.

The tightness in her chest lessened. She was feeling a little better. It didn't seem as if the walls were closing around her out here. Stacey didn't want Tony to wonder where she had gone so she headed back to the party.

The kitchen had changed little when Stacey returned. For once, Jacob was letting someone else speak for a change. A tall woman was talking about something not at all interesting. Allison shot Stacey a bored look. Stacey scanned the room for Tony.

Tony was there, talking to Charlie. She balked at the idea of joining Tony right then. But he must have sensed her because he glanced up and beckoned her over. Charlie saw her at the same moment. His back went stiff as he stared at her.

"There you are. Was wondering where you went," Tony remarked as he pulled her in for a hug.

The sudden hug felt awkward in front of Charlie. She pulled away after a few seconds. Tony swung his arm around her shoulders. He had never been this touchy-feely before and it felt strange. Charlie was looking at her without any expression on his face. She remembered seeing him the last time, storming over to his apartment and wanting him to kiss her.

"So, anyway, like I was saying. I think full coverage of the remodel of the city would be fantastic. My media companies can give you any package you want at a special price."

Charlie flicked his gaze away from Stacey and looked at Tony, "I'm guessing you would want something in return."

Tony laughed and removed his hand from Stacey's shoulders. He hit Charlie playfully on the back and turned him away from Stacey, "Well, naturally."

Tony steered Charlie away from her. Stacey watched as the crowd swallowed them up. She was alone yet again at this stupid party. She should have just bowed out. The only way this party could get worse would be if her ex-boyfriend, Jake, suddenly appeared.

She was saved from loneliness when Allison popped up at her side.

"Hey, I ditched Jacob for the moment. Wanna look around?"

"Are you allowed out of his sight for more than one second?" Stacey joked.

"He's boring some woman in the kitchen. Besides, I saw you standing here completely out of your comfort zone as your ex and your current fuck strolled away together."

"Geez, Allison, still so crass."

"Not going to change. Come on. Let's go upstairs." She grabbed Stacey's hand.

"We aren't allowed upstairs, are we?" she protested.

Allison rolled her eyes, "Which is the exact reason why we are going upstairs."

Stacey didn't have any fight left in her to protest. As Allison dragged her through the crowd, she saw Tony enter the room again. He was looking for her. Charlie was gone. Whatever conversation they had was apparently extremely short. She didn't see Charlie anywhere in the vicinity.

Normally, she would have pulled away from Allison and gone to Tony. But she was exhausted having to deal with people. She was secretly relieved her sister was here. Allison yanked her out of the room and into a hallway.

"The staircase is over—"

"Geez, we aren't going to use the main one. I heard this guy has a bowling alley and I want to see it."

Allison stopped at a thin wooden door. She looked around and opened it. There was a narrow staircase that led upstairs. She looked at Stacey.

"Cool, right?"

"It is sorta cool. How did you know about it?"

"Jacob talks a lot. Come on."

Allison went up the stairs. Stacey glanced around and followed her. The staircase looked like it was used for service or maintenance staff. They opened another small door at the top and stepped out into a hallway upstairs.

"Nothing remarkable here," Stacey remarked.

"Well, what were you expecting? A portal to another universe?" Allison huffed and took off down the hallway.

She stopped to peek into each room. Most of them were bedrooms that were unused. There was seemingly no one else up there. There was a room filled with paintings and statues that were shoved in randomly.

"Probably wants to sell this shit," Allison said before moving on.

At the next door, Stacey noticed it was slightly ajar. But Allison didn't notice. She pushed it open before Stacey could say anything. She heard her sister let out a gasp of surprise. Stacey pushed past her. Her heart fell.

Adele and Charlie were on the bed. Adele's arms were wrapped around Charlie, while her lips were on his mouth. He was on top of her. It was fortunate that they were still fully clothed.

Even so, Stacey felt the shock roll through her. She blindly turned away as the lovers noticed they had been caught.

It was a mistake to come to this party after all.

-To be continued in Book 3-

Book Three – Love Reinstated

Chapter One

THE NEXT few seconds seemed to be a complete blur. As soon as Stacey saw Adele's lips on Charlie, she had turned around blindly and left the room. She had to get out of there right that instant. The last thing she wanted to do was cry. There was no point in crying; she had broken up with Charlie. If he wanted to finally fool around with Adele, then let him.

Allison said something, but Stacey didn't hear it. She was practically jogging down the hallway to the staircase. Allison was hot on her heels. Stacey didn't want to turn around and see if Charlie had followed her or not.

Down the stairs she went. She spilled out into the party and started weaving through the crowd. She was halfway to the entrance when someone grabbed her arm. Startled, she let out a cry and turned around.

It was Tony. It took Stacey a couple of seconds to remember that she had come to the party with him.

"There you are!"

"Uh, yeah, here I am," she mumbled and scanned the crowd for Charlie.

"Listen, come with me to the patio. There is –"

"I can't. I'm sorry." She shook her head. "I have to go. I have a massive headache and I'm in a lot of pain."

Concern flickered across his face, along with something else that Stacey couldn't put her finger on. Tony let go of her. Someone bumped into her as they walked by. The party seemed to have doubled in size in the short time Stacey had been upstairs.

"Thanks for inviting me," she said quickly.

"Wait, how are you getting home?" Tony called after her as she left.

"I'll call a cab!"

She pushed her way through the crowd and out of the front door. Even here the crowd was thick. Her frantic state was starting to mix with feelings of claustrophobia from the mass of bodies surrounding her on all sides. She was on the verge of either passing out or bursting into tears if she didn't get out of this place quickly.

Stacey took off down the driveway toward the gate. Tears were pressing against her eyes. She cursed herself for acting so stupidly. How could she be so upset? She had opted out of dealing with Charlie and his family drama. She had no right to be so upset.

"There you are!"

Stacey froze for a second. But it was enough for Charlie to grab her arm exactly where Tony had. He turned her around. Her heart began to beat rapidly at the sight of him. Music was pouring out of the house. She could hear the heavy beats of the bass even out here on the driveway. The lights from the house seemed to illuminate Charlie from behind. He glowed softly.

"Stacey, let me explain."

"You don't have to explain. It isn't any of my business."

"I'm trying to move on."

Stacey was brought up short. The words swirled in her head. She hadn't been expecting for Charlie to say that.

Taking advantage of her silence, he said, "We're over. I mean, you made it clear. Then Tony tells me you two are dating. I can't really sit around and pine for you any longer, can I?"

"No. I guess not."

"So, Adele was interested and I had never given her a chance before because of my father. So I thought I would."

"Isn't that falling directly into what your father wants?" Stacey asked.

Charlie shrugged. "Maybe. I guess so. I don't care, Stacey. I'm tired. Fighting against my dad like this is downright exhausting. I don't want to do it any longer."

Stacey couldn't keep the bitter tone out of her voice. "So, you'll just date her because she's around and your father already approves."

"No, no, you don't get to do this." He shook his head. "*You* left. You left *me*, remember? Now that I'm moving on, you don't get to be angry about it."

"I'm not angry."

"Yes, you are. Did you expect me to just be miserable for the rest of my life?"

"I expected you to reach out to me after I broke up with you!" Stacey snapped. "You seemed completely fine with the fact I had dumped you. And out of all the people to move on with, you pick Adele. The same woman you made clear that you had no interest in!"

"It doesn't concern you, Stacey! What I do now isn't any of your business! As for why I didn't contact you, I thought that was what you wanted! You broke up with me! I wasn't going to crawl around after you because you didn't want me any longer."

The two of them stared at each other. Charlie's eyes were wide. He had shifted in the middle of his rant. Half of his face was covered in shadows now. Behind him, Stacey could see Adele breaking through the edge of the crowd.

"Maybe you were right," Charlie whispered.

"About what?"

"Maybe we are just from two different worlds."

Stacey felt the air get sucked from her lungs at Charlie's words. She didn't have a chance to reply. Adele had slinked up to Charlie. She wrapped her arms around his waist and rested her chin on his shoulder.

"Everything okay?"

"Yes. I'm just going, actually. Have a good night," Stacey replied stiffly.

She turned around and headed toward the gate, leaving Charlie behind.

Stacey shoved the money for the cab fare into the driver's hand and stepped out into the humid night. Above her, the apartment complex seemed to sag under the weight of its occupants. Without Tina living with her, the place seemed to have lost that little magic touch that had made Stacey feel so kindly toward it. She had once felt so victorious when Charlie had saved it from being knocked down and rebuilt. Now looking at it, Stacey wouldn't have cared if the entire thing was smashed to the ground.

Up in her apartment, Stacey went directly to her bed and fell into it with what felt like all the exhaustion in the world. Her window had a view of another building. From here, she could see someone's light on in the bathroom.

She was to go back to work on Monday. Tony had already given her more days off than she probably should have gotten. At the time, Stacey hadn't thought much of it. She had been too involved with Tina and making sure she was okay. Now that she was thinking about it, however, she wondered if she had been taking too much from Tony. The time off, the payment of the hospital bills and Tina's nursing home – she had been thrilled that Tony had been helping her so much.

But Stacey could practically hear Allison in her head. *You sit there and lecture me for wanting to snag a billionaire yet have no qualms about taking money from Tony.* The worst part was that Stacey had no argument back.

Everything she was starting to get on track had seemingly veered right off the rails. Stacey had somehow let Tony sweep in and start taking care of things. She wanted to date him. But she had to make sure he understood that she wasn't dating him for the handouts.

Tomorrow, she thought sleepily, *I'll figure it out tomorrow.*

Chapter Two

"You really didn't have to get me this," Stacey protested as Tony draped the necklace around her neck.

"Don't be silly. Of course I did. When I saw it, I thought that it would bring out your features beautifully," Tony said in a low voice, dragging his fingers gently across her neck.

The touch made her shiver. She closed her eyes for a moment before protesting feebly. But Tony didn't seem to be listening to her anymore. He was moving over to the poolside bar.

It was the middle of the week. Stacey had returned to work on Monday. If her co-workers cared that Tony had given her the time off, they didn't show it. For some reason, this bothered her more than it should have. Why were none of them, including Ms. Stark, bothered that Tony had given someone new so much time off?

"Want another?"

"No, I'm okay." Stacey held up her own unfinished drink.

This was her first time at Tony's place in the city. It was a penthouse suite, like Charlie's, only it was on the other side of town. He had a pool to himself here, and they were currently lounging next to it. The sun had gone down. The sky had streaks of orange shooting through it.

When Tony had invited her over, Stacey had promised herself to talk to him about how she didn't want him to spend any more money on her. Yet she hadn't gotten a chance to bring it up. Tony had taken her on a tour around his place and then given her the necklace. It felt rude to turn it down.

She fingered the necklace again. It was beautiful, lined with sapphires. In the back of her mind, Stacey wondered what it would fetch if she were to sell it. She quickly pushed the thought out of her head.

"I'm going out of town this weekend," Tony said as he sat down next to her. "I know I mentioned that before. I pushed it off to make sure you were okay, but I really must go this time."

"Back to China?"

"Somewhat," he smiled. "I own a very small island off the coast of mainland China. I have family that lives there. I'll be tending to business in Shanghai and spending time with them."

Stacey couldn't imagine owning an entire island. "Wow," she breathed, "that sounds lovely."

"It is. My family can come and go as they please, but they enjoy the peace and quiet. It will be good to see them again." He leaned back in his chair and looked out at the pool.

Somewhere in the distance there was a boom of thunder. Stacey studied Tony's face. In the darkness, she could just make out the curve of his jaw and his lips. As if sensing that she was staring at him, Tony turned to look at her.

His eyes flicked up to hers. Their gazes locked. Then Tony leaned across the small space between the two of them and kissed her. Like every touch from Tony, a warmth shot through her body. Tony cupped the side of her face with his hand and his tongue slid into her mouth.

Their kiss grew deeper. Anything that Stacey had been thinking about was quickly washed away with Tony's touch. His cologne filled her brain and she pressed her hands against his chest. His t-shirt curled around her fingers as she pressed her mouth against his.

Hungrily, Tony rubbed his hands down her sides. Stacey could feel her heart hammering against her chest. He pulled away from her suddenly. The two of them were out of breath. Something about Tony, being around him, touching him like this, always made Stacey feel as if her head was in a fog.

He took her hand and moved toward one of the lounge beds he had by the pool. It was white and had a sheet of fabric that shielded it from view. Stacey had commented about it when she had first come out on the patio. Tony had explained it was nice to tan or nap on. Now she could see it was going to be used for a different purpose.

When they got close to it, Tony pushed her down onto the lounge bed. Stacey fell down on it as he climbed on top of her. He pressed his mouth against hers. His tongue probed hers as they both yanked each other's clothes off.

Stacey could feel how wet she was. Tony's stiff cock pressed against her thigh. The humid night air weighed down on the two of them. There was another clap of thunder in the distance. Tony ran a finger down her pussy which made her gasp in pleasure. He grunted as he slid his dick into her.

Then he was fucking her. One hand was tangled in her hair, pulling on it. His other hand was propping himself up as he thrust inside of her. Stacey wrapped her legs around his waist. She wanted him to go deeper and harder. She wanted him to make her finish around his cock.

She liked the sound of their flesh slamming against each other. Stacey liked how Tony would close his eyes when he moaned. She liked feeling his hands pulling her hair. His mouth came down around her tits, sucking and biting on her nipples as he vigorously fucked her. She could feel her own orgasm mounting.

Tony let out a loud moan. He grunted – once, twice, a final third time – as he thrust his cock deep inside of her and came. Stacey could feel his climax roll through him. He was shivering with his eyes closed. His mouth was clamped around one of her nipples as he came.

Stacey held him as he climaxed. After a minute, Tony rolled off of her. He lay there next to her out of breath. Part of Stacey couldn't help but feel a little disappointed. She told herself to stop. So what if she hadn't gotten to finish? She had still enjoyed herself, right? That was all that mattered.

Tony turned to look at her. Stacey offered up a wan smile. Tony's eyes were shining.

"I had an idea."

"What?"

He propped himself up. The humidity of the night was cooling off due to the storm rolling in.

"When I come back from China, I'll bring my family here."

"What?" Stacey asked, surprised.

"You can meet them. I won't ask you to come to the island. I know you don't want to leave Tina. So I'll bring them here for you to meet."

Stacey's eyes widened. "Meet your family? Don't you think that it's a little… fast?"

"Is it?" Tony wondered aloud and reached for her hand. "But I want you to meet them. I think you would really like them. Besides, I wanted them to come visit me for a while."

"Who would be coming?"

"My mother. My father died when I was younger. Some cousins. My older sister."

Stacey's head swam. "I didn't know any of this."

Tony brushed his lips gently across her own. The touch was as light as a feather.

"You'll really like them," he whispered. "We should get inside now before it rains."

Stacey nodded as Tony slid off the lounge bed and grabbed his clothes. She watched him stroll away from her. Her lips tingled from where he had touched her. Her fingers played with the necklace around her neck.

Tony was obviously into her. He was taking them being together seriously. She got up and dressed quickly on the patio before stepping into the kitchen. Tony was rummaging around in the fridge. The focused expression on his face looked cute on him. When he saw her, he flashed her a smile that made her knees feel weak. How could she say no to someone like Tony? He was kind and thoughtful. Hadn't he admitted to her earlier that he wasn't ready to settle down? Yet here he was, wanting Stacey to meet his family.

"Hungry?" he asked her.

"Yeah, I am. Thanks."

She went over to Tony as he pulled some food out of the fridge. He leaned over and kissed her. As their lips met, Stacey thought that maybe everything would work itself out in the end.

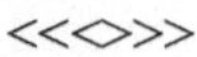

"Does it smell like old people?" Allison asked.

"What?"

Her sister wrinkled her nose. "Does it smell like old people?"

Stacey looked over at the nursing home. It was the first time Allison was going to be seeing it. For some reason, she felt nervous. Her sister had been on edge all day but wouldn't explain why. Stacey had to guess that it had to do with Jacob.

Not only that, but Stacey hadn't technically told Allison that Tony was paying for everything for Tina. She knew that Allison would be furious. It would be the same song and dance about the fact that Stacey was just like her, using money from a rich person to get what she wanted.

They got out of the car. Allison walked toward it as if she was walking to her own funeral. Stacey sighed.

"What?" Allison asked.

"It's just a nursing home. Don't be so dramatic."

"Are you kidding me right now?" Allison hissed. "Don't you remember my first-grade field trip?"

"Oh my God," Stacey groaned, "you're still not over that?"

In first grade, Allison had been taken to a nursing home to sing Christmas carols for the residents there. According to her, the sight of the old people not knowing where they were, all reaching out for her or calling her name in confusion, had been enough to scar her for life. Stacey tried not to roll her eyes.

They entered the nursing home. Allison fell silent when they stepped into the lobby. She took one look around and then pulled Stacey back before she could reach the desk.

"You can't afford this place."

"What?"

"You heard me," Allison said, "You can't afford it.
You have that boyfriend of yours paying for it, don't
you?"

Stacey didn't answer. She hadn't thought that
Allison was going to guess right upon entering. Her
sister took the silence as an answer. She was right.

"My God, sis. Never thought you had it in you.
Using a man for his money." She raised her eyebrows.

Stacey could feel herself start to blush. "It isn't like
that."

"It isn't? So he's paying for this place and what –
you guys are just friends?"

"No. I mean…"

"So, you're fucking him." The delight in her voice
was unmistakable.

"Keep your voice down!" Stacey snapped.

But Allison was grinning. "That is just rich. Well, I
have to admit I am flattered that you decided to try
things out my way."

"I am not trying things out your way."

"Really? What's the difference between you and me
now?"

Stacey got very close to her sister. She could smell
her sister's perfume. It was new. Probably designer. A

gift from Jacob, no doubt. Her mind flashed to the necklace she had shoved in her drawer back at home.

"Yes, Tony paid for this place. But I am doing what I can to make sure our grandmother is in the best place possible and *this* is the best place for her. I am not going to put her in some shithole. You get it?"

"I get it. I do." Her sister pitched her voice down low. "Just make sure you don't lose yourself in the process."

Stacey didn't get a chance to reply. Her sister had turned around and gone to the desk, asking to see Tina. Her throat felt very dry. It was unlike Allison to be accepting of something. The fact that she had accepted it and merely added a cryptic warning had shaken Stacey.

After a few minutes of waiting, they were led to Tina's room. Tina was rolled up to the window and was reading a book. Sunlight poured in through the window. From here, Stacey could see outside. The garden was filled with people doing activities. She could see a small group of women doing yoga off to the side. The chess tables were filled with people as well.

Rebecca, the nurse who had helped Tina settle in, was in the doorway. Stacey turned to her.

Quietly, she asked, "Why isn't she outside in the garden?"

"I tried. But she wanted to stay inside. She said it was too hot."

That was unlike her grandmother. The heat had never seemed to bother her before. Allison had gone over to Tina and was talking to her in a low voice. Stacey couldn't hear what she was saying.

"Is she settling in okay?"

"She forgets often how she got here. Her short-term memory is poor. We have been working with her to try to keep her mind engaged. Coloring. Puzzles. Things like that. Her long-term memory is intact though."

"That's good at the very least."

"Well, if you have any questions, let me know. Feel free to take her to the gardens if you can get her to agree to it. The fresh air might do her some good."

Stacey nodded and Rebecca left them. There was a small TV in the room which was on. Even though Tina had access to probably tons of channels, it was on the weather channel. This small detail made Stacey's chest hurt.

Allison sounded tired, as if she had repeated herself already a few times, "No, this is my first time here."

"No, it isn't," Tina replied. "Weren't you here earlier? You wanted to go to the garden. Or was that your sister?"

Before Allison could get angry, which she always seemed to do instead of getting sad, Stacey stepped in. "Yeah, that was me."

Allison glared at Stacey who ignored it. She sat down next to Tina. The three of them spoke. The conversation was hardly a conversation. Tina's memory was fading quicker with each passing visit, it seemed. She would forget things mid-sentence. Conversations would die on her lips. It was a struggle. Stacey was used to it. Allison, however, left at one point.

"Will you wait right here?" Stacey asked her grandmother who nodded mutely.

She found her sister down the hall. She was leaning against the wall and was staring into one of the rec rooms. Allison was drumming her nails against the wall. Stacey noticed she had fake nails on. They were a bright purple. Currently they were more of a purple blur as she drummed them against the wall.

"Hey, what are you doing?"

"I can't do this," Allison gasped.

"Do what?"

"This." She gestured around her. "We can't even talk to her. You've noticed that, right?"

"Of course I have."

"We can't even talk to her," Allison repeated. "How can her mind have gone so quickly just like that?"

Stacey hesitated and then leaned against the wall. "It wasn't that quick. Her mind has been going for a while now. The seizure just moved the progress along a bit faster. But it was going to happen anyway."

Allison made a strange noise. Stacey knew it well. It was the noise her sister made when she didn't want to cry. Without thinking, she pulled Allison in for a hug which her sister reciprocated without hesitation.

Stacey couldn't recall the last time they had hugged. They were always fighting about something. But for once in their lives, there was no bickering. There was only sadness about their grandmother.

Chapter Three

"Tony, we need to rethink this money situation. I just don't feel as if I can take any more gifts from you. I appreciate everything you have done for my grandmother and the kindness you have given me. But I just can't..." Stacey shook her head. "Sounds so cheesy."

She was driving over to Tony's place that Friday night. After Tony had announced that he was going to be bringing his family into town this weekend, he had been gone all week in Shanghai. He had landed an hour ago. Stacey was determined to speak to him before his family came into town.

Her sister's warning had echoed in her head. It was probably the first time that Allison had warned her about anything, and Stacey couldn't stop thinking about it. Her sister constantly lost herself in men, didn't she? Stacey had seen it first hand over the years. She would alter and change her personality to match whatever billionaire she was trying to win over. Clearly, she was worried the same would happen to Stacey.

"I'm just going to tell him not to buy me anything else," Stacey said aloud.

It sounded simple enough. Yet why was she so nervous? Tony had never been cruel to her. But she knew there was iron underneath that skin. There had to be, to do the sort of business he did. She had never been nervous about that with Charlie.

At the thought of Charlie, Stacey told herself not to go down that road. She had been doing well at not thinking about the fact he was with Adele. If she dwelled on it, she found herself growing angry. All she could hear was what he had mumbled to her before Adele had appeared. His admission that perhaps they were from different worlds after all seemed lodged into her skull.

"Tony isn't Charlie," she said to herself as she stopped at a red light.

And that was a good thing. Surely, that was a good thing.

Her car looked like a hunk of scrap metal in the parking lot of Tony's complex. If Charlie's place had been luxurious, Tony's apartment complex was downright otherworldly. It looked as if it belonged in a science fiction novel. Everything was decorated with different colors and strange sculptures that made no sense to Stacey. The wealth was displayed at every stop to Tony's place. Even the elevators looked as if they were made of pure gold.

The elevator didn't take her directly to Tony's living room. Instead it opened into a beautiful hallway. Mirrors lined the walkway to the door. Secretly, Stacey hated it. Seeing herself in all those mirrors only reminded her of everything she hated about her body.

She reached the door and knocked. It was slightly ajar, which she found odd. She knocked again but Tony didn't answer.

"Tony? I'm going to come in, okay?" Stacey called before pushing the door open slowly.

No one answered. The hallway was empty. Stacey was going to turn around and call Tony to make sure she had the time right when she heard someone laugh. It was a distant laugh, and distinctly female.

Standing there, she suddenly flashed back to coming home and seeing Jake with another woman. Their limbs had been entwined and he had been thrusting into her with a passion that Stacey hadn't seen from Jake in a long time.

She was thinking about this now as she walked down the hallway. Stacey tried to prepare herself for the image of Tony on top of another woman. Of course he would have gotten bored of her. They were from different worlds too, weren't they? She must have been a glutton for punishment.

A woman came around the corner and almost collided into her. She was shorter than Stacey with long, black hair, draped around her shoulders. There was something severe about her face - she looked exactly like Tony.

"Who are you?" she demanded in clipped English.

Stacey was at a loss for words. Luckily, she didn't have to answer. Tony came around the corner as well. When he saw her, he grinned.

"Great! You're here. This is my sister, Michelle. Michelle, this is Stacey, the woman I'm seeing."

Stacey, who moments ago thought she was going to catch Tony cheating on her, suddenly felt foolish. She held out her hand for Michelle to shake. Tony's sister did so but there was a look of slight disgust on her face as if she were smelling fish right under her nose.

"Nice to meet you," Stacey said.

Michelle made a small noise in the back of her throat and looked Stacey up and down. The look was not kind. Stacey wanted to be anywhere else but here. Tony grabbed her hand and steered her away from Michelle toward one of the lounge rooms.

"I thought they were arriving this weekend," Stacey whispered.

"Slight change of plans. It made the most sense this way. My mom and a couple of cousins came as well."

"Great," Stacey replied although she didn't mean it.

Out the window went her plan to discuss money with Tony. She was swept into the room where his mother sat. She was sitting by the window, sipping a cup of tea. She was extremely thin and looked as if she were only thirty years old. When she saw Stacey, she smiled thinly.

Behind Tony's mother were two of his cousins. One was a man who looked more like Tony's brother than cousin. The other was another woman with a round face and large eyes. She was the only one to smile warmly at Stacey.

"This is my mother, Ai. My cousin, Chen." He pointed to the male cousin who nodded at her, "And my other cousin, Mei."

Ai said something in Mandarin that of course Stacey couldn't understand. Chen laughed. It wasn't a kind laugh. Stacey stood next to Tony stiffly. He replied swiftly and his mother fell silent.

"Can I use your bathroom?" Stacey asked him, desperate to get out of that room.

Tony nodded and she left quickly. She went down the hallway and hesitated. On a whim, she decided to go to the bathroom on the other side of the penthouse. It would offer more privacy than being right outside the room with the family that seemed to already not like her.

She closed the bathroom door behind her. This side of the house was silent. She closed her eyes and took a deep breath. Okay, so Stacey hadn't been expecting Tony's family until this weekend. That really didn't matter, right? She knew they were going to be here. They were just here a bit early. Why was she panicking?

She knew the answer deep down. She was panicking because this entire relationship felt as if it were going way too fast for her liking. Already meeting Tony's family felt crazy to her. What was his hurry? To go from saying he didn't want to settle down to someone who now was introducing her to his family didn't make any sense in the least.

Stacey turned and stared at herself in the mirror. Allison had been right; things were out of control. At this rate, she had already lost track of herself. She needed to find a way to stop this before it got ridiculous.

She was about to leave when she heard low voices in the hallway. Stacey pressed her ear against the door. She could hear Tony talking. His voice was rising and falling as if he were irritated. Someone else replied. Stacey strained her ears.

"What is wrong with you?"

"Michelle, stop," Tony replied firmly in English. "I have no idea why you are all overreacting like this."

"I am used to meeting your flavor of the month," Michelle snapped, "but not someone like her! Do you see how she looks? She is double the size of me. Are you bored of the models you usually chase after? Or are you trying to piss off our mother because she's bothering you to settle down?"

A sick feeling was wriggling its way from Stacey's stomach. She knew she should let them know she was here in this bathroom but she felt frozen in place.

"I am not trying to piss off our mother," Tony finally spoke, "and her size shouldn't affect what you think of her. I wasn't expecting much from Mother or our cousins. But I thought you were better than that, Michelle. I really did."

There were footsteps of Tony marching off. She heard Michelle mumble something she couldn't make out before taking off as well. Stacey exhaled slowly.

Talk about a terrible situation.

She left the bathroom and walked back to the room where Tony's family was. The conversation ceased when she stepped inside. Tony went to her side and grabbed her hand, smiling at her as if nothing was wrong. As if his entire family didn't think she was some sort of temporary stop in Tony's dating career.

Even though he was smiling at her, Stacey couldn't help but remember that his sister had said she had met his girlfriends before. What she thought had been special wasn't that special after all. *Then none of this matters,* she told herself firmly, *I'm freaking out over nothing.* She couldn't make them like her after all. If they were convinced Tony wasn't serious about her, Stacey couldn't change that.

The conversation was stilted. There was a language barrier with Tony's mother. Tony did most of the translating. Mei spoke in broken English and Chen hardly spoke at all. It was Michelle and Tony who did the most speaking.

An hour passed before Stacey felt as if she could excuse herself with needing to get home for the night. Tony nodded and was about to show her to the door when Michelle offered to do it. He looked surprised but allowed Michelle to escort Stacey out.

Once they were alone, Michelle turned to look at Stacey. Her eyes were as dark as Tony's. She was staring at Stacey steadily.

"My brother seems quite taken with you," she finally said.

Stacey nodded, unsure of what to say.

Michelle looked away from her and flicked her hair back over her shoulders. "My brother took what my father had and grew it. He tripled the size of the small company our father had. When he died, Tony promised him it would be a glorious company. A company that stays in the family."

"If you think Tony has any plans to give me any hand in the company, I'm afraid you're mistaken," Stacey replied.

"No, I don't think he is going to do that. I think you will ask for it."

Stacey let out a dry laugh, "I have absolutely no interest in Tony's company."

Michelle narrowed her eyes. "Don't you? Tony told me what he did for you. For your sick grandmother. He has an iron will when it comes to business but a frail heart when it comes to people he cares about."

Stacey crossed her arms. She could feel her irritation quickly bubbling underneath her. When she had left Charlie, she had thought she was done with the strange workings of the rich and their dynamics. But now here she was, dealing with the same shit only a different family. *Out of the frying pan and into the fire,* Stacey thought glumly.

Michelle went on, "He won't marry you. You understand that, surely? Tony wants my mother to approve of whomever he decides to marry. She won't ever agree to you."

"What is it with you rich folks constantly getting into each other's business? Is it because you have everything at your fingertips so you have to make up some drama?"

Michelle's eyes widened slightly at Stacey's words. Then her mouth pressed into a thin line.

Irritated, Stacey went on, "For your information, I really do like Tony. He's kind. He's thoughtful beyond belief. But these sort of inner family politics – they don't interest me. I don't understand it. Where I come from with my family, we care about each other. We don't try to backstab or plot and plan. I guess that is where the money makes a real difference."

Before Michelle could reply, Stacey opened the door and left.

Chapter Four

The silence of the apartment seemed to weigh on Stacey like a thick blanket. She locked the door behind her and stood in the living room. The chair where Tina used to sit was sunken in from years of use. The couch where Allison used to sleep looked untouched. Something about it depressed her. Stacey realized for the first time in her life that she missed her sister.

She sat down on the couch and turned on the TV. The weather station popped up. A man was pointing out another summer storm about to rip through later that night. Stacey sighed and closed her eyes.

She must have fallen asleep because soon enough she was dreaming. She was back on the night of her parents' death, young and naïve. She was bent over her homework, trying to solve a math problem. But the numbers on the page kept swirling around and changing. It made it almost impossible to focus.

Next to her, Allison was unchanged. She wasn't a child, like Stacey. She was stretched out in between two chairs and was texting someone on her new phone. Her fingers swept over the touch screen rapidly.

"You should be doing your homework," young Stacey said to older Allison.

Her sister scoffed, "Lame."

"It's not."

Allison looked up at her. Her eyes were glowing a bright purple. Stacey shifted uncomfortably in the dining room chair.

"You run and you run," her sister said. "Why? What are you running from?"

Stacey didn't get to reply. Charlie stepped into the room. He was staring at her and said nothing. Behind him was Tony.

"You aren't supposed to be here," Stacey said to the two of them.

There was a loud noise from the living room. She got out of her chair and ran to the living room. Time seemed to slow down. Behind her, Allison kept texting on her phone. Charlie and Tony gave chase. As Stacey came into the living room, she saw her parents' bodies on the floor. She tried to scream, but no noise came out.

She spun around to get Tina – to try to tell her what was going on. But at her feet lay her grandmother. Her chest wasn't rising or falling. Stacey fell to her knees and tried shaking Tina awake. She didn't budge.

"What are you running away from?" Allison repeated from the dining room as Tony and Charlie stared at her. "What are you going to do about it?"

Stacey woke up with a gasp. Her eyes fluttered open to see the weather channel flickering on the screen. She could hear the rain pounding steadily on the roof. The clock showed an hour had passed. Her mouth felt as if it was filled with cotton. She had a headache.

The dream, once so vivid, was already drifting away from her. Stacey tried to hold onto it, but it was gone like water through her fingertips. She couldn't recall what had jolted her awake like that.

She went to get some water and something for her headache. Stacey then looked out the window and watched the rain drench the city. Tony hadn't called her since she had left. Had Michelle told him what she had said?

Yet Stacey had meant what she had said. What was it about Charlie's and Tony's families that made them poke and prod their way into their families' lives? Charlie, who had to deal with a father who wanted him to marry Adele. And Tony, who wouldn't marry anyone without Ai's approval. Stacey would always like more money, but would she want it at the risk of having her family rule her life?

Not like that mattered. There was no one left in her family besides her grandmother and her sister. There were a few distant cousins scattered around the country but no one she considered close.

A sudden knock on the door snapped Stacey out of wondering what to do. She wondered who it could be. She hoped it wasn't Tony following her home to try to talk about his family. She thought her head would pop if she had to deal with that right now.

Stacey opened the door and blinked in surprise. Allison stood in front of her. Her hair was wet from the rain and stuck to her face. Her dress was soaked through and her make-up was running.

"Are you okay?" Stacey asked.

Allison beamed and stuck out her hand toward her. She wiggled her fingers. Stacey looked down to see a gigantic ring on her sister's hand. The diamond glowed in the dim light of the hallway. She knew what Allison was going to say before she did.

"Jacob asked me to marry him!" she announced and then pushed her way past Stacey into the apartment.

"What?" Stacey replied numbly.

Allison spun in her heels. It was a childish gesture, one that Stacey hadn't seen her do since they were young. Her arms were outstretched and she was smiling.

"He asked me to marry him!" she repeated in a singsong voice.

"And you said yes?"

"Of course I said yes!"

"But..." Stacey tried to find the right words to convey how she was feeling. "But he's so... you know..."

Allison stopped spinning and waved her hand as if she was batting Stacey's feeble protests aside. "He's worth so much money, Stacey."

"That seems really wrong. Like not to be a judge of moral character but..."

Allison came over to her and gripped her by the shoulders. "He's worth so much money," she repeated. "We don't have to rely on Tony or anyone else. I can pay for anything Tina needs. I can get you out of this dump. Everything is going to change. You can come with me. We can travel the world together."

"I don't want to travel the world, Allison. And it isn't as if we aren't still relying on other people. We're relying on Jacob now, aren't we? That's the same thing. I don't want to travel the world on his money."

"Fine. Stay here then." Her sister's tone was flippant. "But we don't need Tony to pay for our grandmother to stay in that nursing home."

"Right, but Jacob will be," Stacey pointed out. "Nothing has changed." She pressed her fingers against her eyelids. "God, what are we both doing? How did shit get so far off track?"

Allison's arms went limp and fell away from Stacey's shoulders, "What do you mean?"

"I mean, we aren't doing anything for ourselves, are we? You're marrying a guy for his money. I've been accepting gifts from Tony because I'm too afraid of hurting his feelings. That isn't how life works. This isn't what Tina wants for us."

"What? Now you're an expert on what she wants for us?"

"Don't get mad. I don't feel like fighting about this, Allison. Seriously. You can't marry Jacob. You don't even *like* him."

"Well, what about you?" Allison retorted. "What are you going to do about it? You expect me to call things off with Jacob but you're still accepting things from Tony. I've seen how you look at him."

"What does that mean?"

Her sister shrugged. "You don't care about him as much as you think you do."

"That isn't true."

"Yes, it is," Allison retorted. "Think about it and you'll know it to be true."

Stacey ran her fingers through her hair. "It's just his family. The rich don't have to worry about paying the bills or keeping a regular job. So they get caught up in family drama instead. Get used to it, sis. I left Charlie because of it. But Tony's family is just as strange and conniving."

"Then go back to Charlie."

"I can't," Stacey said with a pang in her chest.

And it was true. She couldn't leave Tony and go back to Charlie. How could she go back to him now? As Allison stared at her, Stacey felt clammy all over. She moved away from her and sat down on the couch.

"Well, I'm marrying Jacob. I'm sorry if you disagree but I've decided this already."

"Fine," Stacey said, exhausted. "I can't tell you what to do anymore. Not with my own life like this."

Allison opened and closed her mouth before finally replying. "Well. Fine. Alright then." Her tone was off, as if she wasn't sure what to do without a fight from Stacey.

"I have to leave him, don't I?" Stacey mumbled to herself and she knew it was true.

As much as she liked Tony, she was staying with someone who had family drama just like Charlie. The truth was that she didn't like Tony as much as she had liked Charlie. There was a thread connecting her with Charlie. Even if he didn't want her, Stacey couldn't pretend to like Tony more than she did just to try to get over Charlie.

"I like Tony," Stacey said aloud, "I do. But I don't think I like him as much as I fooled myself into thinking I did."

"Then you need to break up with him," Allison said simply.

"Yeah, I do." She had known it, deep down, the first time they had slept together and had been left wanting. She had just pushed it down.

"Well. I just came by to give you the news," Allison said.

"You're leaving already?"

"You have a guy to dump, don't you?"

Stacey sighed. "I hate how you word things."

"I know you do. But sometimes it gets through your head quicker than if I was nice about it." She stopped for a moment and looked back at Stacey. "That Charlie guy. Even if he was a dick when he was trying to ruin the apartment complex… I wouldn't write him off so soon."

Her sister left. Stacey watched her go. She wasn't sure how she was feeling. She couldn't believe Allison was going to be marrying Jacob. She winced at the thought of having to suffer through his boring tales. She also didn't trust him as far as she could throw him.

Yet, if anything, it was enough to spur Stacey into action. She couldn't keep deluding herself into thinking that if she kept at it she could be with Tony. It wasn't fair to him or herself.

Trying to prepare herself, she grabbed her phone.

"I was thinking we could all go out to dinner tonight," Tony was saying. "There is a French place I want to take my family to."

Stacey made a small noise from the back of her throat and looked down at her tea. Tony had come over to her place after she had finished up work that day. He was sitting across from her and had been talking non-stop since he had arrived. Normally, Stacey wouldn't have minded too much. But today, of all days, she was waiting for him to stop so she could end things.

For some reason, she was more nervous about breaking up with Tony then she had been with Charlie. Perhaps it was because she knew Charlie was a sweetheart through and through, whereas Tony always

313

gave off the vibe that there was ice underneath everything.

"Tony," Stacey finally said.

Something in her tone must have alerted him to something because he finally fell silent.

Nervously, she went on, "It was nice meeting your family on Friday."

"Are you upset with me because I couldn't see you this past weekend?" Tony asked her.

"No. No, I'm not. I know you had a lot going on. So have I, with my sister. It's fine." She cleared her throat and tried to restart. "Meeting your family just made me realize that we are going quite fast."

"Are we?" Tony asked, looking surprised.

"Yes. Meeting family is usually a big step forward in a relationship. With that realization, I just think it would be better if we slowed down."

"Slowed down?"

Stacey's throat was going dry. She cleared it and tried to speak. "As friends. I think we would be better if we were friends."

Tony's eyes widened. Silence filled the space between them. For a few moments, he didn't say anything. Stacey looked back down at her tea.

"This is because of Charlie, isn't it?"

Startled, she looked up. "What?"

"You still care about him. I can tell, you know. Especially at that party. I can tell by the way you two look at each other. I thought you'd get over him once we got serious. But I can tell that isn't going to be the case."

Feeling as if a spotlight was shining directly on her, Stacey stammered out, "It isn't just Charlie."

He waved his hand as if he was dismissing anything else she had to say. "Charlie isn't good for you. You understand that, don't you? That's why you left him. I get you, Stacey. I understand where you're coming from. Your struggles are deep within. Starting from the bottom and working your way to the top."

"How?" Stacey asked. "No offense, Tony, but you and I come from different worlds just like me and Charlie."

"I took what my dad left me, and I turned it into something. What did Charlie do? His father had already built the company. He just took it over. Barely, I might add. His father wants nothing more than to get his hands back into the company. He's just too ill. If Charlie can't ward off his sick father, how can you expect him to really love someone like you?"

"Someone like me? What does that mean, exactly?"

"Someone poor," Tony said bluntly. "Someone from the bottom. Someone trying to get out of the bottom they were born into. I get that. I understand what you are trying to do. He doesn't. He never will."

"This isn't just about Charlie. Even without him in the picture, we wouldn't mesh well together. I can't take any more of your money either, Tony. I'll figure out someplace to put Tina, but –"

Tony shook his head. "No. Let your grandmother stay there. Because you'll come back to me, eventually. It might take some time, but you'll realize that Charlie isn't the type of man you want."

He stood up. Stacey felt speechless. What could she say to someone who clearly felt so cocky about the situation? To be so sure that she would run back to him filled her with an irritation she hadn't experienced before.

"See you around, Stacey," Tony said to her as he left the room.

A few seconds later, she heard the front door open and close. Stacey sat there in shock.

"That went great," she mumbled.

She thought about what Tony had said. Even though she thought it was a load of shit, his tone had been so casual and confident. He had hardly stopped to hear her out about why she didn't think they would work out. She really didn't like his assumption that she would change her mind and go back to him. Charlie was never that arrogant.

"It doesn't matter. We're over now at least," she said aloud to herself again.

What now? She had broken up with Tony, but it wasn't as if Charlie was lining up to date her again. She could almost picture him right now, tangled up with Adele, leaving kisses down her neck. The thought of it made her sick.

She regretted leaving him. She wished she had taken that risk and stayed with him to see things through. Now Charlie had moved on and although Stacey was happy she had left Tony, she was alone.

Her tea had gone cold by the time she snapped out of her thoughts. Her mind was whirling with thoughts of Tony and Charlie. She couldn't help but feel as if she had let a chance with someone she truly cared about slip through her fingers. Yet she couldn't deny that she had felt a pull toward Tony as well.

She also still had her sister on her mind. She wished that she could talk Allison out of marrying Jacob. It felt like a huge mistake. Yes, she would have money, but there was more to life than that. Jacob was a bore and seemed selfish. Not to mention there was a nagging feeling that Stacey couldn't shake as to why he was so keen to marry Allison.

She stood up from the table. It was late and her head was pounding. Better to go to bed early and try to get some sleep than struggle with her brain for hours.

Chapter Five

Stacey had been dreaming again when her phone woke her up. She had been running through a maze of trees, trying to catch up to someone when her eyes opened to her bedroom ceiling. On her night table, her phone vibrated loudly. In the quiet of the apartment, it felt as if someone was smashing a gong right next to her.

Her clock showed it was a little after two in the morning. Wondering what in the world her sister had gotten herself involved into this time, Stacey groggily grabbed her phone and answered.

"Hello?"

The voice at the other end spoke and everything changed.

Allison's fingers were wrapped around Stacey's own so hard that she dimly wondered if her bones were going to snap. It was a gesture that her sister used to do when they had stayed up late to watch horror movies together. It meant she was scared and was trying not to show it.

In front of them, they could do nothing but watch Tina's casket being lowered into the ground. Stacey felt as if all emotions had been drained out of her. She felt hollow staring at it. It hardly made sense that Tina was with them one night and gone the next. A heart attack had come out of the blue and snatched their grandmother away from them.

Next to her, Allison let out a noise that sounded as if she were being choked. Jacob was standing next to her dressed in all black. He had one arm wrapped around her shoulders. For once in his life, he was silent.

Allison began to cry. She turned to Stacey – not Jacob – for comfort. Jacob's eyes flickered over to her, but she just blinked back at him. What did he want her to do? Say no to her grieving sister? She stroked Allison's hair and looked around the small group of mourners.

She felt as if she was staring into a fishbowl. Perhaps it was because she felt so outside of herself right now that even the sight of both Tony and Charlie in the crowd didn't stir anything in her. Stacey wasn't sure if she was going to feel anything ever again.

A few people broke off and began to walk to their cars after saying good-bye to the two of them. Tina had outlived most of the people she had called friends. The small group that had arrived were people that Stacey and Allison had known.

Amanda came over to her. "Hey. It was a beautiful service."

"Thank you," Stacey replied, noting that Amanda had shown up with Brad.

"Can I do anything at all to help out? I can come over and cook," Brad offered.

"No, thank you. I really do appreciate it. But I'm alright."

Brad and Amanda said good-bye. Stacey watched them go. Allison moved away from her and furiously wiped her face.

"Fuck. I'm sorry. I told myself I wasn't going to cry."

"It is quite alright, dear." It was Jacob who spoke up, pulling Allison toward him.

She nodded and looked back at Stacey. "Are you okay? You seem…"

"I'm fine."

Her sister narrowed her eyes, clearly not believing her. Stacey didn't know what to say. She wanted to tell Allison that she hadn't felt anything in her heart or soul since the call that Tina had died. Nothing seemed to affect her. It was as if she had been drained completely of emotion. She hadn't even cried. A switch had been flipped, leaving her empty. Nothing mattered.

But her old boss, William, came up to her just then. Besides, Stacey wouldn't have said such things around Jacob.

After giving his condolences, William asked, "No wake then?"

"No. Tina always said she didn't want one," Stacey replied. "She said she didn't want a bunch of people crying over her over poorly made finger food."

"Although I did offer to take everyone out for dinner," Jacob chimed up.

Stacey lazily turned her head to look at him. His mouth, which had been opened to most likely drone on again, shut promptly when he saw the look on Stacey's face. Allison, sensing turmoil, pulled on his sleeve. The two of them turned away from her and headed off toward the parking lot.

"Well, if it's what she would have wanted," William said, oblivious to the moment.

"It is, thank you."

"Listen, Stacey," he cleared his throat, "I know you have a new job. And I bet it's great. But with the money I got from selling the restaurant, I've been debating a new business venture."

"Have you?"

"Yes. I won't bore you with the details now. But how about I call you sometime and we can discuss it? Perhaps you'd be interested and you'd want to give it a shot. Build something from the ground up."

Stacey, hardly hearing him, agreed. William beamed and said good-bye. A couple of Allison's friends came up after to chat. They left after a few moments. The sky was starting to darken with another storm. Stacey stared at the sky. She felt rooted to the spot as if she was going to grow into the soil right there next to Tina's grave.

"Stacey."

She turned her head to see Charlie. There was a time he would have pulled something out of her. An accelerated heartbeat. Her head spinning at the sight of how handsome he looked. Right now, however, she felt nothing as she looked at him.

He hesitated and then walked up to her. He looked tired. His eyes were ringed with dark shadows. He had more stubble on his face than Stacey had ever seen on him before. He ran his fingers through his hair which was slightly messy from the wind.

"I'm sorry for coming but I knew how much Tina meant to you," he said to her, keeping a safe distance between the two of them.

"I appreciate you coming," Stacey said for what felt like the millionth time that day.

Charlie took a step toward her. "Stacey, truly… I am so sorry this happened. I know that you had just gotten her settled into the home. For a heart attack to come out of the blue like that…"

"They normally do, don't they?" Stacey's voice was clipped and sounded distant, as if it belonged to someone else.

Charlie looked slightly taken aback. "I suppose so."

If she had been herself – truly herself – she would have thrown her arms around him and told him to come back to her. It sounded dramatic and perhaps it was. But Stacey wasn't herself. All she could do was stand there and look at Charlie as if he were worlds away.

He looked nervous now as he took another step toward her. They were close now. She could make out the finer details of his face. The way he was looking at her as if he were approaching a deer in the wild. The way his chest was rising and falling quickly.

"I have to talk to you, Stacey."

"Not now. I don't want to discuss it now." She cut him off brutally.

But he didn't let it drop. "Listen, last time. At the party. Things went south and I said some things I didn't mean."

"I don't care about that anymore. Did you come here to make this death all about you?"

Charlie looked aghast. "What? No."

"You told me what you thought about us. You agreed with me that we were too different. So why are you here now, trying to tell me you didn't mean it?" Stacey's words came fast and hard, rolling off her tongue without thinking.

In the back of her mind, the part of her that usually spoke logic and reasoning was eerily silent. All Stacey wanted to do was push Charlie away from her. There was something that overwhelmed her being this close to him. The sight of him and the scent of him made her feel as if she was going to topple over a ledge.

"I know what I said," Charlie fought back, "but I was wrong. I was hasty. I just – I know you feel it. The connection we have."

Her eyes flickered over to her grandmother's grave. Tina, who had been yanked from this world so quickly, had taken the last bit of Stacey's will to keep fighting and keep trying.

Didn't she feel a connection with Charlie? She had. More than she wanted to admit. A week ago, if Charlie had come to her and said these things, she would have jumped at the chance. Now she just wanted to be away from him, away from everyone who had a part in her life that made her feel things. She didn't want to get hurt again. Stacey just simply didn't want to let anyone in.

"I have to go. Thank you again for coming, Charlie."

Stacey brushed past him. In the movement, their hands briefly touched. Something flickered deep in her heart, like a candle trying to illuminate darkness. But Stacey ignored it and walked away from him. The dark clouds had rolled in now, seemingly directly over the cemetery.

She saw Allison ahead of her, talking to a tall, dark-skinned man that seemed like a blast from the past. It was Jake. His head was lowered and he was talking to her. Allison's shoulders were hunched over and she was crying. Stacey didn't see Jacob.

Stacey didn't want to talk to her ex. She changed direction and wandered down one of the rows of gravestones. Better to let Allison handle Jake than herself. She stopped in front of a grave that was covered in weeds. It was obvious no one had been by in quite some time to pay this one a visit.

This is going to be all of us one day, Stacey thought glumly. Her parents were already in the ground. So was her grandfather. And now, so was Tina. For a spilt second, she could feel raw pain shoot through her body as if she had poured salt into a wound.

"Hey."

The wound sealed up at the sound of Tony's voice. Stacey looked up from the grave and turned around. Unlike Charlie, Tony looked the same. There were no dark circles around his eyes. No stubble. His hair was perfectly slicked back. Like Charlie, Stacey felt nothing at seeing him.

"You ran off before I could talk to you," he said.

Stacey didn't reply.

Tony came over to her and stood next to her. Together they stared at the grave where Stacey had stopped.

Finally, he spoke. "My grandfather had always been my biggest supporter. Everyone in my family, they didn't understand what I was trying to do. They thought it was crazy to keep working on the business and build it up. But he always believed in me. When he died, for a while, I felt nothing."

Stacey still didn't answer. She didn't know what he wanted her to say.

Tony went on, "It felt like everything had been yanked out of me. Everything that made me feel like a human was gone. I was struggling."

"Why are you telling me this?"

"I assume you're feeling the same way."

"Because we are so alike, right?" Her tone was frosty.

"Correct. Because we are more alike than you want to admit."

Stacey turned to look at him and crossed her arms. "I can't figure you out. You could have anyone in the world. Any sort of supermodel or high ranking business woman. Yet you seem to think that we are perfect for each other."

"And you don't? I don't want a supermodel. Or some rich woman my father picked out for me." The dig on Charlie was not lost on Stacey. "I want someone who knows what it's like to struggle and who wants more from life. So I made some mistakes with you. I can rectify that. I can change that. If you let me."

"I don't feel like dating anyone."

Tony's hands rested on her shoulders. "Because you're hurting and won't let yourself feel it. So let me take care of things. Come with me."

"Come with you where?"

"To paradise. To wherever you want. Stop fighting how you feel about me and come with me. Forget the shit here and come with me."

Stacey's eyes left Tony's and instead looked around the cemetery. In the distance, she could see Charlie. He was still standing where she had left him. He had wanted her, all of her. He had wanted to try it out again. She could go with him. Stacey could open her heart to Charlie and try it again.

Or she could run away with Tony. What was she really risking there? Even if Tony left her, it would sting but it wouldn't tear her apart as if she had taken a risk on Charlie. It was safer for her… and right now, after losing Tina, what she wanted was safe.

She tore her gaze away from Charlie and looked up at Tony.

"Fine. Let's go."

Chapter Six

"Hey! Get up!"

The voice broke through Stacey's sleepy fog. She rolled over and looked in the doorway of her room. At first she thought that she was imagining it.

"Seriously, you're still in bed? It's one in the afternoon."

"Allison?" Stacey asked, her throat as dry as parchment.

"The one and only. You were supposed to send a car to get me from the airport." Her tone was accusatory as she strolled into Stacey's bedroom.

"I forgot. I thought you were coming on Friday."

"It is Friday."

Stacey propped herself up in bed. How had she lost track of time like that? Although, admittedly, it was easy to do on the island. The last three months that she had been here had been a complete and total blur of long days doing nothing and long nights on the beach.

Allison was looking around the room. She hadn't seen her sister since the day of Tina's funeral. Her sister looked the same besides her hair. She had dyed it a bright blonde which contrasted with her dark skin.

She wrinkled her nose. "Jesus, Stacey, this room really needs to be swept up. Don't you have a maid or something?"

"I don't let her in here."

She did have a point though. As if she could see things through her sister's gaze, Stacey saw the mounds of clothes tossed on the floor. Things were strewn about the room. The vanity was crowded with different types of make-up and tons of perfume bottles. The closet was open with clothes spilling out onto the floor.

The windows had been thrown open in the room, allowing the breeze to roll through. From here, Stacey could see the ocean. It was a bright clear blue and still took her breath away. Her room allowed her to walk directly onto the beach. She usually moved between her bedroom and the beach throughout the day.

"Amazing beach house," Allison remarked. "I walked through it before I stopped by your room. You sleep in separate rooms from Tony?"

"I told you. We aren't dating."

"Right. So you just ran off with him the same night we buried our grandmother to this tropical paradise and have been what, playing chess with him at night?" Allison's tone was dry.

"Is Jacob with you?"

"No. He's at our own place getting ready for the wedding."

The wedding. Since coming here to the island that Tony owned in the Bahamas, she hadn't spoken often with Allison. When she did speak to her, Allison kept her updated on how things were going. Stacey had stopped speaking out about the wedding once she arrived on the island. It wasn't her business anymore. Nothing was.

"Nice of Tony to let us use his island for our big day though." Allison sat down on the edge of the bed. "He has enough guest houses for everyone and plenty of space to hold the wedding."

"Sounds great."

"I guess so." She was playing with the edge of one of Stacey's blankets with some expression on her face that Stacey couldn't make out. "What about you? You ran off so quickly. Sorta just fell off the map. And now here you are! Not dating Tony. Just… doing what, exactly?"

Something about Allison bursting in here and seeing her asleep in the afternoon surrounded by a messy room had Stacey on edge. Maybe it was the fact that she knew she wasn't at her best right now. Perhaps it was because it felt as if real life was finally creeping in on her, trying to yank her back into it. But Stacey would be dragged into it kicking and screaming.

"It's been great. Really lovely. Long days by the beach just relaxing. Best three months I've ever had."

"And you're okay with… with all of this? Tony paying for everything?"

"You're okay with marrying Jacob?" Her tone was openly hostile, challenging Allison.

To her surprise, Allison backed off right away. "Whatever you have to do, Stacey." She stood up.

"Leaving already?"

"Yeah, I should get back to the guest house. We are only two houses down from you. You'll stop by, yeah?"

She didn't wait for an answer and gave Stacey a little wave instead. She closed the door behind her. Stacey was left alone – and for the first time in three months felt as if she had just burst out of a thick fog.

She looked around the room, focusing on how completely messy it was. She hadn't bothered to clean up any of it. Would she have, even if she had remembered her sister was coming by? For some reason, Stacey had just assumed that Allison wasn't actually going to go through with the marriage.

But here they both were, on Tony's private island. It was true that it was perfect for a wedding. There were guest homes across the small island. There was a building in the center for events. Tony had bought the island a couple of years ago. He had told her that he liked taking his yacht out here. Sometimes he would bring groups of people here for vacations.

Yet no one else had been here since Stacey had come here. Tony came by when he could, working from his office on the other side of the island. Yet there were days at a time when he had to go back into the world of the living. Stacey remained behind, spending her days by the beach or reading books.

Once in a while, a reminder of life outside the island would try to get her attention. Allison would ask when she was coming back home. A mention of Charlie in passing by Tony, when talking about business, would make Stacey's heart feel as if it had stopped completely for a few seconds. At night, there would be times when she couldn't sleep because she knew Tina wouldn't have wanted her to grieve this way.

But it was easier to forget. It was easier to go swimming in the beautiful ocean than wonder how long she was going to stay here and what she was going to do afterward. This was her hideout. Stacey didn't want to leave it.

She swung her legs over the king-sized bed and padded into her bathroom. When she had first gotten here, she had marveled at how large and state of the art it was. Now, she barely looked at it as she brushed her teeth and stripped off her clothes.

In the shower, she let the hot water pound against her skin. Something that Allison had said kept bothering her. It was when she had mentioned Tony being in a different room than hers. It was true that they were in different rooms. Stacey hadn't given the two of them much thought, actually. She didn't consider them to be dating, but it was because she hadn't wanted to dwell on it.

She had slept with Tony a handful of times in the three months. Like every time, it was over quickly and left her feeling unsatisfied. There had been no improvement there. Stacey hadn't given it much thought. She had wanted that physical touch from someone some nights. Tony was nearby and it made the most sense.

For the first time since Tina died, a true and terrible emotion rose up inside of her as she stood underneath the shower head. It swept over her like a pure sickness, and for a second she thought she might throw up.

Then Stacey realized what she was feeling. It was a mixture of grief and shame. Grief over her grandmother. Shame at the fact that she had turned tail and run away from all her problems. She had run away from Charlie. Her sister. The entire life she had been trying to carve out back home.

Deep down, she had known what she was doing. But Stacey had buried it so far down and focused only on running away with Tony that it had been easy to trick herself.

She hadn't felt much since getting here. It was so easy to stick her head in the sand and waste her days with Tony. But seeing Allison had reminded her of a life outside of this tropical paradise. Her sister was going to marry someone for money. Wasn't Stacey hiding out here with someone whom she could never feel the way she did about Charlie?

Charlie – she had rejected him that day by Tina's grave. He wanted another shot, but she had been too terrified to let him in. She shut him down and ran away like a scared fool.

Stacey scrubbed her skin extra hard, lost in thought. She had to get out of here. She could leave with Allison. She'd find another job and go back home to her dingy little apartment.

She got out of the shower, dressed quickly, and left her bedroom. Allison had said she was nearby. She'd go see her. Try to talk to her about coming home with her.

But in the foyer, she ran into Tony. He was dressed casually. Spending so much time out here had turned his skin a deep tanned color.

"Saw your sister. Guess we should get ready for the rest of the guests arriving here later on."

"Yeah. I'm actually going to see her to say hi."

He frowned. "She said she came by to see you already. Said you were still in bed." He came over to her and wrapped his arms around her waist. "How are you?"

"Awake," Stacey mumbled, meaning it in more ways than just the one.

Tony laughed. "Well, that's good. Listen, with all the guests arriving, I was thinking I'd buy you something new to wear. Something nice. What do you think?"

She thought of the piles of clothes back in her room and mentally cringed. Tony had been buying her lots of things. She had accepted all of it, barely glancing at whatever he had tossed her way. She had let things get completely out of control.

"No, I'm okay," Stacey replied firmly. "I think I have enough clothes."

Tony frowned again. "Are you sure? We can find something."

"I'm good, really." She untangled herself from his grip and forced herself to smile. "I'm going to go see Allison again though. It's been three months after all."

Before he could say anything else, Stacey ducked past him and went out the front door. It was humid but beautiful. The palm trees looked as if they could touch the sky, which was a beautiful solid blue. There wasn't a cloud in sight. She could hear the ocean as she walked along the pathway to the other houses.

Imagine owning an island. Stacey hadn't given it much thought before. Honestly, ever since she'd arrived, she hadn't given much thought to anything besides trying to forget about Tina. She had been determined to seal off her emotions from anything that could cause her pain.

As she looked around, for the first time it really hit her that Tony owned this entire place. He was rich beyond belief. The yacht and the island alone would be something Stacey could never have afforded in three lifetimes. Yet Tony owned both and was content just letting her stay here. She had hardly walked around the island. She had been in the villa and the beach for most of her time here.

Now she turned the corner on the pathway and came to a row of the guest homes. These were a lot smaller than the main villa but still pretty to look at it. Allison was outside of one with her cellphone raised as if she was trying to get a signal.

"Hey," Stacey called out.

She looked over and waved. She lowered her phone and crossed the short distance toward Stacey.

"Look at you. Out and about."

"I get out and about here."

Allison laughed. "No, you don't. You've been hiding out here for months. You pretty much fled the country just so you didn't have to deal with things. I woke you up, didn't I?"

"Don't start. 'Waking up' is a bit of an exaggeration," Stacey said, unwilling to admit that Allison was right.

"Too late. I've started." She grinned and in spite of Stacey's mood, she found herself grinning back.

"So, come on. Show me around the guest villa."

"You haven't been in any of the guest houses?"

"No," Stacey admitted. "I haven't really left the main villa at all."

"Geez, you've really been doing nothing this whole time, haven't you?" Allison asked as they walked up the front steps.

"Not true," Stacey said defensively. "I know that Tony has this island here mainly for parties. 'The ultimate getaway place' is what he calls it."

"It's pretty impressive. Actually, Jacob is a bit jealous of it," Allison said over her shoulder as they stepped into the house.

Stacey didn't get to ask why he was jealous because Jacob was in the foyer. He was rummaging through a suitcase. He looked unchanged from the last time that Stacey had seen him at Tina's funeral.

"Allison, dear, have you…" He looked up and saw Stacey. "Oh. Stacey. Nice to see you again."

"Same to you," Stacey replied, not really meaning it.

Jacob straightened up. "I was looking for my laptop. I shoved it into one of the suitcases."

"The red one. I put it in our room."

"Ah, great. What would I do without you?" he said and leaned over to kiss the top of Allison's head before leaving without another word.

"He's usually a bit more…"

"Chatty?" Allison finished. "I know. I hope he's just nervous and isn't getting cold feet."

Stacey pulled her sister into the living room and lowered her voice, "Are you sure about this?"

"Oh no. No, no, no."

"What?"

"You don't get to do this now, Stacey. Not after you ran off and hid out with Tony on his *own private island.*"

"I'm just worried. That's all."

"About what?"

"Well. Tony mentioned before at a party how this guy normally doesn't date… people like us."

Allison's eyes narrowed. "So, what, exactly? He's using me? For what, Stacey? I give him nothing. I have no money. I have no business ties to anything he could use me for. He gets nothing out of dating me besides me fawning over him. Perhaps that's what he wants. Someone just to fawn over him no matter what he says."

Stacey felt abashed and looked away. "Yeah, maybe."

"So, not another lecture. Okay? This is happening tomorrow night. That's that."

Stacey nodded, knowing there was nothing else that she could say to change Allison's mind. Not to mention that her sister did have a point. Stacey had been hiding out here, running away from real life. She couldn't exactly lecture Allison about marrying Jacob any longer.

"Great. Come on. Let me show you my dress. You are literally going to die," Allison said with a grin.

Chapter Seven

When Stacey arrived back at the villa later that night, she hadn't been expecting company. In hindsight, she should have. Allison and Jacob's wedding party could all fit on the island, which meant it had to be under two hundred people if each house was filled to the maximum. Tony was in the same social circle as Jacob, so guests were to be expected.

But when she stepped into the living room that night, she hadn't been expecting the guests to be Tony's family again. It was like accidentally walking onto a stage in the middle of a play. All eyes turned to her. Ai cleared her throat softly. Michelle's face looked the same. Chen wrinkled his noise a little. It was Mei who gave her a wave and a smile, which was more than Stacey had gotten last time.

Tony jumped to his feet quickly. He was holding a glass of whiskey. His hand was wrapped firmly around it, which was the only indication that whatever was going on here wasn't a good thing.

"Stacey. Nice time at your sister's?"

"Yes," Stacey replied. "She's very excited."

"Great." He came over to her and turned her to walk her out of the room. Stacey could feel the eyes of his family still on her.

"What is that about? Where did they come from?" Stacey whispered when they were in the hallway.

"Don't freak out."

"What does that mean?"

"Jacob invited them. It was supposed to be a surprise. A thank you for letting him use the island. He thought I hadn't seen them in over a year."

"Well, that was nice of him at least," Stacey said.

"Yeah, well. They aren't too happy that I have you here."

"Of course not," she mumbled.

Tony ignored her. "It isn't anything personal, Stacey. They just thought I'd have either married you or broken up with you by now."

"Isn't personal? Come on, Tony. I know what Michelle thinks of me at the very least. That I'm some fat woman you're taking pity on or something. She said she was used to meeting your girlfriends. So how many do you parade through to see if your family approves?"

"What? How do you –"

"I overheard the two of you back when I met them at your penthouse," Stacey admitted.

Tony's eyes widened slightly. "You should have told me. You shouldn't listen to Michelle. She just doesn't understand… what we have."

"What do we have?" Stacey heard herself say before she could stop herself. "What are we doing? They aren't going to approve of me, Tony. You know it. If you bring every woman you date by your family to find one that sticks, you're going to spend the rest of your life trying to please them."

"Stacey, wait." He grabbed her hand as she turned to leave. "What do you mean? 'What are we doing?' I thought we were doing just fine."

He was looking at Stacey with a pained expression on his face. Not for the first time in their three months together, Stacey wondered what went on in that mind of his. It was a rare glimpse to see what went on in his head. He was kind to her and always thoughtful. But Tony seemed to keep everything close to his heart, refusing to let her in, even when she had pressed him to open up.

"What do you want from us, Tony? Your mother won't approve of us marrying. So, what, you'll try to marry me anyway?"

"I was hoping that they would warm up to you. They don't even know you."

"They aren't going to warm up to me and you know it. I know it too."

"They just need to spend more time around you. Please."

Stacey wavered. She looked back in the direction of Tony's family with a growing sense of dread. Why couldn't she say no? It was as if the time she had spent here had wilted her.

"I have a headache," Stacey finally said. "I have to lie down. Tell your family I'm sorry."

She pushed past Tony, leaving him alone in the hallway.

<<◇>>

Of course Stacey couldn't sleep. She tossed and turned in bed. Even the sound of the ocean, which was once so soothing, bothered her. She felt isolated here on this island, cut off from the rest of human kind.

That was her fault, though. This island that had once been her refuge from dealing with her own feelings and problems now felt like it had her chained to the ankles, dragging her down.

Unable to sleep, Stacey kicked off the sheets and got out of bed. She opened her door very slowly. She had no idea if Tony's family was still here. There weren't enough bedrooms for all of them to stay here, which meant they had to be in one of the guest homes at least.

Stacey flattened herself against the wall and crept down. The entire thing reminded her of when she was a child and used to creep downstairs to see if Santa had left presents under the tree.

She stopped at the end of the hallway. Tony's family members were all speaking in the foyer. As his family left, soon it was just Michelle and Tony.

Michelle was speaking rapidly in Mandarin. Stacey held her breath, hoping that the two siblings would switch to English. She should let them know that she was here. She knew that. But something kept her firmly rooted to the ground.

Finally, Tony spoke in English. "I'm exhausted, Michelle. Need to sleep."

"I just think you're wasting your time. She doesn't love you."

Stacey flinched. Tony answered in Mandarin.

Michelle went on in English, "Stop denying it. You keep trying to woo this woman for some reason none of us understand. But I can tell just by looking at her she loves someone else. The two of you have pulled the wool over your own eyes. She isn't going to marry you, Tony, even if Mother approved. So cut her loose. You're wasting your time. She's holding you back. You're supposed to be in charge of the business and instead you're rotting on this island with her."

With that, Michelle left the house. She heard the door slam shut. Stacey turned to go back to her room when Tony spoke.

"I know you're there."

She froze and then stuck her head out from the corner. Tony was leaning against the wall with his arms crossed. He looked exhausted for the first time since Stacey had met him.

"Sorry. For listening in."

"I'm not angry. Probably the only way you can get answers around here, right?"

Stacey didn't know what to say. She watched as Tony closed his eyes for a few seconds before opening them again to stare at her.

"Is it true?" Tony finally asked.

"Is what true?"

"What Michelle said. That you love someone else."

Stacey felt as if someone had pushed her in front of a speeding train. She could either let it smash into her and let it drag her away. Or she could leap out of the way and break free.

"Yes. I think so."

Tony sucked in a little bit of air through his mouth as if someone had punched him. Then he shook his head and said, "It's Charlie, isn't it? I don't get it. I don't understand why you're still wrapped up in him."

"I didn't know I was. I thought… I thought since he was seeing Adele that it was time to move on. It didn't make sense to be pining after him any longer."

"So, what, you came here?"

"That isn't the only reason I came here and you know it," Stacey replied. "I didn't want to be back home living in that apartment with my grandmother's ghost. All those memories. Allison is leaving too. She's getting married. It was all too much. So yes, I ran. I ran away with you. Maybe it was a hasty decision on my part, but I had to get my mind off all the things that were haunting me, and I don't just mean my grandmother. Sorry, bad joke…"

"You should have stayed," Tony said bitterly. "You should have stayed and gone off to fuck Charlie."

"Hey, that isn't completely fair. I told you before that I didn't think we were going to work out. And you knew even then that I was struggling with Charlie and how I felt about him. When I agreed to come with you, it wasn't because I… because I loved you or anything. I thought you knew that."

Tony pushed off the wall and walked over to her. He grabbed her shoulders. His thumbs dug into her skin. He held her there tightly, staring down at her.

"I told you when you broke up with me, if you remember," he said in a low voice, "that we belong together. We are two sides of the same coin."

"Let go of me," Stacey said, trying to keep her voice calm.

But Tony didn't. He kept speaking. "You're hung up on the illusion of Charlie. Not what he is really like."

"How would you know?"

"I just know. I just know!" He raised his voice suddenly.

Stacey yanked herself away from him. Her heart was pounding rapidly in her chest. She stared at him. She had never seen such emotion from him before. It was unsettling.

"My family – they'll get it in time. That we belong together. My mother will approve. You just have to give me more time." He was pleading now, his voice an octave higher than normal. "You have to let me work on them."

"I don't want you to work on them," Stacey whispered. "Tony, I don't want to marry you. I think I should go, actually."

She turned to head to her room. Her mind was spinning. She planned to pack a few things in a suitcase and go over to Allison's. She would get through the wedding and get back home. Seeing Tony like this was only an indicator of his true nature. Stacey had never seen it before. But now that she had, she knew she had to get out of here.

Tony's hand snapped out and reached for Stacey's. He was pulling her toward him. She tried to dig her feet against the floor but it was tile and made no difference. He wrapped his arms around her and crushed her in a hug.

"Stacey," he whispered, "Stacey, you can't go. I've done all of this for you. Don't you see? All of this was for you. I tried to help you with your grandmother. I tried to help you with the job. From the first time I saw you on the yacht, I knew that I had to have you."

Muffled against his shirt, Stacey said, "You can't own people. They aren't yours to have." She pushed herself away from him. "Jesus, Tony! What is wrong with you?"

"Stacey, you're the first woman that I've felt this for. Don't you get it? All the others – they've meant nothing. They were all nothing. But you and I – I can feel what we have between us. I know you can feel it too! You're just confused."

"I'm not confused. Tony, I'm sorry. I didn't mean to upset you. Truly, I didn't. I'm sorry. I really like you. I do. From the very start. But it just isn't enough. I've been sitting in this villa like I'm in a dream or something. I have to get back to reality. I can't keep doing this." She gestured at the room and hoped it would make sense to him.

"I'll give you whatever you want," Tony pleaded. "Whatever you want. Diamonds. Furs. This island."

"It isn't about things," Stacey said, feeling sad. "It's about that connection. How I feel."

Tony looked stumped. In that moment, Stacey felt nothing but pity for him. He loved her. She knew that. But he also thought loving someone meant owning them. He thought it meant buying them whatever they wanted and allowing them to run away from their problems.

But Stacey didn't want gifts. She didn't want someone who was okay with her hiding out because she couldn't deal with her grandmother's death. She needed someone who would hold her up and push her forward. Make her do things she was struggling to do because it was good for her, not because it was easy.

"Tony, I'm going to go over to my sister's place, alright?" Her voice was soft in an attempt to soothe his ire.

"Stacey, marry me. Tonight. We'll leave the island. Forget about my family. They'll come around."

She shook her head. "No, Tony. Not only because it wouldn't be fair of me to do that to you, but also because you want your family to love who you love, too. And that isn't me. You'd regret it in time. Our similarities are nice. But that's not enough to make a foundation for a relationship, either."

She turned and left the room. Tony didn't come after her which was a relief. Stacey was unnerved by how passionate he was being. She knew that he cared about her, but she hadn't quite understood how deeply until now.

I should have seen it coming. I should have known he was falling too deep, she thought as she opened her suitcase. Stacey knew that she shouldn't blame herself for Tony's feelings. She couldn't control how he felt. But she had assumed they had merely liked each other. She hadn't known he loved her or was thinking about marriage. The thought made her head spin. Talk about too much too soon.

Stacey felt wrong taking anything he had gifted her while she had been here. Not after she had just told him she didn't want anything from him.

Stacey finished packing her suitcase with everything she had brought with her to the island. There was a door in her room that led directly to the beach. She decided she would cut across the beach to get to her sister.

With one last look at the room, Stacey turned around and left. She shut the door quietly behind her. She walked toward the beach as if it had a pull on her. The sand squished in between her toes. The stars were sparkling above her head. The surf crashed against her feet.

Stacey looked back at the villa. All the lights were off. She wasn't sure what Tony was thinking or doing. Her shoulders hurt where he had dug his thumbs into her skin. It had been scary to see him like that. If he was like that over his feelings for her, what would stop Tony from getting that way about other things?

She shivered, and not from the ocean breeze. Then Stacey picked up her suitcase and walked across the beach toward Allison's villa. It came into view in a matter of minutes and was lit up like a Christmas tree. Some of the other villas were illuminated as well. Guests had been arriving all day.

Stacey went over to Allison's bedroom window. She hoped Jacob wasn't in there. She put her head against the glass and rapped on it three times. Nothing. Stacey really didn't want to go through the front door. It was probably swarming with well-wishers and she didn't feel like talking right now.

Stacey was about to tap on the window again when Allison's face popped up. She frowned.

"What the hell are you doing?" she said through the window.

"Can you let me in? Through the bedroom door?"

"Yeah, sure."

Stacey backed away from the window and went over to the bedroom door that opened to the beach. Allison closed it behind her. She was dressed to impress tonight in a shiny purple dress. Her eyes were lined with gold that looked beautiful against her dark skin.

"Wow, you look beautiful," Stacey breathed.

Allison pointed to the suitcase. "What did you do? You couldn't have waited until after the wedding to dump him?"

Before Stacey could stop herself, she launched into the entire story about what had happened. Allison listened with avid interest. When she finished, her sister shook her head.

"Alright, well, he sounds like a fucking weirdo."

"He isn't."

"Why are you defending him? Wait. Don't tell me. Guilt. Fuck that. His reaction was really fucking weird."

Normally, Allison's crass mouth bothered Stacey. Tonight, however, there was something comforting about it.

She went on. "Wanting to get approval like that is old school. Also, his family is never going to like you. They never even gave you a shot. His reaction about wanting you and owning you – creepy."

Something in Stacey's face must have shown conflict because Allison sat down at the edge of the bed. She tugged on Stacey's arm until she was sitting down next to her.

"You fucked up," Allison said simply. "Everyone does it. You got caught up in Tony because he represented what you thought was a way out. You did like him, but he loved you. You can't stay with that imbalance."

"What about Jacob and you?" Stacey asked before she could stop herself.

"Jacob and I are more of a marriage that works out on both sides."

"What do you mean?"

"His money is appealing, right? And Jacob wants to marry someone and start popping out heirs to his fortune. It works out for both of us. He knows I won't be going behind his back to scheme and plot against him. And I get access to his money."

"Scheme and plot? He owns a tea company. Not exactly high stakes stuff," Stacey remarked.

"Hey, there are some serious assholes working in the tea business, alright?" Allison said with a smile.

"So, let me get this straight. He likes you because you have no connections that can mess him over. You're safe, basically. That doesn't bother you that he thinks of you like that?"

"No. It isn't as if I think of him as the love of my life."

"And this doesn't bother you?"

"Stacey, this is what I've wanted. I've looked for this. I know you think it's stupid and you disagree with it. But I want that money. I want that security that I am never going to get on my own. So I'm going to get it this way. And I'm fine with it. Not every marriage is about love. This one is more of a mutual understanding."

"I guess I just have a hard time wrapping my head around it."

"Well, don't. It isn't your problem. No offense, but you pretty much lost your fucking mind when Tina died. You've been living on an island shacking up with some guy that, for reasons beyond me, is in love with you to the point he just thinks if he buys you a lot of shit you'll feel the same way."

"Don't remind me. I feel awful."

"Well, stop feeling bad for yourself. You woke up now. You're going to go back home after the wedding and get your life together on your own terms." Allison stood up. "I have actual guests I need to go talk to. I have to intervene before Jacob literally bores them to death and we have to clean up the corpses."

She turned around to leave when Stacey spoke up, "Allison."

Her sister paused and looked over her shoulder.

"Thanks."

"I'm not as dumb as I look."

"Well, you aren't very good at math."

"Shut up," Allison said, but her tone was light and she was smiling.

For the first time in three months, Stacey felt a little bit of relief bloom in her chest.

Chapter Eight

Jacob actually looked nervous. It was a strange sight for Stacey. She was watching him struggle with his tie. Allison was already at the hall, getting ready in one of the rooms there for the wedding. Yet in all of the insanity, she had somehow forgotten her shoes. Stacey had gone to fetch them.

She hadn't been expecting to see Jacob here. Not only that, but he was alone. Stacey had been expecting a group of people to be floating around him, helping him. But he was struggling with his tie on his own in the middle of the foyer.

Stacey cleared her throat. Jacob almost jumped fifty feet in the air, then looked over at her.

"Sorry," she said. "Allison forgot her shoes."

"It's fine," he said, turning back to the mirror.

She watched his fingers stumble over the tie. Stacey was confident that Jacob knew how to tie a tie properly. To see him nervous was startling. From what she had learned yesterday, Jacob was marrying her sister because it made the most business sense, not because he loved her.

Stacey walked over to him. "Want some help?"

He let out a little groan of frustration and then nodded, turning to face Stacey. She went up to him. Her fingers curled around his tie. She had never been this close to Jacob before. Up close, she still couldn't understand how her sister was going to marry this guy. Billionaire or not, Stacey could only ever see herself marrying for love. To marry him for money just wasn't enough. His skin was so pale today that he was practically transparent. His eyes looked watery, as if he were allergic to something.

"Nervous?" she asked, trying to make conversation.

"Yes. Is Allison?"

Stacey's mind flicked back to Allison only ten minutes ago. Her sister had looked radiant in her gown. Her make-up was flawless. She was glowing in diamond jewelry. There were no nerves in Allison's face. This was what she had wanted, after all. She wasn't going to get jumpy about it now.

But one look at Jacob showed he was clearly nervous. Stacey took pity on him.

"Yes, she is."

He exhaled slowly. "It all happened so quickly."

"There," Stacey said, taking a step back to look at the tie.

Jacob turned back to the mirror and gave a curt nod. "Thank you."

"Not going to leave my sister at the altar, are you?" It was a joke but there was a hitch at the end of her question that made it sound serious.

Jacob shook his head. "No. Definitely not. Just nervous. You know, we were going to wait a little longer, originally. I thought if perhaps she wanted more time… after your grandmother passed."

Stacey didn't know this. Allison had made it sound as if they had jointly wanted it to unfold this quickly.

"Did she say why she wanted to move it up?"

"No, but I just assumed it was her own way of grieving over Tina. She was destroyed when it happened. I think focusing on the wedding helped her process it."

Was that healthier than what Stacey had done? Probably. Stacey had always prided herself on keeping her shit together but doing that after Tina died had been the last thing she had managed to accomplish. How had the tables turned to where Allison was the one who had herself together and not Stacey!

"Listen, I know what you are thinking," Jacob said suddenly.

"What?"

"How quickly it's moving. I know you're seeing Tony, so you at least understand how important business is in our lives."

Stacey didn't bother telling him that she had broken up with Tony. The whole thing still felt too messy to say aloud to someone other than Allison.

Jacob went on. "I don't know if Allison told you that my father is ill. He doesn't have much time left."

"Oh God, I'm sorry," Stacey replied, stricken.

"The control of the company is going to come to me. It is a big responsibility. Not only do I want someone that I can have children with so that the company can stay in the family, but I don't want to be alone either, going through the next few years." He shrugged and looked away from her.

Stacey got the sense that Jacob opening up was a rarity. All she had ever heard from him was a pompous attitude and long, dull stories. This was the first time she saw a real person underneath it all. Not wanting to be alone was something that she could relate to.

"Yeah, I get it," Stacey finally said. "Allison doesn't want to be alone either."

"People have been talking. About her and me, I mean. That she isn't my usual type. That she is just using me for my money. But your sister and I know what we both want out of this and it works out for both of us."

"Like a business deal."

"In a way. Anyway, I'm glad you're here to help her with her nerves."

"Well, I'm going to grab her shoes before she kills me," Stacey said lightly.

"I should get down there as well."

"Do you have anyone going with you?"

"No," Jacob said curtly before turning around.

There was something sad about that, Stacey thought as he nodded at her and left through the front door. She assumed people would be swarming around him. But for the front he put on, Stacey had seen that he was lonely and unsure of himself.

Stacey still didn't quite agree with Allison's way of doing things. Her entire goal had been to marry rich. Now that she was finally accomplishing it, would life be exactly how she had wished it to be? To help Jacob through his father's death, give him children and raise a family with him and be a life boat in the seas of his business struggles – Stacey couldn't picture Allison doing that.

To be fair, Stacey hadn't been able to picture herself losing her mind after Tina's death and hiding out here with Tony. So everyone was full of surprises lately.

With no one to walk Allison down the aisle, she had asked if Stacey would do it. It made the most sense. Allison didn't want someone she hardly knew to walk her. Stacey was the only family around.

It was surreal for Stacey. Her sister glowed next to her like a diamond. Stacey had never seen a more beautiful bride. As they walked together, the crowd hushed, Stacey wondered what it would feel like if she were ever to get married. Surely, it wouldn't be as luxurious as this. Maybe something small and quiet with a handful of people. Her sister could return the favor with walking her down the aisle. She could almost picture it… except for the groom.

At first, Stacey thought she was imagining it. She had been focused on Jacob, who was waiting nervously at the altar. But no, there he was. Charlie was looking at her from one of the seats. Stacey hadn't known that he had been invited. His eyes were resting on her, not Allison.

The sight of him brought back a rush of memories. Their first date by the ocean. Their first kiss. Adele waiting in the lobby. Breaking up with him. Thinking that he was the one who had paid for Tina's nursing home stay. And ultimately, that day at her grandmother's funeral, where he had wanted to give her another chance and she had run away, too afraid to act on her feelings.

She dragged her eyes away from him. This was Allison's wedding. Stacey wasn't going to let herself get distracted by Charlie. They reached the altar. Stacey went to stand off to one side.

Awkwardly, Stacey found herself looking across the aisle at Tony. Jacob must have snagged him as best man at the last minute. Tony was staring at her. His face was like stone. There was no sign of the passionate side of him that she had seen the other night.

She avoided his gaze and turned to watch Jacob and Allison recite their vows. When they finished and leaned in for the kiss, Stacey could only shake her head a little. Her sister had achieved her 'goal,' no matter how silly Stacey thought it was. She married a man who wanted someone to support him during rough times ahead. They both knew it wasn't a marriage based on love, but of mutual caring and understanding, maybe even convenience.

That might work for Allison but it isn't what I want, Stacey thought as she watched the two kiss.

And in spite of her best intentions, she found herself looking over at Charlie once again.

Chapter Nine

Stacey had never seen a wedding reception quite like this before. Tents had been put up on the beach for the reception with room for dancing afterward. Some people lounged on the beach while others even swam. The moon was high up in the sky. The tents were covered in small fairy lights. It was a paradise.

Stacey was standing just outside one of the smaller tents. In front of her, people crowded the dance floor. Allison was in the middle of it. Jacob was spinning her around. Her dress was puffed out and swirling with her. The gems on it shimmered under the low lighting. She looked like a star that had crashed on the island.

A couple of times, Stacey had run into members of Tony's family. They regarded her with a cool indifference. She wondered if he had told them about the breakup. It was impossible to tell with their blank faces. She hadn't seen Tony since the wedding ceremony.

A breeze rolled in off the ocean. Stacey turned to look at it. The waters were dark. The stars reflected off of it, distorted by the waves. She walked away from the tent and headed toward the ocean. There were some people there in small clusters, drinking and laughing loudly.

She slipped her shoes off and let the water touch her feet. It was cold and caused her to shiver when it first rolled over her skin.

"I was going to go swimming, but it ended up being a bit too chilly for my liking."

Stacey froze. She didn't have to turn around to know who was behind her. Charlie walked up next to her and looked out at the ocean. He took in a deep breath and closed his eyes.

"I don't know how you could have stayed here for so long," he said.

"Why?"

"So lonely. I'm not a huge fan of islands. I feel disconnected from everything. Like I'm bobbing around in a giant bathtub." He still hadn't looked at her.

"You know, it's funny you say that. I've thought that before too. All the water in between the next city. It is lonely. Isolating."

"Is that why you're going home?"

"I see you've been talking to Allison."

"Yeah, we've had a little time to talk."

"Is that how you knew I've been staying here?"

Charlie chuckled. "No. No, Tony told me when we ran into each other a couple of months ago. He made sure to slide it in there for me to hear. Which I didn't mind. You just vanished after Tina's funeral. At least you were safely on some island instead of being sad somewhere else."

"Yeah. I guess so."

"Stacey –"

At the same time, she had said, "Charlie –"

The two of them laughed and Charlie ran his fingers through his hair. "Sorry. You go first."

"No, it's okay. You go."

The two of them stared at each other, at a standstill. Stacey had wanted to apologize for how she had acted at Tina's funeral. The words were bubbling in her mouth, waiting to spill out. She wanted to reach out and touch him and tell him that she had fucked things up. She should have gone with him and taken that chance.

But before either of them could say a word, another voice spoke up.

"Get away from her."

Surprised, Stacey looked over to see Tony barreling toward the two of them. His face was contorted with anger and he had his fists clenched. Alarmed, Stacey looked over at Charlie who was positioning himself in front of her.

"Tony, man, why don't you settle down?"

She hadn't smelled it at first due to the breeze from the ocean. But now that Tony was close enough, Stacey could smell the wafts of alcohol rolling off of him. He wasn't just a little drunk. He was completely intoxicated.

"Why don't we go back to that tent over there and talk this through?" Charlie said.

But Tony never replied. Instead, he swung at him. His fist connected with Charlie and sent him tumbling into the sand. A wave promptly rolled over his head which caused him to sputter up water.

"What are you doing?!" Stacey shrieked, alarmed.

Tony grabbed Charlie by the collar of his shirt, getting ready to deck him again. Stacey threw herself against him. The sudden collision threw him off balance. Already drunk, he lost his footing and landed in the sand next to Charlie.

Stacey helped Charlie get to his feet. Tony was slurring drunkenly as a wave rolled in over his head.

"Help me get him up before he drowns or something," Charlie said, rubbing his jaw.

Naturally, a crowd had formed. The sight of usually well composed Tony, drunk as a skunk and punching someone, had generated a lot of interest. Charlie was trying to prop Tony up to get him out of the water. Tony tried to push him off.

It was then that her sister burst through the crowd. She was staring at the three of them. Jacob was hurrying over. Tony pushed Charlie off again and slumped back down in the water.

"I got him," Jacob said to the two of them.

Allison hurried over to them. Stacey was alarmed at the fact that her wedding dress was getting wet, but she didn't seem to notice.

"What the hell happened?"

"Tony's drunk and just punched Charlie."

Charlie's face was already swelling. It had been a good punch. Even in the darkness, she could see his cheek was cut open.

"I'll get him patched up," Stacey said, grabbing his arm. "Allison, I am so sorry."

"What? Why? Tony losing his shit and punching people over you? I never would have pegged that happening. Over me, maybe. Not you." She was teasing her, Stacey realized with relief. She wasn't angry. "Anyway, go get him looked after."

Stacey nodded and grabbed Charlie's arm. She pulled him away from the beach before Tony could wriggle free of Jacob's grip and come after him. They cut through one of the larger tents. This one had a bartender who was busy serving drinks. Stacey tugged Charlie along until she felt him resist.

She turned to look at him. "What?"

"Come on. I want a drink. Whiskey or something."

"You're bleeding."

"It'll help with the pain." He grinned.

Stacey tried to protest but he weaved through the crowd toward the bar. He leaned forward, saying something to the bartender. She watched him and tried to ignore the way her heart was fluttering in her chest. The fairy lights that were looped around the top of the tent seemed to make him glow. It was as if he was the brightest spot in the entire area.

She looked away and told herself to get a grip. After what she had done to Charlie, she didn't deserve another chance with him. She shouldn't even think about it. Not only that, but now Tony had punched him in the face. Wonderful. Why even go near him at this point?

Charlie came back holding a glass of whiskey. He took a swig and winked at her over the rim of the glass. Stacey turned away quickly before her face could betray her thoughts.

"Where are you marching off to? You don't even know which villa is mine," he pointed out.

Stacey slowed down so he could catch up. They were leaving the tent now. Ahead of them were the guest villas. Most were dark. There were a few stragglers here. At one point, their hands brushed against each other. The touch was electric. It felt as if it rocked her to her center, and it was only their hands touching. She felt like a schoolgirl with a crush.

"Here," he said, stopping in front of one of the smaller ones.

A thought struck her out of the blue. "Adele isn't here."

"Ah, yes. That's right," Charlie replied as he opened the front door.

"Why?" Stacey pressed, even though technically it wasn't any of her business.

They stepped into the living room. Stacey had never been in the smaller villas before. She recalled Tony telling her they were the oldest and not used much. He liked bringing big groups to the island, so he had stopped building the smaller homes.

Charlie looked over her shoulder. "Is that any of your concern?"

Stacey felt struck and stammered out, "N-no! It isn't. I'm sorry."

Charlie let out a loud laugh and then winced, gingerly touching his cheek. "Shit. Ow."

"There's a first aid kit in the bathroom. Each place has one," Stacey said as she headed toward the bathroom.

"How thoughtful." His tone was dry.

"Why were you laughing at me?" she asked as she rummaged through the cabinet.

"Because you thought I was being serious about asking about Adele," Charlie said.

She found the kit and pulled it out. Then she pointed to the edge of the tub.

"Yes, nurse," he replied, sitting down on it.

Stacey tilted his face to one side so she could see where Charlie had been punched. His skin was warm under her fingertips. She could feel her own pulse in her fingertips. It was racing. She wondered if he could feel it.

Underneath Charlie's eye was a small gash. She could tell that he luckily wouldn't need stitches.

"I think his ring got you," she mumbled as she looked through the kit.

"Probably. Thought I saw some big shiny thing on his finger." He wrinkled his noise.

"I'm going to clean it up first. You're probably going to end up with a black eye."

Charlie smirked. "I'll look tough, right?"

Stacey rolled her eyes. "This is going to sting."

"I can handle it," he boasted and then cursed when Stacey started to clean it. "Fuck. That hurts."

"Big tough guy, huh?" Stacey quipped.

He laughed. His breath brushed against her cheek. Stacey tried to ignore how close she was to him. As she cleaned up his cut, she refused to look into his eyes. Charlie shifted a little on the edge of the tub.

"I'm not seeing Adele."

"Oh?" She tried to keep her voice neutral.

"It was stupid. I thought – after you left… at the time, it made sense. It was easier just caving to what my dad wanted. For a while, I figured I'd marry her. It would stop all the plotting and planning from my dad and my brother, Eric. Peace and quiet."

"And?"

"I couldn't do it. No matter how hard I tried to tell myself that Adele could work for me, she wasn't you."

Stacey felt her breath catch but she refused to let herself get distracted. She refused to let herself hope, even for a moment, that Charlie would want anything to do with her.

"Why did he punch me?" Charlie said abruptly, changing the subject.

"I don't know," she lied. "Drunk, I guess." It was easier to lie than admit that he had known that she still loved Charlie.

Charlie grabbed her hand. She let out a small gasp, startled.

"Hey," she chastised, "you're lucky I just applied the bandage. You would have messed it up."

Charlie didn't reply. He held her hand gently. Unlike when Tony had grabbed her, she could break free at any time. But Stacey didn't want to break free. Instead, she watched as he pressed his lips against her fingertips. His eyes were on hers.

"When I left Adele, I thought I could win you back. But then I heard from Jacob about Tina dying. I could only imagine your grief. Your anger at how things had turned out." Each word he said gently brushed against her fingers, sending shivers through her. "I could picture a storm inside of you. I had to see you. I thought – I shouldn't have approached you at the funeral like that. It wasn't fair of me."

"What? No, I shouldn't have – I was so stupid that day, Charlie. I should have opened up to you and really listened. But I was so afraid –"

"I should have waited. Instead of trying to convince you to be with me, I should have been there to support you. Maybe if I had, you wouldn't have…"

"What? Run away? I still would have. I was too afraid to let you in. I took the coward's way out. I let myself succumb to my grief and I just didn't want to deal with anything anymore. Allison was right. I lost myself through who I was seeing."

Charlie kissed her fingertips so softly that Stacey thought she could be imagining it. Distantly, she could hear music from the reception. It was the only thing she could hear over the sound of her beating heart.

"You're back now though, aren't you?" he whispered. "You're awake."

"I'm awake," she breathed.

He pulled her toward him. His lips touched hers. The touch was like waking up from a nightmare. The last three months, which had been a fog of hiding her emotions and ignoring reality, seemed to dissipate when Charlie kissed her.

The kiss was gentle and full of longing. There were a lot unspoken words there. Things still needed to be discussed. But for right now, feeling Charlie kiss her like this was more than Stacey had ever wanted in her life.

He broke away from her and said very gently, "Come home, Stacey."

So she did.

Chapter Ten

Seasons were non-existent on Tony's island. It was in a permanent state of constant summer. When Stacey stepped out of the cab to look at her apartment complex for the first time in three months, she was startled to see that it was well into autumn in the city.

The leaves were changing color. One of the trees nearby was already bare. There were no summer storms on the horizon. There was a hint of chill to the wind, as if winter was quietly promising to arrive.

The cab drive home had shown her a lot of construction. Charlie's company was remodeling and rebuilding a lot of the buildings that had fallen into disrepair. The public library was covered in construction signs. There was a park being built where there had once been a junk yard. It was exciting to see positive changes being made to her area of town.

She had also noticed how many people were trying to sell their homes. Everyone was trying to cash in on the remodeling of this section of the city. The sellers were probably hoping to interest someone from a major company like Charlie's in buying their homes and flipping them. Change had steam-rolled in while Stacey had been hiding out.

She opened the door to the lobby and was taken aback. The tile that had once been cracked in places had been repaired. It was jarring. Nothing else seemed to have been fixed down here. But the mere fact that at least that much was accomplished meant the owners of the building were finally starting to fix things.

Stacey climbed the steps. She was oddly nervous about going into her old apartment. She got to her floor and practically ran into Leon. At first she didn't recognize him. He had gotten so tall in the last few months. He had a cigarette dangling from his mouth and was holding a cheap-looking phone in the other hand.

"Holy shit! Stacey!"

"You shouldn't curse like that, Leon," Stacey said automatically.

He let out a loud laugh, "Look at you! Gone for what, four months, and still ready to lecture."

"Three months, actually."

"Everyone was waiting for the apartment to go up for rent or something."

"Nah. I'm back now."

"What about your sister? She's a babe."

"She's a bit too old for you, Leon," Stacey remarked. "Also, she's married."

"Ah, really? Damn. Born a little too early to snag a woman like her," he said wistfully and then looked serious. "I'm sorry about your grandmother. My mom wanted to come by and see if you needed anything. Any help. But you were gone."

"Yeah, I sorta left in a hurry," Stacey replied, feeling guilty.

"Well, you're back now. The building was sold when you were gone. We got new landlords."

"Is that why the tile downstairs is repaired?"

"You noticed that? Yeah, pretty amazing. Anyway, I should go. I have a girlfriend now and don't wanna piss her off. See you around."

Leon moved past her. Stacey watched him leave, marveling again at how tall he was. She wondered who had bought the building. At least they weren't trying to kick anyone out.

Stacey stopped in front of her apartment and unlocked the front door. With a deep breath, she opened it and stepped inside.

Nothing had changed visually, of course. Everything was right where Stacey had left it when she had run away. She stood there, almost afraid to take another step. The dam she had placed around her heart was threatening to crack and let everything she had been holding in free.

Stacey walked into the living room. Everything had a layer of dust over it. She was going to clean the entire place out, she thought idly as she ran her fingers over the coffee table.

She could feel it pulling her. Some sort of force propelling her to what had been Tina's room. Even if Stacey could stop it, she wouldn't. She needed to do this. Her breath caught in her throat. The dam shook violently in her heart. Stacey stopped in front of the door. It was firmly shut. She must have done that. She couldn't remember closing it.

Stacey pushed open Tina's door and looked inside. The bed was a little messy from when they had packed her things up for the nursing home. It had hurt to take her there. But Stacey had thought she was going to have more time.

She stepped inside the room and let the full force of it finally hit her in the face. Tina's loss, still too fresh for Stacey, rolled over her. The dam broke inside of her. Her legs went weak and she sunk to the floor.

For the first time since her grandmother died, Stacey allowed herself to finally grieve. She stayed there on the floor for a long time, sobbing her eyes out, letting herself feel engulfed by the loss.

Stacey had been trying to sleep. She had felt exhausted after crying for so long. She was jet-lagged from the trip. It had made perfect sense to go to bed early. But lying there in bed felt suffocating. She could feel how alone she was. This was one of the things that Stacey had been trying to outrun. The lonely feeling that filled the apartment was enough to make her want to cry again.

Stacey looked at the clock. It was only seven at night. She sat up, deciding not to spend another second in bed. Sleep just wasn't going to happen, and all she was going to do was drive herself crazy.

Charlie had texted her once she had landed, saying that he was happy that she was back home. He had gone up north for a business trip directly after the wedding. Talking things out with him would have to wait until he came back. Nothing else had happened that night, but still, the kiss they had shared in the bathroom had been filled with promise. Stacey was eager to see where that was going to go.

She liked to think that she was going to get another shot with Charlie. Stacey was ready to put her heart on the line and work through the differences in their lives to try again. She had been too quick to break up with him in the first place. If only she had stayed with him, perhaps things would be completely different now.

Her phone went off, breaking her out of her thoughts about Charlie. Stacey looked at it and was surprised to see it was her old boss, William. Dimly, she could recall him back at the funeral. He had been telling her about something. She struggled to remember. Something about a new business, maybe? It was hard to remember anything from Tina's funeral. It was like one hazy bad dream.

"Hello?"

"So, it is true! I can't believe it!" William's booming voice came through the other line. "Allison told me you were back in town, but I thought she was pulling my leg."

"Allison contacted you?" Stacey asked, surprised because she knew Allison and Jacob were on their honeymoon somewhere in Europe.

"Yup. Said you were looking for a job."

"Oh. Yeah. I am, actually." There was no way she was going to ask Tony if she could still work at the office after they had broken up.

"Come meet me at the deli down the street from your apartment."

"Sure. I'll be there soon."

Stacey changed quickly and made sure she looked decent. She knew she probably looked a little rough, but it was nothing that William hadn't seen before. Back when the restaurant had been busy, Stacey had usually looked terrible.

When she walked into the deli, she looked around for him. Someone waved her over. To her surprise, it was Amanda. She hadn't seen Amanda in quite some time. Next to her was Brad. It was nice to see that the two of them were still together. She walked over to their table.

"William call you guys too?" Stacey asked after giving Amanda a hug.

"Not really. We already work for him," Amanda replied as Stacey sat down.

"Really?"

"Yup. I only started a couple of weeks ago. I left the job I had taken when the restaurant closed. William said he'd fit better into my school schedule."

Stacey looked over at Brad, who shrugged. "I needed a job."

"Where is he, anyway?" she asked the two of them, looking around.

"Right here."

Someone had stopped in front of their table. He was holding two coffees. Stacey blinked.

"William?" she asked in surprise.

"I know, I know. I lost a lot of weight."

It was true. William, who had once been the largest man Stacey had known, was now slim. He looked away from her, almost bashful at his progress.

"Wow, that is amazing. What brought that on?" she asked as he sat down next to her.

"Boredom. Losing the restaurant meant I had a lot of free time on my hands. Which sounded great at first. It was nice not worrying about the day-to-day things. But I got bored. My wife – she started talking about going out for walks and things like that to keep me from getting restless. I just started losing weight the more I worked out."

"Well, that's great, really," Stacey replied.

"What about you? Last time we saw you was at Tina's funeral," William said.

"I am still so sorry about what happened with her," Amanda spoke up.

"Thanks, guys. Yeah, I just got back into town. I sort of took off for a while."

"Hid out," Amanda quipped but she smiled gently at Stacey.

"Yeah. I guess I lost my shit there for a little bit," she admitted.

"I've lost my shit more times than I can count," Brad said.

"Well, I'm back now. And ready to hear what you wanted to see me about," Stacey said to William.

"Right. Well," he cleared his throat, "all those times I was out jogging or whatever, I noticed all the renovations going on in the city. And I saw a lot of building owners that were trying to sell their places. They knew companies like Charlie's were interested in remodeling the city or cutting deals with private places to remodel. Over the last few months, I saw that everyone was trying to sell but there weren't a lot of takers."

"So, you want to hop in on it," Stacey finished. "Buy up some of the cheaper places and flip them. Turn a profit."

"We already own one residence," Amanda said.

It clicked in Stacey's head. "You bought the apartment where I live."

William smiled. "Figured it'd be a good place to start. The landlords there didn't seem keen on the place. They had been banking on Charlie's construction company to buy it up. When he changed to remodeling public buildings and parks, they were pretty bitter. It left them wide open for me to swoop in and buy it up."

"So, what? You're going to improve it – hopefully you aren't going to kick anyone out."

"No, of course not. But the top floor of your complex is what… empty?"

"Yeah. Because it fell into such disrepair – oh. I get it now. You're going to rent them out for a higher price. Elite apartments on the top floor."

"Right," William said, rubbing his hands together. "And if it works, we can start doing that all around the city. There is a market there. We just need to grab it."

"Okay. Sounds like a good idea. But what would I be doing?"

"You'd be my assistant, of course. Come with me to any meetings. Help me scope out the properties. I have Amanda working on the paperwork side of things. Dealing with the city. Making sure the deal is clean. I have Brad as…" he trailed off, as if unsure why exactly Brad was there.

"Amanda's assistant," Brad said.

"Sure," William replied slowly. "Amanda's assistant, I guess."

"Well, that sounds great," Stacey said. "Perfect timing, really."

"Great! I'm so happy. It is like the gang is back together. Minus everyone at the restaurant I didn't care about. Let's work out the details," William said, pulling out a folder.

Stacey leaned forward, interested. It was nice knowing that she was going to be doing something on her own. It felt like a fresh start.

Chapter Eleven

Stacey had papers strewn out in front of her. She was looking them over. William had given them to her a few days ago to review. It was a business plan of sorts. This was her third time going over them. It wasn't that she didn't trust William. It was mostly that he hadn't done a fantastic job with the restaurant. She wanted to make sure everything was in place. Perhaps this is where William's talents really were, instead of the restaurant business.

A knock on her door snapped her out of focus. She wondered who it could be. Allison wasn't due back from her honeymoon for another week. Stacey opened the door.

Charlie stood in front of her. He had a suitcase by his feet as if he had just arrived from the airport. He smiled at her.

"Hey," was all he said but it was enough.

Before Stacey could overthink it, she swung her arms around Charlie's and pressed her lips against his. For a spilt second, he didn't do anything. She wondered if he was going to push her away.

But then his hands wrapped around her. They stumbled into her apartment. Stacey almost lost her footing, but Charlie had a firm grip around her waist.

She felt winded, as if she had run a marathon. The sight and feel of him was enough to make her feel dizzy.

He smiled against her lips. "Wait, wait."

"What?" she mumbled, dazed.

He turned around and pulled his suitcase in from the hallway and closed the door. Then Charlie turned back around and pulled her toward him. Their lips met again. Stacey could feel his heart hammering underneath her fingertips as she pressed her hands against his chest. She could feel his muscles underneath. She could feel his stubble scratching against her skin.

"Did you just get into town?" Stacey finally asked when she came back up for air.

"Yeah. But I wanted to see you before I did anything else." He smiled against her cheek before grazing his lips against hers.

The fact that he had come directly to see her made Stacey so happy that she could hardly contain it. She grabbed him by the hand and led him down the hallway toward her bedroom.

"It's a mess," she apologized as she opened the door.

Charlie wrapped his arms around her from behind and whispered, "I don't care."

His mouth left butterfly kisses down her neck. His hands slid down along her body.

"I want to taste you," he whispered in her ear.

Stacey felt her knees go weak. His breath against her neck and his hands along her body was too much. She turned around and practically dragged him to the bed. They collapsed as one onto the springy mattress in a heap.

Together, they fumbled with each other's clothes. Stacey wanted him urgently and she could tell that he was feeling the same way by the way he stripped her. When their bare skin touched, she gasped. His skin was warm against hers. She marveled at feeling him against her. She had thought this would never happen again.

His tongue licked her nipples gently before sucking on each, rolling her breasts around in his hands. Stacey closed her eyes and gave herself over to the sensations. Charlie's mouth was warm around her nipples as he cupped her breasts. Then he dragged his tongue in the middle of them as if he wanted to taste her skin.

He left a trail of kisses down her stomach toward her pussy, which was soaking wet. When his tongue finally probed her wet folds, Stacey let out a moan. Oh, she had missed this. She had missed Charlie's mouth down there, exploring her. He seemed to know exactly what she liked and how good it felt for her.

But Stacey wanted more. Coming out of her haze, she begged, "Let me taste you too."

Charlie moved away from her and lay down on the bed. Stacey got on top of him, moving so her pussy was near his face. He gripped her hips and pulled her pussy down onto his mouth, eating her hungrily. Stacey moaned in pleasure and gripped his cock. Stroking it gently, she moved her tongue up his shaft. It was pulsing in her hand and hard as a rock.

Stacey rolled her tongue along the tip as Charlie worked on her pussy. Waves of intense pleasure were rolling over her as she engulfed the tip of his dick with her mouth. She could hear a muffled moan from Charlie.

Stacey took more of him in her mouth. She liked how full her mouth felt and the sensation it gave her to fit as much of him as she could. She swirled her tongue around. Behind her, Charlie sucked gently on her clit before sliding a finger in her soaking wet pussy.

As her own pleasure mounted, she worked on Charlie's cock. She could feel his cock twitch in her mouth. His fingers wrapped in her hair and moved her head off of his dick.

"Not yet," he growled before his mouth went back on her pussy.

Her orgasm hit her. It was so intense that all she could do was go limp on his body as she quivered and shook. Her climax felt as if it was touching all parts of her, from her head down to her toes. The whole time, Charlie held onto her and rolled his tongue around her pussy.

When her orgasm stopped, he gently rolled her off of him and then slid on top of her. He bent down to kiss her. Stacey could taste herself on him. Then he was guiding his dick deep inside of her.

She had missed this. As he entered her, she pulled him close, looking into his eyes. Stacey had thought that she would never feel this again. She had assumed that she was never going to have sex like this again – where they knew each other so well that everything made perfect sense. Each movement was giving one another the highest amount of pleasure.

As he moved inside of her, Stacey clung to him as if he might suddenly vanish. She rocked her hips along with his movements. Charlie slid his arms under her back and brought her close. His thrusting picked up speed. He began to move urgently, letting out soft moans in her ear.

"Stacey," he grunted as he came close to his climax, "I love you."

The words took what little breath she had out of her. Stacey looked at him in surprise. Her pleasure was momentarily forgotten. All she could focus on was that she had finally heard the words she had hardly let herself dream about hearing. She smiled at him.

"I love you too," she whispered.

Charlie smiled and their lips met. This kiss was different. It was soft and full of promise. Then he moved inside of her and moaned. He was climaxing, Stacey realized, and she pulled him close. His movements were enough to send her over the edge for a second time.

Together, like always, they came. This was how it was supposed to be, Stacey thought to herself as she allowed herself to orgasm. She wanted to be linked with Charlie in this way for the rest of her life.

Afterward, Charlie held her. She rested her head on his chest and listened to his heart beating steadily. His fingers trailed along her back. She could feel him drawing patterns on her skin with the tips of his fingers and it made her smile. She felt completely at peace. How long had it been since she felt this way?

"So, tell me."

"Tell you what?" Stacey asked, peering up at him.

"The last three months. I'll tell you mine if you tell me yours," he joked as his fingers stroked her hair.

"Not much to say, is there? I ran away. Easier not to deal with how I was feeling about Tina than stick around here. Tony offered a way out. I shouldn't have taken it. It was stupid of me."

"Don't be so hard on yourself, Stacey. You had just lost Tina. You were grieving. Scared and hurt. I don't blame you for what you did."

"When you came to me and said that… well, when you were talking about maybe giving us another chance – I wanted that so much. More than anything. But I was so afraid. I was so afraid of opening up and getting hurt. It was easier to run away with Tony because deep down, I think I knew I wasn't in any danger of ever loving him. Like I love you."

Charlie kissed the top of her head. The gesture was small but still made Stacey feel happy. There was something casual about it, as if they had been together forever, that she really enjoyed.

"When you ran off with him, I assumed that it was over and done with. I mean, how could I compete with that? Even though… it bothered me. I don't mean that you had chosen someone else. Mostly that you had chosen Tony. I wasn't sure if he was the best one for you."

"Why is that?" Stacey asked curiously.

Charlie gave a small shrug. "I've worked with him on and off throughout the years. I know what his family is like. I mean, don't get me wrong. Mine is fucked up. But so is his. He goes through all these different women trying to find one that would meet his mother's approval. It's really important to him that they approve of whomever he dates. So far, they never have."

"I thought I was really special, meeting his family," Stacey said with a laugh. "I thought it meant he was interested in me on a whole different level."

"Well, if it makes you feel better, I don't think I've ever seen him punch a man over someone he was dating."

Frowning at the memory, Stacey said, "He said that we were similar. That we both came from nothing and that I was trying to make my way. He wanted to help me. But all I did was let him make everything easier for me. I allowed him to help me with Tina. I allowed him to whisk me off to an island instead of dealing with how I was really feeling. Maybe we are similar. But I didn't want to be coddled like that."

"Did you tell him this?"

"Yeah. It didn't go well, trust me. I had never seen him like that before. He was so upset that I didn't love him in that way. He was… scary, actually."

Charlie's grip tightened around her. "Better now that you're away from him then. If Tony was like that then, who knows what would have come up if you had stayed with him."

Stacey shook her head. "I know. I don't know. I really messed things up."

"Tony has accomplished a ton in his life. He probably just wants someone to share it with."

"He'll find someone," Stacey said although she still felt guilty.

Charlie, sensing her mood, changed the subject. "Still can't believe your sister married Jacob."

"Yeah, that's a whole other thing. I don't get how she could marry someone she doesn't love. But he told me his dad is ill. Probably won't live long. So he wants someone by his side while he takes control of the company. He wants kids too, eventually. Allison is okay with all of this. Perfect… weird match made in heaven."

"So, you couldn't do what your sister did?"

"What?" Stacey shook her head. "No. Allison has always wanted that life. She hated being poor. She hated wanting things and not being able to get them. But I always thought marriage is about love. Nothing else."

Charlie tilted her face up to his. "That's why I love you," he said in all seriousness.

They kissed and when it ended, Stacey said, "Your family…"

He let out a playful groan. "What about them? You don't want to meet them, do you?"

"No, no, not yet. I was just curious why all you rich people have weird families."

Charlie laughed. "Boredom and money."

"Yeah, but surely, you guys could go travel," Stacey pointed out, "or take a class in something. Or literally do anything like fill a swimming pool with money."

"That seems unsanitary."

Stacey rolled her eyes and Charlie laughed. He kissed her again and then looked thoughtful.

"I don't know," he finally admitted. "My dad was pretty thrilled when I finally dated Adele. When I dumped her, he was pretty pissed off. He wants me to hire Eric and give him a high-ranking job in the company."

"Why don't you?"

"My brother is a real asshole," he said without any trace of humor.

"You've mentioned before that you two don't get along. But, surely, he has to accept the fact that the company is yours by now."

"He won't. He isn't nice. He isn't kind. He's all the negatives of my parents in one person. Maybe things would have been different if he had been born first and was trained in the company. But as the younger sibling, all he did was slack off and fool around. Now he wants to be taken seriously, and I'm not prepared to give him that. So he whines to our dad a lot."

"But you said your father had a stroke…"

"Yes. He gets worse with each passing day. I guess that's where Jacob and I are similar. Both of our fathers are dying."

"What happens when he passes away?"

"Insanity. Family coming out of the woodwork like vultures over a corpse, trying to suck up to me. Eric probably planning some stupid shit. The usual."

He sounded exhausted just talking about it. Stacey trailed her fingers along his jaw. He felt tense all over. The pleasure that Charlie had obviously been feeling before had drained from him. She felt bad that his family caused him such stress. She felt nervous at the idea of ever meeting them.

Charlie grabbed her hand and kissed her fingers. "But you're here. So I'll be okay."

"Your family won't like me, will they? I seem to be having bad luck with them."

"Fuck them. Even if they don't, I don't care. I want you and only you. I don't want them." Charlie said seriously.

It was so different from what Tony had wanted. He had wanted full acceptance of her from his family. But Charlie didn't care about that. The fact that he only wanted her made her happier than he could know.

When he brought her in for another kiss, Stacey couldn't believe how content she felt.

Chapter Twelve

Stacey watched as her sister made tea. She had spent five minutes telling Stacey that the tea leaves were from Jacob's own company. It apparently was going to be the best tea that Stacey would ever taste. The way Allison was pitching it, she wondered if Jacob should just let her sell the tea. She was bound to sell a ton.

"You make this sound as if it's some miracle elixir," Stacey finally said, cutting Allison off.

"Hey, it's amazing, alright."

Allison was holding a teapot that probably cost as much as Stacey's monthly rent. It was painted beautifully in bright red and green. The colors swirled together and formed the logo of Jacob's tea company. In the spotless kitchen, Allison stood out. She was wearing a pale pink dress with her hair swept up in a bun. She almost looked like a fifties housewife. It was a strange sight.

"Well, tell me about the honeymoon, at least."

Allison had come back into town yesterday. Stacey had been busy with William, going over things for his new real estate office, so she had missed the welcome back party that was thrown for the newly married couple. Secretly, Stacey was relieved. Allison had told her that Tony was coming, and she was keen on avoiding him.

"It was amazing. I mean, we toured most of Europe. The nice places, anyway."

"Ah, look at you. Sounding like a rich snob already," Stacey joked.

"I'll ignore that because I'm in a good mood. Jacob would stop by some of the offices and see how things were being run. I would explore, tour the city. Bought myself some trinkets."

"Like a new wardrobe?" Stacey asked, pointing to the new dress her sister was wearing.

"Naturally." She slid a cup on a fancy saucer toward Stacey. "Try it."

"It's just tea," Stacey protested.

Allison rolled her eyes. "That cup of tea costs more than you could ever wrap your head around."

"What is it with rich people paying insane prices for things that are really just the same stuff us regular people buy?"

"Because what else are they going to buy, Stacey? A thousand packets of tea or one box for the same price? It's all about the image. Selling a certain lifestyle."

Stacey looked down at her cup of tea, waiting for it to cool off a little. It was slightly purple, which was alarming. She realized she hadn't asked Allison what sort of tea this even was.

"So, now what for you?" she asked Allison.

"Goal achieved. I can relax now. Jacob is at the main office but he's talking about going to Hong Kong next week."

"I guess I won't be seeing you as much, huh?" Stacey asked and for some reason, felt oddly sad.

"Ah, sister. You're finally going to miss me."

"Maybe. I won't admit it though," Stacey said with a laugh. "With everything that has happened… you know, I have to say that I didn't think you would actually go through with marrying Jacob."

"I know. You thought I would suddenly change my mind. Decide to marry for love or whatever. But this is what I wanted. And I finally have it." She sighed happily.

"Yes, but he's so – he's so boring," Stacey whispered, even though Jacob wasn't home.

"He is, but only because of his social anxiety. He gets so nervous in front of groups of people."

"Jacob. We're talking about the same Jacob, right?" Stacey asked, having a hard time picturing this.

"Yes. That's why he talks so much. It was something he learned from his dad. Talk until you feel alright."

"Which is apparently never because he never stops talking."

"Yeah, true. But what can I do about it? I just let him ramble. Listen, I know he's boring everyone. I'm sure deep down he knows it as well. But I'm not about to tell him to stop what works for him. I just pretend that what he has to say is really interesting. Are you going to try the tea or not?"

Stacey had forgotten about the tea. She looked down at it. Little by little, she had been collecting information about Jacob. Perhaps he wasn't as bad as Stacey had assumed.

Allison went on, "I think we'll make a good team together. That's what really matters. You can have some passionate love affair with someone but once the zest fades away, then what? You're stuck with them."

"When did you become so jaded about love?"

"It isn't jaded."

"Sounds jaded to me. What if you find someone else while you're with Jacob?"

"Stacey, honestly." Allison sounded exasperated. "Stop worrying about my life. Focus on yours. Are you back with Charlie yet?"

"Yet? Were you just assuming we would get back together?"

"Yeah, of course. Besides, you have that look on your face."

"What look?"

"The look of getting laid by someone who knows what they are doing." She looked thoughtful. "You never had that look with Tony, now that I think about it."

Not wanting to discuss Tony any further, Stacey said quickly, "Yes, we're back together."

Allison rubbed her hands together as if this was a personal victory for her. "Fantastic. I knew it. That's great. Are you bringing him?"

"Bringing him where?"

"I didn't tell you?"

When Stacey shook her head, her sister said, "This weekend we're having a party. Small event. I promise. Just sort of a little party here for everyone who couldn't make it to the wedding."

"Wait. How many after-parties do you people need to celebrate your crazy marriage?" Stacey said, rolling her eyes.

"Ha ha, very funny," responded Allison, not looking very amused.

Not wanting to get into an argument with her sister, Stacey asked, "Who couldn't make it to the wedding? There were like two hundred people there."

"Some of his business associates and friends couldn't make it." Allison leaned forward. "Come on. You have to come."

"Why?"

"Because."

There was something in her sister's gaze – it was a vulnerability. Stacey hadn't seen that in a long time. Allison, normally confident, felt nervous at the idea of hosting a party as Jacob's wife for the first time. Stacey realized this was important to her.

"Yeah, of course. I'll be there. I'll bring Charlie too."

Allison smiled. "Great. Now, will you try the tea?"

Stacey picked up the tea and hesitantly took a sip. Maybe it was because it was purple or the fact that it was expensive as hell, but she was expecting it to taste weird. Instead, it seemed to explode in her mouth with a vibrant flavor she couldn't pinpoint. Her eyes widened slightly, and she swallowed.

"That is some good fucking tea," Stacey admitted, and Allison laughed.

"Told you," she said, turning away to pour herself a cup. "Stacey… you know if you need anything now, I can get it for you. A new place to live. Or whatever. Anything."

She was touched by Allison's offer. Stacey knew that her sister meant well. But after losing herself to the wealth that Tony had given her, she wasn't eager to fall back into that trap. She had managed to escape her own grief and fog back at that island and didn't want any more handouts.

Stacey gave a small shake of her head. "No, thanks," she replied, and she meant it.

<<◇>>

"You look beautiful, honestly. Stop checking," Charlie said to Stacey as she double-checked her make-up in the compact mirror.

"Sorry. I still hate these sorts of gatherings."

"Allison is going to be there. I'm going to be there. It'll be nice."

It was the weekend of the little party at Allison and Jacob's place. Even though Stacey should be used to going to these events by now, she still felt nervous for some reason.

"Well, you seem nervous too," she pointed out. "You keep fidgeting."

It was true. Ever since Charlie had picked her up, he had been acting a little odd. He was friendly and nothing but a gentleman, but there seemed to be something else going on. She had pointed it out twice already, but he had brushed her off about it.

"I am not," he retorted, brushing her off for a third time.

Stacey rolled her eyes. "Whatever. Like you said, it's just Jacob. I'll be there. My sister will be there."

He smiled at her teasing. He looked incredibly handsome tonight, although Stacey was hard pressed to recall any time when he didn't look handsome. She was happy to be going to this event with him – to be with him in general.

It didn't take long to arrive at the party. They were taken up to the top floor, where Allison now lived.

When they stepped inside, Stacey saw that her sister was true to her word. It seemed to be a small affair. There was a group in the middle which had formed around Jacob. He was telling a story in that typical slightly pompous manner of his. All traces of the man who had been nervous before his wedding had been erased.

Allison saw them first. She waved them over, weaving her way expertly through the small crowd, saying hello to people as she passed.

"She's good." Charlie pointed out as her sister shook the hand of a man three times her size.

"She's always been good with people," Stacey replied, thinking to herself that if anyone could be new to this world and navigate it with ease, it would be her sister.

"You're here!" Allison exclaimed when she got to them.

She brought Stacey in for a hug. At the same moment, Stacey commented, "Everything looks beautiful."

"Thanks. We're going to have snacks and everything served soon. You should go out on the balcony. It's amazing at night." She squeezed her hand and lowered her voice, "I'm really glad you're here."

"Me too."

"All right. I'll leave you two to it. I have to go say hello to George over there," Allison said, motioning her head in the direction of a sour-looking old man who just entered, "or he'll complain for forty years that I was rude to him."

Stacey watched Allison leave to go over to the man. Then she looked back at Charlie who laced his fingers through hers.

"Guess we should mingle," she said to him.

"Come on." He pulled her forward gently and together they walked into the gathering.

Stacey had lost track of Charlie thirty minutes ago. Last she had seen him, someone from Japan had cornered him to discuss construction. She had gone to the bathroom and hadn't seen him since. She had set off to look for him when Allison pulled her over to listen to a dull conversation between Jacob and the old man from earlier.

"Don't leave me alone with this man," she mumbled when she had dragged Stacey over. "He's rude and I want to slap him."

So Stacey stood dutifully by her sister's side. To be honest, she had tuned the conversation out. Social anxiety or not, Jacob was fantastic at droning on to fill any possible gaps in the conversation. George, the old man, was staring Jacob down and seemed very aggressive about tea. It would have been comical if it wasn't so dull.

She was about to tell Allison that she was going off to find Charlie when two more guests entered the party. Their arrival brought Stacey crashing out of her daze.

"No fucking way," she breathed.

George, who had been in the middle of a speech, looked over at her in surprise. "Excuse me?" he said coldly.

But Stacey ignored him. Allison saw instantly what she had seen and mumbled a curse word before excusing the two of them from the conversation.

"What are they doing here together?" Stacey whispered.

"I didn't invite either of them. Jacob must have."

The two sisters turned to watch as Tony and Adele entered the party, arms linked together.

Chapter Thirteen

"Well, makes sense they're dating, right? They both hate Charlie." Allison paused. "And you, I guess. Whatever, don't let it get to you. They can't do anything to you, you know that. If they do the smallest thing, I'll kick them out. They're probably just here to make you feel uncomfortable."

Stacey listened to Allison as she watched Tony and Adele stop to say hello to people. Adele looked as if she had stepped out of a glossy magazine. Tony had outdone himself tonight as well, wearing a suit that she had never seen before. His skin looked as if it was glowing. He was walking with a confidence that Stacey hadn't seen on him. It was almost a swagger.

"Well, I don't like it. I'm going to find Charlie to let him know."

She moved away from her sister and headed down one of the hallways. There were numerous rooms here, each holding a few guests. In one, a group was smoking cigars and discussing politics. In another, a woman had her arms draped around a man as he spoke. In the next, was the man that Charlie had been speaking with, but no Charlie.

Stacey walked into the room and politely interrupted the current conversation, asking where Charlie had gone.

The man shrugged a little. "He cut the conversation short. Said he had forgotten something. Looked slightly sick, actually. Are you his wife? I don't know where he went. He left the room in a hurry though. Looked like he was leaving the party."

He turned away from Stacey, clearly not interested in keeping the conversation going. She felt confused by what he had said. Charlie had left? Why in the world would he leave without saying anything? She knew that he had been acting weird all night but to just ditch her at the party…

Her stomach felt as if she had swallowed an entire jar of live butterflies. She left the room and went into the library, closing the door behind her.

Cut off from the buzzing of the party and the fact Tony and Adele were roaming around, Stacey tried calling Charlie. It went right to voicemail. She sighed and looked out the window of the library.

Below was the city, sprawled out like glittering jewels. In the distance, she could see construction in her section of town. She tapped her fingers against the glass, wondering why Charlie had left like that. Was he having second thoughts? Was he –

"Oh, look who it is."

Stacey cursed inwardly and looked over to see Tony as he entered the library. He closed the door behind him and crossed his arms, blocking her only way out.

"Hi, Tony. Follow me in here?"

"Saw you looking for Charlie like a chicken without a head. Sad. Did he get bored already?" His tone was like dry ice. She could see a smirk dancing at the corners of his mouth.

"Are you allowed off your leash this long to talk to me?" Stacey countered.

"Jealousy doesn't suit you, Stacey," he said casually as he ran his fingers along one of the side tables, walking toward her.

"Jealous of what, exactly?"

"Oh, I don't know. That my date is still here, for one. Although, I'm sure Charlie will come back, right? Probably just had to run to the corner store or something," he said mockingly.

Stacey was trying not to get irritated but was quickly failing. She was already nervous about Charlie suddenly leaving. On top of that, to have Tony here, trying to rub it in her face was not something she wanted to deal with.

"Well, this was nice," she remarked, attempting to move past him to leave.

But Tony's hand gripped her arm. She tried to pull back, but he didn't budge. Stacey looked up at him and tried to ignore the fear that was nestling into her stomach.

"I wasn't sure I would see you so soon after you ran away."

"I wasn't running away. I was going home. Let go of me, Tony." She tried to keep her voice stern.

"Don't you see? He has already blown you off, Stacey. You deserve better than that."

"So, what? I deserve a man who has cornered me in this library and refuses to let me leave? The more you act like this, the more I know that I made the right choice."

Tony looked as if she had slapped him. He loosened his grip a little on her arm but still didn't move his hand. Stacey was unnerved by how he was acting. It was weird that he had seemingly gotten this hung up on her.

"I came here with Adele," he said through clenched teeth.

"Not my problem. No one asked you to bring her here. In fact, everyone probably wished that you hadn't."

"I thought… surely, you see now…"

"See what?" Stacey suddenly felt weary from dealing with Tony and his strange moods. "That I wanted you all along? Tony, this needs to stop. I'm flattered that you feel this strongly about me," she lied swiftly, "but we're over. Now let me leave."

He was looming over Stacey now, staring her down as if she was an enemy that needed to fall in line instead of a woman that he loved. In the back of her mind, she realized that she had dodged a bullet by breaking up with him. Stacey backed up until she was pressing against one of the bookshelves.

"Tony. Let me leave this room or I swear I will scream my head off."

"Stacey, you just have to see. You have to understand. I know if I can only make you see that Charlie doesn't care about you. He left you here alone. What sort of man does that? I would never do that to you."

"No, instead you'd trap me in a room and not listen to me when I tell you to let me leave!" she exclaimed loudly, her fear getting the better of her.

She shoved her hands forward and tried to push Tony out of the way. Yet he was like stone. He didn't budge. His grip only tightened on her. She tried to yank her arm free, but she was pressed against the bookshelf.

"We belong together. Adele, she means nothing to me. She is a means to an end."

"Does she know that?"

"She isn't stupid. She knows how I feel about you. Come with me again. We can go anywhere in the world you'd like."

"I'd like to stay here, actually."

Tony brought his face closer to hers. He was going to kiss her, Stacey realized.

"Stacey," he said, and she could feel his breath lightly against her face, "whatever you want, I can give it to you. I love you, Stacey. You're mine."

Stacey tried to wriggle free. The fear in her stomach was real and alive. She opened her mouth to scream in an attempt to get Tony away from her.

But she never got the chance. Tony was suddenly pulled away from her. It was as if a giant magnet had yanked him away. He went falling to the floor. And above him –

"Charlie," Stacey breathed with relief.

Charlie's face was flushed red. His fists were curling and uncurling. Stacey had never seen him look so angry before. Tony scrambled to his feet.

"Don't get the wrong idea, Charlie," Tony said. "She threw herself at me. At me! I was trying to tell her that I was seeing Adele –"

"Are you fucking serious?" Stacey exclaimed, shocked at his lie.

But Charlie was shaking his head. His hands curled up around the collar of Tony's shirt and he slammed him against one of the bookshelves. The bookshelf shook and a few books clattered to the floor. Stacey watched, holding her breath.

"If you come near her again, you're going to regret it," Charlie growled at Tony in a voice she had never heard before.

Stacey went over to him and hovered behind him, finally managing to say, "Charlie, don't."

Charlie's fingers tightened around Tony's collar, holding him in place. Tony said nothing, only letting out a wheezing noise as he stared at Charlie.

He leaned forward and Stacey heard him say, "The only reason I'm not going to kick your ass is because the lady requested that I don't." He released Tony who began to cough. "Try this shit again and I will put an end to you and your entire fucking company."

Before Tony could say anything, Charlie grabbed Stacey's hand. He turned and practically dragged her out of the library. He stalked down the hallway back into the party. Stacey trailed after him as he went up to Jacob and Allison.

"We have to go," he said to them. "It was a lovely party though. Thank you for having us."

Allison looked surprised and glanced over at Stacey who could only shrug. Then she followed Charlie out of the party and into the elevator.

Chapter Fourteen

The elevator ride down was silent except for Charlie's breathing. He didn't look at Stacey. Instead, he was taking slow breaths, holding them and exhaling them after ten seconds. Their fingers were loosely entwined.

She could picture Tony pressed against the bookshelf and Charlie holding onto him. She had been terrified of Tony then. If Charlie hadn't appeared, what would she have done?

Not to mention she was wondering just what Charlie had run off to do. He came back just in time but what if he hadn't?

The elevator doors opened and the two of them left the elevator in silence. They crossed the lobby into the parking lot. For the first time since she had gotten back home, it was actually chilly outside. Charlie must have noticed because he turned to her.

"Want my jacket?"

"No, I'm okay."

He didn't ask again like Tony would have. Like always, Charlie listened to her. Stacey was about to ask where he had gone when Adele came out of the building. When she saw the two of them, she stormed over. Stacey sighed at the same time Charlie did.

"Try not to throttle this one," Stacey joked under her breath. She saw a ghost of a smile cross Charlie's mouth.

"You!" Adele cried, stopping in front of him. "What did you do to Tony?"

"Nothing. He got off easy," Charlie quipped.

"Why don't you ask what your stupid slutty girlfriend tried to do to him?"

Stacey rolled her eyes at the jab. It was tiresome, and Charlie knew there was no way in hell she would have thrown herself at Tony. Charlie's lips were pressed into a thin line.

"Adele," he said patiently, "what the fuck do you want?"

"I want – I want you to apologize to him –"

"Cut the shit," Charlie interrupted. "Listen. Do me a favor, alright? You still talk to my dad and my brother. Tell them I'm done with them. With their plans and everything else they have plotting. It's done."

"What?" Adele laughed. "What does that even mean? What are you going to do?"

Charlie didn't answer. His gaze was steely and for the first time since Stacey had met her, Adele looked unnerved.

"Tell them," he repeated. "And please, get out of my face."

He turned around and walked toward the parking lot. Stacey gave Adele a mocking wave good-bye and followed Charlie. She tried to keep up with his big steps in her high heels. There was no car waiting for them. She didn't know where he was going.

He cut across the parking lot and Stacey could see now that he was heading toward one of the parks.

"Uh, Charlie?" Stacey called out. "I'm wearing four-inch heels. While I appreciate the walk, can we please find a place to sit?"

He stopped walking at the entrance to the park and shook his head. "Sorry, Stacey. Just wanted some fresh air." He held his hand out to her. "Come on."

Stacey took it. Her hand slid comfortably into his. She could feel his heart rate hammering underneath her hand. He was still full of adrenalin and on edge from whatever was bothering him, aside from his confrontation with Tony.

They walked into the park. In the distance, Stacey could hear a band playing. The park had groups of people enjoying the evening together. Charlie took her to a bench nearby in front of the fountain. They sat down together. He was clutching her hand.

"Charlie, mind telling me where you ran off to in the middle of the party?"

"I forgot something."

She waited for him to say more and when he didn't, she cleared her throat. "And you couldn't tell me?"

"No."

"Well, why not?"

Charlie turned to face her. He looked serious now, instead of aggravated. A thought struck Stacey – *Oh God, I'm getting dumped, aren't I?* It would explain a lot of everything going on. Even with that thought, she remained silent.

"Stacey, I have to tell you something."

Her free hand gripped the side of the bench as if to ward off the bad news. "What?"

"I'm taking the money I have and I'm starting a new company."

She blinked, thrown off by the news. It hadn't been what she was expecting at all.

Taking her silence as a sign to keep going, Charlie spoke, "I've been putting a lot of thought into it. I'm sick of letting my family control me. It won't stop unless I do something about it. So, I'm branching off. Starting my own investment firm with the money I've made."

"That's what you meant when you spoke to Adele," Stacey replied.

"That's right. I'm not going to be listening to their shit anymore. I have no interest in it. Stacey, this is going to be a big deal. Leaving my family to try this out is a big risk. It could all blow up. I could end up with no money."

"Is that what you're worried about? Charlie, I don't care if you have no money by the end of this. I'm here no matter what you want to do. If you want to try this, I support you. I don't care about the money."

Charlie smiled at her. He looked slightly more relaxed and stood up.

"Where are we going?"

"Can you walk a little farther? There's someplace I want to show you."

"Sure," Stacey replied, standing.

He took her hand again and led her through the park. She had never been here before. It was beautiful and sprawling. The trees were so tall that sometimes it blocked out the night sky completely.

Around them, couples walked hand-in-hand. There was something nice about being around other people like this. Everyone looked content and happy. They walked together in silence past a small pond. The moonlight reflected in the water and rippled when someone tossed a rock into the pond.

"Ever been to this park?" Charlie asked her at one point.

"Nope. Too far away from my section of the city."

"It's my favorite. If I lived where Jacob did, I'd be down here all the time," he remarked.

She could picture Charlie by the pond, studying it in the daytime. The question was still in her mouth – where had he gone? – but she didn't want to ruin the moment. After another minute of walking, they stopped in front of an older-looking greenhouse. She couldn't see inside of it very well in the dim lighting.

A man stood guard in front of it. It was clearly closed, but Charlie showed him something and the man allowed him through the door.

"Wow, impressive. Didn't realize your name could get us into the hottest greenhouse in town," Stacey joked.

Charlie laughed. The greenhouse had a dome with the stars glittering down on them. He led her through the darkened flowers. The air was heavy with the scent of different flora. It was a nice smell, pleasant and earthy.

When they reached the back of the greenhouse, Stacey gasped. In front of her, small lights had been draped through the leaves. They seemed to perfectly illuminate the roses that were around the back of the greenhouse. It took her breath away. It was simple yet beautiful.

"Do you like it?" Charlie asked her.

"Is this for me?" she asked in surprise.

"No, I normally decorate like this." Charlie laughed at her.

Stacey took a step toward the roses. She liked how each one looked as if they were glowing. She liked the smell of them mixed with the dirt. Above her, the stars twinkled. She felt far removed from the city, as if she were on another planet.

Charlie came up behind her and kissed her gently on the neck. "I'm glad you like it."

"It's gorgeous. But… why?" she asked and turned around to face him. "Is this where you went earlier?"

"Ah, no. I forgot the most important part of this little thing." He gestured around him. "So, I had to go get it."

"Get what?" Stacey asked.

Charlie brought her in for a kiss. There was something different about this kiss. It was soft and gentle, filled with a promise that she didn't quite understand. She returned the kiss and could feel her heart skip a beat.

"Thank you. For stopping Tony. I didn't know –"

"It isn't your fault for anything to do with Tony. He's an asshole. I'm glad I was there. I'm sorry I didn't tell you that I was leaving. I didn't want to spoil the surprise. I wanted it to mean a lot to you and not be mucked up."

"Well… what is the surprise then?" Stacey whispered.

To her shock, Charlie got down on one knee. Her head went light. She swore that she was dreaming this up. But no, Charlie was down on one knee and he pulled out a small box. Her breath caught.

"Stacey, I love you. I've always loved you. And with this new journey ahead of me, I want you to be the one who comes along with me."

She felt the tears spring to her eyes. Her hands felt as if they were trembling. He opened up the ring box. A beautiful diamond ring sat in the center.

"Will you marry me, Stacey?" Charlie whispered nervously.

His nerves made sense. He had somehow forgotten the engagement ring in all of this. That was why he had left. He had to go back and fetch it. Stacey would have laughed if she wasn't crying.

Furiously wiping her eyes, she nodded.

"Yes. Yes, I will marry you."

-To be continued in Book 4-

Book Four – Love Confirmed

Chapter One

EVEN THOUGH it was autumn, the rain was pouring down as if it was one of those summer storms back in the city. The road here wasn't even made out of pavement, but some sort of gravel that stuck to the tires of the car and bounced Stacey around. Her nose was pressed against the passenger side window, as if she could make anything out.

"You alright?" Charlie asked next to her as he slowly rounded a corner.

Stacey cleared her throat. "Nervous."

"You'll be fine. It'll be me that Dad will be flipping his shit over, not you."

He sounded confident, which made sense since it was his father after all. Even so, Stacey couldn't shake the sense of foreboding that was hanging over her. The storm only made her anxiety worse.

"I'm sure you're right," she finally replied, glancing over at him.

The sudden movement made her ring flicker up at her in the dim light. Stacey still wasn't used to seeing it. She wasn't used to what it represented either. She was *engaged* to Charlie. It had been two weeks since their engagement, but it still didn't feel as if it had truly sunk in.

The night that he had decorated the greenhouse and proposed felt like a dream. She clung to the memory now to help her with her nerves. Sure, she had only heard horror stories about Charlie's family. But he was here and would have her back. She had nothing to fear.

"Anyway, just let me handle most of the talking. Dad will be grumpy, but he's always grumpy. He's been that way ever since Mom died," Charlie joked.

His mother. She was one person Charlie had spoken about at length the past couple of weeks. Stacey had never asked him about his mother, mostly because she always sensed that he hadn't wanted to talk about her.

When he finally did, he told her how she had gotten very sick and died when Charlie was eight years old. Eric, his brother, could hardly recall her.

"Dad changed when that happened," Charlie said to her. "It was as if she was the only driving force of good in him. He had always been able to juggle the company and family, but after Mom died… there was no family anymore. Just the company. Always the company."

The words stuck in her head now as they turned onto a larger road. Charlie's father was at their *vacation home* although it was so far out of state and in the country that it wasn't what Stacey pictured when she heard the term. They had been driving for two hours since leaving the airport.

"We're almost there," Charlie said as if reading her mind. "Rain slowed us down a lot."

"Didn't know it rained like this out here."

"Probably just because my dad is in the area." At seeing her face, he cleared his throat. "That was a joke. Sorry. I'm making you more nervous, aren't I?"

"Yes, but I get it. Joking to cope." Stacey smiled weakly.

"One way of putting it," he replied grimly.

Through the front window of the car, Stacey saw it. It was as if it appeared out of nowhere, conjured up by Charlie's joke. Through each wipe of the windshield, she could see a magnificent house before them. It looked more like a manor than just a house.

"Wow," Stacey breathed. "This looks like something I'd picture out of an old novel or something."

"It isn't haunted," Charlie replied, and she looked at him. "What? Don't those old books always have ghosts around the manors? Or the moors. Or something."

"Did you sleep through your fancy English literature class back in college?" she quipped.

Charlie laughed. "Well, it still isn't haunted. Dad just isn't one for being subtle in any occasion. He had this place built after Mom died. Wanted it to look as if it could be dropped down in Scotland and fit right in."

"Well, it definitely looks like that."

They drove through the open iron gates. In the front of the house was a fountain that Stacey could just barely make out through the storm. She looked up to try to see the top of the house. It was decorated with what looked to be gargoyles which only added to the creepy vibe of the place.

Charlie drove around the circular gravel driveway and stopped in front of the manor. The heavy oak doors opened up and two men stepped out. The taller man was holding an umbrella. Together, they walked over to them. One of them opened the back doors of the car and began removing luggage. The other came over to the passenger door and opened it.

"Peter!" Charlie exclaimed, leaning over. "How are you?"

"Good, sir. I've brought an umbrella to escort your fiancée to the front door. Then I can come back to fetch you."

"I'll catch up with you," Charlie said to Stacey.

She nodded and clutched her purse, feeling oddly nervous. She stepped out of the car and was staring at Peter. He was an older-looking man. His hair had gone completely grey and he was slightly hunched over. She reached for the umbrella, but he shook his head once and then turned around to lead her to the front door.

Stacey hurried after him, not wanting to get wet. At the front doors, he ushered her inside. A quick glance showed that the other man was behind her, holding all their luggage. The rain didn't seem to affect him at all. Even so, she felt badly for him.

The door closed behind her and Stacey looked around. They were in what seemed to be an entrance hallway. There was nothing modern about this place.

Everything looked old-fashioned as if from an old horror movie set. The hallway was narrow, and the floors were made of hard wood. There was a staircase next to her. Not even one of those spiraling staircases she had been seeing so often lately but a cramped one that reminded her a little of the one on Tony's yacht.

The walls were decorated with paintings, mostly landscapes. The place smelled faintly of mothballs. This was not what Stacey had been expecting. This looked like a place someone who came from old money would live in, not a place that someone would intentionally build.

The front door opened again and Charlie came in. He was soaking wet and holding some of the luggage.

"Sir, I was going to come back for you," Peter said.

"I'm fine, thanks. I didn't want to leave Warren with all the luggage," Charlie replied.

Warren, who looked even older than Peter, smiled a toothy grin. "I'll dry these off and bring them to your rooms."

"Thanks. Wait, uh, rooms?" Charlie asked.

Warren's eyes flicked over to Peter, who spoke up, "Yes, sir. Master Terrence has requested you two sleep in separate rooms since you are not married. It would be improper."

I really have stumbled into some sort of time machine, haven't I? Stacey thought glumly. She looked over at Charlie to see if he was going to say anything. He had said before arriving here that he was going to have to pick his battles, especially with his news. Separate rooms would be weird, but it didn't seem like something to kick a fuss over.

Charlie's lips pressed together in a thin line but he nodded his head in agreement. Stacey relaxed a little. Better not to start things off with a fight about bedrooms. Peter moved past Stacey and began to walk up the stairs.

"This way, please," he said to the two of them without looking back.

Stacey shot Charlie a look but all he did was wiggle his eyebrows in an attempt to make her laugh. They walked up the staircase. The first floor had the same décor as the one below. Paintings along the walls. A carpet that was full of dull colors. The windows were opened, showing the pouring rain outside. All the doors were closed. They stopped at one near the end of the hallway.

"This is your room, sir," Peter said to Charlie, opening it for him.

Stacey peered inside. It was a large room with its own bathroom. The bed was huge and could have easily fit the two of them. There was a couch and a bookshelf on the other wall with a table in front of it.

"Warren will bring your bags up once they're cleaned off, sir."

"Great, thanks. Stacey is going to be next to me?" Charlie asked.

"No, sir. Master Terrence has put Stacey on the fifth floor."

"The fifth floor?" Charlie and Stacey exclaimed in unison.

Peter's face didn't change. All he did was nod. She glanced over at Charlie who looked as if he was about to open his mouth and tell Peter off. Stacey rested her hand on his arm.

"It's fine. It's just a big house, right? Not the end of the world to be on the fifth floor."

"The fifth floor is reserved for guests, ma'am, while these rooms are for family. Nothing personal," Peter said to her.

"Of course. Not a problem. I'll see you later." She directed this to Charlie who still looked furious but nodded in reply.

Stacey followed Peter down the hallway. It wasn't that she liked being shoved up to the fifth floor. It was more that she knew Charlie's announcement of leaving the company was going to go off like an atom bomb. She didn't want him to lose his patience early over small things like this.

They went up the flights of stairs to Stacey's guest room. When they stepped into this hallway, Stacey found it hard to believe that it was just for guests. Since it was closest to the roof, it was more cramped than the other hallways. Some of the doors here were open, showing off small rooms filled with mostly clutter. At the end of the hallway was a window that overlooked the gardens. A closet was next to it filled with supplies.

It was the door next to the supply closet that Peter unlocked. The fact it could be locked from the outside was alarming. He opened the door.

"Here you are, ma'am. Master Terrence will see you at dinner. Thank you."

Before she could ask anything, he turned and walked down the hallway. Stacey watched him go and then looked at her own room.

It was a pale comparison to Charlie's room. The room was slanted due to the roof and was cramped. There was a twin bed shoved against the wall and a dresser in the other corner. A rug had been tossed down onto the floor. That was it. Stacey wasn't even sure where the bathroom was on this floor.

She went over and gingerly sat at the edge of the bed which squeaked. It was obvious what Charlie's father meant by this. Putting her up on the fifth floor meant she didn't matter. Putting her in what was basically a broom closet said that he had already made up his mind about her.

"Great," she mumbled to herself.

Chapter Two

The rain didn't stop. Her own small window gave her the view of basically the driveway, but Stacey couldn't make out anything. She wondered if she could go find Charlie. But the fear of pissing off his father made her stay in place. It was probably a good idea that Charlie come to fetch her rather than run the risk of her being caught creeping around the manor.

She wasn't sure what she was waiting for and was busy trying to quell her nerves when there was a knock on the door. Stacey rushed over, hoping it was Charlie, and opened the door.

"Hi, ma'am. Brought the luggage by."

It wasn't Warren who stood before her but someone new. Stacey wondered just how many people worked in this house to keep it running. The situation seemed silly when basically it was only Terry and Charlie's brother, Eric who apparently lived here.

The man in front of her was dressed plainly and smelled of cigarette smoke. Had he snuck off before bringing her the luggage? Stacey felt a little prick of relief. Someone working here who was a bit normal and had a secret. That was something, at least.

"Hi, uh, thanks. Thanks for bringing them up." She went to grab them as she said, "I can put them in here."

"I got it," the man said to her, brushing by her with her luggage.

He put her things down on the floor and looked around. "Man. He sure shoved you into a shit hole, didn't he?"

Stacey blinked. "Excuse me?"

"Master Terrence. This place looks like it used to be a supply closet or something. Probably was. We shove a bunch of stuff on the fifth floor." He turned to look at her. "Not that you're 'just a bunch of stuff', ma'am."

She was surprised by his candor. Peter and Warren had both seemed to be on auto-pilot. They had probably worked here for ages. The man looked around the room as if he was thinking of something. He had a receding hairline and looked older, as if he had been through a lot before settling down here.

"Ah, well." She struggled for something to say. "It's fine."

"Really? Isn't Master Charles on the first floor? Seems a bit unfair but…" He shrugged at her.

"No, it's just – I don't want to rock the boat, you know? Anyway, it's just a room. Besides, this place is really nice."

The man wrinkled his nose. "Yeah, it's alright, I suppose."

"Have you worked here long?" Stacey asked curiously.

"Way too long." He grinned at her and it changed his entire face. He didn't look as run into the ground when he was smiling, Stacey thought.

"Do you happen to know where the bathroom is?"

"Yeah, I'll show you." He motioned for her to leave the room first.

Stacey felt silly at needing someone to show her where the bathroom was, but she followed him anyway. It was located at the very end of the hallway and was just as small as the rest of the rooms. She peered inside.

"Thanks so much."

"No problem. Sorry it's like a dollhouse up here."

"It's completely fine, trust me. From where I came from, even these small rooms are nice." She turned to look at him. "I didn't get your name."

"Devin."

"Nice to meet you. I'm Stacey." She held out her hand.

Devin smiled at her, a slow smile that seemed to spread out across his face as he shook her hand. "Nice to meet you too."

"Well, I should probably freshen up before dinner. Do I just… sorta stick around or what?"

"Someone will let you know when it's ready." He leaned forward and lowered his voice, "Listen, Terry and Eric are assholes. Between you and me."

"Yeah, I haven't exactly heard kind things," she whispered back.

Devin's eyes flicked up to hers. "From Charlie?"

"Yeah. Anyway, I'm sure it'll be okay. I'll just keep my head down. Try not to attract any attention. Are they the only two here?"

Devin clicked his tongue against the roof of his mouth, "Yup. Well, listen, you do that. Don't attract attention. Just let Terry and Eric deal with Charlie. Terry, you know, he'll be furious over the fact you aren't Adele, but he's always pissed off nowadays. Probably because he's dying and all."

Once again, Stacey was surprised at how open Devin was. Secretly, she was glad for the advice. It felt as if someone here was at least on her side. Still, she wasn't sure what to say about Terry being ill from his stroke.

Devin seemed to sense this. He leaned forward even more. They were quite close now and it made her feel a little uncomfortable. She could smell mint on his breath, as if he had tried to cover up the cigarette smell.

"See you later."

She nodded and watched as he turned to go. Devin looked back once and smiled at her. Then he was down the stairs without another word. Stacey shut the bathroom door behind her. Stay low. Don't attract attention. It was advice she was going to listen to as much as she could.

<<<>>>

When Charlie appeared at her door an hour later, she swung her arms around him and crushed him in a hug.

"Whoa, everything okay? You didn't see a ghost, did you?" Then he gently pushed her away and stepped into the room. "What the fuck is this?"

"My room."

"This is not a room," he said, pointing to the floor. "This was a fucking supply closet or something before." He kicked the rug out of its position. "Look. You can see marks from where they dragged stuff out of here."

He was right. Even from here, Stacey could see deep marks in the wood from where something had been dragged away. She shrugged.

"It's fine. I was told that anyway."

But Charlie wasn't listening. "This is so like him. So like my father to pull this shit. God, you know what? I was nervous before about telling him I was leaving the company. But why? We won't have to tolerate stuff like this once we get married and I'm working on my new business. Dad can put Eric in charge or take control again on his own. It won't matter."

"Whoa, whoa, calm down," Stacey said, coming over to him. "Don't get worked up before we go downstairs."

Charlie ran his hand through his hair, looking frustrated. "I know. Dad does things like this just to throw me off. Listen, he's going to be an asshole. So will Eric. But, just let me handle it, alright? Ignore whatever they throw your way. Eric is a moron to begin with."

"When are you going to tell them about the business?" Stacey asked.

"I don't know. When the time is right. Dad thinks this is just for him to meet you since I told him we were engaged."

Stacey thought about what Devin had said and replied, "He isn't going to like me very much. I'm not Adele."

"Thank God for that. Come on. I don't want to be late."

He looped his arm around hers and together they headed downstairs. Stacey tried not to feel nervous, but it was proving difficult.

"No elevator before you ask," Charlie said to her as they looped down to the third floor.

"Any reason why?"

"Didn't fit in with the manor."

As they made it back down to the first floor, Charlie stopped for a moment. Stacey paused and looked down the stairs. The entrance was empty. She was trying to collect herself. This was just Charlie's father. A human being. She had to stop making it worse than it really was. How much had she gone through to be with Charlie? They were engaged now. She wasn't going to let some old man run her off.

"Wait," Charlie said to her. "Who told you that room was a supply closet?"

"One of the people working here. What do you call them? I'm not calling them servants. That feels so old-fashioned. Butler or something?"

"Which one? Warren? Because Peter would have never told you that," Charlie said urgently.

As if he had heard his name, Peter was suddenly at the base of the stairs. "Sir and ma'am, dinner is about to be served. If you could please come this way." He bowed his head.

Charlie gripped her hand tightly. Whatever he was going to ask died on his lips when Peter appeared. Stacey had no choice but to follow him, wondering why he seemed so bothered. They walked down the steps and headed down the hallway.

They were in the living room now. A fire was roaring in the fireplace. Books lined the shelves. There was no TV here. The floor was covered in a thick carpet and the windows had the curtains drawn. It was hot in here and Stacey hoped it wasn't going to feel like this in the dining room.

She lowered her voice as they walked through, "This place is…"

"Creepy? Weird? Mom would have fucking hated it," Charlie whispered back grimly.

They were led down another short hallway before entering the dining room. Here there were more windows. The curtains weren't drawn, allowing Stacey to see the lit patio. It was still raining, so all she could see were puddles and darkness just outside the light. The table in the center looked to be one solid piece of oak. There were places set for everyone. Stacey noticed one of the places was separate from the rest.

"No," Charlie said simply and crossed the marble flooring to move the place setting with the rest.

"Sir –" Peter began to say but Charlie raised his hand to cut him off.

Then he motioned for Stacey to come over. He pulled out the chair and she sat down. He sat down next to her. No one else was there. Peter came over and served them wine. Neither of them moved to take a sip.

Peter left and they sat there in silence for a full minute.

"Are we early?" Stacey finally asked.

Charlie slid out his phone from his pocket and began checking his e-mails. "No. Just my father being his typical self."

"You get service here?"

"Don't be fooled. This place has wi-fi and one of the rooms on the first floor is completely modern; TV, video game systems, state of the art computer. Eric threw a fit when he was younger." He looked away from his phone. "Which reminds me –"

"My older brother!" A voice rang out, breaking the silence and ending Charlie's question.

Charlie stood up and Stacey followed. It felt sort of silly, standing up like that when someone entered the room. But she realized shortly after it wasn't because Eric was coming in. It looked more as if Charlie was trying to get to Eric first. He walked past Stacey toward the dining room entrance.

Eric came into view and Stacey's eyes widened in surprise. He was wearing a tuxedo, while Charlie was just wearing a suit. Yet it wasn't the tux that was taking her back.

It was the fact that Eric was Devin.

Chapter Three

Eric's gaze landed on Stacey and a lazy grin bloomed across his face. Stacey felt her mouth go dry. She was sure that she was blushing. Stupid, stupid. Charlie had his hand gripping Eric's arm. She could practically see the lecture falling out of his mouth. He had figured it out. That was why he had been trying to ask her about it.

Stacey was wondering if he was wearing the tuxedo as more of a joke than anything else. He didn't seem to be listening to Charlie at all. From this view, she couldn't understand how Eric was the younger sibling. There didn't seem to be anything of Charlie in him. He looked almost ten years older than his brother.

"Man, are you done yet?" Eric finally spoke up. "We should all be sitting down when Dad gets here or he's gonna flip."

He broke free of Charlie's grip and sauntered over to the table. Stacey still felt embarrassed. She had honestly fallen for his trick. She had even told him that Charlie had called him basically an asshole. Great.

He stopped in front of Stacey. He was still smiling. Now that she knew he was Charlie's brother, she tried to see any similarities between the two. Yet there was nothing.

"Nice to meet you," Eric said to her through his grin.

Part of her wanted to smack him. The other part of her knew he would probably like it. So she exhaled slowly and forced her own smile on her face.

"We met earlier. Is your memory alright?"

Something flickered behind Eric's gaze. It was unreadable.

"We did, didn't we?" he laughed. "How is the supply closet?"

"Lovely. How is it living up to your reputation as an asshole?" It rolled off her tongue before she could stop herself.

Behind her, Charlie snorted in both laughter and surprise. Eric didn't lose the grin on his face. It was as if her insult hadn't affected him at all. He just chuckled and walked past her. He pulled out the chair across from Charlie and sat down.

Stacey and Charlie sat down as well. She wished she didn't have to be at this dinner. Having Eric successfully trick her made her feel stupid.

Eric pulled out his own phone and began to play a game on it. He had the volume turned up as loud it could go, and it seemed to bounce off the walls. Stacey leaned over to Charlie and lowered her voice as much as she could.

"I thought you said that he was younger than you."

"He is."

"He looks a lot older than you."

"It's the receding hairline. Going bald early.
Anyway, he looks like my father. I'm pretty sure my
dad was born looking eighty."

She was going to ask more when two large doors on
the other side of the room opened. Peter walked in first,
helping a man with a cane. Eric didn't stop playing the
game on his phone. But Charlie stood up to go over to
him.

"Want some help?" he asked.

"No! I can sit down by myself," his father barked.

"No problem, Dad," Charlie replied quickly,
hurrying back to his seat.

Terry grunted and slowly made his way toward the
table. For the first time, Stacey could see him clearly.
He was small, as if he had shrunk over the years. The
cane wobbled with each step. She was half worried he
was going to topple over. He sat down at the head of the
table. Peter helped him push in his chair.

"You can go," Terry said to him and he nodded his
head, moving away from the table.

Charlie had been right. Now that she was seeing his
father, she could see how Eric looked similar. They
both looked older than their age. In Terry's case, he
looked positively ancient. Lines were deeply etched in
his face and he was balding. His clothes were a size too
large for him as if he had lost a lot of weight recently.

Even though he looked feeble, there was a confidence in his movements, as if he didn't care that he was moving slowly or he appeared ill. His eyes had a sort of mischievous look to them – the same sort of look Eric had in his eyes. Yes, Charlie's brother definitely took after their father.

Two more people came out of the kitchen carrying bowls which were served to each person at the table. Stacey looked down to see it was some sort of stew. It smelled delicious, but she didn't want to start eating until Charlie did just in case there was some strange rule in place here.

"Eric, put your fucking phone away. And why the hell are you wearing a tuxedo?" Terry snapped.

Eric made a show of sighing heavily before shoving his phone in his pocket and replied, "Big brother is here. I thought we were all going to dress up. I guess I misjudged his importance." He lingered on the last word.

"We never wear tuxedos to dinner," Terry said. "Don't be stupid."

"That's all he knows how to be," Stacey heard Charlie mumble under his breath.

"Careful, brother. You wouldn't want to rock the boat."

Charlie's face scrunched up as he tried to figure out Eric's meaning. Stacey got it, however. She had said something similar, back when she had thought Eric was

Devin. She refused to look at him now and instead became fixated on her spoon in front of her.

"Enough," Terry said and his booming voice caused the two brothers to fall silent. "I'm starving."

He still hadn't said anything to her. Stacey felt almost invisible. In fact, if it hadn't been for Eric's jab at her just now, she could have sworn that she had vanished into thin air. Charlie began to eat. She did as well. The meal was delicious. It had been a long time since Stacey had eaten stew. If only the company were better.

No one spoke. Stacey could hear the rain against the window. Somewhere nearby a clock was ticking. She could probably hear a pin drop at this rate. She glanced at Charlie out of the corner of her eye as if to say *what the hell*? but he didn't look at her.

It was Eric who finally spoke, "So. Stacey. Tell us about yourself."

"Don't," Charlie answered.

"Don't what?" he replied with a cool indifference.

"I know what you're doing."

"Oh, do you?" Eric's tone was mocking now.

"Yes, so why don't you just focus on your dinner instead of starting things?"

Stacey couldn't help but look at Terry. He kept his eyes down on his bowl and ate silently. Eric and Charlie continued to bicker. She suddenly wished she could be anywhere but here.

"You sure have a bad attitude," Eric was saying, "probably because you only hang out with assholes. No offense, Stacey."

The fact that Eric was the only one actively engaging her was weird enough. She knew that Terry would be furious she wasn't Adele but to go so far as to shove her to the fifth floor, move her placement down the table, and now actively ignore her felt like she was dealing with a high school mean girl rather than an old man.

"Charlie," Terry finally spoke up and the two brothers went silent as if someone had unplugged them. "We need to go over the financials while you're here."

"I have people hired to do that."

"Subpar accountants. I want to look at them."

"Dad, that isn't needed. I have it under control –"

Terry held up one of his hands to silence him. His fingers were long and so skinny they looked more skeletal than anything else. Charlie fell silent. Stacey had never seen him act like this before. Bickering with his brother and falling silent when his father ordered it – it was a new side to Charlie, from her point of view.

Everyone went back to eating. Eric finished first. He made a show of dropping his spoon in the bowl. Then he looked at Charlie as if the two were in a race or something. Stacey was full but made herself finish the entire bowl. She was scared of looking rude for not eating all of it.

When Terry finished, he looked up and shouted for Peter. He appeared in the doorway and helped Terry get to his feet.

Charlie stood up and spoke quickly, "Dad, you can't be leaving already?"

"Tired," was all Terry replied.

"But Stacey –" Charlie said, motioning to her.

"Tomorrow we go over the financials. Goodnight."

Charlie stood there, his hands clenching into fists, as Terry was escorted out of the room by Peter. Someone came out of the kitchen and began to clear the dishes. Eric clapped his hands together loudly, which made Stacey flinch.

"Good job."

"What?" Charlie snapped.

"Dad didn't say one word to your fiancée the entire meal. Off to a great start, don't you think?"

"He'll come around."

"Will he? It isn't as if you really put your best foot forward there."

"What the hell does that mean?"

Eric stood up and yawned, as if the entire dinner had bored him to tears. "You're smart. Figure it out. Now, it was a truly wonderful dinner but I'm simply exhausted. Stacey, hope you had a nice time."

He gave her a small wave and left the room. The two of them were alone in the cavernous dining hall. She looked at Charlie. In this lighting, he looked exhausted. Even when he had spent long nights at the office he didn't look this tired. Feeling sorry for him, she reached out and took his hand in hers.

"Sorry," he said to her.

"For what?"

"I had this big plan in my head for how that dinner should go. I was going to introduce you and run through all sorts of conversations. But as soon as I saw Dad, it was as if all of that just flew away. Instead, I acted like the same pathetic little kid like I always do."

"Hey, it's okay. I mean, your dad is sorta scary for an old guy. He just doesn't even look nice," Stacey said, shaking his hand a little to try to make him smile.

Charlie did smile but it looked forced. "Everything he does, he does as some sort of passive-aggressive insult. It's all his childish way of saying he doesn't accept you. I should have stuck up for you. I'm sorry."

"It's only the first night. Don't be so hard on yourself."

"I just don't want to make things bad before I drop the bomb on him about me leaving," he said, lowering his voice.

"I get it. Come on. Let's get out of this room. It's cold and uninviting," Stacey remarked, pulling him toward the hallway.

"That's the entire house," he quipped.

Chapter Four

"How did you know it was Eric?" Stacey asked as they made their way toward the first floor.

"What?"

"When I mentioned that someone had told me the room was a supply closet. You knew."

"Dad has Peter and Warren to help out around the house and a couple of different people to help out in the kitchen. None of them would have told you that it used to be a supply closet. Eric is the only person here who would pull something like that."

"I fell for it too. I should have known."

"Don't blame yourself. You had no idea it was him. He doesn't look like my brother at all. And unfortunately, he is." They stopped in front of his bedroom door.

Stacey wanted to ask more – about his family and the house – but Charlie wrapped his arms around her waist and pulled her in for a kiss. It felt like ages since she had touched his lips. In reality, it hadn't been that long. But every second without him touching her felt like decades.

He pulled her into the bedroom, closing the door behind him. His lips were on her neck so softly that she could barely feel them, yet it was just enough to send goosebumps along her skin.

Their lips met again. This time the kiss was deeper. Charlie's tongue met her own and he made a tiny gasp of pleasure, pressing himself against her. She was against the wall now. His hands were trailing along her arms, pinning them above her head as he kissed her harder.

Stacey liked feeling him flattened against her like this. She liked the thrill of being pinned against the wall. She could feel her heart hammering in her chest as his fingers laced through hers.

Charlie moved down to her neck again, biting it gently before switching to kisses. Stacey closed her eyes, marveling at how each touch seemed to bring her alive. She should be used to it by now, surely. Didn't people say it wore off after time? Yet with Charlie, each time felt like the first time he had touched her.

His hands slid off hers, moving down to her waist. Her dress, which she had changed quickly into before dinner, bunched up around her thighs. Stacey could hear his labored breathing against her ear as he shuffled her skirt up.

Their lips crushed together now so hard that she could feel his teeth against her lips. He bit on her bottom lip, tugging on it. Her hands wrapped around his neck, bringing him as close as possible.

Charlie raised her dress up around her hips. The cold air of the room struck her skin. She shivered, and she could feel him smile against her neck. His hands were fumbling with her belt now. Finally, he loosened the buckle allowing the belt to drop onto the floor.

Stacey yanked on his pants, eager to unzip them. She could feel how hard he was against the fabric, straining for release. She unzipped his pants and tried to lower them. Yet his hand gripped her wrist and moved it away.

"So impatient," he teased, his voice sounding hoarse. "Now, you have to be quiet."

Stacey wasn't sure exactly what he meant until he hooked her underwear aside with one finger and ran another finger down the front of her exposed wet pussy. The touch was sudden and caused her to gasp in surprise.

"Shush, shush," Charlie mumbled in her ear which only made her feel light-headed.

He moved his finger down again, teasing her once more. His fingers were warm, contrasting with how cold the room felt. She breathed heavily. With his other free hand, he kept her wrists pinned above her head against the wall. Stacey couldn't move. All she could do was try to wiggle her hips to have Charlie give her more.

Finally, he relented. He moved his index finger inside of her pussy so slowly that Stacey could hardly stand it. She exhaled and swallowed her moan before she made too much noise. Charlie was studying her face. His lips were parted a little from their kissing and his face was flushed. She could still feel his hard cock through his pants, pressing against her leg.

He began to move his finger in and out of her, so slowly that Stacey wanted to snap at him to give her more. But she didn't – it would only encourage Charlie to continue teasing her. After a minute of this, he slid another finger into her. Stacey's eyes fluttered and she breathed hard.

"You have to keep quiet. Do you think you'll be able to do that for me?" he whispered in her ear.

"Yes," she pleaded.

"Ah, too loud. What did I just say?" he replied, shoving his fingers all the way inside of her.

The sudden motion caused her to gasp. Charlie smiled at her and leaned forward, dragging his lips across her neck. His grip on her wrists was still tight.

"I'll be quiet," she whispered.

Charlie pulled his fingers out from her. Stacey could hardly think straight. All she wanted was to feel him inside of her before she exploded. He kissed her hard, her own lips pressing against her teeth as he took his hand off her wrists and his pants dropped down to his knees. Both of his hands gripped her waist now and he suddenly picked her up.

Stacey wrapped her legs around his waist. Her back was pressed against the wall. Charlie's cock entered her in one swift motion. Going from nothing inside of her to his thick dick made her moan in surprise.

One of his hands covered her mouth swiftly. He began to fuck her like that – Stacey pinned against the wall with his cock deep inside of her and his hand covering her mouth. She whimpered against it, the sound muffled as he thrust deep inside of her.

Charlie himself was quiet. He was breathing heavily but otherwise didn't make a sound. Somehow, that turned her on even more than if he had been moaning. Her hands gripped his back. Her nails dug into the fabric of his shirt. Her dress clung to her, and she could feel sweat on the back of her neck.

Stacey couldn't hold back any longer. She gasped against his hand and closed her eyes. Her climax rolled through like a wave, sending warmth throughout her entire body. Charlie grunted as well. She could feel his cock twitch inside of her as he came. She shuddered against him and buried her face in his neck as they climaxed together.

They clung to each other like this for a full minute. Stacey couldn't even feel her legs. Her entire body felt like jelly. Slowly, Charlie pulled away from her and gently lowered her feet to the floor. Stacey wavered for a moment and pressed her hands against the wall.

"You alright?" he whispered.

"Yeah, just sort of feel like a tire iron hit me. In a good way," she added on quickly.

Charlie laughed shakily and went over to the bed before collapsing on it. He motioned for her, but she shook her head.

"No way. I won't ever get up. I don't want your dad finding us like this," she replied.

It hadn't mattered. Charlie let out a loud snore. He had fallen asleep instantaneously. Stacey marveled at how quickly that had been. She was jealous, actually, mostly because it usually took her ages to fall asleep.

With one last look at him, she crept out of the room.

Stacey quietly closed the bedroom door behind her. Even out here in the hallway, she could hear Charlie snoring. She knew that she could stay in bed with him if she wanted to. But she was still hoping to impress Terry somehow. It would cast a favorable light on her if Terry knew she had respected his wishes. Better to go back to her small bedroom and sleep there.

Yet the silence of the manor seemed to be overwhelming as she stood there in the hallway. She didn't feel tired at all. Stacey walked down the hallway slowly. At one point, she stopped in front of one of the closed doors. She looked around, as if someone were just hanging around spying on her, and then opened it.

It was a guest bedroom. It was ready for someone to use it. Eric and Charlie had been right. Terry had shoved her up on the fifth floor as a dig against her. There were clearly rooms to spare here.

Suddenly feeling awake and slightly rebellious, Stacey went downstairs instead of up. She strolled into the living room. The fire had been put out. There were lamps against the walls which were on the lowest setting. The dimly lit room looked like something she would have dreamt about as a kid. There were strange shadows cast everywhere, and the portraits of people she didn't know looked spookier at night.

Stacey went over to the mantle by the fireplace, drawn to the fact she had thought she had seen framed photos. She stopped in front of it and peered at one of them. It was an old photo of a much younger Terry standing next to a beautiful pale woman. Her hair was chestnut brown and looped up in a simple bun. She was wearing a plain yet striking white dress and holding a bouquet of flowers.

Stacey realized this was most likely Charlie's mother. She picked up the framed photo to get a closer look. Terry was dressed in a tuxedo and was beaming into the camera. There was a thin layer of dust over the photo which she rubbed off to try to see it better.

It was hard to make out the exact features of Charlie's mother, but she could see how they looked similar. Their smiles were almost exactly the same. Their hair color was the same as well. There was also something gentle that Charlie had that his mother had in the photo too.

She put the photo down and looked at the rest of them. They were all older photos. Eric, looking old even as a teenager, dressed up for prom. His arm was slung around a pretty woman and he was grinning into the camera as if he were on top of the world. A photo of Charlie graduating from college. He was standing next to Terry. His posture was stiff. Terry looked grumpy even in this picture. If Stacey hadn't just seen him smiling in his wedding photo, she would have wondered if he was capable of smiling at all.

There was one more photo at the end of the mantle. It caught her eye because the frame was a bright silver and decorated with flowers. Stacey picked it up and stared at it.

It showed Charlie standing next to Adele. Her throat tightened at the sight of them. Adele was dressed in a sleek black suit. She had her arm looped around Charlie's. Her smile looked similar to a great white before it ate its prey. Charlie was looking off to the side as if he was distracted. It was a bad photo. Adele looked as if she had won a prize and Charlie looked as if he were trying to escape.

Even so, Terry had deigned that it was important enough to make it onto the mantle, next to Charlie's graduation portrait and his own wedding photo. It was clear that he had thought they were really going to get married. He'd had his heart set on Adele marrying into the family.

The room felt very musty all of a sudden. Stacey wanted some fresh air. She put the photo down, resisting the urge to place it face down. There were doors leading outside on the other side of the living room and she went to them quickly. Stacey wanted to get away from the cloying scent of mothballs and that photo on the mantle.

It was cold outside. Luckily, the rain had stopped and the sky had cleared. The moon was full in the sky, illuminating the gardens in front of her. It felt as if they went on forever. She could probably wander into them and get lost.

Stacey stepped off the patio and took in a deep breath. The air felt clean compared to the stale air back in the manor. She followed the pathway, letting it take her along the grounds. It was nice to be out of the house. It felt as if she had the entire place to herself.

Just as she was thinking about how nice it was being alone, she saw Eric by one of the fountains. His back was to her. She could see the smoke trail from his cigarette. He hadn't seen her yet. Stacey decided she'd turn around and go the other way.

Yet as she turned, Eric spoke, "I know you're there."

Stacey froze and cursed inwardly. How childish would it be to break out in a run? Knowing Eric, he would probably chase after her just to piss her off. She stayed in place. He turned around and took a long drag off his cigarette.

"Wow, you know, I didn't know anyone even smoked anymore," Stacey remarked.

He exhaled, and the smoke formed a perfect circle. She fought the urge to roll her eyes.

"Didn't expect you to be creeping around. Figured you'd be safe in bed."

"Needed some air. Not like it's any of your business."

"Have a nice dinner?" Eric asked her as he walked over to her.

"The stew was good," she said honestly.

He laughed, "Sure was. Conversation though… not so good."

Stacey shrugged. She didn't know what to say. She felt as if she had babbled enough when she had thought he was part of the house staff. The last thing she was going to do was babble to Eric about how uncomfortable dinner was.

"You know what my favorite part was?" Eric said as he took another drag off his cigarette. "The fact that Charlie didn't mention you at all. I mean, you noticed that, right?"

She had. But the last thing she was going to do was tell Eric that it had bothered her or made her feel uncomfortable.

Eric took her silence as a sign to keep going because he said, "Actually. Now that I'm reflecting on the meal, I think I mentioned you. I did, didn't I? Twice or something."

Stacey fought down her annoyance and turned her head to look at him, "How kind of you."

Eric turned his face away from hers and blew out smoke. Stacey watched it waft up to the sky before it dissipated. In the distance, she could faintly hear thunder.

"Just saying. Kinda shitty of him. You're his fiancée, yet he didn't even bring you up. Guess he's still afraid of Dad."

"Says the guy who sneaks out here for a smoke and then shoves mints in his mouth to try to mask the scent."

Eric actually looked surprised at this. He turned to look at her. His eyes squinted as if she were far away.

A slow smile spread out across his face. "You're not like the other women he's been with. Has he told you that?"

"I don't really care about his old relationships."

"Well. That's half true, right? You care about Adele."

"Why would I care about her?" Stacey asked stiffly.

"Because Dad is so keen on her."

"Why don't you marry her then?"

His cigarette finished, Eric dropped it and crushed the butt under his shoe. Then he pulled out a pack from his pocket. He had changed from his tuxedo into sweatpants and a black t-shirt. He pulled out another smoke and offered the pack to her.

"Want one?"

"No," she paused and added, "thanks though."

Eric slipped the cigarette in between his lips and brought out his lighter. "I don't want to marry Adele. I don't want to get married at all." He flicked the lighter and the flame flickered in the darkness. "No thanks."

Stacey watched the tip of the cigarette glow. She couldn't help but ask, "Why not?"

Eric inhaled deeply before answering, as if he were thinking of a proper way to reply. In spite of her best attempts, she found herself curious to hear his answer.

"Why bother? I don't want to be tied down. Maybe Charlie has to get married because Dad wants him to have a wife and kids to eventually take over the company, but since I'm not in charge, who cares?"

Stacey thought of Charlie's announcement and tried to ask casually, "What if you were?"

"What?"

"What if you were in charge? Would you get married then?"

Eric stared at her for a long moment and she wondered if he was going to figure out that Charlie was leaving.

But instead, he replied with, "Doesn't matter. I'm not in charge. Although… I guess if I was, I'd probably find someone who just wanted to marry me for money."

"What?" Stacey exclaimed, thinking of her sister and Jacob.

"Yeah, why not?" He puffed on his cigarette thoughtfully. "That way, I wouldn't really be tied down. She'd have the money and be happy. I'd have the marriage, so Dad would leave me the hell alone. I'd still have the girlfriends. All works out."

Stacey wrinkled her nose. What was it with these people and marrying just to sort things out for the business? She couldn't wrap her head around it. She was glad that she was marrying Charlie for love.

"What, you don't approve?" Eric asked, seeing her facial expression. "Oh no!"

"Don't be a smartass."

"Why not?"

"Is that your answer for everything?"

"Why not?" he replied and then smirked at her.

"Well, this was a lovely conversation." Stacey turned to leave.

"Hey, wait, you didn't answer me."

She turned to look at him. "About what?"

"The fact that Charlie didn't bring you up at dinner. It didn't bother you?"

"No," she lied.

Eric looked at her closely. She was starting to hate how much he studied her face after every answer she gave.

"Charlie has brought girls home before. They always leave. This time, he changed it up. Proposed to you first. Probably to make it harder for you to leave."

"I'm not leaving," Stacey replied coolly.

He took another drag off his cigarette and said, "We'll see."

Her eyes narrowed. "I guess we will."

She turned around and walked away. Something about the entire conversation had unnerved her. Before Stacey went back into the house, she paused and looked back at Eric. He had turned away from her and was looking up at the moon. The moonlight illuminated his hair and made it look as if he was slightly glowing. She could barely make out the tip of his cigarette, glowing like a cooling ember.

Chapter Five

She dreamt again that night. It had been a while since Stacey had dreamt anything so vivid. After Tina had died, and she had run off to live on Tony's island, her dreams had been dull, as if the color had been drained from them.

Tonight, however, her dream was bright and bold as if a painting had exploded across the wall of her brain. She was walking through the manor, only it was so brightly lit that it felt as if it was a different house all together.

Stacey walked into the kitchen. The marble flooring was replaced with what looked like blood-red tile. Tina sat at the dining room table. She was at the head of the table. A steak was in front of her, which she was slicing very slowly. It didn't even look like it had been cooked. Blood splashed across the plate.

Stacey moved toward her grandmother. She was anxious to touch her again and to hug her. But when she went to do so, Tina suddenly vanished, disappearing into thin air. She turned around, trying to see where her grandmother had gone.

She gasped in surprise. Charlie had startled her. He was standing in the doorway of the dining room.

"Tina. Tina was here," Stacey said to him although her voice sounded far away.

Charlie didn't answer. He just stared at her blankly as if he didn't know her. She went over to him, trying to snap him back into focus but he turned to mist when she got close. Panic started to surge through Stacey. She was afraid that she was never going to get out of here. Where had Tina and Charlie gone?

Someone was laughing behind her. Stacey turned around and saw Eric, sitting where Tina had been just moments before. The sight of him filled her with a rage. He had something to do with them vanishing – she just knew it.

Stacey began to run but Eric just got farther and farther away. She could never get closer to him. He laughed the whole time with a cigarette dangling out of his mouth.

She woke up in a cold sweat and sat up. It took her a few seconds to remember where she was as she looked around the tiny room. The blanket that she had found in the dresser was wrapped around her legs. She yanked it off and took in a deep breath.

The clock on the wall showed it was a little past eight in the morning. Sunlight poked through the blinds. She could hear birds outside. Even though Stacey had slept through the night, she felt exhausted, as if she had run a marathon.

She got out of bed. Her stomach was grumbling, and she wanted to see Charlie. She peeked her head out of the doorway to make sure no one was in the hallway, then went to the bathroom.

After Stacey showered, she decided she'd see if Charlie was awake. They could eat breakfast together and figure out how to tell Terry that Charlie was leaving the business. The manor, like always, was deathly silent.

She walked to the first floor and went to Charlie's room. She knocked twice but there was no answer. She turned the door handle and slowly looked inside. Would it be wrong of her to wake him up?

It didn't matter. His bed was empty. The covers were thrown back as if he had gotten up suddenly. Stacey stood there, feeling a little confused. Where had he gone? She made sure he wasn't in the bathroom before deciding to go look for him.

She wandered into the living room again. Sunlight poured in through the windows which had the curtains pulled back. The room didn't look so scary in the bright sun. It was empty, however. Stacey stuck her head in the kitchen, but no one was there either. She wasn't sure where else to look. She didn't want to get caught creeping around.

As she stood in the kitchen entrance way, debating what to do, Eric strolled in. Stacey closed her eyes briefly, cursing her luck. She really didn't feel like talking to him. Both major interactions she'd had with him had either been based on lies or full of irritation about Charlie.

This morning, he was wearing the same clothes he had been wearing last night. His hair was messy from sleep but his eyes were alert as ever.

"Good morning," he said to her, going over to the coffee maker, "want some coffee?"

She did, but hesitated to ask for some. That meant she would have to stick around with Eric. On the other hand, she could fish around for information about where in the world Charlie had gone.

"While you stand there and debate the coffee conundrum, I'll make some extra," he said when she didn't reply right away.

His back was to her and she fought the urge to flick him off. The more she hung around Eric, the more she understood why Charlie wasn't his brother's biggest fan. He was cocky to a fault and held himself with a composure that just wouldn't seem to crack. He glanced over his shoulder.

"You just going to stand there or what?"

"No, I was going to meet up with Charlie," she lied swiftly.

Eric turned back to the coffee machine and she heard a low chuckle from him, "Were you?"

Something about his tone put her on edge. Stacey had wanted to appear as if she had known where Charlie was, yet now she was getting the sinking feeling that he knew more than she did.

"Yes, that's right."

"Wow, well, you might want to leave now, then. Takes about an hour to get into town. Did you sleep through the alarm or something?"

After saying this, he flicked on the coffee maker and turned to face her. He crossed his arms casually as he leaned against the counter. Stacey could tell that he was trying not to smirk at her, which just made it worse.

"You have no idea where he is, do you?" Eric asked her.

"No, I – I just slept in. That's all."

"Ah, right. So, you're going with Charlie and Dad to check the financials on a company that isn't yours? Sounds logical. On top of that, Dad, who literally pretended you didn't exist last night, is completely okay with this."

Stacey sighed and shrugged. "Fine. You caught me."

Eric rubbed his hands together as if he had discovered a treasure or something equally interesting. "Charlie didn't tell you he was going to town this morning?"

Stacey felt oddly defensive. "He did. I forgot."

The scent of brewing coffee filled the air. Her stomach grumbled loudly. Eric laughed at the noise.

"Want something to eat?"

"Don't you have like, people to cook for you?"

"We do but only Dad calls them. I can make my own eggs, thank you very much," Eric replied, opening the fridge and rummaging around.

Stacey gave up on the idea that she was going to see Charlie this morning and sat down at the breakfast bar. She tried to tell herself that it was fine that he had left without telling her. He probably would have assumed she'd sleep through the entire trip. Nothing to be irritated over.

Eric turned away from the fridge but wasn't holding anything to make for breakfast. He put the objects down on the counter and Stacey raised her eyebrows.

"Isn't it a little early to start drinking?"

"What? That's why the Bloody Mary was invented. So we can drink this early and not be judged," he remarked. "Want one?"

"No thanks."

"Good idea. If Dad saw you drinking this early, he would like you even less."

"But he's fine with you doing it?"

Eric shrugged. "He doesn't care much what I do."

This took Stacey by surprise. From what Charlie had told her, Eric had been scheming to take control of the company his whole life. Surely that would mean that Terry held an interest in what he was up to?

"Eggs are in the fridge," Eric said to her from over his shoulder.

Stacey balked at the idea of cooking in here. The last thing she wanted was for Terry and Charlie to come back while she was cooking and run the risk of Terry making a backhanded comment about her taking liberties in his home. She was clearly not welcomed here at all, let alone allowed to use his kitchen to cook for herself. The coffee maker beeped.

"Your coffee is ready."

"I thought it was yours too," Stacey said.

"Well, now I want a Bloody Mary."

Stacey slid off the stool and went over to the coffee maker. It was some state-of-the-art one with roughly a thousand different buttons and settings. She looked around for where the mugs could be but there were so many cabinets it was impossible to begin to guess.

Eric leaned over and opened the cupboard above the coffee maker to show her where the cups were. Stacey could smell the faint scent of cigarette smoke clinging to his clothes and a thought struck her.

"If he doesn't care what you do, why hide the fact you smoke?"

Eric looked surprised at this. "Really?"

"Yeah."

"Well, because of how my mom died."

Something must have shown on Stacey's face because Eric took a step back and was shaking his head. He mumbled something under his breath. She couldn't catch what he said, but it sounded like *unbelievable*.

"I know she got sick and passed away but…" Stacey trailed off.

"She died of lung cancer. Mom smoked like a chimney. She practically ate cigarettes her entire life. Even after she got diagnosed, Dad said she still kept smoking. That's why I hide it." Eric peered at her. "That's all Charlie told you? That our mom got sick and died? And what, that was enough for you?"

Stacey felt embarrassed. More embarrassed than the rest of the times she had been suffering through that emotion recently. Eric had turned back to making his drink. His shoulders were hunched as if he was holding something in. She silently turned back to the cupboard and pulled down a mug.

"Creamer is in the fridge," he mumbled to her.

"Thanks."

She poured the coffee and went over to the fridge, opening it. It was brimming with all sorts of food and drinks. Stacey leaned forward and looked closer to try to find the creamer.

Suddenly, the door of the fridge was yanked open farther and Eric leaned in. He snatched the creamer off the top shelf and handed it to her.

"Thanks," she repeated lamely.

"I'm not mad at you," he said suddenly to her, "I just don't understand why Charlie didn't tell you how Mom died."

"I should have asked him about her more. He said she got sick and passed away and he looked upset – I didn't want to press him for details."

"Word of advice," Eric said to her, "press Charlie for details or you won't ever find out anything at all."

Stacey opened her mouth to respond when she heard a loud creaking noise from the main hall. It sounded like something breaking in half and it startled her. Eric shot her a grin.

"They're back," was all he said and pulled away from her.

Stacey looked down at the creamer in her hand, trying to steady her beating heart. Eric's advice lingered in her head. It wasn't something she could just throw away. Charlie should have told her how his mother had died. Maybe she *should* have asked him for more details.

Bitter memories swirled to the surface. The fact that he hadn't told her the truth about being a billionaire, and how he hadn't told her about Adele until she had asked. Perhaps there was some truth to Eric's words after all.

Chapter Six

Charlie and Terry entered the kitchen a few moments later. Peter was behind them, positioned almost as if he could catch Terry if he lost his balance. Stacey was over by the counter again, pouring some creamer into her coffee. Next to her, Eric had finished making his drink and was marveling at his work.

"Nice presentation, right?" he said to her and playfully hit her on the shoulder.

She could see Charlie's eyes narrow at the interaction as she turned around to face him.

"What's going on here?" he asked, trying to keep his tone light but failing.

Before Stacey could speak, Eric chimed up, "Your fiancée here woke up early. Guess you forgot to tell her where you were going. Anyway, don't worry. I took good care of her."

"Are you drinking?" Charlie asked him.

"Geez, it's just tomato juice. Loosen up," Eric remarked, walking past Charlie and punching him in the shoulder.

The gesture, similar to the one he had just done to her, was clearly not meant to be playful for Charlie. His fist thudded against Charlie's shoulder. Stacey watched him take a deep breath as Eric slid onto the stool at the breakfast bar.

Stacey decided to take the bull by the horns. She positioned herself in front of Terry and forced a giant smile on her face.

"We made coffee. Would you like some?"

Terry finally looked up at her. Stacey wasn't sure what she was expecting. She was waiting to see how he was going to ignore her this close. He couldn't walk past her from this angle. Maybe he would just yell at her.

Instead, he grunted and shook his head. "No. I don't like coffee."

Then he moved forward as if he was going to run her over. All Stacey could do was flatten herself against the fridge as Peter escorted him through the dining room toward the living room. Stacey and the two brothers watched him leave.

Then she turned to face Charlie. "Look!" she said excitedly. "He acknowledged my existence!"

"Nice one," Eric replied, raising his glass to her.

But Charlie ran his hand over his face. "Please be careful. Don't corner him like that."

Stacey, who had just considered it a personal victory, felt as if someone had stuck a needle in her balloon. "Why not?"

"Cornering him won't endear him to you," Charlie replied.

Eric scoffed. "Nothing she does will endear him to her. He'll accept her once he is either on his deathbed or you two have kids. Doesn't really matter what she does now."

"We don't know that. She could win him over."

"Can you stop talking about me like I'm not in the room?" Stacey snapped, feeling irritated all of a sudden.

Charlie looked alarmed. "We weren't –"

"I wasn't. You were," Eric quipped.

"I was not," Charlie hissed, turning to his brother.

"I'm still here!" Stacey exclaimed.

Charlie turned back to her. "I didn't mean to speak to you like that. I just meant that we should try as best we can to have Dad like you. That's all."

Stacey shook her head. The emotions she had been holding in threatened to bubble over. Eric watched her curiously as if she were an exhibit in the zoo.

"No, your brother is right," she finally said.

Charlie looked alarmed while Eric looked victorious.

"What the hell does that mean?" he asked her.

"Your father isn't going to like me. I could cure cancer and he wouldn't like me. Speaking of cancer," the words rolled off her tongue, hot and venomous,

"Thank you for once again making me look like a moron."

She pushed past him before he could stop her. She could hear him asking Eric what he had done. Eric proclaimed his innocence. Stacey walked through the hallway toward the staircase. She wished she could leave. Coming to this place had been a mistake. Charlie was right – his family was messed up. Not only that, but it seemed to bring out the worst in him.

Stacey had made it up the first flight of stairs when she heard Charlie chasing after her. He caught up with her as she reached the second floor. He turned her around and looked at her.

"What's wrong? I don't – listen, Eric told me. That he told you our mother died of lung cancer. But I don't get what you are so upset about."

Stacey let out a dry laugh, "Are you serious?"

"It isn't as if I told you she was still alive or something. I told you – I told you she passed."

"All you said was she got sick and died. You didn't tell me how. And you know what, I didn't ask. I never ask! I just assume you are going to tell me. I don't know why I keep assuming that, because you don't."

"That isn't fair," Charlie protested. "I tell you everything. You can't keep throwing the past in my face. About who I said I was. I thought we moved past that."

"Me too," Stacey said sadly, and she could feel her throat close. "You should just tell me things. Straight up. You didn't tell me you were going to be gone this morning either."

"What? You're upset about that?" His eyes widened in surprise. "I didn't think it was a big deal."

"I woke up and I didn't know where you were. I ran into Eric and he knew. He knew where you were, but not me. It's embarrassing to be kept so little in the loop with you. How can you expect your father to accept me when you won't even tell me where you're going?"

"How are those two things even connected?" Charlie snapped, and Stacey could see that he was bubbling over now as well.

"If you don't think that I am important enough to tell things to, what does that tell your dad? It isn't exactly a vote of confidence!"

"Don't start this. Not now. Not here." He pointed to the floor. "Not while we are in this house."

"You can't tell me what to do. I don't work for you! I am your fiancée! All I'm asking for is to be kept in the loop! Tell me what is going on with you!"

"What is going on with me? Stacey, I am stuck back in this stupid fucking house dealing with my father. My father, who spent the entire morning making jabbing little cutting remarks about what I am doing with my life. And I try to ignore it because I want to tell him gently that I am leaving the company and trying to set out on my own. I want him in the best mood possible for this – I want to be in the best mood possible for this." He was very close to her now, his voice hushed and struggling to remain so. "But that is difficult when I am also dealing with you being upset because I left the house this morning."

Stacey took a step away from him. Her breathing came quickly now as she tried to keep herself in control.

"Oh, well, excuse me! I had no idea that I was here to make sure your mood was stable enough to stand up to your dad! I guess I should be completely okay with you leaving out how your mom died or that you left the house or anything else. Why don't you just do whatever the fuck you want while we're here? Whatever works for you, your royal highness."

Charlie's features colored with anger. "I just assumed you could handle yourself if I left the house for a couple of hours, so excuse me."

"I took care of myself just fine. I'm not a child!" she snapped.

"Well, I'm glad that Eric was there to help you out." His voice was dripping with bitterness and Stacey blinked.

Then she let out a loud bark of laughter. "Are you serious right now? Eric was helping me figure out where the coffee creamer was. Why, are you jealous?"

"I'm not!" he said loudly and then lowered his voice swiftly. "Don't listen to him. Don't even speak to him. He is never up to anything good. He's a liar. Trust me. I know I sound crazy –"

"You do sound crazy."

Charlie ignored her. "He's just a bored kid. He has nothing to do. He just hangs out and causes problems for everyone. Whatever he told you, just ignore it."

"He told me where you were. He told me how your mother died. Both things you failed to tell me yourself," she replied in disgust.

"Fine, if he's so fucking wonderful, go hang out with him then. I'm done with this conversation."

Charlie turned around and began walking down the hallway. Stacey stood there with her mouth slightly open. She couldn't believe that he was *walking away* from her instead of wanting to work things out. Charlie went to his room in a pout like a teenager.

She couldn't remember the last time she had felt so furious. She refused to chase after him. He probably wanted that. Instead, Stacey stormed down the steps back down to the main floor. *Let him sulk in his room then*, she thought to herself.

She cut across the living room and stopped by the kitchen. It was empty. She poured herself a new cup of coffee to replace the one that had cooled down and set off outside.

It was even chillier today. With the sun high up in the sky, Stacey walked toward the gardens. Better to get lost in the fields than deal with anyone from that family. Her heart was pounding in her chest.

Stacey couldn't recall a time she had ever been this angry at Charlie. Even when he had lied about being a billionaire. Even when she had left him because of the craziness with Adele. She had been afraid of being with him – afraid of taking that leap and seeing what would happen. He had always spoken poorly of his family. Now that she was among them, and saw how he acted, she could see why he wanted to run away.

Even so, Stacey didn't think that it excused his behavior. In spite of her best attempts, she did feel as if she didn't exist here. It wasn't a great feeling. She had assumed Charlie would be on her side throughout this. He would defend her and make Terry notice her.

But he hadn't done any of those things. To hear him speak about trying to keep both his mood and Terry's mood intact had angered her. What about her? She was his fiancée. He was supposed to make sure she was okay too, wasn't he?

Stacey looked around. She had wandered into a section of the garden that was a little wild compared to the other areas. There was a bench nearby. She sat down on it and breathed deeply before taking a sip of her coffee. She wondered why this section was untamed. Stacey could ask Charlie – but would he tell her the complete story?

All she wanted was to be kept in the loop on things. She had thought for sure once she got his father to speak to her, it would be a personal victory for the two of them. But he had been irritated with her for even that simple gesture.

Stacey ran her finger over the rim of her coffee cup. Both Eric and Charlie's words floated around in her head, buzzing loudly.

Don't listen to him. Don't even speak to him. He is never up to anything good. He's a liar.

Word of advice. Press Charlie for details or you won't ever find out anything at all.

Hearing the two brothers bicker and insult each other behind their backs suddenly made her miss Allison. It was odd how different her own relationship with her sister had been. Growing up, they had been similar to Charlie and Eric. Yet something had shifted after Tina passed away. Allison had been the one to wake her out of her fog when she had been hiding out on Tony's island.

She slipped her phone out of her pocket and on a whim called Allison. She was sure that she was going to wake her sister up, but she was willing to deal with being snapped at.

"Hey!" Allison answered on the second ring, sounding alarmingly awake for someone who hated getting up before noon.

"Hey. Did I wake you?"

"No, no. I'm up early. I have a flight to catch in an hour. We're going to Belgium for like, three days."

"Wow, Belgium. That should be fun."

"Yeah, I'm excited. I'm on like three cups of coffee already though. Why are you up so early? How awful is it there?"

"How do you know it's awful?"

"Because you're calling me," Allison replied.

Stacey laughed a little shakily. "Yeah. It isn't as great as I thought it'd be."

"I have approximately ten minutes before Jacob gets here. Spill it."

Stacey talked as fast as she could. She told Allison everything from how creepy the manor house was, how Terry ignored her, how Eric had fooled her into thinking he worked here up to the fight she had just had with Charlie. When she finished, she exhaled slowly and waited for Allison to reply.

"Wow, sounds shitty," she finally said.

"Is that all you have to say?" Stacey asked.

"What? What do you want me to say?"

"I don't know. Advice?"

"Well, both you and Charlie need to cool off. Honestly, I wouldn't bother even discussing this stuff until after he tells Terry his news. It's probably weighing really heavily on him. After he tells him and there is the nuclear fallout that will eventually clear, then talk to him. He would be more open to talking and apologizing then, I think."

"Wow," Stacey said, feeling impressed, "when did you get so smart?"

"I think it comes with being married. Soon, you won't need my advice. I have two minutes left. Tell me more about Eric."

"What? Why?"

"He sounds cute."

"Seriously, Allison? You're married."

"Married but not dead," her sister replied solemnly. "Come on. You know I like troublemakers."

"That's because you *are* a troublemaker. I'm going to go now."

"Alright," Allison sighed. "Well, text me later, okay? And don't do anything stupid."

The call ended. Stacey had to admit that she felt a little bit better having vented to Allison. She mulled over her sister's advice. It seemed sound. Charlie was under a lot of stress. Trying to discuss it with him now would only lead to more trouble.

They were here for two more days. Better to just suck it up and deal with it the best that she could.

Chapter Seven

Stacey didn't see Charlie for the rest of the day. She spent most of the day in the garden and once she got bored of that, read a book in one of the sitting rooms in the manor. No one bothered her. She didn't hear anything.

By the time dinner rolled around, her anger had cooled off and had turned into just regular irritation. Peter came to fetch her for the meal. Stacey trailed after him. When she got there, Eric was already there. He was on his phone, typing furiously. Charlie and Terry weren't there yet.

She was about to sit down next to Charlie's seat but not before yanking the place setting that had been set for her three seats down to where he was. Eric glanced up.

"Where were you all day?" he asked.

"One of the thousand sitting rooms this place has."

His phone chimed and he looked back down at it with a roll of his eyes. "Trying to set up a date with this chick and she's making things difficult."

"'Chick?' Really?" Stacey asked, arching an eyebrow.

"Woman. Female. Whatever."

Stacey wasn't interested in his woman problems. She felt on edge, as if she were waiting for the other shoe to drop.

Eric went on, "Anyway. Bad thing about being stuck at this manor is it makes it a bit hard to hook up."

"I don't care," Stacey remarked, glancing over at the doors where Terry had come through last time.

"Wow, you're charming tonight."

"What, like you?"

Eric held his hands up as if he were warding off an attack. "Fight with Charlie, eh?"

She bristled at his comments and looked over at him. "Whatever happened with Charlie isn't any of your business."

That slow, lazy grin moved across his face and he leaned forward as if he were waiting to hear a secret. His phone was on the table now, and it vibrated loudly against the oak table.

"He's jealous, isn't he?"

"Of what?" She played dumb.

"Us. Getting along." He motioned between the two of them.

"Is that what this is? Getting along? It doesn't feel like getting along. Feels more like you talk to me to piss off your brother because the two of you act like children together.”

Eric’s grin didn’t diminish. He didn’t get to reply because that was when Charlie entered. His eyes fell on the two of them. Eric was still leaning forward, smiling widely. Stacey could see Charlie’s shoulders stiffen at the sight. *Great,* Stacey thought.

He sat down next to her. Eric leaned back in his chair and rubbed his stomach.

“I’m starving,” he said.

Neither Stacey nor Charlie replied. Eric picked up his phone and began texting again. The doors opened and Peter came in, helping Terry walk in on his cane. He looked unchanged from this morning. He didn’t smile as he sat down.

Instead, he looked over at Eric. “Put your phone away! Every time I see you, you’re on that damn thing.”

“Sorry, Dad,” Eric drawled, shoving the phone into his pocket.

The two same servers came out of the kitchen and put a plate of steak and potatoes in front of everyone. Stacey had a flashback to her dream – Tina, cutting the raw steak, blood pouring out on the plate, and felt her appetite wane.

They began to eat in silence again. Stacey wondered if the meal was going to be as awkward as last night’s dinner, when Charlie suddenly cleared his throat.

“I have to tell you something, Dad.”

She froze. Eric's eyes fell on her and he squinted at her. He must know she knew whatever Charlie was going to announce. For some reason, she hadn't thought Charlie was going to announce it right now. They still had two days left. She had pictured him mumbling it very quickly as they left.

Terry looked up and grunted, "What?"

Charlie took a deep breath and said the words, "I'm leaving the company. I'm giving up the position of president. I'm walking away."

The reaction was instantaneous. Eric dropped his knife and fork directly onto his plate, looking stunned. Terry practically choked on the piece of steak in his mouth and started coughing. Peter began to hit him on the back. Stacey was concerned he was going to stop breathing.

"Are you serious?" It was Eric who spoke first – Stacey couldn't read the expression on his face.

Terry finally stopped coughing and shook his head. "Don't be stupid, boy."

"I'm not. I'm serious. I should have told you before we went into town today but…" He shook his head. "Anyway, I'm leaving at the end of this quarter. That gives you –"

"Enough!" Terry barked, and he slammed his hand down on the table. "No more of this madness!"

"It isn't madness. I'm leaving, Dad."

But Terry stoutly ignored him by turning to Eric and doing something Stacey hadn't ever seen him do before – ask his son a question. "How was your day?"

Eric's face would have been comical if there hadn't been such a serious thing going on. He cleared his throat but didn't get a chance to reply.

"Dad. Dad, stop. I'm leaving the company. I know you can hear me. Give it to Eric. He's always wanted it, anyway."

Terry turned to look at the two of them. Stacey was reminded of when she was a little girl and had gotten in trouble. Tina used to have the same expression on her face before she grounded her.

But instead of directing his words to Charlie, he looked directly now at Stacey. "Is this your fault?"

"What?" Her throat felt dry at suddenly being put on the spot.

"You heard me. Is this your stupid idea, girl?"

"I'm not a girl," she bristled.

"Listen to me, Charlie. Whatever stupid ideas this one –" and he jabbed his finger toward her, "has put into your head, forget it."

"She didn't put any ideas in my head. You take control of the company then. You were furious you were too sick to run it anyway."

Terry went on as if Charlie hadn't spoken, "This never would have happened if you were marrying Adele."

Charlie slammed the palm of his hand down on the table which made her jump. "But I'm not! I'm not marrying Adele, Dad. I was never going to marry her. I've made that clear over the years. Have her marry Eric if you love her so much."

"Hey, what the fuck? Will you stop doing that?" Eric spoke up now.

"Doing what?"

"Just being like 'Oh, give this shit to Eric, no one cares about him'."

"Not this right now," Charlie snapped. "Feeling badly for yourself so quickly?"

"I'm not feeling badly for myself, just asking for a little human decency from my own brother," he growled back.

Charlie began to shake his head. "No, don't pull that shit."

"What shit?"

"You know exactly what you're doing!" he hissed at his brother.

Eric's muscles tensed. Stacey half expected him to lean over the table and swing at Charlie.

Instead, he said very softly in a controlled voice, "What, just trying to get some respect? I can tell you can't give it. I've spoken to Stacey, you know."

Charlie stood up. So did Eric. They looked like two little boys at the playground about to fist fight over lunch money. The two of them stared each other down. It was Terry who spoke.

"Enough! Both of you! Idiots! Sit back down!" When they didn't move, he exclaimed louder, "Now!"

Charlie took in a slow breath and sat down. The remark that he wasn't treating Stacey with respect seemed to have hit him hard. Eric knew exactly what to say to him to piss him off.

Eric sat down next, crossing his arms. Terry glanced at him before turning to the two of them again.

Charlie cut him off before he could speak. "Stacey didn't even know about this until after I told her. No, listen to me. I don't care if you believe me or not. I'm still leaving at the end of this quarter. I can help you or Eric get things settled. I'm willing to do that."

"Generous," Eric mumbled under his breath.

"Why are you doing this? What brought this on?" Terry demanded.

"I don't want to work here any longer. I'm sick of worrying about you. Worrying about this idiot over here." He gestured to Eric who glowered. "Dealing with you two trying to run it behind my back. I kept fighting you two, but why? I'll leave and start my own thing. It was a matter of pride that kept me here, but I don't care any longer."

"So, you're giving up?" Terry grunted. "I didn't raise you to be a quitter."

"You hardly raised me at all. So just stop, alright? Years and years I've put up with your nonsense and general insanity and for what?"

"Aw, what do you want, boy? Me to tell you that I'm proud of you? Looking for my approval?" Terry sneered at him.

"No, not anymore. Hence why I am leaving." He stood up again. "You two can figure out who is going to take over. If Eric here realizes he can't handle it, maybe you can give it to Adele. We all know you probably want to fuck her anyway, Dad." He dragged out the final word – a slap in the face.

For the first time since Stacey had met him, she saw color fill Terry's face. But Charlie didn't give him a chance to respond. He was already leaving the room. Stacey stood up quickly, not wanting to be alone in the dining room and ran after him.

When they got to the living room, she finally caught up with him and grabbed his arm. "Charlie –"

"No." He shook her off. "I don't want to talk right now."

She felt as if she had been punched in the stomach. All she could do was watch him leave the room. A few seconds later, she heard the front door open and slam shut, leaving her alone in the manor.

Chapter Eight

Stacey heard a knock at her door later on that night and hurried over to answer it. It had been almost six hours since Charlie had stormed out of the house. She had been by the window, straining to see when he was returning.

She had gone up to her room right after Charlie had rebuffed her. She found herself crying, which only made her feel stupid. Was it silly of her to have thought something from their fight earlier would have sunken into that thick skull of his? She had just wanted to be there for him, to lend support to him. The fact that he had rejected her hurt more than Stacey had expected.

So it was with hope that she hurried over to the door and opened it. To her bitter disappointment, it wasn't Charlie, but Eric. The disappointment was so strong she could taste it in her mouth. Stacey fought the urge not to slam the door in his face.

"What?" she asked.

"Charlie back yet?"

"No. You came all this way to ask me that?"

Eric ran his fingers through his hair. "Well, I went to his room first, but it was empty. Thought he might be up here."

"Well, he isn't, so…" She began to push the door shut.

Eric shoved his foot against it, stopping her from closing it. "You knew, right? That he was planning this."

"He told me before he proposed." Eric looked thoughtful at this so she added, "Are we done?"

"Not yet. Want to go for a walk?"

"No. Absolutely not. Not with you, anyway. Can you also stop?"

"Stop what?"

"Don't play innocent with me," Stacey sighed. "Your little jab at Charlie at dinner. About respect and me. Don't think I didn't notice. I'm sick of it. You pretending you know me or how I'm feeling toward him. So just stop."

Eric clicked his tongue against the top of his mouth and shrugged. "But it bothers him so much." He grinned.

"Get out," Stacey said and closed the door firmly.

She waited to hear him leave but he didn't. She could hear him on the other side of the door. Charlie was right – he was annoying.

"Hey, listen, Stace – I can call you that, right? You're going to be my sister-in-law, so… you know," he said through the door.

Stacey didn't say anything. Maybe if she ignored him, he would go away.

"Well, be that way. But tell him that he's making a mistake. He probably hasn't thought this all the way through. You know, because he's an idiot."

In spite of herself, she replied through the door, "How so?"

She could hear him walking away. She cursed inwardly and opened the door. He was strolling down the hallway with his hands shoved into his pockets. His posture was clear – he knew he had hooked her even though she had tried to shut him out.

Stacey hurried after him. For the second time in one night, she was chasing after one of the brothers. It was irritating, to say the least.

"What did you mean by that?"

Eric turned around slowly and feigned surprise as if he hadn't seen her there. "Thought you went to bed."

"Oh, cut the shit, Eric," Stacey snapped. "Tell me what you mean."

"Dad isn't just going to let this slide. He isn't the sort of man who just lets things like this happen. He will crush Charlie and his new business just to prove a point."

"Well, maybe he knows this," she replied uncertainly.

"If he does, then he *is* an idiot. Pulling this shit now. Why?"

"Why not?" she asked, mimicking Eric's own phrase from the night in the garden.

He narrowed his eyes at her and took a step toward her. "You have no idea the shit storm Charlie is leading you into."

"Why do you even care?"

"You're being dumb," he said simply.

Stacey snapped. Before she could stop herself, her hand went flying across his face. She instantly regretted having slapped him. She couldn't recall ever slapping anyone before. She stood there, her hand by her side limply and her breathing coming quickly.

Eric rubbed his cheek idly and regarded her with an expression she couldn't read. He didn't look angry. Stacey wasn't sure what he was feeling.

"Well, you sure showed me," he finally said, and turned to walk down the stairs.

Stacey listened to him go. Somewhere downstairs, a clock chimed midnight. She listened to it count out twelve beats before the manor was shrouded in silence again.

Someone was shaking her. Stacey groaned softly and twisted in her bed. The shaking got worse. Her eyes fluttered open. Her eyes were still blurry from sleep, so she wasn't quite sure what she was looking at.

Charlie sat beside her on the bed. Surprised, she sat up and looked at him. He appeared exhausted. There were dark circles under his eyes. He was still in the clothes from last night. His hair was messy and he smelled faintly of booze.

"Stacey," he said and cupped her face with his hand. "Hey."

"Charlie? What time is it?"

"Six in the morning."

"Did you just get home? What's going on?"

"We're leaving."

Stacey propped herself up and asked groggily, "What?"

"Yeah. I can't stay here any longer. I'm sorry. I feel like I'm losing my mind. We'll head back to the city early. It'll be better for us."

"What about your dad?"

"Who cares?" he mumbled, standing up.

"No, I mean, with your announcement. He's going to want to discuss things, right?"

"There isn't anything to discuss. He can decide who is going to replace me and I'll help them settle in with things. Even if it's Eric."

At the mention of Eric, memories flickered across her mind. She saw him warning her about Terry. She recalled the way she had slapped him and his final words to her as he walked away. She wanted to apologize for the way she reacted but there apparently wasn't going to be any time.

"Come on. Pack up. We're leaving in an hour," Charlie said and left the room, closing the door behind him.

Stacey sat there in bed. Charlie had still been distant. Sure, they were leaving, which was a good thing. But she couldn't help but think they were leaving on a bad note with everyone involved.

There had been no good-bye to Terry or Eric. They had left an hour later, packed and driven to the airport in silence. Charlie had the radio on, making it clear that he didn't want to talk. Stacey wanted to reach out to him and talk to him, but she was too afraid of being rebuffed.

Even though she was making her best attempt at not stressing out, it was failing. She felt as if Charlie was drifting away and she was trying to catch up. When he had told her he was going to talk to his father about leaving, she had been picturing something completely different. There had been no fights in that scenario. Just the two of them working together and facing down his father.

On the plane ride home, Charlie slept. Yet another chance for them to speak was gone. What if he didn't want to discuss it at all? What would she do then? She watched him sleep, her heart aching at the fear that she should have stuck with her choice. The choice she made that day in the graveyard at Tina's funeral, when she had shut the world out, and decided to shut down her feelings for Charlie.

She had been afraid to take that leap with him. Afraid of getting her heart broken. If that ended up actually happening now, Stacey wasn't sure what she was going to do.

A car was waiting for them at the airport. Charlie was on his phone, checking e-mails and tending to business. Stacey idly thought about William and the real estate office. She would be happy to go back to it. It would give her something to focus on.

"Stacey," Charlie's voice came through her fog and she turned to look at him. "Did you hear me?"

"No. I'm sorry. What is it?"

"Do you want to come home with me first?"

The offer took her by surprise, but she nodded that she did. She had been expecting him to drop her off at her place without another word. Charlie seemed to be relieved that she had agreed with him.

By the time they got to the penthouse, Stacey felt exhausted. It was nice to be back in the city. It felt as if she were back on solid ground. The manor, besides being creepy and odd, seemed to have brought out the worst in everyone. She was glad that she was back home.

Charlie dropped his bags to the floor and yawned, "Man, I am tired."

"Me too."

"Last few days sucked."

"They sure did," Stacey replied.

Charlie stared at her for a beat and then threw himself down on the couch, "I'm sorry."

Stacey looked over at him in shock. Her sister had been right. Once he was free of that atmosphere, he was open to talk. Feeling boosted by this, she went over and sat down next to him on the couch.

"I'm sorry too," she said. "I didn't mean to piss you off or make you feel cornered."

He waved his hand. "Don't worry about it. I should have stuck up for you more. I should have made Dad take notice of you. I thought I wasn't rocking the boat but honestly, I was letting him control me. I always do that."

"I get it. Your dad is…"

"Believe me, I've heard it all before," Charlie mumbled.

"That must have been hard. Growing up with that, I mean."

He sighed, "It wasn't fun. I don't mean to sound like 'oh, poor rich kid, woe is me' or anything. But Dad wasn't kind. Like I said before, when Mom died it was as if all the kindness was sucked right out of him. He wanted me to be groomed for the company and that was all he cared about."

"Do you think Eric will take it over?" Stacey asked thoughtfully.

"I don't know. I would assume so, yes. He's always wanted to. Let him have it."

"You know…" She hesitated for a moment. She wanted to tell him what Eric had said but didn't want to upset Charlie by letting him know that Eric had come to her room.

"What?" he asked her. "Why do you look funny?"

"Sorry. Just tired," she said swiftly. "I don't remember what I was going to say."

She should have just told him. But Charlie seemed extremely sensitive about Eric. She had bickered with Eric as if he was her own brother, yet Charlie didn't see it that way. He thought the worst of him – most likely for good reason. If she told him that Eric had told her Terry was going to have it out for him, he would probably be upset. Maybe even angry with her for not mentioning it sooner.

On top of that, she had slapped Eric. Stacey still felt guilty about it. No, better not to let Charlie know. He had probably accounted for Terry's anger, anyway.

"Come here," he said and pulled her toward him.

She went willingly, draping her arms around his neck and bringing her lips to his. It was nice feeling him like this – no more anger or awkwardness between the two of them.

"I'll be honest with you. I'm sorry," he whispered against her neck. "I don't even realize I'm doing it."

He left butterfly kisses down her neck and Stacey closed her eyes. "It's okay. Families always bring out the worst in people."

Charlie chuckled. "They sure do. But we don't have to worry about it any longer."

Being back home with just Charlie felt nice and relaxing. The tensions of dealing with the family seemed to have faded into the background. For a while, they did nothing but watch TV. Stacey had her head on his shoulder as they flipped through the channels together. Stacey even dozed off at one point, finally able to unwind a little.

When she woke up, she let out a yawn and looked up. She was curled against Charlie who looked down at her and smiled.

"Sleep well?"

"Yeah, I needed that," she replied, sitting up and turning to face him. "Did I miss anything exciting?"

Charlie shook his head and grinned, "No, but you look cute sleeping."

Stacey laughed and he leaned forward to kiss her. His hands trailed down her sides. He slid his hand down her pants and ran a finger down the front of her underwear, causing her to shiver.

His lips found hers and he tugged on her bottom lip, whispering, "We don't have to worry about anything."

He moved her underwear to the side. His fingers were cold against the heat of her body. She tingled all over as Charlie gently probed her pussy with his finger. She buried her face in his shoulder, closing her eyes.

Very slowly, his finger entered her. She was already wet. The smallest touch from Charlie made her melt. His finger moved deep inside of her, promising her more, but making her wait for it.

Then another finger slipped into her pussy. Stacey's grip on his shoulders tightened as Charlie began to move them in and out quickly. His other hand was on the small of her back, holding her in place. Stacey grinded her hips against his fingers, wanting more.

Charlie pulled his fingers out of her and then moved them to her mouth. She wrapped her lips around them, rolling her tongue around his fingertips. He watched her with his eyes wide. His mouth was slightly parted as if he was in the middle of a gasp.

Then he pulled her clothes off. Stacey yanked his clothes off just as urgently. When their bare skin finally touched, she was in ecstasy.

Charlie leaned against the couch and pulled her toward him. She moved into his lap. His cock pressed against her now. She could feel it throbbing. He cradled the back of her neck and their lips met. This kiss was feverish with desire, an urgency that hadn't been in their lovemaking in quite some time.

If the manor had worked to crush what they had, being out of it and back home was bringing it all back to life. Stacey could feel herself blooming under every touch of Charlie's. She could feel every detail of him – his fingertips pressed against the back of her neck, his tongue in her mouth, his heart racing against her own.

With his free hand, he positioned himself so he could enter her. Stacey held onto him as his cock slipped into her pussy. She moaned into his mouth as she felt him fill her up with his dick. With his tongue still in her mouth, Charlie leaned back and let her ride him.

Stacey rocked her hips at first, getting used to how he filled her from that angle. She felt stuffed, as if he had taken her completely over. His mouth moved to her breasts, biting and tugging on her nipples. She threw her head back and began to pick up speed.

The sound of their skin smacking together filled the room. Charlie cupped her breasts and buried his face in them as she brought her hips down on his cock again and again.

"You look so good," he said between gasps for air as she fucked him on the couch.

Stacey couldn't reply. Her body felt frozen as if every nerve in her body was vibrating. From this angle, he felt incredible. His dick was warm and hard inside of her. Her pussy accepted every inch of him. She could feel herself on the verge.

Charlie gripped her hips so hard that Stacey couldn't moan anymore. Her eyes fluttered open.

"What are you doing?" she asked dizzily.

"This." He moved her so they were almost falling off the couch onto the floor.

Before she could say anything, Charlie's head was in between her legs. He buried his tongue deep in her pussy and flicked it out to her clit. Stacey let out a moan of surprise, rolling her head back against the floor. Behind her, she could see the city spread out like a jewel. Upside down, dizzy with pleasure, it looked full of possibilities. She felt like a queen in a tower.

Charlie's tongue rolled across her clit before darting back down the length of her pussy. His face pressed against her as she shuddered and rolled her hips against him. She was going to finish – she was going to come right now.

As if sensing this, he was suddenly gone. Stacey let out a groan of frustration from having been on the brink both times. Her eyes had been closed and when she opened them, Charlie was on his knees next to her. His dick was hard in her face, dripping with pre-cum.

"Suck it," he ordered huskily.

Stacey obeyed, rolling over onto her stomach and engulfing him with her mouth. His cock was warm and twitching in her mouth as she lapped at it with her tongue. She gripped his dick at the base with one hand. She covered it in her spit before bobbing her head up and down on his thick shaft.

Charlie groaned and shut his eyes. Stacey took as much of him as she could in her mouth until he hit the back of her throat. Then it popped out of her mouth, slick with her spit. She jacked him off with her hand before taking him in her mouth again.

He grunted and pulled away. He pushed her onto the floor and climbed on top of her. Without pausing, he entered her fluidly. He began to fuck her hard and fast on the floor. Her body shook with each thrust, her tits jiggling as he fucked her.

It didn't take long to finish. They were both so close. After a few thrusts, Stacey's orgasm exploded over her. She arched her back and let out a loud guttural moan as she came. Charlie came at the same time, grunting and breathing hard. She had her legs wrapped around his waist as she came.

After it was done, he collapsed on top of her. They were both sticky with sweat and the air smelled of sex. Stacey gasped for breath. Her body felt numb, although her scalp was still tingling from the remnants of her orgasm.

He kissed her gently before rolling off of her. They lay on the floor as if they had both melted there. She turned her head and smiled at him.

Everything felt okay now.

Chapter Nine

The next two weeks went by in a blur of activity. Stacey threw herself into helping William, Amanda, and Brad set up the real estate office. On top of that, she was helping William figure out repairs on her own building.

She was so busy that everything else seemed to fade into the background. She would get up early, work late into the night, and come home to fall asleep. Charlie had to go to Europe for a business trip the second week. Part of her wanted to go with him but she refused to leave William hanging. He had been kind enough to give her time off to go meet Charlie's family. She didn't want to ask for more time off.

Stacey had learned a lot during her time with Tony. It had been easy to slip into a role she didn't even realize she was falling into. She had been comfortable with him paying for things, and she had allowed herself to ruin a job just to run away with him.

It was going to be different with William. This was a chance to build an office from the ground up. Stacey didn't want to blow it. She said good-bye to Charlie at the airport and then went back to work.

It wasn't until one night when she was staying late that Amanda poked her head into the room. Their office was small and on the outskirts of the city. They could have gotten someplace nicer, but William wanted to start small. Stacey couldn't blame him. There was a chance this could all go under. Amanda had been taking classes to get her real estate license in the meantime, so they would have at least one agent in the office.

"You're still here?" Amanda had said.

Stacey looked up. "Yeah. Just finishing up some things. Why are you here?"

"I left my phone here before I went to class." She held her phone up as if it were proof. "Had to come back to get it."

"Aren't you overwhelmed?" Stacey asked. "You're taking college courses on top of real estate courses and popping by here."

Amanda sat at the edge of the desk that William had put in the room earlier today, "Massively, stupidly busy. But I don't mind. I hate being idle."

"Well, don't overdo it."

"You either," Amanda crossed her arms. "Don't you have a wedding to plan?"

"We haven't set a date yet."

"Why not?"

Stacey paused and then shrugged, "Just haven't."

"What's the hold-up? You guys are clearly in love. Just hire a planner and be done with it."

"I hadn't thought about it before."

To be honest, Stacey hadn't been thinking about the wedding much lately. Between dealing with Charlie's family and being busy with work, the wedding had been something in the back of her mind. Both she and Charlie had such busy schedules that planning a wedding had felt daunting.

A planner, however…

"I'll talk to Charlie about it."

Amanda clapped her hands together. "Great! I'm expecting the largest wedding I've ever attended. Don't let me down," she joked as she waved good-bye.

The largest wedding I've ever attended. Something about those words left Stacey feeling uneasy. She just couldn't put her finger on it.

"Meredith is supposed to be the best," Charlie reminded her as they walked into the building. "She organized a couple of my friends' weddings and they were crazy. Ice sculptures, for one."

"Ice sculptures?" Stacey asked, balking at the idea.

Something must have shown on her face because he quickly amended with, "We don't need those though."

After Charlie had gotten back into town, Stacey had told him about the wedding planner idea. He was thrilled and promptly set up a meeting. She wasn't sure what to expect. This was a whole new arena for her. Most things in her relationship with Charlie were like that.

The office was on the first floor. The waiting room looked more like a living room, with a large couch and TV. They were offered freshly brewed coffee as they waited. After five minutes, the door on the other end of the room opened and a woman burst out of it.

"Charlie!" she trilled. "I can't believe you're getting married!"

"Meredith," Charlie smiled, standing up.

Stacey got a good look at Meredith, apparently the golden girl of wedding planning. She was rail thin and tottering on four-inch-high heels. She was also a lot older than Stacey had been expecting, seeing as her hair was completely white and skin wrinkled in places. Her face was frozen, as if she had injected more Botox in it than necessary, especially since there were still deep lines around her mouth. On top of that, she was a hideous shade of orange, as if she lived for fake tanning.

"Is this the woman who stole your heart?" Meredith cooed, turning to Stacey.

"The one and only," Charlie said, gently shoving her forward.

She stuck out her hand toward Stacey. There were massive rings on each finger, all of them sparkling under the lights of the office. She shook Meredith's hand, which was freezing cold.

"Great. Amazing. Wonderful," she kept adding on adjectives as her eyes raked over Stacey.

She felt exposed in front of this woman, even though Meredith looked ridiculous. Stacey was now hyper aware of her size next to how freakishly skinny this woman was. She pushed her concerns to the side. Now was not the time to let them get to her.

"Come on back to my office, darling, we must speak," she said, resting her hand on Stacey's shoulder and steering her down the hallway as if she were a car.

She glanced behind her to see Charlie following. He wore a bemused expression on his face as if he was getting a kick out of all of this. They went into the first room. The windows had the blinds raised up, allowing them to see the view of the river that cut through the city.

On the walls were photographs of happily married couples. There were fresh flowers on the desk, filling the room with a pleasant scent. Stacey and Charlie sat down on the opposite side of the desk as Meredith held a tablet in her perfectly manicured hands.

"Okay, hit me. What are you thinking? What do you envision?" She swept one of her hands in the air and the bangles on her arm jangled loudly.

Stacey glanced at Charlie who spoke first.

"Well, we don't have anything particular in mind. We don't even have a date set."

Meredith drummed her fingernails against her desk. They were long and fake, making clickity noises that sounded like a typewriter. She glanced at a calendar.

"Have you thought about a winter wedding?"

"That's really close," Stacey remarked. "Is that even possible?"

Meredith laughed loudly, as if Stacey had said something very funny. "Dear, I can make anything possible. What about January? Holidays are over. Everyone is winding down. It'd be nice then." She had already turned her attention to her tablet, swiping her bony fingers across the screen.

Charlie looked at her and asked, "What do you think?"

Stacey wasn't sure what to think. To be honest, the entire thing was a bit overwhelming.

"I can get you January twentieth at the House Gardens," Meredith declared.

"House Gardens?" Stacey asked.

Meredith lowered the tablet and smiled at the two of them. "I like this girl." She pointed at Stacey as if she was declaring something. "She's cute. She's fresh."

Even though it was a compliment, it felt more as if she were being called cute for not understanding what the House Gardens was.

Charlie cleared his throat and said, "The House Gardens is about an hour away. It's a lush estate filled with flowers and amazing landscapes. It's a hotel. A retreat."

"An hour away?" Stacey asked, thinking about the logistics of having a wedding there.

Meredith slid the tablet across the desk and tapped her finger on the screen, "Look, look!"

Stacey did. The screen was full of images. She gingerly held the tablet and looked at them. The estate was old fashioned, like something out of a novel. It looked faintly like the manor that Terry lived in, only draped in bright colors surrounded by beautiful vivid grounds. The images of the gardens were especially striking. All sorts of different flowers and plants sprawled across it. There was also a view of the ocean, twinkling like a gem.

"Wow," she said and meant it – it was stunning.

Meredith rattled on, "Make a weekend of it. The estate can only hold three hundred guests, however, so we will have to trim the guest list."

She froze and looked up, "Three hundred?"

Meredith pouted, looking childish for a woman her age. "Ah, I know it will be hard. But I think we can manage it."

"No, no, I mean – we aren't inviting three hundred people. We aren't going to be even close to that," Stacey remarked, turning to look at Charlie.

He didn't reply. He was looking at her a bit uncomfortably before he finally said, "How many were you thinking?"

"I don't know." She began to mentally count on her fingers. "Maybe like twenty?"

"Twenty?" Charlie exclaimed at the same time Meredith did.

"Yeah, why?" She looked at the two of them, confused. "Charlie… how many were you expecting?"

"I had it pegged for around two hundred and fifty to three hundred," he admitted.

This time it was Stacey's turn to exclaim. Meredith swept the tablet out of her hands and smiled at them.

"My, my, lots to discuss! I'm sure you two will agree on a guest list! The House Gardens then?"

Charlie looked at Stacey, who wasn't sure what to say. She couldn't imagine having that many people attending their wedding. Meredith, sensing the mood change, stood up.

"Excuse me for a moment," she said politely and shut the office door behind her.

"Charlie, that is way too many people," Stacey said as soon as the door closed. "I don't even know that many people."

"It'll just be business people mostly. Especially since I am starting the investment firm. Inviting them to our wedding would be prudent."

She scowled. "Our wedding shouldn't be about business deals."

"No, no, that isn't what I meant," he said hastily. "I just meant that I think everyone being involved would be good all around. You can invite anyone you want too."

"That's like five or six people," Stacey protested. "So, what, two hundred and forty-five of them will be for you?"

"You have distant family though. Cousins."

"That I haven't spoken to in years!"

Charlie reached for her hand and looked her in the eyes. "I know it's a big deal. January is soon and it's a bit daunting to think it's coming that quickly. But I want to give you the best. Including a big wedding. We'll cut it down. A hundred people, tops."

"That's a bit better," she said, feeling her will start to give.

Charlie smiled. "Perfect. I'll just figure out who to not invite."

"Your brother," she joked, and Charlie cracked a smile.

As if she knew the topic had been resolved, the office door opened and Meredith breezed into the room. She sat behind the desk and smiled brightly.

"All set?"

"Yes," Stacey said firmly. "Book the House Gardens."

"Perfect!" Meredith trilled.

Charlie met her eyes and smiled.

Chapter Ten

When they got back to Charlie's penthouse, Stacey was in a good mood. She had felt overwhelmed by the wedding plans when she had first met Meredith, but at least now it was being taken care of by someone who knew what they were doing. The House Gardens was beautiful. Even though the guest list was still too large, she could deal with it. It was still going to be their special day, no matter what.

Charlie had been saying as much as they walked into the living room. It was Stacey who saw Eric first. He was in the living room, flopped down on the couch, making himself at home. The TV was on but muted, and he was flipping through the channels at a rapid rate.

"Charlie… Charlie." She had to say it twice to get him to stop talking and look to where she was pointing.

He turned around and stared at Eric on the couch. Eric stopped flipping channels. He had a bag of chips in his lap, and had shoved a handful into his mouth as he waved at them with his free hand.

"What the fuck are you doing in here?" Charlie demanded.

"Whoa," Eric said through a mouthful of chips, "Is that any way to greet your brother?"

Charlie stalked over to the couch and yanked the bag of chips out of Eric's hands. He protested as Charlie tossed them on the coffee table.

"Why are you here?" he asked again.

Eric swallowed the chips. "What do you mean? You invited me."

Charlie's brow furrowed. "No, I didn't."

"Yeah, you did. Remember, when you told Dad you were leaving the company? You said you'd train anyone who was taking over. Well, you're looking at him."

Stacey heard Charlie scoff before replying, "I was hoping Dad was actually going to pick someone capable to run it."

Eric ignored the jab and turned his head to look at Stacey. She felt her insides twist a little at the sight of him. She could recall the slap she had given him and his last words. *Well, you sure showed me.*

"Hey there, future sister-in-law."

"Eric," she said with a slight nod of her head.

"Get out. Get a hotel. You aren't staying here."

"Dad said I have to."

"I don't care," Charlie snapped, "You're not staying here."

"Why, too cramped for three people?"

"Stacey doesn't live here, but anywhere with you is too cramped."

"Wait, wait, wait," Eric said, holding his hands up. "Stacey doesn't live here?"

Already sensing where this was going, she quickly walked forward. "There's that hotel down the street. Eric could stay there."

"I told you already. Dad said I have to stay here."

"And I told you that I don't care. So get your shit and go."

"That really hurts." He rested his hand on his heart. "That hurts deeply."

Charlie rolled his eyes. Eric suddenly showing up wasn't good for anyone, Stacey thought to herself. It was going to put Charlie on edge. Why did Eric have to appear now?

"How did you get in here anyway?" Stacey asked him.

"Dad has a key."

"For emergencies," Charlie added, "not so you could come in here and eat my chips."

"They were almost stale. I was doing you a favor."

"Out. Hotel down the street. Take it up with Dad if you don't like it."

Eric shrugged. "If you want. Don't know why you'd want to piss him off more though."

"Don't care," Charlie snapped, brushing his words aside. "I'm going to change. I want you gone by the time I'm done. We will discuss training at another time."

He stalked out of the room, leaving Stacey alone with Eric. He was getting to his feet, brushing crumbs off his shirt. He wore a baggy t-shirt and jeans with holes in them. Stacey couldn't imagine Charlie ever wearing such an ensemble.

He picked up a backpack and slung it over his shoulder.

"Is that all you brought?" she asked, not wanting to have any silence in between the two of them.

"Yeah. I can just buy whatever I need when I have to so…" he shrugged.

He started walking down the hallway. Stacey watched him go, then propelled herself forward toward him. Her fingers wrapped around the sleeve of his grungy t-shirt and yanked gently. Eric paused and looked over his shoulder.

"I'm sorry. For slapping you. I didn't get a chance to apologize."

For a few seconds, Stacey wondered if he was going to lecture her or tell her he was mad at her. She didn't want to make things worse between members of Charlie's family.

But then that lazy grin swept across Eric's face. "Worried, Stace?"

"It was wrong to slap you, but don't tempt me to do it again," she said firmly.

"Sure. Whatever you say," his grin only got wider and he leaned forward, bringing his voice down to a whisper, "I forgive you though."

The bedroom door slammed shut and Stacey took a step away from him.

"I better leave before I get in trouble," he said, turning around with a wave and heading toward the front door.

Charlie came out and stood next to Stacey, watching his brother depart. Once Eric was gone, Charlie sighed heavily.

"What the hell?" he mumbled.

Stacey turned to him. "Don't let him bother you. He knows all your weak points. I'm sure your dad sent him here just to bother you. Throw you off your game."

Charlie ran his hand over his face. "Probably. Just what I need right now."

"We can handle Eric. Together." She laced her fingers through his and smiled brightly.

He returned the smile. "You're right. Hey, we aren't at the manor. So we can handle it however we want."

"Exactly."

Charlie pulled her in for a kiss and all thoughts of Eric were quickly forgotten.

Chapter Eleven

Allison was coming over to meet Meredith and help plan some of the wedding details. She had put together that beautiful wedding on Tony's island, after all, and was better at this sort of thing. It was a no-brainer for Stacey to make her sister the maid of honor.

Meredith was meeting them at Charlie's place. He was still at the office, trying to finish up in order to make the meeting, although Stacey doubted that would be possible. At least Allison would be there. Meredith was slightly weird, and that unnerved Stacey. She knew that her sister would help make her feel more secure with any choices she made.

This was the first time Stacey had been here alone in Charlie's place. She had wandered through it, feeling a little like a ghost. Something was bothering her, although she couldn't quite put her finger on it. It was as if there were a small bud of anxiety in her chest, waiting to bloom.

By the time she sat down to get ready for Meredith, Stacey felt oddly jittery, as if she had drank two coffees one after another. She heard the elevator emit a soft ding and stood up, brushing her skirt smooth.

But it was Eric who waltzed into the room, not Meredith. Stacey tried to keep the scowl off her face.

She was determined to have the two brothers eventually patch things up. If she had to play peacemaker between them, she couldn't lob insults at him as casually as Eric did to everyone else.

"Eric!" she exclaimed stiffly. "What are you doing here?"

"Nice to see you too, Stace." He drawled on the nickname he had given her before cutting into the kitchen.

She trailed after him. He had opened the fridge and was rummaging around in it as if he lived here. Like the other day, Eric was dressed down, looking like he was going to spend all day playing video games instead of training for a job.

"Ah, there it is," he said from behind the fridge door and then poked his head out, dangling a can of iced coffee.

"You came all this way for an iced coffee?"

He shut the fridge door. "No. Charlie told me to meet him here."

"I have a meeting with the wedding planner in like, ten minutes here," Stacey said urgently.

"What, am I not allowed to see her or something? I might woo her over with my charms."

For someone who wasn't handsome and who easily looked older than Charlie by ten years, Eric sure was cocky.

"Somehow, I don't think she's your type," Stacey replied, going back into the dining room.

Eric opened up the can of iced coffee and took a swig. "Well, I'll stick around, anyway."

"Don't. My sister is coming by to help."

"She the one that married Jacob?" When Stacey nodded, he went on, "Man. Imagine being married to that guy. Talking to him is like watching paint dry. I would rather sit through a lecture from my dad than have to talk to Jacob."

"He's a good guy. Just a little dry."

"That's putting it mildly. He's like taking a depressant. I'm going to assume your sister is with him for the money or something like that."

Stacey looked over at him, alarmed. Even though it was true, she wasn't exactly comfortable with everyone guessing that so easily. Eric saw her face and let out a laugh.

"Don't worry. I'm sure no one else knows."

"How did you?" she asked slowly.

"Previous experience," was all he said when the elevator dinged again.

Stacey quickly excused herself and walked over to the foyer. Allison was there, dressed in a sleek purple pantsuit. Stacey couldn't recall ever seeing her sister wearing one of those before. Her hair was pulled up in a high ponytail and draped over one of her shoulders like a sleek curtain.

"Hey," she said to Allison and lowered her voice, "Charlie is going to try to make it. His brother is here."

Allison's eyebrows raised. "The one that everyone dislikes?"

"Yeah. He said he's waiting for Charlie, I guess. Listen, play nice, okay?"

"Play nice? Am I ten?"

Stacey cast a glance in the direction of where Eric was and replied, "No but he has a way of annoying everyone he comes in contact with."

"Sounds great to me. I love troublemakers."

She breezed past Stacey, leaving a trail of perfume wafting behind her as she went into the dining room. Stacey followed.

Eric was sitting at the dining room table, flipping through some of the wedding materials that had been strewn across it. He was looking at each one intently, as if any part of this wedding had anything to do with him.

He looked up and stopped when he saw Allison. He straightened in his chair and smiled at her easily. "You must be Meredith," he said in a tone of voice that Stacey had never heard from him before.

Of course, Stacey sighed inwardly. At first glance, most people didn't think Allison and Stacey looked related. The truth was most people couldn't see past their size difference. If they had, they would have seen that both sisters shared the same button nose and wide eyes. But Eric, clearly already thinking with his dick, wasn't interested in looking for any sort of family resemblance.

Allison sat down on one side of the table and flipped open one of the wedding magazines. She glanced up at him and replied simply with a "No."

Eric's gaze flicked between Allison and then back to Stacey. She could see it finally click. He leaned back in his chair and took a sip of his coffee.

"Of course. You must be Allison."

"That's right. And you're Eric. Heard a lot about you."

"Is that so? Good things, I hope," he said lazily, his gaze still fixed on Allison as if he was determined to flirt his way into a longer conversation with her.

"Not really," Allison quipped and then turned to Stacey. "Have you thought about a dress?"

Stacey risked a glance over at Eric who had turned his attention back to a magazine about flower arrangements, and then answered her sister, "Not really."

"You need to. This wedding is happening quickly. You need to make plans fast. I know you like to take your time, but big choices have to be made right away," her sister lectured.

That strange feeling was swooping over Stacey again. She clutched her stomach and swayed on her feet for a few seconds. Eric noticed first, and he squinted at her.

"Are you okay?"

"I think I'm going to be sick," she mumbled before taking off down the hallway.

There was a guest bathroom here. She pushed open the door and aimed her head over the toilet. Nothing happened. Stacey sunk to her knees, clutching the side of the bowl. Her knuckles were white from gripping it and she closed her eyes.

"Stacey?" her sister's voice rang out.

Stacey couldn't answer, afraid if she opened her mouth that she would start to throw up. Allison knocked on the door and then slowly opened it. When she saw Stacey with her head over the bowl, she sunk to the floor next to her and began to rub her back.

"Hey, whoa, are you alright?"

"Just feel sick. I thought I was going to throw up. Sorry, I'm fine," Stacey mumbled.

In the distance, she heard the elevator ding and tried to move. But Allison's hands were firmly on her.

"Eric can handle it," Allison said.

The thought of leaving Eric alone with Meredith wasn't exactly filling her with joy but she had no choice. Her sister got to her feet and went over to the sink. A few seconds later, she came back with a cup of water.

"Here, take a sip."

Stacey moved away from the toilet and pressed her back against wall. The tile was cold against her legs although she could feel a thin layer of sweat on the back of her neck. She took the cup from Allison and gulped it down. Allison got her more and handed it to her, warning her to sip this one.

Stacey did. She could hear mumbled voices – Meredith's high pitch, mile a minute voice and the low rumble from Eric.

After she finished the second cup of water, the sick feeling had mostly dissipated. Stacey exhaled slowly and handed the cup to a concerned looking Allison.

"I'm okay. I've been feeling off all day."

"Stress, I'm sure. You're probably overthinking this entire wedding."

"Yeah," she mumbled back, not wanting to go into how stressed she truly was.

Allison brushed a lock of hair from her face. The gesture was small but touched her anyway. It was just more proof of how much their relationship had changed over the last few months.

"Come on," she said to Stacey. "Let's go make sure Eric hasn't done anything awful."

"I thought you said he could handle it," Stacey replied, alarmed.

"Not sure what Eric could handle to be honest," Allison said and stood up, offering her hand to Stacey.

She took it, getting to her feet. The two of them headed toward the dining room.

Chapter Twelve

Stacey wasn't sure what she was expecting when she went into the dining room. Meredith looking horrified, perhaps, at having to talk to Eric for so long.

She certainly hadn't been expecting the two of them to be talking in front of the dining room table. They were standing close together. Meredith was twirling a lock of her vividly white hair and was laughing loudly. Eric was joking about something. When he finished, she laughed again and rested her hand on his shoulder.

He saw them first and looked at Stacey with the sort of expression on his face that said *what did you expect me to do?*

"Meredith, I'm so sorry for the delay," Stacey said, stepping in between them before Meredith could tackle Eric to the floor.

"I was sick," Allison lied swiftly. "My fault. I'm sorry."

Meredith, who had looked irritated at Stacey being late, suddenly softened when Allison blamed herself. She rested her hand on Stacey's shoulder.

"Things happen! Normally, I cannot stand anything off schedule but when family comes into play, what can you do!" she said loudly, a bright smile plastered on her face.

"Yes, of course," Stacey replied although she didn't know why it mattered if she were sick or her sister.

Somehow Allison had known though. She looked over at her sister who only shrugged. She would ask her later.

"Would you like something to drink?" Stacey asked Meredith, who was back to staring at Eric.

"Yes, please. Some water would be lovely."

"I'll help," Eric said quickly, using the opportunity to get a break from Meredith and her man-eating grin.

He followed Stacey into the kitchen. She turned to look at him and couldn't help but ask, "What the hell was that about?"

"Allison said to distract her," Eric said in a low voice. "She said Meredith drops clients all the time for the smallest things because she's super picky. If you were late, even if you were sick, Allison said Meredith would be extremely put off and drop you as a client. She sounds unreasonable as hell. Charlie really thought she'd be good for your wedding?"

Before this could turn into an anti-Charlie rant, she interrupted him, "I was maybe three minutes late."

"Ask your sister. I don't know. Anyway, I just started flirting." He shrugged, as if this made sense.

"Well, she seems super into you now."

"Can't blame her," he said as he opened the fridge to pull out bottles of water. "I'll just have to ward her off, I guess."

"Good luck with that."

"Are you sure you trust a woman so orange she looks like one of those cheese puffs to plan your wedding?" Eric suddenly asked her.

"She comes highly recommended," Stacey said defensively.

"Doesn't mean she's the right fit for you," Eric said and looked at her for a long moment before adding, "Come on. Wouldn't want to make her wait any longer."

He turned and left the kitchen. Stacey watched him leave, that queasy feeling back in her stomach. As much as she hated to admit it, Eric had a point.

By the time Meredith left, Stacey had a gigantic headache. It felt as if a tornado had swept through the dining room. The table was covered with plans and other ideas. There was a guest list in the middle of the table that was close to 300 people. Meredith had been trying to convince her to do a fireworks show, which Allison swooped in and put an end to after seeing how annoyed Stacey was getting.

Even though the fireworks show was off the table, there were still tons of other things that felt as if they were being planned with hardly any input from her.

When Meredith left, Stacey sat there, feeling dazed. She could hardly recall everything that had been planned.

Allison came back into the room from the foyer. "Guess we should clean some of this shit up."

"Guess so."

Eric followed in after her sister. "She asked for my number! Can you believe that?"

"Wow, you have a suitor," Allison replied.

He ran his hand over his face – a gesture that Charlie did regularly. At the memory of him, Stacey looked around the room. He hadn't shown up. She had been expecting that he wasn't going to be able to make it. Even so, she felt a kernel of disappointment in her chest. He was the one who had wanted this many guests, after all. If he had been here, maybe Meredith would have been more likely to listen to them about how they had agreed to trim it down.

"Not a suitor I want," Eric grumbled.

"Stacey, you should go lie down," Allison said, ignoring Eric, "you look awful."

She nodded numbly and got to her feet, "Yeah, I still don't feel a hundred percent."

"Eric and I will clean up. Go lie down."

Too tired, with a headache too strong to protest, Stacey nodded and headed off to Charlie's room. She opened the door and didn't waste any time sinking into his bed. She pulled the sheets over her.

For a few seconds, she thought that she wasn't going to be able to sleep but exhaustion overtook her and soon there was only darkness.

<<<>>>

Stacey had been dreaming that she was wading in a pool of water. The ocean was stretched out in front of her. Behind her was Tony's island. She didn't want to go back there. There was an urgency to her wading out deeper in the water, as if Tony's island was trying to pull her back.

She woke suddenly and blinked, trying to clear the fog from her brain. Stacey propped herself up and looked around. The window showed that it was dark outside now. The city twinkled against the darkness.

There was a loud voice followed by low rumbling. That must have been what had woken her up. Stacey threw her legs over the side of the bed and slid out of it, still feeling tired. The carpet felt plush against her feet and kept her footsteps silent as she padded out of the room into the hallway.

"Why aren't you listening to me at all?" It was Eric, sounding more annoyed than she had ever heard him before.

"Because you never say anything important enough to listen to," Charlie snapped in return.

"Will you stop already? Can't even talk to you at all about anything!"

Stacey hesitated. Part of her felt she should go back to bed but she remained glued to the spot. Charlie sounded angry and Eric sounded irritated. Instead of sneaking back into the bedroom, perhaps she should go in and try to break up the fight.

"Listen, that Meredith lady doesn't know what sort of wedding your fiancée wants. How can you want a wedding like that? Some big event?" Eric was saying to her surprise.

"Why don't you mind your own business? I don't remember asking you at all for any advice."

"Well, I'm giving you some because you clearly don't know what you're doing. I could see today that she didn't want a fireworks show or a huge number of guests or whatever else you're adding on."

Charlie's voice was a controlled fury. "If Stacey has an issue with the wedding plans, she can come to me."

"When? You aren't around. Weren't you supposed to meet me here and be part of the wedding planner meeting? But you didn't get home until an hour ago. When would Stacey have told you?"

Charlie said something that Stacey couldn't hear. Eric replied but their voices were distant now as if they were moving to the other side of the penthouse. She felt stuck in place, letting Eric's words wash over her.

It was true, wasn't it? The wedding wasn't what she wanted. It was growing, like a wild beast that couldn't be tamed. But Charlie had a point too – she hadn't told him. As far as he knew, she was only hesitant about the guest list.

Propelling herself forward across the carpet and walking down the long hallway, Stacey heard the voices grow louder. Charlie's office was close by and she could hear them talking in it. The door was halfway shut. Part of her told herself to wait until later to tell Charlie – but she was afraid if she didn't tell him right now that she never would. She would end up going along with this giant wedding she didn't want.

Before she could stop herself, she pushed the door open and stepped into the office. Charlie had his arms crossed and was leaning against the wall behind his desk. Eric was on the opposite side of the room, near one of the bookshelves. Both of them looked at her when she entered.

"Did we wake you up?" Charlie asked, looking abashed.

Stacey cleared her throat, hesitated for just a moment, and then said, "The wedding plans aren't turning out the way I want. It's getting out of hand."

Eric looked victorious, turning to look at Charlie who looked startled by her declaration. He moved toward her and grabbed her arm gently, steering her out of the room. He closed the office door, leaving Eric inside.

"What do you mean?"

"Exactly what I said." The words were rushing out of her mouth now. "It isn't just the guest list. The meeting with Meredith today was overwhelming. All the things she wants – the things Allison wants – the guest list is back up to three hundred because Allison wants to invite Jacob's business partners and investors. It doesn't even feel like our wedding. It feels like a party we're throwing so people can make business connections. Including you," she added gently, remembering how Charlie had said he wanted to invite people who could help his new investment firm.

Charlie looked stunned and his arm dropped from her side. "I had no idea."

"It's okay. I didn't say anything. I should have brought it up again."

"I just assumed. Big weddings… that's what everyone wants, right? I'm sorry," he said. "I didn't mean to upset you."

"I know you meant well. And I thought it would be fun too. But the thought of throwing this massive wedding… Meredith actually had a list of people we should invite and their personality quirks that we should 'tend to'."

Charlie ran his hand over his face. "That's not what I want either. Listen, we'll let it all go. We won't have a wedding like that. We'll do whatever you want. Small wedding. Handful of people. No people at all. We can just go to the courthouse instead."

Stacey looked up at him when he said the last word. He studied her closely.

Then he nodded. "That's right, the courthouse," he said again, this time more confidently.

A buzz of energy swept through her now all the way down to her toes. She couldn't help but smile up at him. "Yes, the courthouse."

Charlie bent down to kiss her when the office door flew open. Eric stood in the doorway. He still had that smug look on his face. Maybe she should have told Charlie when Eric wasn't around, Stacey thought as she looked at his face. Surely Eric was going to use this to drive Charlie even crazier.

But it was too late now.

"You can't just lock me in a room like I'm a kid," Eric scowled. "I'm going to the hotel."

"Good riddance," Charlie sneered.

"You guys, please," Stacey sighed.

Eric wriggled in between the two of them, breaking up their hug as he headed down the hallway. Charlie shook his head and went back into his office, calling Stacey after him. She turned to watch Eric leave. He turned around and began to walk out of the hallway, shooting her a wink before he turned forward and headed into the living room.

Chapter Thirteen

"Are you sure about this?" Charlie asked her for the thousandth time today.

"Yes," Stacey repeated through her smile.

He nodded and exhaled slowly. The car was winding through the city to the courthouse downtown. He was dressed in a suit but kept playing with his tie nervously. Stacey, however, remained calm. She had felt ill earlier in the morning, but it had passed quickly. Now that she was going to marry Charlie, all she could feel were butterflies in her stomach.

It had been five days since they had agreed to forego the large wedding they were planning with Meredith, and had opted for a quiet ceremony at the courthouse instead. Stacey would have been fine going the very next day. But they had to get the wedding license and find rings. Not only that, but Allison was travelling with Jacob out of town for a couple of days and demanded to be there.

"You need a witness," she had proclaimed on the phone, "and I'm the only one who counts."

Stacey had relented. She wanted Allison there. It was the other two hundred and ninety-nine people that she could live without.

Now they were on their way to the courthouse. It was cold outside today with the tree branches stark and a wind slicing its way through the city. Stacey hardly felt it. She was buzzing with excitement.

"Allison is meeting us there, right?" asked Charlie.

"Yeah. She's bringing Jacob as well."

"Great. Are you nervous? I'm nervous," he said.

Stacey smiled. "If you're nervous about this, imagine if we had been married in front of that enormous crowd of people."

"Stupid idea in hindsight." He exhaled slowly through his mouth. "This is better. I can panic in peace."

"I won't tell anyone," Stacey joked, leaning forward and kissing him gently on the cheek.

Charlie turned to look at her. "You look beautiful."

"Thanks. It isn't as extravagant as the dress Meredith would have wanted but I still love it," she replied, gesturing to the simple white dress she was wearing underneath her coat.

Stacey did love it. She had found it downtown while looking for something understated yet pretty. It wasn't technically a wedding dress, but she felt like a bride in it. It had long sleeves made out of lace and beads along the top. In her lap was a small bouquet of red roses that Charlie had given her. She had splurged and gotten her nails done that morning. They were red to match her flowers and reflected the light back at her from the shine of the lacquer.

The car pulled into the parking lot of the courthouse and the driver parked near the front. Charlie got out of the car first and went over to the other side, helping her out of it. The wind cut through her coat and she shivered.

"Winter is definitely coming," Charlie remarked as he pulled his own jacket tighter around him.

"Let's get inside. My toes are going to freeze off." She gestured to her open toed shoes.

He gripped her hand which was warm and a little sweaty. He was really nervous, Stacey thought, as she glanced at him. They walked into the courthouse. Allison was already in the lobby, talking Jacob's ear off. He was standing stiffly next to her, still as pale and dull-looking as ever.

When Allison saw the two of them, she cut her conversation short and rushed over. She crushed Stacey in a hug so hard that she thought her bones were going to pop.

"You look beautiful. Honestly. That dress is really nice."

"Thanks," Stacey said as Jacob went over to Charlie to offer his congrats.

"Come on. I already looked, and we have to go to the second floor. Are you ready?" Allison said, grabbing her wrist and pulling her forward.

Charlie followed at her heels. Jacob had launched into a story about the tea company. Stacey could tell that Charlie was barely listening, just nodding his head a lot. She glanced over at Allison as they piled into the elevator.

She clapped her hands together. "Alright, second floor," she declared so loudly that Jacob stopped speaking as she pressed the button.

The ride was fast, and soon enough they were in a small waiting room. It was empty except for one person.

"What is he doing here?" Stacey asked, wondering if Charlie had invited him.

"No idea," he mumbled before stalking over to where his brother stood.

Eric wasn't dressed up. He was wearing jeans and a baggy yellow t-shirt with some logo Stacey didn't recognize. He had his hands shoved in his pocket. From here she could see the pack of cigarettes in his pocket, straining the fabric. The jeans looked new, Stacey noted, as if he had decided to buy them just for this occasion.

"I should go over there in case Charlie decides to swing," Stacey said to her sister and quickly hurried over.

"–not invited." Charlie was finishing up his lecture.

Eric saw Stacey and smiled brightly at her, as if his brother hadn't just been ranting at him. "You look lovely."

“Thank you.”

“You need to go.”

“You need a witness.”

“We have them.” Charlie jerked his head in the direction of Allison and Jacob.

“How did you even find out about this?” Stacey asked curiously.

Eric rolled his eyes. “Meredith. She got my number somehow, can you believe it? She called me up after you let her go. She was spitting mad. Ranting about how she had been disrespected. Anyway, she let it slip that you two were running off to the courthouse sometime this week. After she propositioned me,” he had to add.

“Did you say yes?” Stacey wondered at the same time Charlie asked, “How did you find out the time?”

Charlie glanced over at her as if to say *who cares* that Meredith had any interest in Eric. She shrugged and said, “I think it’s pretty funny she’s so into him.”

“Bribes. We have a lot of money, in case you forgot, brother,” Eric responded to Charlie first before looking at Stacey. “And no. I had to let her down. Which just made her even angrier.”

“Some things just aren’t meant to work out,” she joked.

Eric laughed at that and even Charlie looked amused before shaking his head and trying to scowl. Stacey rested her hand on his arm to get his attention.

"Just let him stay."

"What?"

"He's your brother. That has to count for something."

"Yeah, come on. I'm your brother," Eric chimed.

Stacey shot him a look that said *shut up, you aren't helping* before turning back to look at Charlie.

"You should have someone of your own at the wedding too. Even if it is Eric."

Charlie paused and then relented, tossing his hands up in the air. "Fine. Fine, he can stay."

"Great," Eric replied, rubbing his hands together.

Someone tapped Stacey on the shoulder. "Sorry to interrupt the family reunion but can I talk to you for a second?"

It was Allison.

"How long until your wedding?" she asked.

Charlie looked at his watch. "Twenty minutes."

"Great, come with me," Allison said, yanking on Stacey's arm toward the hallway.

Confused, Stacey let herself be pulled along. They stopped in front of the bathroom and Allison opened it, pushing Stacey inside. The bathroom wasn't one of those with a lot of stalls but simply a small tiled room with a sink and a toilet. The lighting in it made Stacey look ghastly and she avoided looking in the mirror.

"Okay, what is going on?" Stacey asked, crossing her arms.

Allison was rummaging around in her purse. After a couple of seconds, she pulled something out and handed it to her. Stacey blinked and took it slowly, looking down at it.

"A pregnancy test?"

"You've been sick lately, right?"

It was true. The past few days, Stacey had been feeling ill, even throwing up a couple of times. But she had chalked it up to stress from the wedding. She suddenly felt dizzy.

"Yeah but…"

"Just take it."

"Why now? This could wait."

"You probably waited too long already." She began to feel around Stacey's belly, as if she was far enough along and the baby bump would be easy to feel.

Startled, she smacked Allison's hands away. "Stop! Stop it, you weirdo!"

Allison dropped her hands and laughed. "Whatever. You know it's true. Pee on the stick so you can see if you're pregnant or not. Rather you know now than go into your wedding completely unaware of what's happening with your own body."

"I'm telling you. It's just stress," Stacey said stubbornly as Allison turned to face the corner.

She leaned against the sink, opened the package and read the instructions. She suddenly felt very nervous. Her hands were shaking slightly. She hadn't considered being sick with having anything to do with being pregnant. The instructions seemed to swirl in front of her eyes. She closed them briefly and refocused when she opened them again and looked at her sister.

"I can't pee with you nearby," Stacey snapped.

"Why not?"

"Wait outside. Go stand guard or something."

"Fine, fine." Allison left, closing the bathroom door behind her.

In the sudden silence of the bathroom, Stacey exhaled slowly. Of course her sister couldn't have let this wait. Finding out now or finding out tonight – did it matter? Apparently, this was so urgent that it absolutely had to happen right now, even though Allison had had an entire week to bring this up.

Since Allison had left, it was easier to do the test. Afterward, she knocked twice to let Allison know to come back in. Then she thrust the stick toward her.

"What? I don't want it, fool," Allison said with disgust. "It's covered in your pee. Rest it on the counter."

Stacey obeyed and then asked, "What did you tell the others?"

"Said it was pre-wedding girl stuff." She shrugged. "Charlie is too nervous to care. Eric is too involved in bothering Charlie. And Jacob is just Jacob."

"How is he lately?" she asked, trying to whittle the wait time down with small talk.

"He's okay. He still tends to drone on, but I've been trying to help him see you don't have to yammer on to fill up the silence. It's good to let things breathe."

"Is it weird? Being married to him? Especially when you don't…" She made a small gesture with her hands that really didn't mean anything.

"Love him? I've come to respect him in his own way just like he has with me. I help him with the business sometimes. I think he likes the fact that I'm always honest with him, no matter what. I don't think he gets that with the people who he works with."

"Sounds like everything worked out then."

"Of course it did!" her sister replied flippantly. "I knew it would."

"Right. You always had things figured out."

"Not really. I just had something I was fixated on. Money. Power too, in a way. But this is your day, not mine. Are you nervous?"

"I was before. Now I'm extra nervous," Stacey said, glancing over at the pregnancy test.

"What if it's positive?"

She ran her hand over her belly. "Then I guess I'm having a baby."

Allison smiled. "Tina would be so happy about that. She always wanted you to have kids."

This surprised Stacey. "Really? I didn't know that. She never mentioned anything like that to me."

"Yeah, she would talk about it sometimes. I don't think she ever expected me to have children, so she was hoping you would."

Silence filled the space between the two sisters before Stacey said quietly, "I miss her."

"Me too," Allison replied honestly and then looked at the small watch on her wrist. "Time to check."

Stacey blew air out of her mouth and turned around to the counter. Her sister stood behind her nervously. She reached out for the test and looked at it. In the tiny screen of the stick, a small plus sign had appeared.

Allison exclaimed something, but Stacey heard a roaring in her ears. She couldn't believe it. She had thought for sure she was just stressed out.

"Hey, hey," her sister's voice was coming back to her now, "are you okay?"

"Just surprised," Stacey said as she stared at the stick.

"Come on. You have to tell Charlie."

"What?" she replied, snapping out of her mood. "We have like ten minutes before our appointment."

"Plenty of time." Allison practically yanked her out of the bathroom.

Stacey was holding the stick in her hand, hardly noticing that she was being tugged back into the waiting room. Pregnant. She was pregnant! It hardly felt real.

Back in the waiting room, Charlie and Eric were listening to Jacob tell a story. Stacey glanced at Allison.

"So much for letting the silence breathe, right?" she joked.

Allison rolled her eyes. "Don't worry about him. Go, go!"

Charlie had seen her by now and was coming over to her. Stacey's heart began to pound in her chest as she stared at him. He looked at her worriedly.

"Are you okay?" He led her away from the rest of the group into the corner of the waiting room. "Are you having second thoughts?"

"No."

"Then what is it?"

His eyes fell on the stick she was clenching in her hand. He frowned in confusion and then attempted to take it away from her. Reflexes kicked in for some reason and Stacey held onto the stick tighter.

Charlie gently pried her fingers open yanked removed the stick. He raised it up to look at it. Stacey studied him silently. There were two seconds of him letting the information register and then his eyes widened in surprise.

"Is this yours?" he asked, lowering it.

"Well, it's covered in my pee," she blurted out.

"You're pregnant." It came out more as a statement than a question.

She nodded silently and watched him. Was he going to be angry? He hadn't ever brought up children before. But a smile broke out across his face, as radiant as the sun. Charlie leaned over and brought her in for a hug. He held her tightly before suddenly letting her go.

"Sorry. Sorry. The baby. I shouldn't be…" He trailed off and smiled at her again. "We're going to be parents."

"Well, I'll go to the doctor. To confirm it," she said quickly.

"I believe it's right." He smiled at her.

Allison came over then. "Sorry to interrupt but we have to get going. They called your name already."

Charlie looked back at Stacey. She was so nervous that she thought she might faint. Her brain was battling so many different emotions that her head felt light. Charlie grabbed hold of her hand tightly, as if he was never going to let go.

Together, they headed toward the room to be married.

Chapter Fourteen

The next week, Allison hosted a small get together at Jacob's place. It was mostly a business dinner, but Stacey was looking forward to going anyway. She liked seeing her sister. On top of that, she had been so busy since she had gotten married that she hardly had any time to enjoy herself.

After moving in with Charlie, Stacey had put her apartment up for sale. It felt odd saying good-bye to the place. She had cried on the floor of what had been Tina's room and had trailed through the apartment like a ghost. There had been a lot of memories, both good and bad.

On top of moving, she had been helping William at work. Stacey had found herself hitting a groove there that made the long days go by quickly. She was working quickly, keeping herself organized and task-oriented. It felt different from the other jobs she had, even the short time she worked for Tony.

After going to the doctor and confirming her pregnancy, Stacey knew there was even more that would have to get done. They would have to redecorate one of the rooms for the baby, for one thing. Stacey had to deal with being sick in the mornings, and she worried about feeling even worse as more time went on.

Even so, she was in a fantastic mood when they arrived at the small party. Her sister was glowing in a light blue dress lined with lace. Jacob was by her side as always. To her relief, there were no signs of Tony or Adele. She hadn't seen them since the last party here, when Charlie had proposed.

Eric had wangled his way into the event. Stacey assumed that it was because her sister seemed to have a soft spot for him, although who knew why. Her sister loved troublemakers and general annoyances; both which described Eric.

Charlie had been busy trying to train Eric on the business, but had told her he wasn't having much luck.

"It's like he doesn't care at all," Charlie had said to her the other night. "I mean, he's made it perfectly clear he wanted this over the years. Now he has it and he's acting like it's ruining his day."

"I don't get it," Stacey had replied. "Doesn't make much sense. Are you worried?"

"When it comes to Eric, I'm always worried," he said with a resigned tone.

Now, however, he offered a small wave to his brother from across the room. Eric waved back but was clearly busy trying to charm a tall, pretty woman.

"Is that all your brother does?" she asked Charlie.

"Flirt? Yeah, basically. Never understood how it comes so easily to him. I always tried to be careful. People hear you have money and that's all they care about."

Stacey watched Eric laugh and lean in toward to the woman. He had a slight smile on his face and was holding a glass of whiskey in one hand. *Because he doesn't care if they just want his money,* she thought to Charlie, *he doesn't care about much at all.*

"Great! You're here!" Allison had seen them and swooped over, hugging Charlie and kissing Stacey on her cheek. "I put some sparkling grape soda aside for you," she said in a low voice. "That way you look like you're drinking and no one will notice you aren't. Better to keep the pregnancy a secret as long as you can."

"You sure know your stuff," Charlie replied.

"Are you telling me that I'm wrong?" Allison asked, almost defensively.

He shook his head. "No, not at all. You're right. We don't want everyone to know yet."

"Great, you go mingle," she ordered Charlie. "I want some time with my sister."

She pulled Stacey toward the kitchen. Stacey waved at Charlie and allowed herself to be pulled inside. The massive kitchen was brimming with servers and people preparing food. They greeted Allison when she came in.

"Why are you always pulling me around like a dog?" Stacey joked, loosening her arm from Allison's grip.

"You overthink things and move too slowly," she replied as she opened the fridge.

"Good point."

Allison pulled out the soda and poured her some in a champagne flute and handed it to her. Stacey thanked her and took a sip.

"Do you remember…" Allison started to say.

"Drinking this stuff as kids and pretending it was wine?" Stacey finished.

Allison laughed, "We drank so much our mouths were purple. We looked so silly."

Stacey grinned, replying, "We had purple tongues for hours. Tina was so annoyed."

Allison looped her arm through Stacey's. "Come on. Let's head out."

<<◇>>

Halfway through the party, Stacey was actually feeling a little queasy. It didn't help that, like always, more people had shown up, making the penthouse feel crowded. She brushed it aside. The last thing she wanted was to leave early.

She looked over at Charlie and Eric, who were currently laughing at the fact they had stuck a sticker on Jacob's back and he hadn't noticed. Both were drunk. It was such a rare sight to see them both getting along that there was no way Stacey was going to cut that short.

Charlie was laughing so hard that he snorted which only made Eric laugh harder. She couldn't hear what they were saying, but they kept gesturing to Jacob. The sticker they had stuck to his back was of a baby wearing a silly party hat, exclaiming 'Happy New Year!' Stacey had no idea where in the world they had found something like that.

Jacob had no idea the sticker was on his back. The longer it went on, the more the two brothers laughed. Stacey tried to find the resemblance between them. Their eyes crinkled the same way when they were laughing, she decided. But that was about it.

Allison came out of the side hallway and saw what they were laughing about. Her face flushed and she stormed over to Jacob. Then she casually circled her arm around his waist and swiftly pulled the sticker off. Jacob didn't notice anything at all.

Bunching up the sticker, she moved away from Jacob and went over to the two brothers. Stacey watched as she flicked the sticker at Eric and began to lecture the two of them. They were too drunk to care however, and Allison gave up.

That was when she saw Stacey sitting in the corner. She went over to her and sat in the chair next to her.

"I saw," Stacey said before her sister tried to explain.

"What is up with them?"

"They're drunk."

"And getting along. And making a fool out of Jacob."

Stacey took a sip from her glass. Peering over the rim, she widened her eyes innocently to hide the fact that she found it amusing.

Allison shrugged, "At least they're getting along, right?"

"Do you think it'll stick?" Stacey asked curiously.

"No, probably not. Everything is better when you're drunk. But reality will kick in eventually."

"Yeah," Stacey replied, feeling disappointed. "True, I guess."

She looked back over at the brothers. Her stomach tightened hard suddenly, and she winced and rubbed her belly.

"You okay?" Allison asked.

"Crowded in here."

"Tell me about it. We're going to run out of food," she grumbled.

Stacey forced a smile through her discomfort but managed to say, "I'm okay. Go, tend to the guests."

"Alright. If you need me though, find me."

"Will do."

Stacey watched her sister head back into the fray. She turned to look over at Charlie, but the brothers were gone. She stood up to try to find them and make sure they weren't getting into more trouble. When she stood up, however, a wave of dizziness swept over. Stacey closed her eyes. It was hot in here, she realized.

Charlie and Eric were big boys. They could handle themselves. In the meantime, she needed some fresh air. She walked out to the balcony. There was a cluster of people on one side of it, smoking cigars. Stacey opted to go to the opposite side where it was more secluded.

She pulled a chair close to the edge of railing of the balcony and sat down. Allison had a great view. Even now, married to Charlie and pregnant with his child, there were some things about her new life that still took her by surprise. Small things, like a view such as this, was one of them.

It was chilly outside with winter quickly approaching. But Stacey's skin felt hot and the cold against her skin was pleasant. Her stomach was grumbling, as if she hadn't eaten just an hour ago. The last thing she wanted was to be sick here tonight. Not with Charlie having a good time.

There was a loud boom of laughter and Stacey looked over at the group of people on the other side of the balcony. Eric was in the middle of them now, a cigar hanging out of his lips as he told them a story. She couldn't hear it, but it must have been hilarious. She wondered where Charlie was.

Eric finished the story and was listening to someone else speaking when he saw Stacey. He took the cigar out of his mouth and handed it to a woman next to him. Then he walked over to her.

"Where's Charlie?" she asked him.

"He's inside. He drank way too much and thought he was going to be sick," Eric grinned.

"And you?"

"I'm drunk but I never get sick."

"Is that so?" Stacey asked dryly.

Eric pulled a chair up next to hers and sat down. He was fiddling with his lighter, most likely resisting the urge to smoke around her.

"What are you doing out here?"

"I didn't feel too well inside. It was a bit too crowded."

"You should tell Charlie so you two can leave before you both start getting sick at the same time," he remarked, looking over the balcony.

"Yeah, I will," she said, trying to ignore the sick feeling that was blooming in her stomach.

"So," he said, leaning back in his chair. "You excited? For the kid, I mean. I heard that's exciting, anyway."

"Yeah, I'm really excited," Stacey replied honestly. "I still can't believe it."

"Lots of changes coming," Eric said and something in his voice made her look at him more closely.

"Yeah. All good changes though. Even for you. I mean, you're finally getting to control the company, right?"

Eric let out a dry laugh, "Yeah, sure."

She frowned, "What does that mean?"

He cleared his throat and then leaned toward her. She could smell the booze wafting off of him. When he spoke, she could smell it off of his mouth.

"It means that this is all bullshit."

"What is?"

"All of it. Didn't I tell you before? Dad isn't just going to let Charlie walk away. He'll interfere with Charlie soon enough. Then he will have to come back to the company. He'll become president again."

"Why? I don't get it. Why doesn't your dad just let it go?"

"No one goes against our father, Stace. No one. Not even his sons."

"That's why you aren't taking anything seriously," she said, realization dawning on her.

He snapped his fingers. "Bingo," he slurred.

Stacey shook her head. "Charlie needs to know this."

She went to get up when Eric's hand grabbed her arm. The touch was sudden, and she stopped, looking down at him.

"Didn't you warn him?"

"What?"

"I told you this before. About Dad not letting this slide." His voice was a little more urgent now. "You told him, didn't you?"

"What? No." She sat back down next to Eric because he looked as if he was turning an ugly shade of green. "I just thought he would know."

"I told you so you would tell him!"

"You tell him!" she snapped. "How was I supposed to know you meant for me to tell him?"

"Why didn't you tell him?" Eric asked, his head lolling drunkenly to one side before turning to look at her.

Stacey hesitated and then replied, "He doesn't like us getting along, I think. It bothers him. I thought if he knew we talked about it, he'd be angry."

Eric stared at her but didn't saying anything. He looked as if he wanted to say something, but no words came out. Stacey stared back at him for a few seconds before standing up.

"I have to get Charlie," she said, fighting another wave of dizziness.

Eric stood up now. "I'll come with you."

They walked back into the apartment. The crowd had thinned a little. Allison was talking to someone near the kitchen. Jacob was sitting at a table with an old man. They were looking at what appeared to be a map. Stacey didn't even want to know what that was about.

They headed down one of the hallways. Stacey thought of how she had been down this hallway before. She had been looking for Charlie then too. Tony had been trailing after her and had cornered her in the library. She pushed the thought from her mind.

They stopped at one of the bathrooms and knocked. There was no answer.

"Charlie? It's Stacey."

This time there was a groaning noise and the door unlocked. She pushed herself in and found Charlie slouched over the toilet, looking worse for wear. Behind her, she could hear Eric snickering.

"Come on," she said, knowing she wasn't going to be able to discuss Terry with him in this state. "We're going home."

"Good idea. I think I drank too much," Charlie mumbled.

"Never could hold the booze," Eric boasted.

"Just shut up and help me," she said to him.

The two of them went over to Charlie and helped him to his feet. He leaned back against the wall and steadied himself on Stacey.

"Never seen you this drunk before."

"Eric brings the worst out in me," Charlie hiccupped.

"Are you going to tell him?" Eric nudged her.

She tried not to feel irritated and glared at him. She knew he was just as drunk but hopefully, Eric would get the point and shut up.

"Tell me what?"

"Nothing," Stacey replied.

But Eric was too drunk to let it go. He pushed past her and got in Charlie's face. "Dad is gonna fuck up your business."

"Huh?"

"Eric, not now," she snapped.

"No – yes, I mean. Yes, now. Dad isn't serious about me learning about the business from you. Or learning about it period. He said it's pointless," he slurred. "He's going to take away anyone interested in your company until you come crawling back to be president."

"What?" Charlie mumbled, his eyes widening drunkenly at the two of them.

Eric kept going on, much to Stacey's chagrin. "I shouldn't even be telling you this. I told Stacey and I thought – I thought she'd tell you, dude. You gotta come back or you'll just get run into the ground. Dad harps on you all the time but he doesn't want me in charge of the company!"

Charlie was looking at her now. "You knew about this?" he asked, sounding as if he was sobering up magically.

"He told me that your father was going to do something like this, yes, although I had no idea Eric wasn't taking it seriously for those reasons."

He nudged past Eric and came close to her. He stunk of alcohol and vomit, and his eyes were glazed over. That cold sick feeling was spreading across her body. Her back pressed up against the counter and she gripped it with her hands behind her.

"Why didn't you tell me?"

"I thought you knew."

Stacey felt as if someone had splashed cold water on her insides.

"Charlie, wait," she said, trying to explain. "I thought you knew going into it that your dad would be like this."

She couldn't bring herself to tell him just yet that she hadn't told him because he had already seemed to be jealous of Eric being friendly with her. The fact he had warned her had just seemed like it would upset Charlie. She had been trying to do the right thing. But he looked away from her.

Charlie shook his head and without another word he stumbled from the bathroom. She watched him go, feeling upset.

She spun on Eric who was slouching in the corner. "Why did you tell him?"

"I thought that's why we were going to find him," he said with eyes wide open.

"He's drunk! He didn't have to hear that now. I have to go get him," she mumbled mostly to herself and turned around.

"Stacey, wait," Eric said, clamoring after her before she could leave, "I have to tell you something. Don't go just yet."

She whirled on him, angrier than she should be and lashing out at Eric, "Let me tell you something. I am not a messenger. If you have to tell your brother something, then tell him yourself instead of going through me. I tried to do the right thing. I just didn't want to upset him. And now he's probably furious with me all because you didn't have the balls to do your own dirty work!"

Eric had the good sense to look abashed even though he was hiccupping now. "I'm sorry."

"I have to go get him. So whatever you have to tell me, tell me quickly." Her words were harsh even to her own ears.

"Stacey, listen, I…"

But she didn't hear whatever Eric ended up saying because suddenly her stomach kicked up in such pain that she doubled over, clutching her mid-riff. It felt as if her entire body was going to collapse into itself. She sunk to her knees.

Eric was panicked now, hovering over her and opening the bathroom door, calling for help. He sounded far away. Stacey was hunched over with her nose practically touching the floor. The pain was so intense that she was worried she was going to black out.

People were coming to the door now. She wasn't sure who was behind her. The only thing she could focus on was the acute pain in her body. Something else was nagging her at the back of her mind – a sensation that was sticking out from above the rest.

Her sister's voice swam to the front of her brain and Stacey managed to raise her face enough to look at her. Allison was asking her questions, but Stacey couldn't reply. Then Allison's eyes cast down and she made a horrified strangled noise.

Stacey looked down to see what had scared her sister. At first, she just saw something dark on the floor – a few spots, nothing more.

But then it clicked through the pain.

It was blood, dripping out of the bottom of her dress.

-To be continued in Book 5-

Book Five – Love Divine

Chapter One

"**WALK SLOWLY**. Maybe you should wait here. I can get a wheelchair."

"From where?" Stacey asked. "I'm fine, really."

Charlie frowned and reached out for her anyway. He slid his arm around her waist to help her walk into the lobby of their apartment complex. Stacey knew that she could walk fine without his help but didn't want to shrug him off.

She had spent the night in the hospital. There were those terrifying moments that Stacey had been utterly convinced something dreadful had happened to the baby. She felt sore all over as if a train hit her.

But the doctor said the baby was okay. She was a high-risk pregnancy and would have to take things slowly. He told her to cut back on work and stress. Stacey couldn't help but think of Charlie and his family, her new job with William, and Charlie's own investment firm starting up. Cut back on stress. How in the world was she going to do that?

There was no time to talk to Charlie about what his brother, Eric, had told her. Eric warned her that their father, Terry, was going to move against Charlie. At the time, Stacey decided not to tell Charlie because she didn't want to upset him. Now that Eric had drunkenly blathered about it, she saw it in a new light. Charlie perceived it as Stacey keeping a secret from him, something she only shared with Eric, his brother, of all people.

As they made their way up to the penthouse, she wondered how she should apologize and try to make what happened clear to him. Charlie, who became incredibly drunk last night, was now extremely hungover. His skin was sick looking, with a slight yellow tinge to it. His hair was messy and he still wore the same clothes from the other night. He was now drinking water and coffee non-stop. Both of them needed a nap.

At home, Charlie led her directly to bed. Stacey sunk into the massive bed gratefully, pulling the sheets over her. She knew that she needed to talk to him about Eric and what he had said, but she suddenly felt more exhausted than ever. Everything that had happened seemed to sweep over her all at once and she felt as if she had emotional whiplash.

"Charlie…" she mumbled as he crawled into bed next to her.

"It's okay," he whispered back and brought her close against him.

Stacey could hear the steady beat of his heart. Her eyelids closed without effort. All her limbs felt as if they each weighed a thousand pounds. Before she could utter another word, she fell fast asleep.

<<<>>>

In her dream, there was a baby crying in the distance. Stacey knew that this was hers. She was in Tina's old house, at the dining room table. She felt rooted to the chair as if she couldn't move. Next to her was Allison. She was ignoring her homework again, covering her page in doodles.

Stacey could hear the TV playing in the living room. Some part of her realized this was the night she found out about her parents' deaths. The baby cried louder in the distance.

Fighting against the pull that was keeping her to her chair, she managed to stand up. Allison didn't glance at her – it was as if Stacey wasn't even there. Stacey felt hot all over, as though she suddenly came down with a fever.

The phone rang. She knew what the news was going to be. Quickly, she darted out of the dining room. If she kept running, she wouldn't have to hear the news. She just had to keep moving.

She ran to the front door and yanked it open. Behind her, Tina was letting out a wailing cry. Stacey stepped outside and slammed the door shut. The front yard was covered in a thick layer of snow. The moon was covered by clouds and almost everything was dark.

She cut across the yard. The crying got louder now. She could see a cradle in the distance. She hurried, anxious to get to it.

But as Stacey approached the cradle, a sharp pain shot through her body. It felt like she was getting stabbed. Her knees weakened and she hit the ground. The snow around her turned red. She let out a gasp.

"You're okay! You're okay, Stacey. It was just a dream."

Stacey's eyes opened and she found herself staring up at Charlie. His arms were wrapped firmly around her, and he was clutching her close to his chest. Her breathing was coming hard and fast as if she just ran a mile. She could still see the snow around her, turning dark with her own blood as her baby in the cradle cried.

She shivered and said, "I'm okay. Sorry. Did I wake you up?"

"Yeah. You were making a whimpering noise." He pushed back a strand of hair that fell in front of her eyes. "You sounded terrified."

Stacey's mouth felt dry, as if it was stuffed full of cotton. The room was dark except for the hallway light shining through the crack in the door. They must have forgotten to shut it off when they got home.

"What time is it?" she asked.

"Little after three in the morning."

"And I woke you up. I'm sorry," she said again.

"Hey, it's okay. Really. Do you want to talk about the dream?"

Stacey thought about Tina answering that phone call that changed everything. The thought of her parents and Tina, now all gone, made her heart ache. She silently shook her head. Charlie nodded and then got out of bed.

"Need some water. Want some?"

"Yes, please."

She watched him go and tried to calm down her racing heart. She told herself it was just a dream. She had weird dreams all the time. This one was no different. How could she not have crazy dreams after what she just went through?

Stacey sat up and brought the blanket around her. It was slightly chilly in the room. She reached over to check her phone. There were two missed calls from Allison, who left shortly before Stacey was discharged from the hospital. She left only because Jacob's father recently fell and had been sent to a hospital out of state. Stacey ordered her sister to leave, telling her over and over again that she was fine and so was the baby. Stacey felt it was important for Allison to be with Jacob.

She made a mental note to call Allison first thing to try to calm her nerves. She could picture her sister right now, nervously pacing the hotel room, torn between her and Jacob.

Charlie came back with two glasses of water and handed one to her. Then he sat down next to her and took a swig from his glass. Stacey mumbled a thank you and drank half of her water in one gulp. She was incredibly thirsty for some reason.

"I shouldn't have stormed out of the party like that," he finally said.

Out of everything for him to say, Stacey was surprised by this. She wasn't even thinking about how he hadn't been there right at the start of things. She was too busy trying to form an apology in her head.

"You don't have to be sorry," she replied.

"Yeah, I do. If I'd stayed – if I'd stayed even a minute longer…" he trailed off.

Stacey grabbed his hand, shaking her head. "No, Charlie. It wouldn't have changed anything."

"If I hadn't gotten angry with you over what Eric said. Being drunk isn't an excuse. I should have stopped myself and discussed it with you. Instead, I got angry and you ended up in the hospital."

"One has nothing to do with the other," she said firmly.

But Charlie shrugged and looked morosely at his glass before saying, "Maybe not."

"They don't. And even if you were there, nothing would have changed. Eric found you a minute later, didn't he?"

"I know. I know it's pointless to beat myself up over it. I was terrified that you were hurt or something happened to the baby."

"Well, I'm okay. I just need to relax."

"You're so good at that," he joked and smiled at her.

"Well, just keep me in check." She poked his abs playfully and smiled back.

Charlie leaned over and kissed her gently before saying, "I'm sorry that I got angry. I'm basically sorry for the entire night. Made me remember why I don't drink like that."

"No, I'm sorry for not telling you about what Eric warned me about."

She hesitated for a moment and then decided to tell him the entire thing. She told him of how Eric had warned her about Terry not being pleased back in the hallway at the manor. She admitted to slapping him and feeling ashamed at having done so. Stacey then finished with Eric telling her that his becoming president was bullshit and wouldn't happen.

Charlie leaned back in bed. "I knew there must have been a reason why Eric wasn't taking things seriously. I mean, don't get me wrong. He never takes things seriously. But this was different. This was something he had been saying for years he deserved. It lands in his lap yet he doesn't want it? It didn't make sense."

"What are you going to do about your father?"

He shrugged. "Ignore him."

"No, Charlie, I'm serious."

"So am I."

Stacey shook her head. "Eric seems to be taking this really seriously. When he mentioned it in the hallway, I just assumed he was trying to start things and that you knew already what Terry was up to. But you don't. You could lose this entire business before it even gets off the ground."

"Stacey, do not worry about it. Please. It isn't going to help you at all to fret about it. Eric warned you, but I know now. I'll figure it out."

"I don't get why he didn't just go to you in the first place."

Charlie laughed at that. "Really? I do. He wanted to help me out but didn't want to come to me directly. Easier to go through you."

"I just thought…"

"Thought what?"

"Well, sometimes you seemed upset that Eric was speaking to me. So, I thought he told me this just to piss you off. As if he and I were close," she said this all quickly, as if she was yanking off a bandage that had been on for too long.

There was a small intake of breath from Charlie. For a second, Stacey was worried that she pissed him off. He was touchy when it came to Eric, who seemed to know every nerve to press against his older brother.

"Jealous. Maybe a little," he admitted.

"Why in the world? No offense but your brother is maddening, to say the least."

He chuckled. "Tell me about it. I don't know. I guess it's because I knew what he was doing. He was buddy-buddy with you. I've had it happen before where —" He cut himself off as if he was saying too much.

But Stacey pressed, "What? Had what happen before?"

As if remembering their last fight about him keeping things close to his chest, Charlie said quickly, "Him flirting with past girlfriends before. And I've had them… go for it."

Stacey was aghast, "What? How?"

"He's funny and charming. You've seen him. He enters a room like he owns it."

"So do you," she countered.

But Charlie shook his head. "No, Eric is different. He's cocky. He's got this sort of swagger to him that some women just eat up. Including some ex-girlfriends."

"So, what, exactly? You thought I'd be tempted?" Stacey asked, aghast.

"No! No, no, this is coming out wrong. There was no way I thought you'd ever make a move on Eric. But I didn't trust him with you. I could just picture him, feeding you all these little secrets or stupid notions. Suggesting I wasn't on your side. I didn't think he'd swoop in and kiss you or anything. No, I thought he'd just keep stirring the pot. Making you think I wasn't on your side when it came to my dad."

"So… when he told you that he warned me about Terry…"

"Drunken me just sort of panicked. I took that as a sign you two were getting close. That whatever Eric was scheming was working." He looked at her seriously. "I'm sober now though. I know that isn't the case. I know that I overreacted. I just…"

"What?"

"I just don't trust Eric with you."

"I know he's a cocky bastard, but I saw you two drunk together. You were laughing and having fun. Surely, somewhere deep down you two want to be like that all the time."

Charlie didn't reply. He shrugged a little and avoided looking at her.

But Stacey didn't want to drop it just yet. "You two are still brothers. There is still a connection there, somewhere. It's just gotten mangled up with everything going on."

"Stacey, I know what you're trying to do. And I appreciate it. Really, I do. But Eric and I aren't going to be like you and Allison. There isn't any understanding to be found between us. There's too much bad blood. And frankly, being around him this much lately has reminded me why we don't just casually hang out."

"I guess," she mumbled although she still wasn't convinced.

Charlie leaned over to her and kissed the top of her head, "Don't worry about me and Eric. I'm used to how we are. It's just how it has to be. We should try to sleep now."

She nodded and Charlie tucked her into bed. He curled up next to her. Stacey could feel the warmth from his body. Before she could say anything else, he was already snoring.

Yet Stacey couldn't fall asleep right off the bat. Her mind was swirling with all sorts of different things. She was worried about the baby. She was worried about work and Charlie. And even though he said there was no reconciliation with Eric, she wasn't yet convinced.

She focused on her breathing. It took a little while but eventually Stacey drifted back to sleep.

Chapter Two

"I'm okay. I promise. How is Jacob?"

"Alright. Actually," Allison lowered her voice, "it all feels weird. Like, we're all just waiting around for his dad to pass on. Maybe it's a rich person thing."

Stacey snorted, "I doubt it."

"Well, in any case, I'm just sitting here like we're on death watch. He's been sick for months, so no one is too surprised or anything. Jacob is pretty quiet. Honestly, I wish I was there with you."

"I'm fine, really."

"The doctor said no stress and to relax. You're shitty at both of those things," Allison replied.

"I'm a quick learner."

"Well, as soon as I get back into town, I'm keeping an eye on you. Strict bed rest. Going to corner William and make sure he doesn't keep you overworked."

"William was really sweet about the whole thing. Said I could work from home."

"You shouldn't be working at all."

"I'm not going to sit around and do nothing all day," Stacey replied, "so don't start."

She heard her sister sigh before saying, "We'll discuss it later. Keep me posted, okay?"

With the call over, Stacey leaned back against the couch. Charlie had gone into the office even though he hadn't wanted to. But Stacey didn't want to keep him. She was sure that whatever his father was planning was already underway.

Daytime television hadn't improved since the last time Stacey watched it. Charlie had every channel under the sun; the kind of selection that would have left Tina dizzy with options. However, Stacey ended up watching one of those terrible day time court room shows.

She was feeling restless - it snuck up on her. The thought of spending every day like this annoyed her. She was used to being on the go. For her entire life, Stacey worked as hard as possible. She put long hours in at William's diner. She worked at Tony's with the goal of achieving more. She was on the path she wanted until she lost her way with Tony.

Now, the idea of sitting around and letting life pass her by because she was on bed rest left a bad taste in her mouth. Her laptop was in the other room. She was going to check her e-mails at least.

She had just gotten up when the elevator made a soft noise and someone stepped in.

"Charlie," she sighed, "I'm fine. I told you. I can handle it."

"I'll let him know."

Eric came into the living room. He was awkwardly holding a vase of flowers and stood in the doorway. Stacey was surprised to see him. She hadn't seen him since the night in the bathroom.

"Eric, hey. What are you doing here?"

"Uh, these are for you. 'Get well' flowers. Or… 'Glad you're well' flowers? I don't know." He held them out at her and looked like a child holding out a test with a good grade on it.

Stacey took the vase from him gingerly. Eric ran his hands through his hair and looked away from her. The vase was brimming with freshly cut flowers, all vividly colored and beautiful to look at.

"Wow, thanks. You didn't have to do this," she replied.

"I did. I was a dick the other night."

"Just the other night?"

He looked abashed. "Well, I can't give you flowers for *all* the times I was a dick. I'd be giving you flowers all day and Charlie might get angry."

"You weren't that bad the other night. Just drunk."

"I wasn't *that* drunk, Stace. I remember you being furious with me."

It was true. She had flipped out on him, furious that he went to Charlie and babbled about their father. In hindsight, she should have kept her cool. Eric was drunk and wasn't thinking clearly.

She shrugged. "It's fine now." She turned around to go put the flowers on the coffee table.

Eric trailed after her. "You and Charlie talked?"

"Yeah. We're fine. We worked it out." She skipped the details of how Charlie didn't trust Eric or the fact she knew he slept with his ex-girlfriends.

"Great. Good." He shoved his hands into his pockets.

She frowned. "What's wrong with you?"

"Nothing. Nothing new, anyway. I just – it was scary, you know? You ending up in the hospital. I just wanted to make sure you were okay."

Stacey sat back down on the couch. "I'm fine. Thanks for checking in."

Before Eric could say anything, the elevator doors opened. This time it had to be Charlie. Eric straightened and took his hands out of his pockets. Any sort of vulnerability he was showing in giving her the flowers was quickly erased.

Charlie hurried in and stopped when he saw Eric. "Uh. Hi."

"Hey," Eric said stiffly.

Her mind flickered back to the two of them drunkenly laughing and she stood up. "Eric brought me get well flowers."

Charlie narrowed his eyes. "How kind of him."

Stacey held back a sigh and stared at Charlie directly. She was going to have these two get along. She just had to keep at it.

Something in her glare must have struck Charlie because he turned to Eric and said, "Nice of you."

Eric looked disarmed for a moment before mumbling a 'no problem.' Stacey took control of the conversation.

"You're home early."

"I wanted to make sure you were doing alright. And…" He hesitated and glanced over at Eric. "Weren't you supposed to be at the office?"

"Was I?"

"Yes," Charlie said, clearly trying not to lose his patience. "Stacey, can I speak to you in private?"

"Yeah, sure," she replied, confused.

She followed Charlie down to his office where the two brothers had been recently bickering. He closed the door behind her and sat down in one of the chairs. For the first time since he got home, Stacey got a good look at him. He looked deflated, as if someone had sapped all the energy out of him.

"What's wrong?" she asked, sitting in the chair next to him.

"I don't want to stress you out, but whatever Eric warned us about… it's already happening. I lost two investors today."

"Already? I thought things were going smoothly."

"Yeah. Probably too smoothly, now that I think about it. You know last night, how you mentioned I should talk to Terry?"

"Yeah."

"Well, I think I'm going to."

"What are you going to tell him?"

"I don't know yet. Something. I have to make him stop this stupid shit. What sort of father does this? Complains about how his son runs things and then tries to botch the son's plan to branch out?"

"Someone very controlling, I would imagine."

"Well, I'm going to head up to the manor tomorrow. I know Allison is out of town, but I could get –"

"Whoa, whoa. Wait. You think you're going to confront your father and leave me at home?" Stacey asked.

Charlie blinked. "You can't come with me. The doctor said no stress."

"It isn't me confronting my father. It's you," she replied.

"Even so! Last time we went to see my father, we fought. A lot. And you slapped Eric. Which is amazing, don't get me wrong. But it was stressful."

"I want to be there to support you. You're going to need someone on your side, maybe even to back you up, if need be. Also, I know what to expect this time. I can handle myself," she protested.

Charlie sighed. There was a knock at the door.

"What?!" he snapped.

Eric opened the door and leaned into the room. "Couldn't help but overhear."

"Really?" Charlie drawled.

"You're gonna tell off Dad? You think that'll work?"

"What's your fantastic idea then?"

Eric strolled into the room and leaned against one of the bookshelves. He looked almost thoughtful, "Definitely wouldn't go with that. I mean, Dad won't care what you say. Nothing will change his mind. He wants you back in control of the company. It's just a pride thing. Come on, Charlie. Even you have to know how he gets."

"Yeah, but this is stupid. Even for him," Charlie replied.

"Doesn't matter what we think either way. Dad wants you in charge. Not me."

"Why not you? Why does it matter? I mean, Charlie is leaving but the company will still be in the family," Stacey said.

Charlie didn't answer. Eric's mouth twisted for a moment before he mumbled something she didn't make out.

"What?"

"I said because Charlie was groomed for this sort of thing. Not me," Eric said loudly. "In any case, Dad won't care if you want him to stop. You could ask him a thousand times and he won't care. But I'll come with you anyway."

"Why? I don't want you there," said Charlie sternly.

"Maybe we both can team up."

"Yeah. Maybe," Charlie replied, suddenly looking thoughtful.

Stacey could see by the way the two brothers stared at each other that neither one of them was completely sold on the idea of teaming up against Terry.

Chapter Three

The manor didn't seem to be nearly as scary as the last time Stacey was there. Perhaps it was because she had given up hope of impressing Terry. She cared more about remaining relaxed and supporting Charlie than caring what Terry thought of her. She rubbed her belly absently as the manor came into sight.

Next to her, Charlie was gripping the steering wheel of the rental car. His knuckles turned white from the force of it. She reached out and touched his shoulder. He glanced at her out of the corner of his eye before looking back at the road.

"I'm fine," he said.

Behind them came a snort followed by, "Yeah, right. The way you're sitting is enough to give you a back ache."

Stacey glanced at Eric. He was taking up the entire backseat as if it were a bed. He had his phone in his hands and had been texting with someone ever since they landed. Probably a woman, she thought as he looked up at her.

"Relaxing?" she asked him.

"No point in stressing out about trying to talk to Dad."

"If you think it won't work then why are you here?" she asked him.

Eric ignored the question and instead directed one toward Charlie, "I know it's a rental, but I'll blow the smoke out the window."

"No," Charlie replied firmly.

Variations of this conversation had unfolded since they had piled into the rental car. Eric rolled his eyes and fiddled with the cigarette pack he was holding in his lap as if just being near it helped him relax.

"I'm just going to chain smoke like, this entire pack once we get there."

"I don't care if you eat them. The rental car is non-smoking."

"Well, good for the car that it doesn't smoke but I, unfortunately, am not non-smoking," Eric quipped.

"Seriously, why are you here?" Stacey pressed with her question. "If you think Terry won't budge on this thing."

Eric looked at her for a long moment and then finally said, "Well, Charlie and I have never teamed up to try to talk to him before."

"It isn't teaming up," Charlie snapped. "We're just going to be in the same room."

"Talking to him about the same stuff and trying to make him not sound like an asshole," Eric replied swiftly, "I would consider that to be on the same side."

Charlie was about to say something no doubt unhelpful when Stacey said, "Can you two not fight about if you're on the same side about a fight? Honestly. Charlie."

"Not just me," he mumbled as if he were a five-year-old.

"Not just me either," Eric shot back.

Stacey threw her hands up in the air. "You two – *both of you,* might I add – are acting ridiculous. Charlie, your father is literally trying to ruin your investment firm before it takes off, and you're too busy debating semantics with Eric instead of being glad he is here."

Charlie fell silent. A smug look crossed Eric's face but Stacey turned to look at him.

"And you shouldn't be focused on bothering Charlie. This affects you too, doesn't it? Stop treating everything like a joke and be a little more active in what's going on."

Eric's lips pressed firmly together but he didn't say anything. The car filled with silence for the first time since they had gotten into it. Stacey turned and leaned back in her seat.

"If you both really want to talk to Terry, you have to put up a united front. He'll try to get you two to fight with each other instead of him."

"And how do you know that?" Eric drawled from behind.

"Makes sense, doesn't it? He knows you two don't get along. He won't take you guys seriously until you show him you mean business."

The car fell silent again. Stacey pulled out a thin paperback book she had brought with her and began to read, signaling the end of the conversation. Both Charlie and Eric were mercifully quiet.

It was funny, Stacey thought, how much the two brothers didn't get along. The more she watched them interact and the more she learned about Terry, the more Stacey became convinced it was nothing more than the fact the two of them were pitted against each other since their mother died.

Maybe it was a fool's errand, but Stacey was still convinced that the two of them could mend the broken bridge between them and become close again.

By the time they pulled up to the manor, snow had begun to fall. It was the first time that Stacey saw snow since winter officially began. She pulled her coat around her tightly as they got out of the car.

"We aren't welcome," Eric pointed out when no one came out to greet them.

"That's not new for me," Stacey joked although Charlie frowned in response.

"Come on," he said.

Stacey and Eric followed him to the large front doors. The manor looked even more dark and foreboding with the winter sky behind it. Next to her, Eric slid a cigarette out and lit it up.

"I thought you were trying to hide that from him."

"What's the point now?" Eric replied as he took a long drag off of it and sighed in pleasure. "He's going to be furious with us soon anyway. This way I can just slide the smoking part in so it gets lumped with everything else."

He puffed out a smoke circle and watched it warp and twist up into the sky. Charlie pulled a key out of his coat pocket and shoved it in the lock. It turned and opened with a click. He yanked the door open and looked behind him.

"Come on. And Eric, hurry up. We don't have time to sit around so you can smoke."

"One more puff," he replied quickly.

Stacey followed Charlie into the hallway. The manor was as silent as a tomb. Eric hurried in after them, reeking of cigarette smoke. Peter didn't magically appear to greet them. Stacey glanced at Charlie who looked as if he was wavering.

"Maybe he isn't here," he said to her.

"No, he's here," Eric replied. "Where would he go? No one likes him, remember."

Charlie grabbed Stacey's hand. Even though it was cold outside, his hand was warm from his nerves. Eric made a noise that she couldn't make out. The three of them headed toward the living room.

"Hear that?" Eric mumbled.

She did. Voices. She relaxed slightly. At least someone was here. She was starting to wonder if Terry went somewhere and hadn't bothered to tell them. Showing up here would have been for nothing.

They entered the living room. Charlie stopped abruptly which caused Stacey to run into his back. Eric reached out and steadied her. His hand was warm like Charlie's. He must have been just as nervous as Charlie was.

"What is this?"

Stacey moved so she could see into the living room. It was Charlie who spoke and when she looked in the room she could see why.

Terry was sitting on the couch with Peter standing behind him. On a chair across from Terry sat, of all people, Adele.

Stacey hadn't seen her since the night Charlie proposed. She had cut her hair. It was angled to frame her face perfectly. Her eyes looked wide and luminous. A slow smile spread across her face when she saw the three of them. She looked like a cat that had just cornered a mouse.

"Charlie. Eric. So nice to see you," Adele said, crossing her legs to show them off.

Charlie ignored her and turned to Terry, "We have to speak to you."

"As you can see, I'm busy," his father replied and then looked over at Eric. "Why are you here, boy?"

"He said 'we,' Dad. Not just him. *We* have to speak to you," Eric replied.

Terry scoffed, "Go wait outside for me. Peter will show you to one of the sitting rooms."

"No," Charlie replied and crossed his arms.

"Eric, take your brother and his…. wife," he lingered on the word as if it left a dirty taste in his mouth, "and go sit in one of the other rooms."

"No, we're fine here. Besides, you shouldn't be alone with Adele. I heard the way she unhinges her jaw in order to engulf an entire man is a mighty sight to behold but ultimately deadly," said Charlie, keeping a straight face.

Stacey stifled a laugh and avoided looking at Adele. Terry's jaw set. His eyes jumped from the brothers to her. No doubt he was getting ready to blame her for the brothers standing against him. Even so, she felt oddly calm. It was as if she was watching the events unfold through a window.

"Oh, let them stay," Adele spoke up, leaning back in the chair. "No harm in it."

"I know what you're doing. With the investment firm and getting my backers to jump ship. Whatever else you have up your sleeve, I want you to stop it. This is my business, not yours. Put Eric in control of the company and leave me out of it. I told you I was leaving. I need you to respect that, Father." Charlie spoke quickly and looked slightly sick but kept going, "I need you to respect that I'm going out on my own. I don't understand what the issue is. You hated not being in control of the company when you got too ill."

Then Eric spoke, "Also, I don't want to be in charge of it either. Not like this, anyway. You know, I've been thinking a lot about how much you spoke about the company after Mom died. You groomed Charlie to run it so why do I want the stupid thing so badly? I've come to the conclusion that you *wanted* me to want it. Speaking soft words here and there as if Charlie stole something from me. But he didn't take anything from me. I just thought he did. So take the company and find someone else to run it because I don't want it," and then he added, almost as an afterthought, "and, by the way, I'm a smoker. So there."

Terry didn't reply. He looked carefully at Charlie and then at Eric. The two of them were silent.

Then Terry laughed. Stacey was startled. It was the first time she had heard him laugh like that. It wasn't a nice laugh. It sounded hoarse, like sandpaper being dragged across glass. She flinched as if she had been struck.

"I see what is going on here," Terry finally said after laughing. "You two idiots think you can come in here and tell me what's going to happen. Did *she* put that into your heads?" He jerked his head toward Stacey.

"This isn't about me. This is about you," Stacey replied calmly.

A flicker of surprise crossed Terry's face as if he couldn't believe she actually had the nerve to speak to him. But Stacey realized she wasn't afraid of him. He was a bully, wasn't he? He bullied his own sons and used them against each other. Her parents always loved her. Tina always loved her. She was lucky enough to have a family that cared about her. Terry let his heart die with his wife. She pitied him.

"I don't want you meddling any more in my life or in what I'm doing. Stacey is pregnant, Dad. And if you act like this, you won't see my child because I wouldn't want the baby around you."

Stacey looked over at Charlie in surprise. He never mentioned this to her. He glanced at her nervously but she only nodded slightly in agreement.

"And I just want you to leave me alone too," Eric said. "I'm sick of being your errand boy."

Terry turned his gaze to Eric. The expression on his face was openly hostile. There was something raw about it that unsettled Stacey. For some reason, she felt as if she had to throw herself over Eric to protect him from whatever his father was about to unleash.

"Leave you alone? To do what, exactly? You have amounted to exactly nothing, boy. Now that you can finally do something, you back down. You don't want to control the company. You don't want to help out your brother. You don't want to help me out anymore. What if I cut you out of the will and left you with nothing? What would you do?" he snorted. "Absolutely nothing, I bet! Because you *are* nothing. It's this family name that gives you any worth and you're trying to toss that aside. Do it then. Rot for all I care. You haven't proven yourself to be good at anything besides dirtying yourself with low class women and slacking off."

Eric's chest was rising and falling rapidly. Stacey felt a flash of anger shoot through her after Terry finished speaking. The expression on Eric's face was something she had never seen before. The mask of arrogance he usually wore was now yanked away. He suddenly didn't look like a grown man but a child being scolded. His bottom lip quivered and for one terrible moment she wondered if Eric was going to cry. She didn't think she could stand it if he did. It seemed so unlike him.

Before Eric could say anything in response, Terry swung his gaze to Charlie. "And you, boy. You have been groomed for this since you were young. It's true. I didn't want to give you the company. Often I feel as if you make stupid choices and are blundering through things. That business with the city renovation, for one thing. Losing that entire profit for a woman." His face contorted into a sneer as his gaze shot over to Stacey for a moment. "Stupidity through and through. And now you want to leave – after everything I've done for you? I have supported you through the good and bad. You want to embarrass me and make me look like a fool. It's a matter of pride, Charlie. I am doing this so that you can see what mistakes you're making. Your firm will never take off because I won't allow it. Come back to the company before I have to ruin you completely."

Charlie went completely still. He looked as if he was carved out of marble. Stacey didn't dare look at Eric. She couldn't imagine what he looked like right now. Terry's speech to Charlie was kinder although that wasn't saying much. She hadn't considered Terry to have favorites before today. Now it was clear that he preferred Charlie.

He still didn't reply. Terry took this as a sign to keep going, as if sensing it as an advantage. "I only did what I did because I am trying to have you see how foolish this all is. You want to leave the company you were made for. I only ever objected to things you did to help you learn. When I die, this company is yours, Charlie. I can't allow you to give up being president to run off on this folly."

"You're right," Charlie finally said.

Behind her, Eric called his brother something terrible. Stacey felt shocked herself and turned to look at him. She was about to ask him how he could agree with his father when Charlie kept going.

"I mean, you're not right about this. You're right about something you told me when I was thirteen. I broke some stupid vase accidentally when Eric and I were playing a game. Smashed it to pieces. I remember you looming over me, larger than life, telling me that once you ruin something like that, it can't be fixed. I could spend hours gluing the pieces together and you'd see the cracks all over it."

Terry didn't say anything.

"And you're right. Once something is broken like that, those cracks are there. In vases and in humans. And frankly, I'm sick of patching up all the cracks from your insanity and your stupid lessons. So, if you want to crush your own son's business, go ahead. But I'm not coming back to control the company, no matter what you do."

Terry's face darkened to an ugly shade of red. Stacey was glad he was so feeble; otherwise, she could see him lunging at Charlie.

"You're an idiot. Just like your brother. No different," he finally hissed at Charlie.

Next to her, Eric sucked in a small breath as if he was being physically wounded. Stacey wanted to reach out for him but she knew he'd shrug her off.

"Fine," their father said. "If that is how you want things done, then so be it. I'll go on with my own plan."

"And you're going to tell us what it is now, aren't you?" Eric finally spoke up. "As if you're going to really prove us wrong."

"Found your voice again, did you?" Terry sneered at Eric who balked. "I don't need you posing as president anymore. I'm marrying Adele."

Both Charlie and Eric exclaimed in surprise. Stacey wrinkled her nose. Terry looked ancient. Adele sat in the chair, looking smugly at them.

"What the hell is wrong with you?" It was Eric who spoke first. "That's disgusting. She's young enough to be your daughter."

"Adele's family and I will merge our companies through the agreement that she gets by marrying into our family. Since neither of you two morons will take it, once again I have to step up."

"Step up, really? To fucking someone that young? Wow, Dad, you're so brave. Mom would be so fucking proud of you," Eric spat angrily and then turned around, storming out of the living room.

Charlie watched him go and then looked with disgust at his father. He didn't say anything else. Instead, he grabbed Stacey's hand and pulled her out of the living room. He was yanking her down the hallway now. She allowed herself to be pulled along until they went into one of the small sitting rooms. Charlie shut the door behind them and ran his fingers through his hair.

Eric must have followed them because they didn't even get a chance to speak before the door bursted back open.

"Let's go. Come on. Book a flight or whatever," he gestured to Charlie.

"I'm not leaving yet," Charlie replied, "I'm just cooling off."

"What?" He got close to him. "Why aren't you leaving? There isn't anything left to do here."

"I have to talk Dad out of this, okay? He can't marry Adele. That's insanity."

"Who cares? It isn't our business what that crazy old man decides to do!" Eric yelled. "If he wants to marry that witch and merge with them, let him! Why do you care?"

"Mom wouldn't want this."

"Mom is dead!" Eric shouted so loudly that Charlie took a step back. "She's dead. She won't care what Dad does or doesn't do. She isn't going to come down from Heaven to bless us if we stop him from making irrational life choices!"

"He's still family, Eric! He's still our dad."

"No." He was backing up now as if he had been slapped, shaking his head. "No. He's nothing. He's not a fucking thing."

He threw one look at Stacey and then stormed out of the sitting room, slamming the door shut behind him so hard that the wall rattled.

Chapter Four

"Maybe we should go," Stacey said very softly after Eric stormed out.

Charlie threw himself down onto the nearest chair. The sitting room was full of bookshelves filled with books that gave off a slight musty scent. Dust swirled in the light from the windows. She sat down in a chair across from Charlie.

"He's going to marry Adele. I can't wrap my head around it."

"Yes. But he's a grown man. He can make his own choices."

He let out a bitter laugh. "He can make choices for everyone else. His own end up seeming questionable at best."

"I'm not trying to pick sides," Stacey said carefully, "but Eric does have a point. He hasn't treated either of you with kindness. There were no heartfelt emotions expressed in there, Charlie. Just poison spewing out of his mouth."

"He's always like that."

"That doesn't mean you and your brother should be accepting of it." When he didn't reply, she tried again. "What do you think will happen if he marries Adele?"

"He's only doing this because I'm leaving, I know that. I know he's doing it as some kind of control method. As if I'd *want* him to marry Adele. And she'll marry anyone in this family for the money. All this talk about a merger is bullshit. It's just to get under my skin. And it's working! Of course it's working. Dad, the master manipulator."

"So, call his bluff. Let him marry her."

Charlie was drumming his fingers against the arm of the chair but at this moment he stopped. "What do you mean?"

"Your dad is clearly doing an awful lot to get you to come back to the company. That means he needs you, Charlie. He needs you more than you need him. That's why he's trying so desperately to get you to come back, including this stunt with Adele. So let him marry her. I doubt he'll really go through with it."

"You don't know my dad like I do," he mumbled.

"So, if he wants to marry a snake like that, let him. I think you should just live your life the way you want and not let your dad manipulate you into coming back to the company. He's grasping at straws because you're doing what you want without his approval."

He met her gaze. His eyes softened a little and a small smile crossed his face. "You're a smart woman, Stacey."

She smiled back. "I know. Someone has to be the smart one in this relationship."

He stood up. "Let's leave. And get Eric before he punches someone in the face. Hopefully not me."

Charlie held his hand out to her. Stacey took it and stood up. His hand was firm, not as nervously warm as it previously was. He leaned over and kissed her gently on the lips. In that moment, Stacey couldn't have been more proud of him.

The trio hit a patch of bad luck trying to get a flight home. They missed the last flight back to the city, leaving them driving to the nearest town to try to find a hotel for the night.

The drive in was silent. Stacey could feel waves of anger and irritation rolling off of Eric. It felt as if it was filling the car with nothing but negativity. At one point, he pulled out a cigarette and lit it, rolling down the window to blow the smoke out. The entire time, he stared at Charlie as if challenging him about the fact he was smoking in the car. To Stacey's relief, he didn't say anything to Eric.

The nearest town to the manor was small and offered a tourist trap museum claiming to be the *World's Biggest Collection of Smallest Teapots*. They drove past it on the way to the hotel.

"Wow, that place looks riveting," Stacey joked as they drove by.

She heard Charlie laugh quietly but Eric's expression remained unchanged. He was opening his pack for another cigarette but Stacey saw that it was empty. He made an irritated noise in the back of his throat and slumped against the back seat.

They stopped at a fast food place for dinner and ate quietly. A light snow covered the car as they got in to drive to the hotel.

The place looked run down. The neon sign illuminating the name of *Neptune Suites* was half burnt out. The snow was coming down heavier now, sticking to the sign and melting against the lights that were working. The hotel itself was all ground level with a tiny pool in the center that had a CLOSED sign on the gate.

"Sure you can stay here, Charlie? Might not be nice enough for you," Eric sneered.

For once, Charlie didn't reply. He seemed to sense that Eric was looking for a fight and that it was better not to go after him. They walked into the lobby where a sleepy-looking man gave them two room keys.

Eric went into his without saying a word and shut the door firmly behind him. Stacey and Charlie took the other room. It was barebones, with a bed and a small television that looked ancient. A lone painting of a beach was thrown up on one of the walls.

"It'll do. I'm exhausted," Charlie said as he tossed his bag onto the floor.

He yanked the sheets down and crawled under them, pulling the covers over. Stacey rummaged through her bag for her toothbrush. She couldn't sleep without brushing her teeth first.

Charlie mumbled something into his pillow and Stacey replied, "What?"

He pushed himself up and looked at her. "Thanks. For everything you did today. I would have stayed to try to convince Dad not to marry her. I would have fallen right into his stupid trap. But you helped me… helped give me the strength to leave."

"You were always strong enough to do that. You just needed a little push. What do you think Terry thought when you left?"

"I don't know. I don't know if he figured we'd leave and then go crawling back, or what."

"What about Eric? Terry wasn't nice to you, but he was downright cruel to your brother," Stacey said.

Disgust crossed Charlie's face. "How could he just tell his own son that he was nothing?" He rolled onto his back and sat up. "Eric and I have never gotten along but I've been thinking about what you've said. And just about me and Eric in general as we drove over here."

Stacey went over and sat down next to him on the bed. "What are you thinking?"

"Dad was always harder on Eric. Like, not in a way to help him succeed but just in an asshole sort of way. I wonder if it's because he's like our mom."

"Eric is like your mom?" Stacey asked, surprised and trying to picture Charlie's mother as a sarcastic smart ass.

"From what I remember, she was really great with people. They flocked to her. Sort of like what Eric can do in a room. Mom was funny too. She was witty and a quick thinker. Eric is too."

"So, your father takes things out on Eric because he reminds him of your mother. Makes sense but still completely wrong and terrible."

"I wonder if Dad just takes out his anger about Mom dying on Eric. It's still fucked up either way. I don't know what Eric is going to do now. We've both always wanted Dad's approval for so long. Living with that desire… neither one of us are just going to be able to shake it off, you know?"

"Your dad sounds like he thrived off manipulating his own sons. That's what he lived for. And with you about to break free and start things on your own, it sounds as if he's trying everything to keep you under his thumb," Stacey remarked.

"Yeah, it's a good plan. Dad was always good at figuring out what would drive the other person crazy. In business and with me and Eric. He knew I'd be disgusted with him marrying Adele. He has to think that I'm going to agree to come back to the business just so he doesn't marry her."

"Why do you think he said those things to Eric?" Stacey asked curiously. "Trying to marry Adele to manipulate you into coming back – I understand it even though it's insane. But he was downright cruel to him."

"I don't know. Maybe he thought full on force like that was enough to bring Eric back. He did threaten to cut him out of the will too. He probably thinks Eric wouldn't be able to function without any money. Honestly, Dad might have a point there. Eric enjoys a certain lifestyle."

Just then, Charlie yawned. Stacey leaned over and kissed him before saying, "You should get some sleep."

His eyes were already closing as he snuggled down into bed. He mumbled good-night as Stacey went over to the bathroom to brush her teeth. By the time she finished, Charlie was fast asleep, snoring quietly.

Stacey studied his face. The face of her husband. She still wasn't used to that word. So much had happened lately. Everything felt as if it was moving at hyper speed. Their court house wedding followed by her pregnancy felt like a whirlwind. She rested her hand on her belly, marveling at the fact that there was a life growing inside of her.

She thought of Terry and how he treated his sons. Stacey vowed to never speak or treat her own children that way. She couldn't fathom telling them that they were nothing. Charlie shifted a little in his sleep. Picturing his father with Adele was gross. What kind of man marries a woman like that just to try to get his son to do his bidding? She couldn't wrap her head around it.

Stacey was still worried that things would only get worse from here. She was hoping confronting Terry like this would have shown him how serious his sons were. Instead, it simply backed him into a corner. He lashed out at Eric and was trying to force Charlie to give up his dream. She was sure a shrink would have a field day with Charlie's family.

Eric had gone to his room without them saying a word. Stacey had been so caught up in her thoughts that she had failed to even ask him how he was doing. The brothers hadn't turned on each other in the confrontation with Terry. That counted for something, right?

She decided she'd go make sure Eric wasn't trashing the hotel room. She grabbed her coat and quietly shut the hotel door behind her. The snow covered everything in a thin blanket. Stacey went over and knocked on the door to Eric's room.

There was no answer. Maybe he fell asleep and she was going to wake him up. Even when she thought it, however, she knew that she was wrong. There was no way Eric could calm down enough to let himself rest. He was too wound up. Stacey knocked again when she heard a shuffling noise behind her.

She turned around and saw Eric walking down the pathway toward his room. He carried a small plastic bag from the gas station around the corner. A cigarette hung out of his mouth. The tip glowed dimly in the darkness.

"What are you doing here?" Eric asked her.

"Just wanted to see how you were doing."

Eric held the bag up and it made a clattering noise. "Doing great."

"What's in the bag? Besides probably ten more packs of cigarettes."

"Booze. Now, if you'll excuse me." He walked past her toward the door.

"The room is non-smoking," she pointed to his cigarette.

"Everywhere is non-smoking now," Eric replied, the cigarette still in his mouth.

"So, you're just going to drink tonight?"

Eric stopped looking for his room key and looked up at her. She couldn't read his facial expression. It was completely blank. For some reason, this unsettled her more than if he were angry or irritated with her.

"Why not? You heard dear old Dad. Doesn't really matter what I do. I could do anything I want now because he doesn't expect anything out of me anyway."

"You're going to let what he said affect you like this?" Stacey argued.

Eric sneered, "Please, don't start with me. What am I supposed to do?"

"Live your life. Don't cater to your father anymore. You won't ever please him. Neither you nor Charlie –"

He made a disgusted noise in the back of his throat, "Don't. Don't even compare what Dad said to me to what he said to Charlie. Dad is going to marry Adele just to get Charlie back. In his own warped way, that's the highest compliment he's ever given either one of us. But there isn't anything like that for me, is there? No."

"Eric, I don't think –"

"No, you don't *know*. You don't know anything about my dad, Stacey. My whole life, I've tried to make him think better of me. I did whatever he wanted. I was basically his fucking errand boy. It was pounded into my head that if I only did whatever he wanted, maybe he'd give the company to me instead of Charlie. Well, that didn't happen. Not even close. And you know what? I'm not even fit to run a fucking company worth billions of dollars. Because I was so concerned with impressing Dad that I didn't ever improve myself anywhere else. I didn't learn anything of importance. I did nothing."

Stacey took a step back, unsure of what to say. She didn't expect an outburst like this. For some reason, she thought she was going to be able to speak to him rationally like when she spoke to Charlie.

But the rage in Eric kept spewing forth out of his mouth. "So, while Charlie got everything he ever wanted, I let myself do nothing. That's my own fault. Not Charlie's or my dad's. At any time, I could have told Dad that I wasn't going to do this shit anymore. But I tricked myself. I thought if I got his approval –" His voice caught for a moment and an irritated look crossed his face. "Fuck it. Don't know why I'm telling you this anyway. Besides, I'm smoking. You shouldn't stand near me. Bad for the baby."

He pulled away from her and went over to stand by the edge of the sidewalk, looking at the closed pool. Stacey could only see his back. Eric was hunched over as if he were preparing to run from an attack. His shoulders were tense. Stacey realized he wasn't wearing a coat. He had to have been cold on top of everything else.

The smoke from his cigarette swirled above his head. She watched as he crushed the butt underneath his feet and pulled out another. Stacey went over to him and grabbed his wrist.

"Wait, don't light it yet."

He stared at her and slipped the cigarette in his mouth but didn't light it.

"Eric, please, talk to Charlie about this. You two need a real heart-to heart."

He scoffed, "We need more than a heart-to-heart."

"Then start with it. I know you have a lot of history between the two of you. But if you are both going against Terry and trying to move on from what he has put the two of you through, then you need each other. You're family. You can mend the bridges burned between you two."

"Why? Because you and your sister did?"

"Allison and I had our differences, but we didn't have parents or grandparents like Terry raising us. We just needed to grow up and accept each other for who we are. You and Charlie need to do the same."

"I'm not interested," Eric replied stubbornly.

Stacey stared at him. "Why not?"

"I'm more into self-sabotage," he said darkly.

"I'm afraid I don't follow."

"The night you ended up in the hospital, there was something that I needed to tell you. At the time, I was glad I didn't. But now – fuck it, right? Who cares anymore? I'm leaving town after tonight anyway."

Stacey was still confused as Eric turned around to face her. He tossed the unlit cigarette to the pavement. Her mind was still registering what he said as he grabbed her shoulders firmly and kissed her.

She tasted the cigarette in his mouth. The stubble around his mouth grazed against her skin. Her brain finally caught up to everything that was happening and she pushed against Eric, shoving him off of her.

He stumbled yet didn't try to kiss her again. Stacey felt as if the wind was knocked out of her. She stared at him in shock, unable to speak. Eric's face was blank again. The rage that propelled through him apparently ran out. He bent over and picked up the bag at his feet along with the unlit cigarette.

Then he straightened himself and said, "I had to do that just once."

Before Stacey could reply, he turned and went into his hotel room. She heard the door lock, leaving her alone on the pathway.

Stacey brushed her teeth for the second time in a row. She could still taste Eric's kiss in her mouth – the taste of cigarettes unwilling to leave. She spit the toothpaste into the sink and then took a swig of water.

In the other room, Charlie snored. She gripped the edge of the counter, trying to figure out what to do next. Yet her mind felt as if it was plunged into a fog.

What was it that Charlie told her? *Eric had done this before,* meaning he was accustomed to his brother throwing himself at Charlie's previous girlfriends. At the time, Stacey didn't think much of it. She wasn't like the other girlfriends. She was *married* to his brother. They weren't just a short-term dating situation. She was pregnant with Charlie's baby. For some reason, she thought that meant she wouldn't have to worry about Eric doing something like that.

The night you ended up in the hospital, there was something that I needed to tell you.

Oh no! she thought to herself. He was going to kiss her then, wasn't he? Right after Charlie stormed out, Eric was drunkenly blathering about telling her something. This wasn't something he did on a whim. He had been wanting to do this for some time.

Stacey took the cup of water with her back to the bedroom. She turned on the TV when she came in. It only got two channels. One of them was the weather channel. It was oddly comforting. It reminded her of Tina. She sat at the edge of the bed and stared at the grainy image.

Something else Eric said was nagging in her brain. He said he was into self-sabotage. He must have known kissing her would get back to Charlie. That would ruin any chance of them making amends and becoming close brothers again. Charlie wouldn't want to see Eric anymore, for certain. Eric wouldn't go back to Terry.

He'd just drift around on his own. He said he was leaving town, didn't he? He must have assumed that she was going to tell Charlie tonight.

She suddenly felt exhausted. She was supposed to be avoiding stress, but this was not the way to go about it. She finished her water and curled up in bed next to Charlie, who barely stirred when she got in. His back was to her and she gently pressed her hand against his skin.

His skin was warm to the touch and comforting. She was going to have to tell Charlie. Eric played her just right, knowing that there was no way she could keep such a thing from him.

Her eyelids growing heavy, she thought about his last words to her.

I had to do that just once.

Stacey's eyes fluttered open. She was staring at the ceiling of the hotel room. The door shut loudly, jolting her awake. She propped herself up to see Charlie pacing the small room, holding his phone in his hands as he typed.

"What's going on?" she mumbled, still half asleep.

"Eric is gone. I went over there to see how he was doing and the room is empty. I don't know where he is. I'm afraid he went back to Dad's or something. Up to something stupid."

"Charlie..."

Something in her voice caught his attention and he looked up at her, "What?"

"Eric left town."

"How do you know?"

She took a deep breath and then proceeded to tell him the events of last night. When she got to the kiss, Charlie went stiff. His face drained of the little color that was left.

When she finished, Charlie was silent and remained that way for a few moments. He was frozen like a statue. Stacey wondered if the stress had gotten to him and he wasn't going to speak for a while, but just stare ahead at the wall.

"Uh, Charlie?"

"He said what? What did he say?"

She recited what Eric said, but slower, afraid it didn't sink in the first time. When she finished, Charlie shook his head and mumbled *idiot* over and over again.

"What is it? I mean, I know he's an idiot but…"

"Don't you get it? All that talk about self-sabotage and leaving town. He likes you, obviously. And whatever was holding him back from acting on it died when our father pointed out he's a piece of shit. He thinks he's a piece of shit now. So he kissed you and has run off to go do… God knows what."

"I don't think he really feels that way about me," Stacey protested. "He's just confused."

Charlie yanked some clothes out of his bag along with a few toiletries they had bought the night before. "He's confused about nothing. He's just a fucking idiot. You know…for a second – a split second – after everything happened last night, I thought we could fix things." He shook his head.

"You still can. We'll find him and –"

"I don't want to find him. He kissed you, Stacey. You're my wife! I can't trust him around you. If he is so keen on believing the stuff Dad said about him, then let him. I'm not going to track down a brother who's betrayed me yet again and try to convince him to come home."

He stormed out of the room, leaving Stacey in bed. This was what she was afraid of, she thought dully.

She listened to Charlie in the shower and could feel a wave of nausea roll over her. She sucked in air through her mouth and got to her feet, bursting into the bathroom and leaning over the toilet to vomit.

Behind the shower curtain, Charlie stuck his head out, alarmed, "Are you okay?"

"Fine," she mumbled. "Morning sickness."

"No, it's Eric sickness. He's putting you through his own bullshit," Charlie said furiously.

She limply waved her arm for him to stop as another wave washed over her. She didn't want to talk about Eric any longer. Charlie was right about one thing – she was going to stress herself out at this rate. Easier to put it behind her and let Charlie worry about his brother.

Stacey had tried everything she could and all attempts had blown up in her face.

Charlie finished his shower and helped her lie down. She protested, saying she was fine, but he refused to listen.

"We leave in an hour. Just try to get some rest until then," Charlie said sternly to her as he flipped on the TV.

He began to go through the channels and looked confused when it kept cycling through the same two. Stacey, in spite of feeling sickly, laughed. He looked back at her.

"Only two channels," she pointed out. "You gonna be okay with that?"

Charlie smiled at her teasing tone and looked back at the TV. "Guess we're stuck with the weather."

"I don't mind. Tina used to watch it all the time," Stacey replied, shifting so that she could see it better.

"What do you think Tina would say? About all of this? Eric and… my family."

Stacey found the question interesting and thought about it for a few moments before replying, "She would probably find it all ridiculous. And guaranteed she wouldn't want you to give up on Eric."

"Even though he kissed you?"

"She'd say he was lost. She always told me not to brush Allison aside and that we were sisters. She would want you to remember that too. You two are brothers and nothing can change that. You both were loved by your mother and withstood whatever Terry threw at you. I don't think she would want you to give up on him, because he's having a hard time."

Charlie ran his hand over his face, looking tired. "Still doesn't change the fact that he kissed you. And has feelings for you, or whatever he's thinking. I don't care what Dad is doing to make me come back to the company. It doesn't give Eric a free rein to do whatever he wants."

"I know, and I agree. I just don't want you to brush him off completely. He's still your brother."

But Charlie shook his head decisively, "I don't care. I'm done with him."

She wanted to say more but knew at this moment it would be useless. She could see in the set of Charlie's jaw that he was done talking about it. As of right now, he didn't consider Eric to be his brother at all.

Chapter Five

The next two months passed by in a blur. Stacey worked from home, helping William's real estate office as much as she could from the comfort of her living room. Working kept her mind active and gave her a reason to get out of bed in the morning even when she felt incredibly sick from the pregnancy.

Allison was busy helping Jacob after his father's death. With complete control of the tea empire falling to him, her sister was making sure he remembered basic things like eating since he would tend to forget when he was busy. Allison always made sure to come by to see Stacey when she was in town, however, to make sure that everything was going well.

Charlie struggled with getting his company off the ground. The conversation with Terry, as it turned out, didn't matter. By the time he formally left the company, Terry stepped up as temporary president because no one had seen or heard from Eric.

Well, almost no one. A month after he kissed Stacey, Eric sent one postcard to Charlie. It showed a cheesy photo of a cat sleepily lying in a tree. It was post marked from Puerto Rico.

On the back it simply read: *Hanging in there. Hope you're well.*

Charlie threw it out almost immediately. Stacey didn't stop him. She told herself that they would never reconcile. If Eric intended the kiss to ruin things for good, it was a fantastic idea. Charlie undoubtedly meant what he had said in the hotel room – he was done with Eric.

Stacey could hardly believe it was Christmas Eve already. There was a thick blanket of snow that draped the city last week. She worked in the living room, admiring the way the snow looked from this high up.

They decorated their place together and put a giant tree in the living room. A couple weeks ago, Charlie had surprised her with a cat after she said she was a little lonely during the day. The cat, Munchkin, had curled up underneath the tree, sleeping away as Stacey came into the room.

"Ready?" Charlie asked her.

"Yup. Let's go."

Charlie took her hand firmly as they left the penthouse to go see Allison. She was throwing a small Christmas party. Stacey made sure to grab their gifts on the way out and held them tightly.

"You know, it's so weird buying gifts this year. I never know what to get Allison. Some years, I didn't get her anything."

"Why is that?"

"We weren't talking. Or we were fighting about something stupid. The usual. But this year, so much has changed. Allison has everything she ever wanted. So what do I get her?"

"What *did* you get her?" Charlie asked her curiously as they cut across the lobby.

Stacey grinned. "When she was six, there was this limited-edition cupcake maker. It was one of those little oven things where you mix the gross powder and make cakes or something. They had one that made cupcakes and it was too expensive for Mom and Dad to buy for Allison. It had a fancy oven and came with sprinkles and all sorts of extra toppings. Allison was heartbroken that she couldn't get it."

Charlie laughed. "You got her that?"

"I tracked it down online! I mean, hopefully she'll know not to use any of the ingredients or anything. They're all expired. But she's going to totally flip. I know it," Stacey grinned.

He shook his head at her and smiled, "You amaze me."

He leaned in and gave her a kiss before opening the lobby door and getting into the car that pulled up for them. The ride to Allison's place was comfortable, with Stacey bundled up in her coat and listening to Charlie talk about his day.

"And tomorrow, I figured it'd be just the two of us, relaxing," he said as he held her hand. "What do you think?"

Stacey smiled. "Sounds nice. Relaxing. I'm sure Allison will have gone all out tonight so it's better to spend our first Christmas together like that. I just want to relax. Everything has been so crazy lately."

"The entire year has been crazy," Charlie remarked.

Stacey nodded. "A lot has changed. I can hardly believe how quickly everything unfolded."

He nodded and looked lost in thought. Stacey couldn't blame him. The entire year, beginning in the summer, was a whirlwind of events. Strange to think that at the start of the year she was struggling to make enough money at William's diner to pay her bills. And look where everyone was now.

By the time they pulled up to Allison's building, Stacey really needed to pee. Her bladder felt like it was shrinking every day she was pregnant. Charlie took one look at her face as they entered the lobby and laughed.

"Go, go. I'll wait for you here and then we can go up."

"Great, thank you," she said and hurried off toward the restroom.

It was empty for a brief moment before two women burst in. From the stall, Stacey could hear their heels clatter against the tile as they stalked over to the mirror.

"Security was too tight to get to the top floor," one of the women commented, "I thought it'd be busy up there so we could get in but I guess not. Usually Christmas parties are easy to crash."

These two women must have been trying to sneak into Allison's party, Stacey realized. She hadn't even thought about that before – that people would willingly try to get into her sister's parties. Curiously, she stayed still, wondering if they would say anything about why they thought it would be fun to try such a thing.

"So, where are we going next?"

"I think there's a bigger event across town," the first woman replied. "That guy. What was his name?" Stacey heard the woman snap her fingers as if she was trying to jog her memory. "Tony. Tony something."

"The one that was dating Adele?"

"They broke up. She's engaged to some old guy now. I bet one of us could get his interest," the woman said confidently.

"Great. Let's go there, then. If he's hosting a giant party, then I'm game."

Stacey listened as the two women left. Hearing Tony mentioned unexpectedly like that conjured him up in her mind. She hadn't given him much thought after Charlie proposed. This person she was once fond of and seemed like such a kind man; who cornered her in the library one night and frightened her, making her see how controlling he was, was better not to think about.

Even so, Stacey realized that she hadn't thought about him in all of this time for even a brief moment. Was he furious with Adele for leaving him for Charlie's father? There was no way she could have told him it had anything to do with love.

The women in the bathroom sounded as if they knew Adele. They probably ran in the same circle. At the start of this year, Stacey always thought what her sister did with her life was shallow. It never dawned on her that there were probably groups of women who tried to crash parties to find a rich man.

Stacey left the restroom to see Charlie waiting for her. He was checking something on his phone and slipped it in his jacket pocket when she came over.

"Everything okay?" he asked her.

"Yeah. Sorry, there were two women in the ladies' room talking about Tony."

"Mel and Marge. The two M's."

"You know them?" Stacey asked, surprised.

"I saw them coming out. And yes, I know them. They hung out with Adele a lot."

"They tried to get into Allison's party, apparently. Now they're going to try to woo Tony," Stacey explained as they headed over to the elevator.

"Good luck with that."

Something in his tone got Stacey's attention. "What do you mean?"

Charlie avoided her stare. "Heard he wasn't doing very well, that's all." He pressed the button on the elevator to take them to Allison's place.

Stacey blinked and followed him into the elevator. "What do you mean?"

"Well, Adele dumped him for my dad. You saw him that night at the library. I've never seen him like that before. And everything else you told me… how he acted on the island. How keen he was on trying to find someone his parents were interested in…"

"I'm not following."

Charlie shrugged. "Just heard that he parties a lot now. I wouldn't let it concern you. Tony made his bed and has to lie in it now. If he's lost his head over his weird fixation on finding someone to marry, that's his issue."

Stacey leaned against the elevator wall as it took them up. "He did seem fixated on it."

"He's always been like that. I don't know why. He probably thought he had you and then I fucked it up. Then he probably thought he had Adele. He never spoke of her very kindly before. But she was always willing to marry anyone who could tolerate her."

"He wanted his family to approve of whomever he married. He wouldn't go with Adele. There is no way that his parents would approve."

"Adele already met his family a couple of years back. She got along great with them. They loved her. But, mind you, she was a completely different person around them. She met them a few times at social events. He would have married her if she had stuck it out a bit longer."

Stacey thought about this as they walked into Allison's place. Adele changing herself to have people like her didn't come as a surprise. It was more surprising that Tony was partying a lot lately. He never struck her as the type.

There was a dark side to him that she saw that night in the library, and flashes of it when she ran away to his island. She was safe, Stacey thought to herself, now that she was away from Tony. Let him have his parties and his billions of dollars. She would have never been happy with him.

Allison saw them immediately when they entered the party and swooped over to them. She wore a pinched expression on her face and practically cornered the two of them.

"Are you okay?" Stacey asked her curiously.

"I didn't invite him," she said.

For a wild second, Stacey thought her sister meant Tony. It would be just her luck, wouldn't it, that one of her ex-boyfriends appeared at this party. But Charlie seemed to understand exactly what Allison was saying because he pushed past her into the penthouse.

"What is it?" Stacey asked her.

But Allison was chasing after Charlie in her stiletto heels. Confused, Stacey slipped out of her jacket and hung it up. She looked into the living room and was greeted by William, Amanda, and Brad, whom she wasn't expecting but was thrilled to see. Jacob was in the middle of the room, talking to someone she didn't know.

Stacey hadn't seen Jacob in a while. He looked thinner than usual and there were circles around his eyes. Allison mentioned that he was taking his father's death harder than even he had expected. She could hear him speaking now. His voice sounded quieter than usual. She waved at him as she walked by and he acknowledged her with a nod.

Amanda came over and hugged her gently. "Sorry, I'm hyper paranoid about hurting the baby but I had to hug you. I only ever talk to you on the phone now or through e-mail. I never get to see you!"

"Believe me, it's pretty dull to be working from home."

"Better to be resting and working from home than overdoing it at the office," William said seriously.

"Even so, I want to talk a little business with you."

"Come on, Stacey, it's a party," Brad protested.

Stacey smiled. "You're right, you're right. Christmas Eve and all." She sighed, "Could you excuse me a moment. I'll be back." She rushed off in search of the bathroom. The baby was really dancing on her bladder this evening.

She crossed the living room and went down the nearest hallway which had a guest room and a bathroom. She grabbed the handle, but it was locked. She bobbed on the balls of her feet, considering if she should go to the other bathroom near Allison's room. This place was spread out and there was no need to wait here for the door to open.

As she turned around to leave, the door opened. Her heart felt as if it stopped for a moment.

Out came Eric.

Chapter Six

Allison's apology of 'I didn't invite him' floated back to Stacey and it all finally clicked. She didn't mean Tony, she meant Eric. He was standing in front of her with a bored expression on his face. He wore a rumpled white button-up shirt that was a size too large for him. The sleeves hung over his wrists as if he were a child playing dress up with his father's clothes.

"Eric!" Stacey said, surprised.

"That's my name," Eric deadpanned, moving past her.

He didn't say anything else. She watched him saunter off down the hallway back into the fray of the party. Stacey headed into the bathroom and closed the door behind her. She couldn't believe that he was here.

All hopes of the party being enjoyable and Charlie having a relaxing time was out the window. She was expecting Charlie to punch Eric in the face as soon as he saw him. Her only hope was that he wouldn't do it at the party, but would wait until they were alone.

She finished quickly, washed her hands and headed back to join the party. Allison was by her side within a few seconds.

"Where did you go?" asked Allison.

She shook her head when Stacey tried to reply.

"I don't care, please, just keep Charlie occupied and make sure he doesn't murder his brother in front of everyone."

Stacey nodded and walked into the dining room. There were a few more people that she didn't know there. Charlie was on the balcony, staring out at the city. Eric was in the corner of the dining room. Stacey did a double take.

There was a woman with her arms draped around Eric. She was a platinum blonde, shorter than he was, wearing a baggy t-shirt and cut off denim shorts, noticeably dressed down from everyone else at the party. How was she not freezing to death? On top of that, she was wearing red platform heels that must have been six inches high. For a moment, Stacey wondered if Eric brought a prostitute or a stripper to the party just to cause trouble.

Eric's gaze flicked around the room before stopping at Stacey. He motioned for her to come over. When she took a step away instead to go toward Charlie, Eric tugged his date toward her.

"Stacey," he said. "This is my date, Kailyn."

Stacey thought she misheard, "Kailyn?"

"Yes, that's right," the woman, Kailyn, trilled in a loud voice. "Pleasure to meet you!"

They shook hands. Kailyn was wearing a strong perfume that made Stacey's eyes water. She took a small step back hoping to avoid the invisible perfume cloud that seemed to engulf the woman.

Up close, Eric's lady friend looked a bit older than she did from afar. There were deep lines around her eyes and her lips looked a size too large to be natural. She looked as if she had stepped out of a comic book. It hardly felt as if Stacey was looking at a real person.

Eric watched her with a detached expression on his face. She had no idea what he was thinking. Why did he turn up out of nowhere like this?

"It's lovely to meet you," Stacey lied, smiling. "I just have to speak with my husband for a moment. I'll be back later."

Kailyn nodded and said something so quickly that Stacey couldn't even make it out. She was thankful for the fresh air when she got outside. Charlie stared blankly at the city. Stacey approached and stood next to him.

"Okay," she said slowly, "what the hell is that about?"

"Which part? Eric coming back and crashing Allison's party or the fact he brought someone who belongs on a reality show?"

"Both, I guess."

He shook his head. "No idea. I avoided him as soon as I saw him. Whatever reason he has for coming back isn't anything I want to be a part of."

"He's going to try to talk to you eventually," Stacey pointed out.

"Let him. I'm not causing a scene at your sister's party."

"Good. Because she asked me to make sure of that."

"Nah, not here."

Stacey rubbed his back, unsure of what to say. She had been looking forward to a relaxing evening. Eric appearing with a date named Kailyn wasn't exactly her idea of a fantastic Christmas Eve. She felt irritation blooming in her chest and tried to ignore it.

"Maybe he came here to apologize or make things right." Even as the words left her mouth, however, she knew they weren't true. That wasn't Eric's style.

Charlie scoffed in reply and didn't say anything else. She could practically see the dark cloud over her husband's head.

"Well, just don't pay any attention to him. I ran into him in the hallway and he barely even spoke to me. Even when he introduced Kailyn –"

"Wait, wait. Kailyn?"

"Yeah, that's her name, apparently."

Charlie sighed, "Really? Kailyn? Where the hell did he find her?"

"I don't know. She seems uh… nice," she said almost apologetically.

Charlie laughed at this and threw his arm around her, bringing her in close. She could smell the cologne on him – a welcome scent after Kailyn's cloying perfume. She closed her eyes and for a few seconds, everything washed away. There was just her, Charlie and their child.

"You always want to see the good in people. I wish I could be similar."

"There has to be a time when you and Eric got along," she said, her words muffled by his jacket which he still hadn't removed.

He looked down at her. "Maybe before our mom died. I remember us wearing socks that were too big. I think they were our dad's. Anyway, we use to slide around on the floor in his socks. We'd pretend we were in martial arts films."

Stacey tried to picture it but it proved to be impossible. She couldn't imagine the two brothers sliding around the floor like that, laughing and having fun. Instead, the memory of them being drunk together at the last party floated in her head. She could see them with their heads bent together, laughing hysterically as they stuck that sticker on Jacob.

"You have a lighter?"

Charlie released his arm from Stacey as she stood back and looked behind them. Eric stood there. She could see dark circles under his eyes that mirrored Jacob's. Only he wasn't dealing with his father dying like Jacob was – so why was he so tired?

"Why would I have a lighter?" Charlie said roughly.

Eric shrugged and turned behind him. "Babe, I need a lighter."

Kailyn teetered up to him in her heels and pulled out a silver lighter. She bent over and lit the tip of Eric's cigarette, smiling at him the entire time. He took a drag from his cigarette and waved the smoke away from his face.

"Thanks. This is my brother, Charlie. He's married to Stacey."

Kailyn turned to look at Charlie who had a funny expression on his face. It was half irritation and half trying not to laugh. The end result made his mouth twist in a strange manner.

"You're Eric's brother? I've heard so much about you!" she exclaimed loudly. "All nice things, naturally. Anyway, he said you're starting your own business! How exciting!"

This woman, Kailyn, was drunk, Stacey realized. She was so caught up in Eric appearing here that she didn't notice it at first. Yet in front of her, Kailyn swayed uncertainly on her feet and her eyes looked glassy.

"How long have you been seeing Eric?" Charlie asked kindly.

"Uhhhh…," she dragged it out as she thought, sucking on her bottom lip. "Like a week?"

"Wow, a whole week," Charlie remarked although Kailyn was too drunk to notice the dig, "Amazing. How did you two meet?"

"I was a waitress at this diner down south that Eric stopped by almost every day just to see me. And then he said he was going back home and wanted to know if I wanted to come with him and how could I resist that?" She slurred a little at the final word but otherwise was masking her voice well enough.

"Romantic," Charlie quipped, and Stacey nudged him with her elbow in a silent voice of 'be nice'.

Kailyn beamed at the two of them but before she could say anything else, Eric spoke up, "Honey, can you get me another drink?"

She nodded and left to go back into the penthouse. They watched her go and when she was out of ear shot, it was Charlie who spoke first.

"Honestly, what the hell are you doing?"

"What, you don't like her?" Eric asked and then waved his hand around his face. "Fuck, sorry, Stacey. The baby."

"You could put the cigarette out, you know," Charlie snapped.

"I could but I really want this," he replied stubbornly.

"It's okay. I'll go," Stacey said even though she didn't like the idea of leaving the brothers alone.

She made her way back into the penthouse. Christmas music was playing now, although her festive mood seemed to have vanished. Kailyn had gotten distracted on the way to another drink and was talking to Brad who was looking as if he were talking to a side show exhibit.

What was the deal with Eric just bringing someone like Kailyn to this event? Was that what he was doing all these months – just shacking up with various women and taking them around with him? If so, Kailyn was probably the feather in his cap. There was no way she'd fit in here. Eric probably didn't even care for her too much.

Stacey suddenly felt bad for the woman. Out of her element, already drunk – there were probably more issues with Kailyn than she was letting on. Maybe it was her motherly protective urges kicking in, but she made her way over to Kailyn.

"Hey, what's up?" she asked nicely.

Brad raised his eyebrows. "Uh, not much. Kailyn… Kailyn?" When she nodded to confirm her name, he went on, "Kailyn was just telling me about how she's dating your brother-in-law."

"That's right. Actually, Kailyn, I'd love to hear more about how that has been. Why don't we go over here?" She linked arms with the woman.

She nodded and Stacey was able to steer her away from Brad, who mouthed a 'thank you' to her. She led Kailyn into another room that had a pool table and a bar. A TV was on, playing some sports program that three men were watching. They didn't pay the two of them any attention. She allowed Kailyn to seat herself on a couch in the back of the room before sitting down next to her.

"So, Eric, huh? Must be fun," Stacey remarked, hoping she didn't sound phony.

If she did, Kailyn didn't notice and replied, "So much fun. He said he'd take care of everything money-wise. Which is good because I'm low on funds right now. It's been a pretty crazy week."

"What have you guys been up to?"

"Drinking, mostly. Partying. Eric knows where all the great parties are. You know, he didn't mention a brother until last night though. And I was like 'oh why is that?' and he said his brother was a jerk but he seemed quite nice out there! No offense. You're married to his brother, right?"

"Ah, yeah but it's fine. No offense taken. He didn't say why he decided to come back here?"

Kailyn shook her head and her snowman earrings bobbed against her thin neck. "Nope. He doesn't like to talk too much about the past."

"What about you? I mean, it's Christmas Eve. No family to stay with?"

Kailyn leaned over Stacey and grabbed a drink that was left on the table. Stacey was about to suggest getting a fresh one, but Kailyn downed the remaining whiskey in one gulp before settling back down on the couch.

"Didn't want it to go to waste," she explained before saying, "No. My parents are dead. I was an only child. Been working at that diner for years and years. Figured well, why the fuck not? Eric has money, too. Did you know that?"

"Yes."

"That's right, sorry," Kailyn replied. "Anyway, when a rich man wants to take me around the town, I'm not going to say no!"

Stacey nodded in agreement but something nagged at the back of her mind. She felt as if the hairs on the back of her neck were standing up. Dead end job. Parents dead. The only difference was Kailyn was an only child. Stacey was staring at herself in an alternate universe.

"Will you excuse me for a moment?" she said quickly, standing up.

"Yeah, tell Eric I'm in here, will you? Do you think the woman who owns this place would care if we snuck off somewhere?" The implication of what 'sneaking off' meant was clear.

"Probably, yes," Stacey said, and left the room, heading back to find Charlie and Eric.

Chapter Seven

The brothers weren't on the balcony. Stacey turned around and discovered Allison standing next to her. She jumped in surprise.

"How do you do that? You're just magically appearing everywhere tonight," Stacey remarked.

"What's the deal with that woman Eric brought? Is he dating her? Has he lost his mind?"

"Yes and yes."

Allison clicked her tongue against the roof of her mouth. "She looks like she's on something. Where is she?"

"Wanting Eric to fuck her in one of your rooms. Don't look at me like that! I told her you would mind."

"Oh, that'll show her," Allison scoffed and marched off to probably go drag Kailyn into her line of sight.

Stacey watched her go and sighed. She went into the kitchen to see if Charlie and Eric were in there. Amanda was in the corner talking to Brad. William got sucked into a conversation with Jacob and looked like he was falling asleep on the spot.

She went over to Amanda and Brad. "Have you guys seen Charlie?"

"Yeah, they went to the other side of the penthouse. This place is massive. I feel like I'd get lost and be found, like, a week later starving to death," Brad remarked.

"Thanks," she said quickly and hurried out of the kitchen.

Always this hallway, Stacey thought to herself as she walked down past the bathroom where she had started bleeding and past the library where Tony had grabbed her. She made a mental note to tell her sister that this side of the place was cursed or something.

She stopped in front of one of the guest rooms. She could hear voices and opened the door, hoping it wasn't the two people she dreaded them to be.

It wasn't. Inside, Charlie had Eric pinned against the wall and was raising his fist as if to punch him. Stacey cried out and ran over, grabbing his arm. Charlie looked back in surprise. Eric took advantage of this and pushed Charlie hard. He toppled backward onto the bed.

Stacey reached out and grabbed Eric, trying to tug him away from his brother. But he shrugged her off and tackled Charlie.

Stacey stood and watched the two grown men wrestle like children on the bed. There was a solid thud of Charlie's fist connecting with Eric's shoulder, who grunted in return and kicked Charlie off the bed. He hit the floor and Eric lunged after him.

Sibling rivalries were the worst, Stacey declared to herself. They turned grown adults into children, no matter the age. There was no way she was going to get in the middle of the fray. The last thing she needed was to trip and fall in her condition. She felt weary of both Charlie and Eric in that moment.

Maybe they just needed to wrestle like absolute idiots together. Stacey took a step back with her back against the door and crossed her arms. She was mentally forming a lecture in her head when Charlie finally stood up.

"Enough!" he strained through a ragged breath. "Get off me!" He pushed Eric away when he tried to swing another punch.

"Are you two finished?" Stacey said in a clipped tone. "Honestly, you guys aren't twelve anymore."

"He kissed you!" Charlie exclaimed. "I've been wanting to punch him ever since!"

He jerked his arms as if to gesture to Eric. But Eric's head was bent, looking down at something on his shirt. Charlie's elbow accidently slammed into Eric's nose and sent him jolting back.

"Fuck!" he exclaimed in surprise.

Blood gushed out of his nose all over the white button-up shirt. It bloomed across his chest like roses. Charlie began to apologize but Eric jerked away from him in irritation.

It was then that someone tried to get into the bedroom. Stacey was pushed forward as Allison wedged her way into the room.

"What the fuck is going on in here?! It sounds like people are either fucking or murdering each other!" she snapped in irritation, looking around the room. When her eyes landed on Eric bleeding, she huffed.

"Allison, let me explain –" Charlie began, but his sister-in-law raised her hand up to fend him off.

"No, I don't want to hear it. If you weren't married to my sister, I'd kick you out. No offense, Charlie, but you're always a handful at my parties."

He opened his mouth as if to protest but thought better of it and closed it instead.

"And you, Eric – you weren't even invited. So take yourself, your bleeding nose and your weird girlfriend and please leave," Allison said firmly.

Eric covered his nose but the blood kept dripping through his fingers. Allison turned around and left, shutting the door behind her. Stacey went over to the two of them and led Eric into the ensuite bathroom.

Behind her, Charlie spoke. "I didn't mean to connect like that. It was an accident."

"Does it matter?" Stacey asked tiredly. "You two were fighting like little kids anyway. Come here, Eric."

She tore off a wad of toilet paper and had him try to stop the bleeding. His shirt looked as if he had been in a bar fight. She made a clucking noise as Eric held the toilet paper against his nose.

"Go lie down on the bed," she ordered him.

Without any protest, he moved past Charlie and flopped down on the bed they were just fighting on, holding the tissue against his nose. Then she turned to Charlie.

"What is wrong with you two? This is how you settle differences? Fist fighting? This isn't some playground spat. I left you alone before and you two were talking. What the hell happened?"

From the bed, muffled due to his nose, Eric spoke up, "He's a dick."

"No, that isn't a reason. You two need to actually hold a conversation and work things out. How long are you going to do this for?"

"He kissed you, Stacey. Why am I supposed to forgive him for that?" Charlie protested. "We tried to speak and he's just – he's impossible to talk to! He isn't going to change."

"Me?" Eric protested from the bed. "Why do I have to change? You need to change… asshole."

"You're the one who couldn't handle Dad being mean to you so you've spent months running away, probably drinking and fucking your way around the country!" Charlie said.

"Enough! This is exactly what I mean!" Stacey exclaimed. "This isn't a conversation. It's just fighting.

Charlie, I know. I know what he did, okay. But Eric knew what he was doing too. He knew kissing me was just a way to ruin things," she lowered her voice. "He knew he could run away then. It gave him a way out."

Charlie exhaled slowly as if fending off the urge to go over and punch Eric again, who was lying silently on the bed, waiting for his nose to stop bleeding.

"You two can't keep doing this," she said.

"Why not? Looks to be working just fine," Eric replied, his voice sounding clogged.

Stacey turned to look at him. "You aren't helping things and you know it. Whatever you went through since Terry said those things to you – you can't just sit on them forever. Is this what you want? To be absolved from doing anything because your father said you were nothing? Makes life easier, doesn't it? You can go anywhere you want and not be expected to do anything because of your father. And when you're bored, you come back here and cause trouble. That's what you want life to be?"

Eric didn't reply. He was very still on the bed. Stacey turned back to Charlie.

"You're going to be a father soon. Is that what you want your child seeing? At this rate, you and Eric won't have any relationship at all, which means our child won't have an uncle. Are you okay with that?"

Charlie didn't reply right away. He just stared at her, wide-eyed, before he mumbled, "I hadn't considered that."

"No, of course not." She shook her head and walked toward the door. "I'm going to spend some time with Allison. Eric, you should leave once your nose is done bleeding or she'll flip."

With that, she closed the door behind her.

Chapter Eight

When Charlie and Stacey got home that night, she could feel that he wanted to talk about what happened. But Stacey didn't feel like it. She was tired. Her feet were sore. She had spent most of the party on her feet, clinging to Allison as if she could ward off the bad vibes of Charlie and Eric.

She had seen Eric take Kailyn by the hand and leave twenty minutes later. Kailyn had protested, trying to explain that she wanted another drink. By this time, she was so drunk that Stacey couldn't understand how she was even standing.

Charlie, as if sensing her mood, had kept a safe distance from her for the rest of the party. He probably thought she was angry. The truth was that Stacey wasn't angry – just mostly tired.

Yet she couldn't help but wonder why she was putting so much energy into Charlie's familial problems. Perhaps she saw something of how she and Allison used to be in them. She thought if Allison could become someone she eventually grew to have such a great relationship with, surely Charlie could get that way with Eric.

But, she thought, as she took her shoes off in the entranceway of their home, it was time to focus on her pregnancy and getting ready for the baby's arrival. She was putting too much energy into getting the two brothers to be friendly to each other.

"Can I get you anything?" Charlie asked her.

"Just a water, actually. Thanks," she replied as she plopped down onto the couch.

A minute later, Charlie returned with a bottle of water. She took it, mumbling a 'thanks' and opened it. He sat down next to her. For a split second, he looked like a child waiting for a lecture. If Stacey didn't feel so tired, she would have found it funny.

Munchkin was under the tree, sleeping soundly. Stacey wished she could be a cat. Imagine just sleeping anywhere like that.

"Can we talk about Eric?"

She sighed, "I'm tired, Charlie. Physically tired and also just in general about your brother."

"He has that effect on people," he replied and when he saw the warning look on her face, he cleared his throat. "I mean, just… like, he has a lot of effects on people."

"Nice save." She rolled her eyes.

"Maybe I haven't been… trying as hard as I could be. With Eric. Although, I don't know if I should be the one making all the effort, because he did kiss you. I don't think I've mentioned that enough."

"You might have brought it up like, once or twice," Stacey joked.

Charlie ran his fingers through his hair. "I didn't mean to make him bleed. I was holding back that entire fight. I could have really decked him if I wanted to."

"So kind of you," she replied dryly.

"Come on, I don't get a little credit for that?"

"For not pummeling your brother senseless at my sister's Christmas Eve party?"

"Well, when you word it like that…" He cleared his throat. "There's history with my brother. Nothing good."

"I already know this, Charlie," she said with a sigh. "Honestly, I can't stand having this conversation yet again. I meant what I said earlier. Think of it this way – if you two don't work out your grievances, then your father won here too. Do you want that?"

She stood up, ready for bed. Charlie didn't say anything. Before she left she paused, looked back at him, and sighed.

"I'm not angry. You know that, right? But I can't just keep going around in circles about Eric. I know what he did. I know it was a shitty thing to do. But I also know that he reminds you of your mother. You said that's why Terry has an issue with him, but what about you?"

A funny look crossed Charlie's face. Stacey shrugged, too weary to say anything. Then she turned around and headed to the bedroom to sleep.

<<<>>>

In her dream that night, she was at Terry's manor. It was storming outside and the power had been knocked out. Stacey was walking down the stairs to get to the living room. For some reason, she knew Charlie was down there with her child. She could hear them whispering. Her steps quickened.

Yet when she got to the living room, it was empty. Stacey looked around for them but they weren't there. A sudden noise made her turn around. Eric was standing in the doorway. His shirt was covered in blood and he was smoking a cigarette.

"Looking for your kid?" he said to her and when she nodded, he said, "No idea. Can't see the kid, remember?"

Stacey looked to the right to see that long hallway again. There was a door at the end. She headed toward it, knowing that Charlie was there. Someone reached out and grabbed her wrist, yanking her back.

"What are you doing?" It was Eric.

"I have to go," Stacey said, although her words came out slowly and slurred.

"They don't want to see you. They don't want you as a part of their lives any longer. You're stuck here with me."

Alarmed, she tried to pull away from Eric's hand. But his grip was iron-tight, and he didn't budge. With his free hand, he held out a cigarette.

"Want one?"

Stacey felt a wail swell in her throat – a panicked cry at never seeing Charlie and her child again –

<<<>>>

"I'm here, I'm here. It's just a dream!" Charlie's arms were around her and she woke up with her face pressed into his neck.

For a second, she was still in the dream with Eric pulling on her wrist. She could smell the cigarette smoke wafting off of him and tried to push herself away.

"Stacey, it's me! You're awake!" he exclaimed.

His voice cut through the dream fog that was still wafting within her brain. She took a deep breath and stopped trying to break free. Charlie moved so that he could see her face. It was dark in the room but she could make out the outline of his jaw and his eyes on hers.

"Just a dream," he repeated and kissed her gently.

"S-sorry. Sorry. I woke you up again. I'm sorry," she blathered.

"No, it's fine. Do you need anything? Some water?"

Now that he mentioned it, she was feeling parched. It was as if she had crossed the desert or something. She nodded and he slid out of bed, going into the bathroom and coming back with a glass of water.

She drank it quickly and could feel her heart beat slowing down.

"Dreams have been more vivid since I got pregnant."

"I wish you could have dreams of you just watching TV or reading… something mellow," Charlie said.

"Me too. There's always something just out of reach or I'm being kept away from something." Even now, the dream was fading and no matter how hard she tried, it was harder to cling to the images that had terrorized her before.

"Can I help you relax?" Charlie asked her, brushing a lock of her hair off her face.

"I might watch some TV. I don't think I'll be able to sleep."

"I have a different idea."

Something in his tone caught her attention. She turned to look at him. He leaned forward and kissed her gently on the lips.

She shook her head. "Charlie, I don't –"

"I don't mean that," he whispered in her ear.

Stacey didn't follow until his hand slid under her pajama bottoms and trailed across the front of her underwear. The sudden touch sent a shock through her. It had been a while since they had fooled around. Charlie, after working long hours, would come home exhausted and fall promptly asleep. Some nights, Stacey just wasn't feeling up to it. To feel his touch now sparked something inside of her.

Charlie gently pressed her down against the bed and moved her underwear aside. His fingers were warm and probed along her skin. She closed her eyes, letting the feeling of him wash over her.

One of his fingers slid gently inside of her. He moved it around, letting her get used to the sensation. She could hear Charlie breathing in her ear as he pumped his finger inside of her.

Then his finger was gone. Alarmed, she opened her eyes, wanting to protest. But Charlie pressed his lips to hers before he began to slide down her body. She felt him tug off her pajama bottoms.

His finger trailed down the front of her pussy again and then he slowly lowered her panties. In the darkness, she could just make out his head down by her thighs. She felt butterfly kisses along her thighs which caused goosebumps to pebble her skin.

Then Charlie flicked his tongue along her wetness, causing her to gasp in surprise. The sensation was so sudden that she raised her hips slightly. Charlie took that as a sign she wanted more.

Gripping her thighs, Charlie began to flick his tongue along her clit. Stacey let out a small moan as his tongue flicked and rolled over her clit. His fingers dug into her thighs as he moved his tongue around her wet pussy.

Then, one of his fingers entered her. He alternated between pumping his finger inside of her and rolling his tongue across her clit. Sliding a second finger inside of her, Stacey's hips bucked as she felt her orgasm mounting.

Charlie was buried in between her thighs with his tongue moving swiftly along her pussy. Two fingers were moving in and out of her quickly, hitting just the right spot, her G-spot. Her entire body tingled with pleasure.

He wrapped his lips around her clit and jammed his fingers deep inside of her. As he continued to massage her pleasure spot, Stacey felt an urge to pee. She tensed up momentarily, causing Charlie to look up and say, "Let it go. It's okay. Give in to this."

Trusting Charlie's words, she relaxed and gave in to the sensation. Charlie continued the rhythmic massage with his two fingers and lapping at her clit with his tongue.

That was enough to send her over the edge. Stacey moaned loudly as her love juices flowed freely, practically squirting into Charlie's mouth. Her entire body shuddered as she felt her orgasm spasm through her whole being. Charlie kept his face down there, moving his fingers still deep inside her.

The sensation was so intense as the waves of pleasure rolled through her that Stacey went limp immediately afterward. She had never experienced a deep G-spot orgasm before. He moved away from her and slid up to kiss her. She could taste herself on him and she kissed him passionately. Already her eyes were trying to close. She could feel sleep coming for her.

Against her skin, she could feel Charlie smile and she knew all was right in the world. He kissed the top of her head and sleep came for her swiftly.

<<<>>>

Christmas morning was a quiet affair. Charlie told Stacey she could invite anyone she wanted, yet she opted for spending it with him and their cat. He gave her a beautiful necklace. In return, Stacey gave him a sweater she knitted during the time she had been resting.

"I didn't even know you took up knitting," he said as he held up the sweater.

"It was a secret. You could buy anything you want so I decided to make you something one-of-a-kind."

He smiled and said, "I love it," as he slipped it on.

It was a little large but Charlie said he didn't care. He brought her in for a big kiss before asking, "What did Allison think of the gift?"

"She said she was going to open it today. I think she was too annoyed with how the party unfolded to open any gifts. I'm sure she'll call me when she does."

"Well, what do you want for dinner tonight? I'll cook everything."

Stacey cringed. "Last time you cooked, dinner was a disaster."

It was true. Charlie had made dinner a month ago. It was supposed to be a surprise for her, but he practically burnt the kitchen down.

"That was just an unfortunate pasta related incident," Charlie said, as if reading her mind.

Stacey laughed. "Oh, is that what we're calling it now?"

He grinned when the elevator doors dinged, alerting them to someone coming in. Alarmed, Charlie got up and went over to see who it was. Stacey couldn't imagine who would be coming to their home on Christmas Day.

She hurried after Charlie and watched in surprise as, of all people, his father, Terry, stepped in, followed by Adele.

"Merry fucking Christmas," she heard Charlie mumble under his breath.

Chapter Nine

Terry and Adele were followed by Eric and Kailyn. The sight of all of them in their home was a shock. Stacey could tell by the look on Charlie's face that he was not expecting this either.

Terry looked as if he had aged ten years since the last time she saw him. He was hunched over and clutching his cane. Adele was helping him by resting one arm on his shoulder as if to steer him. Was Stacey imagining things or did she have dark circles under her eyes?

Behind them, Eric looked just as exhausted. Kailyn was exclaiming loudly about how nice the foyer looked. Her high heels lit up when they hit the floor, Stacey noticed, and she was pretty sure they were something only strippers wore.

Charlie went up to them and said, "This is a surprise. What do I owe this… pleasure?" He paused on the last word as he looked over at his brother.

"Dad here surprised me at the hotel I was staying at," Eric replied. "Said he wanted to spend Christmas with us. He came by this morning."

He looked over at Terry but it was Adele who said, "He wanted it to be a surprise. So we didn't call you."

"What if we'd had plans?" Charlie crossed his arms.

At this Terry snorted, "I knew you'd be holed up in here with your wife."

He pushed past Charlie to go farther into the penthouse. Charlie's face turned to stone as he turned back to look at Eric. The two of them were whispering now but Stacey couldn't hear anything they were saying.

Terry and Adele stopped in front of her. Terry mumbled a greeting before heading over to the kitchen. Stacey watched him go at a snail's pace. Then she turned back to Adele who was wrinkling her nose.

"Do you have a cat in here?"

"Yes. Why?"

"I'm allergic," Adele replied, offended at the mere idea that there was a cat in the same space as her.

"That's a real shame," Stacey said. "Guess you'll have to spend Christmas elsewhere."

Irritation flickered across Adele's eyes and she pressed her lips into a thin line. "No, I'm fine."

"Great," Stacey drawled as she took off to follow Terry, who sounded as if he was rummaging around in the kitchen.

Kailyn came over to her and crushed her in a hug as if they were best friends. Her eyeliner was smudged, and she smelled of whisky and that same perfume she had worn the night before. The scent made Stacey's eyes water.

"Merry Christmas!" she said in Stacey's ear before heading off into the kitchen.

Stacey went over to Charlie and Eric. Their heads were bowed together as if they were almost praying. They didn't seem to be fighting at all. It was a strange sight. Stacey lowered her voice to ask what the hell was going on.

Eric replied, "It was exactly as I said. Dad stopped by out of the blue. Adele was with him and said he wanted to spend Christmas with us. I told him that was a bad idea, but he said he was going over anyway and I could either come along or not. So, I came because I thought it'd be better than just having Dad come after you."

"Why didn't you call me?"

"I did!" Eric protested. "Your phone went straight to voicemail."

"Shit, I forgot to charge it last night." Charlie rubbed his face with his hands before turning to Stacey. "What do you want to do?"

"We can't kick them out. It's Christmas."

"It's also my dad."

"Yeah but," Stacey looked over her shoulder and lowered her voice. "There has to be a reason he came here. Think about it. You haven't heard from him in months and he shows up for Christmas?"

Eric begrudgingly said, "She has a point."

"Why did you have to bring Kailyn?" Charlie asked Eric.

"Hey listen, don't get mad at me for that. She was with me when Dad came over. What am I supposed to say?"

"You need to break up with her," Stacey remarked.

He looked at her, surprised. "Why?"

"Come on. She's a mess, first off. And I know you only brought her here to piss off Charlie." Stacey crossed her arms.

Eric looked abashed. "I will. After this trip, okay? I'm not going to dump her now. Not when Dad is here. He's going to loathe her."

"What a beautiful relationship you have," Charlie replied.

Eric shrugged and moved past the two of them before turning around and saying, "Let's go enjoy Christmas with our father."

Stacey watched him go into the kitchen and looked over at Charlie. His lips were tightly pressed and he looked as if he wanted to go right to bed. Munchkin appeared at the end of the hallway and sauntered down toward them.

"Adele said she's allergic to cats," Stacey remembered out loud to Charlie as she scooped up Munchkin.

"Great, maybe she'll have to leave sooner," Charlie replied as he turned to look at her. "Do you really think Dad has another reason for being here?"

"Yes. It's not like him, correct? There has to be a reason he showed up. Just don't lose your cool and try to stay on Eric's side. If he sees that you two are getting along, it might throw a wrench in his plans."

He nodded and took a deep breath, "Alright. Let's go."

He reached over and grabbed Stacey's hand. Together, they went into the kitchen. Kailyn cornered Eric by the fridge and threw her arms around his neck. She was cooing in his ear. Eric's arm was around her waist and he was mumbling in her ear. It felt as if Stacey walked into the beginning of a pornographic film.

Terry stared at them in distaste but didn't say anything, which was shocking enough. Stacey cleared her throat.

Eric turned his head. "Well, I could go for a Bloody Mary."

A scowl crossed Terry's face. "Drinking already?" he remarked.

"Come on, Dad, it's like nine in the morning. An hour later than I usually start," Eric replied as he pulled out everything to make the drinks.

Stacey was taken back to that morning in the manor when Charlie left to go into town with Terry. It was one of the first times that she had been around Eric. A sense of déjà vu washed over her. It was the sight of Charlie looking at his father warily and Eric making a drink just to get under Terry's skin that propelled her forward.

"What would you like to drink?" she directed this to Terry who eyed her warily.

"Coffee."

"Great, I'll make you some." She moved toward the coffee machine, aware that Terry was watching her.

"Charlie, you want a Bloody Mary?" Eric asked him over his shoulder.

Stacey couldn't help but flick her gaze over to her husband. This was it, she thought to herself. Was Charlie going to show a united front with Eric or not? She found herself holding her breath as she turned away to pull down the coffee from the cupboard above her head.

"Yes," Charlie replied, "I'll take one."

She looked over at Eric, who donned what could only be described as a 'shit-eating grin' on his face. "Wonderful."

She heard Terry make a disgusted sound in his throat, "Really, boy?"

Charlie ignored him and looked at Stacey, "You got the coffee?"

"Yup! You know, I think we have some pastries over there. We can all snack on those and catch up."

Kailyn clasped her hands together and chimed, "Eric, make me a drink too, will you?"

"Of course. Drinks for everyone. Except for Stacey, for obvious reasons."

Stacey turned back to the coffee machine and tried to hide the smile that was forming on her face.

They settled in around the dining room table. The pastries were placed in the center along with a carafe of coffee. Adele was perched at the end of her chair as if she was getting ready to flee at any sign of their cat. Kailyn was drinking her Bloody Mary as if she was suffering from dehydration. Terry was seated and looking shrunken. There was an odd expression on his face that Stacey had never seen before. He looked almost uncertain. Could he ever be uncertain?

Yet it was Charlie and Eric who looked the most at ease. Eric was leaning back in the chair, wobbling on the back legs. It was the sort of thing a child did to irritate a parent which was apparently working. Terry kept glancing over. Charlie was next to his brother, looking at something on his cellphone.

The entire situation was surreal, Stacey thought. Whatever Terry's reason was for coming over here on Christmas, if he thought he had the upper hand, he was mistaken.

"Been a while since we saw you, Dad. So, how have things been?" Eric spoke up, slamming the legs of the chair hard against the floor.

Terry flinched and then his face turned to stone again, "We've been planning the wedding."

"Ah, the wedding. And what a wedding it'll be, right? Going to be beautiful," Eric said in a tone so dry that if Stacey didn't know him at all, she would have thought that he was serious.

"How is the planning going?" Charlie asked, jumping into the conversation.

"Fine," Terry said at the same time Adele said, "Stressful."

The brothers glanced at each other. Something passed between them. It was so quick that Stacey thought she might have imagined it. Eric leaned forward toward his dad.

"Stressful? Ah, that's no good. You should do what Stacey and Charlie did. The courthouse. Skip that mess."

"No, thank you. I would like a proper wedding," Adele replied primly.

"Well, what do I know, right?" Eric said and held up his hands in front of his chest. "I'm not getting married any time soon."

From the other side of the table, Kailyn laughed loudly, "Yet! You mean 'yet'!"

"Right," Eric swiftly corrected. "Yet. Who knows what could happen?"

Stacey cleared her throat. She was all for making their father squirm, but she wasn't going to give Kailyn any hope of Eric proposing. He must have sensed what she was thinking because he quickly changed the subject.

"Where are you guys going to get hitched? I mean, this is going to be a pretty big deal, right? Merging of the companies. Fantastic."

"It doesn't concern you, boy," Terry said, finding renewed vigor. "You won't be attending. I've been trying to get in touch with you for months and you have been off doing Lord knows what. I don't need you mucking up the wedding."

"I'm crushed, truly," Eric replied in a voice that sounded decidedly *not* crushed. "But what can I do?" He picked up a pastry and crammed the entire thing in his mouth as he shrugged at his father.

Terry looked disgusted and turned his attention to Charlie. "What about you, boy? You haven't been speaking to me either. Here I am, planning a wedding and you haven't offered to help."

"Been a little busy," Charlie replied lightly.

Terry scoffed, "With what? Not your business, I'm sure. I've been hearing things –"

"You've been hearing things because you're pulling the strings. That means you're all caught up so there's no need to talk about it. Let's just focus on the wedding. Must be exciting to remarry after all these years."

Terry stared at Charlie for a long moment. His eyes went to Eric who was still attempting to chew the pastry he had shoved into his mouth. Kailyn yawned loudly. Stacey turned to look at her.

"Are you tired?"

"Yeah, I didn't get much sleep last night, if you know what I mean," she said and laughed loudly.

Behind her, she heard Adele make a disapproving noise. Terry looked disgusted. Eric winked at Kailyn, who pursed her lips and blew a kiss back at him.

"Would you like to nap? Why don't I show you to one of the guest rooms?" Stacey offered, getting to her feet.

Kailyn agreed, to Stacey's relief. Yes, the woman was a mess, but Stacey felt strangely protective of her. She didn't deserve to be put on display just to piss off Terry. She got Kailyn into one of the guest rooms, who fell asleep almost the instant her head hit the pillow. Covering her with a blanket, Stacey went back into the dining room.

Adele launched into a story about searching for the perfect wedding dress. There was something monotone and mechanical to her story, as if she had been repeating it for days on end. Terry looked bored as he stared into his coffee cup. Stacey wished she could cut through the garbage and figure out why he was really here.

Eric, of course, was taking everything very seriously. He was pretending to be so fascinated by

Adele's story that it was almost comical. He moved to the opposite side of the table and was leaning forward, nodding his head often.

Stacey sat down next to him and glanced over at her husband. He wasn't acting as over the top as his brother, but he was still actively nodding his head while Adele told her story.

"Anyway, so I get it back and the dress didn't fit. For the third time, if you can believe it," Adele was saying.

"No!" Eric exclaimed, "That's ridiculous."

Stacey shot him a look but he ignored her. Even so, up this close she could see that he was fighting the urge to laugh. Something caught her eye, however, on his collarbone. She hadn't noticed it before. The night before, he had worn a shirt with a collar that covered it. Not to mention, she had been preoccupied with helping him staunch the blood from his nose.

Without thinking, Stacey exclaimed, "Did you get a tattoo?"

Adele stopped speaking, looking annoyed at having been interrupted. Eric looked down at his collarbone and yanked his shirt down a little. There was a tattoo there – two very small birds circling around each other in blue ink. It was a simple tattoo and ultimately generic. She had no idea why he would have gotten it.

But the reaction from Terry was almost immediate. "A *tattoo*? This is what you do? You run off and get tattoos? Disgusting!"

"I think I was drunk," Eric replied with obvious glee at bothering Terry. "Am I grounded, Dad?"

"Disgusting. I can't believe I raised a son who's smoking and getting tattoos. Charlie, tell your brother. Tell him how disgusting that is."

Eric pulled out a pack of cigarettes. "Wow, speaking of cigarettes. Been about an hour since my last one." He stood up and looked over at Charlie. "Are you going to lecture me?"

But Charlie shook his head, "Nah, I could go for a smoke myself."

"What?!" Terry exclaimed, also getting to his feet. "Stop this! Your mother wouldn't approve of any of this."

But the brothers didn't reply. Charlie opened the balcony door, allowing Eric to step out first. Stacey watched them as he slid out a cigarette and handed one to Charlie. Then he pulled out his lighter and leaned over, lighting up the cigarette. Terry watched as Charlie took a drag from it. Then Eric lit his up and did the same. The two of them then turned their backs on Terry as they smoked.

Terry turned toward Stacey. She braced herself for a lecture – how could she do this, what did she do to his boys – but instead he asked for more coffee.

Surprised, Stacey nodded and took the empty carafe into the kitchen to refill it. As she was doing so, Adele came into the kitchen, eying Stacey warily.

"Need something?" she asked Adele.

"How did you get them to get along?"

"What?"

"Eric and Charlie. It's clear what they're doing. Trying to show Terry he has no power over them anymore. I'm assuming that it's your doing."

Stacey poured the carafe full of coffee and then replied, "I can't force those things. Whatever happened, it was ultimately up to them."

Adele marched over and yanked the coffee away from Stacey. She turned to look at her yet didn't feel afraid. She used to feel insecure when it came to Adele. Here was a woman that Terry wanted in the family. He had wanted her to marry Charlie and help control the company. But Stacey had been allowing Adele to have that power.

Staring at Adele now, she felt only pity. This person who wanted nothing more than to marry into this family at any cost. Why did Stacey feel so insecure around her?

"He's going to call off the wedding. He hasn't said it yet. But I can feel it. I'm going to lose everything I have spent planning," Adele said to her in a thin voice.

"I'm sorry," Stacey said, and then corrected herself. "No. Not really. But I am sorry that you think this is the only way to live your life. Because you're pretty and rich and bored. So, you've made getting into this family your entire life goal. And I'm sorry for that, because you are wasting real talents."

Adele looked as if she had been smacked in the face before replying, "You're the one who ruined it. Charlie would have married me. I was so close and then you swept in with your sob story about being poor. He ate it up."

"I'm not interested in discussing me or whatever you think of me, Adele. Terry is here because he doesn't want to marry you, right? This whole thing is some Christmas guilt trip in disguise. He thought Charlie would come back when he said he was going to marry you and now he realizes that isn't the case."

"Yes. Yes, okay, you're right. Is that what you want me to say? You seem to forget that I have known this family a lot longer than you have, Stacey. I know what Terry is like. There isn't a kind bone left in his body. He needs Charlie's leadership. He keeps trying to bribe people not to work with Charlie or to not leave the company to go work for Charlie. But the truth is that his son has a strong following there. They respect him as a leader and they hate that he left."

"You mean…"

"Yes," Adele said quickly, "I mean that Terry is bleeding money trying to bribe people to stay. Most of the people who work higher up want to jump ship and help Charlie out with this new company. And instead of just stopping this madness, Terry has come here in one final attempt to bring Charlie back."

"It won't work," Stacey said simply. "Charlie has put too much into this. He knows what his father is doing and just refuses to go back to him. Terry can marry you, he can bleed himself dry in bribing people to stay but time will tell."

"Eric and Charlie are getting along," Adele said. "At least for now. Terry wasn't expecting that. He never wants them to get along. Surely, you've noticed that by now. Easier to keep them separated than friendly. If they get along now…"

"Tell Terry it's over. It's over for you too, Adele. Get a hobby or something. Go travel. I don't know. Just don't waste time on this anymore."

She gently took the coffee out of Adele's hands and went out to the dining room. Terry watched the brothers out on the balcony. Eric was lighting up a second cigarette. Charlie, who was only smoking to irritate his father, took a slow, deep drag. Stacey poured a cup of coffee for Terry, who turned to look at her.

"Would you like a pastry?" Stacey offered.

"Where is Adele?"

"In the kitchen."

He made a clucking noise and then looked down at his coffee, "Is there any sugar in this place?"

"Sugar, coming right up," Stacey said politely and slid the sugar bowl from the other end of the table over to him.

Terry eyed her warily as she sat back down. He scooped two spoonsful of sugar into the mug as Stacey grabbed a pastry. She took a bite of it and smiled at Terry.

"You're an interesting woman," he finally said to her.

"Is that right?"

"At first, I thought all of this was your fault. That you were some poor girl looking for hand-outs. I heard about your sister marrying Jacob. No one could love that boy."

"He's quite nice."

"He's a dullard," Terry retorted.

"Still nice," Stacey smiled.

There was a beat of silence before Terry went on, "But I can see now you aren't going anywhere. Charlie is quite taken with you. Eric seems to be fond of you too."

She remained silent. It almost felt as if Terry was fishing for something and she wasn't going to give him any information. She wasn't stupid enough to mention that Eric kissed her all those months ago.

When she didn't reply, Terry said, "You should tell Charlie. Tell him that the company is for him. His mother wouldn't want him to throw this out the window. This investment firm – it's foolish. What sort of billionaire walks away from a company he was in charge of to start an investment firm?"

To get away from you. To make it on his own and not be in your shadow. But instead, Stacey nibbled on the pastry in silence.

Terry seemed almost unnerved by the fact she wasn't speaking because he continued on. "It's funny seeing the two of them getting along. They were always against each other, you know. It didn't help that Eric always chased after Charlie's girlfriends. I'm sure it is just a matter of time until he throws himself at you. What will you do then, I wonder? Most people find Eric very alluring even though he isn't as good-looking as Charlie. Do you know why that is?"

Stacey took another bite of the pastry. She could see Charlie lean over to tell Eric something who glanced over at the dining room table. She gave him a small wave and he grinned before turning back to Charlie.

"Are you listening to me? Do you hear me?" Terry was bothered now. "I'm trying to warn you about Eric."

"Eric is fine," Stacey replied. "The only reason he has any issues, I believe, is because of you. Would your wife really be okay with you telling her sons that one of them is worthless? Would she be okay with you trying to ruin a business your other son is starting? I never met their mother but if she was anything like her sons, I doubt that she would think kindly of you. Now, if you will excuse me…"

She stood up and grabbed her hoodie that was tossed on the counter. Terry stared at her with an expression that could only be described as shock. Adele came into the dining room just then, carrying a Bloody Mary. Stacey made her way to the balcony and slid the door shut behind her.

Charlie was laughing at something Eric had said. His head was thrown back and he was laughing loudly.

It wasn't a phony laugh to get Terry's attention either. It was genuine.

"Everything okay out here?" Stacey asked.

Charlie pulled her in close to him and kissed the top of her head. "Yeah, Eric was just telling me about some bar fight he got into a month ago."

"Put your smoke out, idiot." Eric swiped the cigarette out of Charlie's mouth, butting it out along with his.

"Aw, you're cramping our Piss off Dad session," Charlie joked and kissed her – he tasted of smoke.

"Was he mad?" Eric asked. "When Charlie agreed to have one, I thought he was gonna have a stroke."

"Yeah, he doesn't understand why you two are getting along now. He's freaked."

"Those cigarettes taste disgusting. I have no idea how you can smoke them," Charlie said.

Eric shrugged. "Crippling addiction? I don't know. I hardly notice anymore."

"You should quit." When Eric shrugged, he kept on. "I'm serious. How are you going to be around our kid if you die of lung cancer?"

Surprise crossed Eric's face and he said uncertainly, "Figured I wouldn't be around the kid at all."

"Yeah, well," Charlie exhaled slowly, "wouldn't be fair to my kid, would it? They should see for themselves what a complete idiot their uncle is. It's high comedy."

Eric playfully punched Charlie in the arm but he was laughing. Stacey felt as if she had stepped through the looking glass into an alternate universe. She could practically feel Terry staring at them through it.

"Dad say anything?" Charlie asked her.

Stacey nodded and told the brothers what had unfolded between Adele and then Terry. They listened and both of them wore identical looks of focus on their faces. For the first time since she had been around the two of them, they actually looked related.

When they finished, Charlie spoke first. "So, he's cornered, basically. He needs me to come back."

"Fuck it. You better not cave now," Eric said gruffly.

"I'm not going to. But I don't want the entire company to go to shit because of me. Are you sure you won't take it over?"

"Positive. I thought I wanted that. But I just wanted it because Dad put the idea in my head. I don't want it now."

"Then I have an idea but it will depend on making Dad admit he's fucked up."

"Good luck," Eric snorted.

"No, I think you might have a chance now," Stacey replied. "He seemed sort of all over the place."

"Yeah, plus you just told him our dead mother would think he's an asshole," Eric pointed out and crossed his arms. "I'm pretty impressed."

Charlie looked at Stacey. "I'm going to go try to talk to him." He looked over at Eric. "Try not to murder Adele, or fuck Kailyn while I deal with Dad."

"Yeah, yeah. I'll be fine." Eric waved his hand.

Charlie kissed Stacey again before heading back inside the penthouse. She watched as he said something to Terry who then got to his feet and followed him out of the dining room. Adele was on her phone, texting away.

Stacey pulled her hoodie around her and exhaled nervously.

Chapter Ten

"So," Eric said as he turned to look over at the city, "I actually did want to talk to you."

"Well, if you're going to kiss me, I'd like to suggest holding off. I don't feel like cleaning up blood today."

He laughed and ran his fingers through his hair. "No, no kissing. I wanted to apologize for that. For obvious reasons. At the time, it made sense. You know, Dad said all that shit about me and it was easier to just become what he called me instead of fighting against it."

"That's what you've been doing these past few months, haven't you?"

"Yes. Basically just going from town to town, drinking and sleeping my way around. When I came here with Kailyn, it was just in a moment of ultimate self-destruction. I was hoping secretly that Charlie would beat the shit out of me for what I did."

"Pretty sure he did just that."

"No. We were both holding back. I think even then he didn't want to attack me. After Allison kicked me out like that, I thought to myself *what am I doing? Why did I really come back to the party?*"

Stacey shivered as a gust of wind kicked up over the balcony. Eric noticed and offered his jacket. She declined but he slid out of his jacket and handed it to her anyway.

"Come on. I'm not the pregnant one," he said.

She relented and slipped into the jacket, pulling it over her hoodie, asking, "So, why did you come back to the party?"

"I guess I wanted to see Charlie again. He is my brother, after all. And I was just going down this road of doing whatever I wanted and ultimately, I wanted to see him. I didn't realize it until after I left the party though. I was trying to figure out how to make things right when Dad showed up."

"Well, that's a big step from before when the two of you were content to fight every second. And that isn't just you. Charlie was quick to fight with you no matter what as well."

"I just wanted to apologize to you. For what I did. And I knew when I did it that it was wrong."

"Can I ask you something?" When he nodded, she said, "You said that you wanted to do it that night you were drunk, but you stopped yourself. What did you mean? Mess things up between Charlie and yourself?"

Eric looked surprised for a moment.

A thought struck her. "Eric – you don't… I mean, I assumed that you kissed me to get to Charlie, not because –"

He cut her off swiftly, "I'm over it. Whatever I was feeling at the time, it's gone now. It was stupid to begin with. It won't ever happen again. It shouldn't have happened in the first place. I just hope we can move on from it and you can forgive me for overstepping a serious line."

"Yeah. Yeah, I forgive you. Of course."

Eric visibly relaxed and nodded. "Great. And listen – thanks. For everything. I know you were pushing really hard for me and Charlie to make up. And I think we still have a lot to work through together, but I think this is an important start."

"Me too," Stacey said, and she meant it.

Eric smiled that slow grin that she had come to know well over the past year, and he said, "Remember when I introduced myself as Devin? That was one of my better ones."

She rolled her eyes. "Don't start. Remember when I slapped you?"

"You felt so bad about it too! I should have told you I'm used to being slapped regularly by women I piss off."

She laughed. That was when the sliding door opened and Charlie stepped out. His face was unreadable. Stacey could feel her heart skip a beat and she went over to him.

"How did it go?"

For a split second, she wondered if he was going back to the company. It would be a blow, Stacey decided, not only to her but to Eric, who was looking forward to having a brother again and moving on.

But then a smile broke out across Charlie's face and he smiled brightly, "I'm going to be merging my investment firm with Dad's company. He's relinquishing control. He would rather step down completely than see the company melt. He's calling off the wedding with Adele."

Stacey exclaimed in surprise as Eric said, "That was fast!"

"He crumbled almost right away. Stacey was right. He was nervous and on edge. I just had to give the little push."

Charlie was beaming now, and he brought Stacey in for a hug. His lips pressed against hers and she could feel the warmth from his body. It cut through the jacket and the hoodie she was wearing. She could feel his heart racing with excitement.

Eric came over and brought Charlie in for a hug. She couldn't recall ever seeing them hug before.

"So, what now?" he asked Charlie.

"Paperwork will be drawn up and we'll go from there. Going to be crazy busy for a while but it's always busy. We'll get things ready for the baby too."

Stacey smiled and then looked at Eric, "What about you? What are you going to do?"

"Take Kailyn home. Break up with her. Then, I don't know."

"You know, if you want to come help me out…" Charlie offered.

He shook his head. "Not yet. I need some air from the whole company. Might travel a bit. Properly travel this time, not just party. Figure out what the hell I'm doing."

"Well, if you decide that you want to be involved, let me know."

"Thanks," Eric said, and he smiled.

Stacey stared at the brothers with happiness filling her heart.

"So, is Dad leaving? Maybe we can enjoy this holiday after all," Eric said, playing with a cigarette, clearly trying to bury the urge to light it.

"He said he's going to stay for lunch and then leave with Adele."

"Man, when is he going to tell Adele the wedding is off? She's going to be pissed," Eric said.

As if in reply, Adele's voice rang out, "Are you fucking serious?"

Stacey widened her eyes. "I guess now. Man, your dad doesn't like to wait, does he?"

Charlie shook his head. "No, guess not. Although he could have easily waited until tomorrow."

"Look at the bright side," Eric offered.

"What? That Charlie is going to get his own company and merge it with his father's? I guess that is the bright side."

"No," Eric shook his head. "One less person to feed."

Charlie groaned and Stacey sighed. Eric grinned at them and then moved away to the other side of the balcony, waving his cigarette at them.

"Gotta quit those!" Charlie called after him.

He flipped off Charlie and Stacey watched him light the cigarette. The gesture was a teasing one, not serious. Stacey looked over at Charlie who was smiling and looking like he was on top of the world. How could he not be? Terry came here for one last guilt trip, but it was finally Charlie's time to shine. There was no more control over him.

Even as Adele was freaking out indoors, Stacey decided that this was going to be a good Christmas after all.

Epilogue

Stacey yawned and waited for the coffee machine to beep. She had been up most of the night and was feeling as if someone had smacked her across the head with a frying pan. Next to her, Charlie was rummaging around in the fridge.

"No Bloody Mary mix," he remarked.

"He'll have to get over it." Stacey yawned.

Charlie laughed at that. Jessica padded in and looked up at the two of them with wide brown eyes. "Bloody Mary mix?"

"Not as gross as it sounds," Charlie replied, scooping their daughter up in his arms.

"More gross, actually," Stacey joked.

There was the sound of rushing feet as Alex burst into the kitchen. He was about ten now, all long limbed and awkward looking. His glasses were slipping down the bridge of his nose and he was clutching a tablet in one hand.

"Wow, what's the rush?" Charlie asked him.

"The internet is down. Can I reset the router?"

"Sure, I guess, but it might just be down from the snow storm last night," Stacey said, but Alex was already taking off again like a shot.

She sighed and shook her head. Charlie laughed and looked at Jessica in his arms. "Your brother is silly."

The doorbell rang and Stacey glanced at the clock. "Can't be him already, can it?"

"Might be Allison."

"She said she'd come by later because of all the snow. I'll go see."

Stacey left the dining room and walked toward the front door. She opened the door and was surprised to see Allison and Jacob on the doorstep.

"Hey! I thought you'd come by later!"

"They plowed our streets early. It only took us like, an hour to get here," her sister joked. "You know, instead of the normal twenty. Merry Christmas!"

She threw her arms around Stacey. Allison, Jacob, and their son, Vinny, had been out of the country for the past three months. It was a surprise when they had come home a week ago. However, both women had been too busy to see each other.

"Get inside so you guys don't catch a chill or something. Vinny, how are you?" Stacey asked the seven-year-old.

"I'm okay. Mom got me this." He shoved something toward Stacey who looked at it.

"Looks cool," Stacey said, even though she didn't know what she was looking at.

"I'm gonna go show Alex," he said, and ran inside the house.

In the foyer, Allison explained, "It's a tablet that comes with games. That way he doesn't break Jacob's again. It's sturdier too, since he tends to throw them around."

Stacey recalled last Christmas when Vinny, in a burst of excited energy, accidentally knocked her cell phone off the counter and shattered the screen. Allison's son was like a hurricane in human form. He would sweep into rooms full of energy and didn't seem to ever run out. He was more like Allison than Jacob, although sometimes he would get very serious about things.

"Well, hopefully the house remains unscathed," Stacey remarked as they took off their coats.

Jacob lifted up a bag he was holding. "Gifts. Just put them under the tree?"

"Yeah, please. You guys want anything to drink?"

"Coffee," they said in unison.

As Jacob went over to the large Christmas tree and began to put their gifts under it, Allison looked around. Alex was greeting Jacob, talking to him excitedly about computers or something that Stacey didn't understand.

"Kid is going to be a tech whiz," Allison remarked.

"He's already too smart for his own good," Stacey joked as they went into the kitchen.

"Maybe Vinny and Alex can team up. Create a brand new business or something. Imagine that."

"Seems a long time away."

"Maybe. But they're already growing up so fast. Before you know it, Jessica is going to be a teenager, driving you crazy."

"That's if I survive Alex. For some reason, I think he's going to be a handful. Not as much as Vinny though. Pretty amazing, your child is basically just like you. What goes around comes around."

"I was never that bad," Allison protested. "You just didn't like what I was doing. That's all."

"Yeah, yeah," Stacey began pouring her sister a cup of coffee. "So, you have a good trip?"

"Mostly, but it was just Jacob working on the expansion. I tried to keep Vinny in line and not have him cause an international incident."

"How did that go?"

"Couple of close calls but I think we made it through all right." She smiled.

"Things have been pretty quiet here."

"As quiet as things can be with Charlie. I saw his article in that magazine last month. I don't even remember the name of it. That fancy business one. Pretty impressive."

Stacey looked over at Charlie, who was now in the living room with Jacob and the kids. Vinny was showing Alex his new tablet. Jessica hovered behind Charlie and Jacob as if the business conversation they were having made complete and utter sense to her.

"Well, Charlie gets bored if he isn't working on new projects."

"Sort of like you."

Stacey shrugged, "Maybe a little."

"Come on, you're selling yourself short again –"

There was a sudden thud of something dropping, followed by Vinny saying, "Oops."

Stacey and Allison grabbed their coffees and went out to the living room. Vinny had knocked over a small statue that they brought back from China a couple years ago. Luckily, it wasn't broken. Stacey bent over and picked it up as her sister lectured her son.

"Sorry, I was showing Alex the photo mode on the tablet," Vinny replied.

"Just be more careful. I swear, you're all flying limbs," Allison said.

"Dad said he was like that when he was little," Vinny protested.

"Were you really?" Stacey asked, surprised. "I can't picture that."

Jacob looked sheepish. In the years he had been with Allison, the long endless conversations had faded as he became comfortable with silence. The nervous, social anxiety that had once compelled him to fill every moment with stories about himself had slowly tapered off, due to Allison's touch.

Even with the changes that had happened over the last few years, trying to imagine Jacob as a clumsy lanky ball of energy took everyone in the room by surprise.

"Always finding out something new," Allison finally said.

"I grew too fast. Had a hard time controlling my limbs," Jacob remarked primly.

"Does this mean I can't control my limbs?" Vinny inquired.

"You can control your limbs just fine," Alex chimed up. "Just look around once in a while."

Vinny looked as if he was thinking about this when Stacey's son turned to her and asked, "When is Uncle Eric getting here?"

"Soon. We won't open gifts until he gets here."

"I hope he likes what I got him."

"I'm sure he will."

He nodded and flopped onto the couch next to Jessica, who was holding onto her doll and making it talk in a high-pitched voice. Jacob turned back to Charlie, picking up where their conversation had left off. Allison glanced over at Stacey.

"Today is going to be a tiring day."

"Holidays always are."

"Worse for you. I've seen how Alex gets when Eric is around."

Stacey smothered a groan and shook her head. "He idolizes him though. At least he's not the same Eric he was when I met him. And I know Eric loves him too. We couldn't ask for a better uncle for our kids."

"Been a while since you saw him, right?"

"Three years," Stacey replied.

"And what has he been doing? Writing or something?"

She nodded. "Yup. Traveling the world and writing about it. I still can't imagine him writing. But he sort of floated around for those five years and then started putting everything to paper, remember?"

"Can't imagine Eric writing anything that people could relate to."

"It's been a long time since you saw him, though." Stacey pointed out.

It was true. The last time Eric came down to visit, Allison had been in Asia with Jacob. It had been easily about four or five years since her sister had seen Eric. She was still picturing the mess of a man that he was while everything unfolded with Terry. That was a far cry from who he was now.

Alex turned around on the couch, "When is he gonna get here?"

"Soon. Snow delays everything. Just be patient."

"Be patient," Jessica repeated next to him.

Alex rolled his eyes at his younger sister. Sensing a possible fight, Stacey clapped her hands together, "Let's get breakfast started. Who wants to help?"

Jessica hopped to her feet and hurried over. Stacey grabbed her hand. She knew Alex wasn't going to want to help with breakfast.

Allison, Jessica and Stacey got to work in the kitchen. As Stacey looked around at everyone, she felt happiness wash over her. It was nice having everyone home for the holidays.

"I want another chocolate Santa!" Vinny pleaded with Allison later on that day.

"No way. No more sugar. You're cut off."

Changing tactics, he turned to look at Jacob. "Dad, I want a chocolate Santa. Come on."

"You heard your mother. Let it go, Vinny."

Vinny pouted and plopped down on the couch, crossing his arms. He looked away from his parents.

Allison whispered, "He'll be asleep in moments."

Stacey stifled a laugh. There was a knock on the door. Before she could even move, Alex took off like an arrow, running toward the door. Stacey trailed after him. She could hear him exclaim in excitement and then heard the low timber of Eric's voice.

She paused in the foyer. Eric stood there, talking to Alex, who was beaming up at him. He was bouncing on the balls of his feet, telling Eric about some computer program. Eric caught sight of Stacey and looked up at her.

In the three years since she had seen Charlie's brother, he looked mostly unchanged. Eric had always looked older than he really was. Ten years ago, Stacey thought that had been a detriment. Now, however, he appeared to be almost frozen in time.

"New tattoo," she remarked.

His hand went to his neck where she could just make out the top of a tattoo. Alex was bobbing around at his feet.

"A new tattoo? Cool! Dad said I can't get any tattoos until I'm an adult. But I'm gonna get one like yours, Uncle Eric."

Eric put his hands gently on Alex's shoulders, steering him away from the front door. "Well, don't tell your dad that, okay? But you *can* go tell him that I'm here though?"

Alex nodded and took off again. Eric took off his jacket and hung it up. He turned to look at Stacey.

"You look good."

"Thanks. You look the same."

"You mean devilishly handsome? Thanks sis!" He gestured to his face as he took a step toward her.

"Well, you look good. Healthy, at least. Must be from all that traveling."

"Yeah, I've gotten in shape from all that climbing around. Although, I was just in Mexico. Didn't do anything there besides just sit by the beach."

"You as a writer. Who would have thought that would ever happen?" Stacey asked.

"Not me. Books have been selling well though. They want me to go on a book tour for my next one but…" He shrugged.

"You don't want to?"

"I don't know. Nervous, I guess. Seems weird to be surrounded by people wanting to talk about my books. Not used to the idea yet."

"Well, don't worry about it for today. Come on." She gestured for him to come into the living room.

Eric hesitated and asked, "Anyone here smoke?"

Puzzled, she replied, "No. Allison and Jacob are here. That's it. Why?"

He cleared his throat. "I quit three years ago but I still get really antsy around anyone who does."

Stacey's eyes widened and she said in disbelief, "You quit?"

"Don't get excited. You know I've tried it before."

That was true. Eric struggled on and off with quitting smoking. Sometimes he'd go months without touching one only to cave one night at a social event. He said he wanted to quit so he could be around as an uncle. Even so, it hadn't been easy. For him not to have a cigarette in three years was a Christmas miracle unto itself.

"Yeah, but three whole years! That's your longest time yet."

"Well, don't make a big deal out of it, alright? I still don't feel like it's going to stick."

"No one smokes here. Smoke free zone. Come on and say hi to Charlie."

The living room was empty. Jacob, Charlie and the children were in the family room at the back of the house. Allison stuck her head out of the kitchen.

"Eric. Great, you're here. I need you."

"Wow, wasn't expecting that turn of events. I know you haven't seen me in a while but…"

Allison rolled her eyes, "I can't open this jar, idiot."

Eric went into the kitchen to help her. The jar lid popped off and he opened the fridge.

"Don't bother. No Bloody Mary mix," Stacey casually warned.

"What? Seriously? Come on."

"We had a snow storm come through, in case you didn't notice. You're lucky that you're here at all," Stacey remarked.

"Man, what a let-down. Here I am for the entire week and I can't have a Bloody Mary."

"If you want some so badly, then you can go out into this weather and get some."

"Better not. Your son would want to go with me and I would probably lose him or something in the snow," Eric replied before turning to look at Allison. "Everything well with you?"

"Yeah, thanks. Just trying to keep Vinny under control."

Eric grabbed an energy drink out from the back of the fridge. Stacey couldn't recall ever buying any of those things. He always managed to find the weirdest stuff in their fridge.

Cracking it open, he said to Allison, "Can't believe you two are still married." When Allison glared at him, he added quickly, "Because you two were so different at the start of everything. And Jacob was so dull."

"He isn't anymore. He just needed support and some understanding," Allison replied. "And we love each other now. It just took time."

Eric shrugged. "Who am I to judge? I don't have any sort of family life going on."

"Can't imagine why," Allison quipped as she left the kitchen.

Stacey looked at him. "Still great at annoying people, I see."

"Come on, everyone thought they'd be divorced by now. But they've been together longer than most marriages these days. Besides you and Charlie, of course."

"Well, they're happy together. Like Allison said, just took some time. But things worked out. What about you, anyway? No girlfriend or anything?"

"Nah. I mean, there's been lots of women, don't get me wrong. But I'm not interested in settling down."

"Always going to be a bachelor?"

"Most likely."

"What's going on in here?"

Stacey turned around to see Charlie walking into the kitchen with a grin on his face. He went over to his brother and brought him in for a hug. Even now, after all these years, it was still such a strange sight to see the two of them hugging one another.

"Nothing much. Telling Stacey here that I don't have any girlfriends."

"I think everyone has given up on you getting married," Charlie replied.

Eric shrugged. "Ah, well… what can I say? They like you because they think you're a starving artist. Or they like you because they figured out you have a bunch of money."

"Not everyone is like that," Charlie replied.

"Well, for the time being…" He trailed off as if he didn't know what else to say.

Sensing the subject coming to a close, Stacey spoke up, "Eric hasn't smoked in three years."

"No shit. Are you serious?"

"It's not a big deal, come on. I wanna hear what you've been up to. Besides what you've told me, I mean, in short phone calls. You've been busy since Dad died."

Terry had died of cancer four years ago. The death left Charlie and Eric with mixed feelings. Stacey couldn't blame them. After Charlie merged his new company with his father's, Terry still sprung up once in a while to be a thorn in his side. He never completely gave either of his sons the respect they deserved.

The death plunged Eric into a deep depression, causing him to go to Africa for a full year before coming back to see them. He later said that it was because he still felt as if he never lived up to what his father wanted or fully forgave him for what he put him through.

Charlie handled his father's death by throwing himself into work. He worked on expanding the company worldwide in the years after Terry died. The construction company was booming. Not to mention he had his investment company on the side. Recently, he was debating getting involved in media as well.

When Eric said that Charlie was keeping busy, it wasn't an exaggeration. Everything that Charlie had held off doing because of Terry came into full focus after his death.

Stacey brought Terry up a few times. He was always kind to their children, although Charlie had him on a tight leash. Even so, there was never any sort of forgiveness on either side.

Stacey was sometimes concerned the brothers had issues stemming from Terry that they never came to terms with while he was alive. But when she said as much to Charlie, he brushed her off.

"Eric is grieving in his own way. So am I," he said and hadn't brought up his father since.

"Busy, yes. But things are starting to settle down now. I was thinking about traveling a little. I think the kids should see more of the world."

"What about you? You want to travel?" This was directed at Stacey.

She knew what Eric was asking – could she leave to go travel? The real estate company that she had started with William had turned into a success. He had opened a few more branches across the country, with Stacey firmly entrenched as his 'right-hand.' Brad still worked there as well, although Amanda had quit once the two of them broke up. She went back to school full-time and became a history teacher.

"William has been bothering me to take a vacation for a while now. He wouldn't have a problem with it. I wouldn't mind taking a break either."

"Working and taking care of two kids. I don't know how the both of you do it. I get exhausted after hiking. Imaging hiking and then taking care of some kid on top of it."

"That's why you're the favorite uncle. You appear with all the cool stuff now and then and Alex and Jessica love you for it."

"Speaking of Alex, I should find him before he freaks," Eric said and headed toward the family room.

The two of them watched him leave and Stacey turned to look at Charlie. "So?"

"So, what?"

"You gonna ask him?"

"I don't know. I don't think he wants to take control of any branch office overseas. I know we thought maybe he would but seeing him now…"

"Yeah, I agree with you. I think he likes what he's doing. But I still think you should ask."

"Why?" Charlie looked puzzled.

"It'd be a good gesture. I think he'd like it. A formal invitation to work for you – ten years ago he never would have thought that would happen."

Charlie ran his fingers through his hair and watched as Eric was stalked over to Alex who began to show him something on his tablet.

"I'd like him to be around more."

"Never thought I'd hear you say that," Stacey said.

"Me neither," Charlie admitted. "But it's true. Sometimes I wish he would stay here a little longer."

"Well, we have the whole week with him. Think about asking him to stay for longer then."

She could tell Charlie was thinking about it. She grabbed some snacks and headed off toward the rest of the family.

Later that night, once Jessica and Alex were safely in bed, they sat around the fireplace in the living room. Allison and Jacob left after Vinny fell asleep in his father's lap.

Eric was staring at the fire, holding a glass of whiskey as Stacey cleaned up some wrapping paper that was scattered around. Charlie was also drinking.

"Nah," Eric was saying. "I don't want to be in charge of an office. But the offer is appreciated. Thank you for thinking of me."

Stacey wasn't surprised. Eric had seemed against any kind of office job ever since Terry told him off that night.

Charlie, however, still looked a little crestfallen. "Well, I think you'd be perfect for it."

"Probably," he replied, cocky as ever, "but it just isn't my thing."

Charlie glanced at Stacey who nodded at him to keep going. He looked vulnerable, which was an expression she rarely saw on him.

"What could I do to convince you to stay around longer?"

Eric looked taken aback by this and blinked. "Stay around where? Here? The city?"

"That's right."

"Why would I stick around here?"

Charlie seemed to falter again. In the progress they had made over the years, coming right out and saying he wanted to spend more time around his own brother felt to be the biggest task yet.

He cleared his throat. "I think it'd be good for Alex if you were around. He's taken to you. Jessica likes you too. And with Terry gone, we don't have a lot of family left. I think it'd be good for the kids to be around their uncle."

Eric took a sip from his glass and glanced at Stacey. "What about you?"

"What?"

"You think I should be around your kids more?"

"They do really like you… for some reason," Stacey teased.

He looked back at Charlie and then grinned. It was the same grin from all those years ago when he knew he had someone where he wanted them.

"You miss me, huh, bro?"

Charlie groaned.

But Eric didn't stop. "You do! You really do. You miss your little brother. I don't blame you. I've been traveling the world a long time now, making my own way. No one has been around to drive you crazy like me. I'm flattered, really."

"Come on, would you stop?" Charlie protested but he was smiling.

"I suppose I could work on my next book here in the city. Might help me focus. Or completely ruin my focus in which I will then blame you."

"Fine, blame me. But you'll stay?"

Eric leaned back in the couch. "Yeah. I'll stay."

A smile broke out across Charlie's face and Stacey felt a warmth spread out across her body. Never, in a thousand years, did she ever think that this could have happened. The mere idea of Charlie asking Eric to stick around for longer felt like something conjured up in a dream.

But it was reality. The brothers, torn asunder by whatever hold Terry had over them, were finally and completely reconciled again. Stacey had her husband and her two wonderful children. She had a job that she loved and family and friends she adored.

Standing behind them, she watched as Eric flipped on the TV. The two began to instantly bicker about what to watch. Eric wanted to watch sports. Charlie wanted to watch a movie.

She glanced out the window. It felt like a lifetime ago when Charlie announced Terry was allowing the company merger. It was the book end of a whirlwind year.

Who would have thought that so much could have happened so quickly? Looking back at it now, Stacey had very few regrets. She knew that somewhere, Tina was looking down at her and smiling.

Everything was finally just right.

-The End-

If you enjoyed this series, I would appreciate your leaving a review of the book. Good reviews encourage an author to write as well as help books to sell. Good reviews can be just a few short sentences describing what you liked about the book without having a spoiler. If you could spend 30 seconds writing a review, I would appreciate it: you can review this title right now at your favorite retailer.

Here is a preview of **another story** you may enjoy:

Love Deceived: Tenacious Billionaire BWWM Romance Series, Book 1

"**I LIKE** your buns." The customer's voice was creamy, with a hint of spice. "How much are they?"

"Excuse me?" Adalia glanced up from behind the cash register and glared at the man.

"Your buns," he answered, flashing a naughty grin at her.

Heat erupted in her core.

It was him. The guy. He came in every day in that Prada suit, no suitcase, and flaunted his perfect jawline and wavy blond hair. Adalia's stomach did a turn, but she steadied herself mentally.

Come on, it's just a customer. Same as any other in the bakery.

"Can I help you with something?" She asked the same question each day when he came in. Then it would begin.

"That depends." The gorgeous man strolled over and rested his elbows on the glass of the counter that displayed treats and sweets.

"On what, exactly? It's pretty simple," she answered. "Either you want the buns or you don't."

"Oh," he replied, interlocking his fingers and resting his chin on them. "I want the buns. You can count on that." He reached out and brushed her forearm with the tips of his fingers. Sparks danced across her ebony skin.

Adalia cleared her throat gently, but didn't move away. It was the first time he'd touched her, and she'd honestly fantasized about the moment for weeks.

"Which buns would you like?" She breathed the words, and he leaned in close enough that she caught a whiff of his cologne. It was a masculine, woody scent and it suited him perfectly.

Warning alarms went off in her head – this guy was clearly a player, well put together, with that easy charm – but they were drowned out by her attraction to him.

"Yours," he uttered, "every day, for the next month. Every night, too."

Adalia narrowed her chocolate brown eyes at him. She'd given up trusting anyone a long time ago, let alone suave white strangers with a clear desire for more than a carb fix.

"I wouldn't advise you eat that many carbs. And you've yet to specify which type of buns you'd like, sir." She gave a sweet smile she didn't feel in her gut.

Why couldn't she shake her attraction to this guy? She'd just gotten out of a relationship with DeShawn, just started the healing process. She had to focus on getting the bakery on track, not on some sexy dude with a fetish for curvy women.

God, wouldn't it be nice if he had a fetish for – No!

He studied her expression with a grin that made her insides go melty like tempered chocolate.

"I think you know which buns I want."

"Cinnamon," she answered, reaching over for a brown paper bag beneath the glass fronted cabinet. In the back, one of her bakers slammed a tray in the oven and cursed.

Irritation flickered through her – they never treated those ovens with respect – but she kept a straight face.

"No, no," he answered, then grasped her wrist again, and heat waves assaulted her. "I'm in the mood for chocolate today."

She stared him dead in the eye, willing the arousal to back the hell down. "Smooth," she said wryly.

"Excuse me, miss. I'd like to pay?" said a hunched over granny, clasping a box of éclairs.

"Sorry, ma'am," Adalia replied, sparing a frown for the handsome businessman. He winked a blue eye at her and she swallowed hard. "That will be five dollars."

"Five dollars," the lady answered, squinting a little and stretching to pat her curlers. Adalia glanced at 'Handsome Guy' again. He hadn't looked away, and their gazes were glued for a moment. "I'll tell you, it's a pity these éclairs are so good, dearie. You're going to have me on the streets at this rate."

"I'm glad you like them," Adalia replied. That was the plain truth: with the bills piling up, every happy customer helped pave the pathway to financial success. Losing her lifelong dream wasn't an option. "Can I get you anything else?"

"Oh no, dear. Perhaps the recipe so I can make these for myself at home." The old woman's wrinkled façade split into a friendly smile. "No, I'm joking, of course. I quite enjoy the trip into the city for these treasures." She lifted one from the bag and took a bite. Cream squished out the sides and smeared onto her cheek.

"I'll get you a napkin." Adalia fumbled for them beside the register, but Handsome Guy was already on it.

He swept out a handkerchief and handed it to the customer with a courteous bob of his head.

"Thank you," the lady breathed, accepting it with a flutter of her eyelids. "My, what a dashing young fellow. You certainly are a lucky woman." She directed that at Adalia.

"What? He's not my –"

"Not as lucky as I am," he put in, and gestured for the customer to keep the soft square of linen. She thanked him and shuffled out with a cheery wave, pink slippers slapping on the linoleum.

Adalia had given the bakery a fifties' style look. She'd loved the idea of a parlor where customers could sit and have a milkshake while they ate their baked goods. So far, the idea hadn't taken off.

The booths and chairs were empty. A pang of regret stabbed at her stomach, and she wiped down her flowered apron with a grimace.

"I'll get those chocolate buns for you," she said to the businessman, but the stare he gave her made her stop dead in her tracks. "What is it? You don't want them anymore?"

"I do, but I'd prefer it if you had a few with me. Do you make coffee here?"

"We do," she said, "but I've got way too much to do to take a break."

"I wasn't asking."

"Look, I don't even know your name. What makes you think you can come in here, flirt with me and make a fool out of me in front of my customers?" Adalia allowed anger to gutter through her and override the desperate need to reach out and spank that cute butt. "Now, if you want buns, I'll give you buns, but I'm going to have to ask you to leave."

"I assume you don't normally treat your customers this way." He glanced left and right, searching the empty storefront with mock intrigue.

If you enjoyed this sample then look for **Love Deceived: Tenacious Billionaire BWWM Romance Series, Book 1**.

Here is a preview of **another story** you may enjoy:

DEIRDRE CLARKE stepped out of her apartment into the hot Los Angeles sun; dusk had fallen, but the temperature still sat near 100 degrees. Deirdre was already running late for her gig, so the sight of her ex-boyfriend Carl standing by her car irritated her even more than usual. She stomped down the single flight of stairs and greeted him with hostility.

"I'm late. What the hell do you want?" Deirdre demanded.

"Can't a man just stop by to see his best girl?" Carl smiled. His green eyes complimented his mocha skin and for a moment Deirdre forgot why she'd put up with his shit for so long. Then she remembered why she'd stopped.

"I guess you'd better go see her then," she said roughly. "And let me be on my way."

"Dee… you know I'm talking about you."

"I'm not your girl no more," she answered, "and I've got somewhere to be."

"Don't be mad, Dee I just came here to check on you… you alright? What about D'Angelo? You two need anything? You got rent covered?"

Deirdre's blood boiled and she met his eyes with a defiant stare. "I don't need a damn thing from you. D'Angelo and I are not your business anymore." Deirdre had been responsible for her younger brother since their mother had gone to prison. D'Angelo was one of the reasons she'd known she had to get away from Carl in the first place. The last thing she wanted was for her brother to see her thug ex-boyfriend as a role model.

"When are you going to understand that you can't buy your way back here?" She glared at him.

"Deirdre, we were together almost our whole lives. I love you. But I'm not trying to buy my way back. I have a business proposition for you."

"I don't need a job, I have two," she snapped, trying to open her car door. Carl blocked her way.

"Its easy money Dee… you wouldn't even know it was here."

"Ah, I see. You think I'll hide drugs or hot shit for you, after all of the hell you put me through? You think I'd take that risk for you and your 'boys'?" She snorted back at him.

"It's just herb, Dee… it's practically legal. And I don't know why you're so pissed at me. Nothing that went down was my FAULT!"

"Our windows were SHOT OUT, Carl. You can stand there all you want and claim it was a random drive-by, swear it wasn't personal, but I'm not a moron! You think I didn't know you'd fallen in with Derrick and his thugs? You think I believed your lies about where all the money was coming from? I KNEW what you were doing, and you just denied, denied, denied. Until our home was shot up... with my brother inside. Take your shit and get out of my face." Deirdre shoved him out of the way of her car and escaped inside. She checked her face in the rearview mirror, and then prayed she'd have time to fix her make-up before she had to go onstage.

She stood on stage, in her element. As Lou played along on the black grand piano, Deirdre let all of her emotions flow out to the music. The small crowd gave her their undivided attention as she belted out Trouble, Stormy Weather, and Summertime. Her white, full length gown stood in stark contrast to the milk-chocolate color of her skin.

Deirdre couldn't remember a time when she didn't love to sing. When she was still a young girl, before her father left, her family went to church every Sunday. She loved listening to the soloists in the choir and dreamed of one day standing next to them. But they'd stopped going to church once her father was gone. When D'Angelo was born, Deirdre had tried to get her mother to go back, but she'd refused; D'Angelo's father was against the idea. But soon, he was gone too. Looking back, Deirdre was sure that was when her mother started using drugs, though she didn't realize what was happening at the time. Three years ago, right after Deirdre graduated from high-school, Pauline Clarke had been busted and sentenced to twenty years in a federal prison. Deirdre became D'Angelo's legal guardian, though in all honesty she'd raised him since he was born.

D'Angelo was a good kid, especially considering everything he'd been through. And he was the reason Deirdre hadn't fallen into the same kind of traps the other girls in her neighborhood had found themselves in. She hadn't had any kids, she hadn't gotten messed up on drugs, and she didn't take her clothes off for money. Instead, Deirdre worked as a hotel maid and took college courses online. She'd have loved to go to school on an actual campus, but she couldn't afford childcare for D'Angelo and she refused to turn him into a latchkey kid at eight years old. Deirdre worked while he was at school, and then after dinner they did their homework together.

Thursday nights were different. Those nights were all for Deirdre. She had a standing gig at Fuseli's, an upscale jazz club in the Hollywood foothills. The gig paid just enough for Deirdre to afford her stage-clothes, but she didn't do it for the money.

When she finished her last set, Deirdre took a seat at the bar and ordered herself a beer and a sandwich. As the bartender walked towards the tap, a tall, broad stranger signaled his attention. When he returned to Deirdre, he carried a martini with her draft.

"Dee, a kind gentleman asked me to bring you this and wondered if you'd mind some company?"

Deirdre looked up at Steve and sighed. After her encounter with Carl, she was in no mood to put up with anyone's advances. "Tell him thank you, but I can't possibly accept."

"I don't know… this one's pretty hot, Dee… he's the one down there, in the suit."

"Really Steve, I'm not up for it right now."

"Alright, fine…" he answered in a disapproving, sing-song voice.

Deirdre thought the issue was dealt with as she watched Steve approach the end of the bar to deliver the message. The gorgeous blonde man took the martini, rose, and headed Deirdre's way.

"I'm sorry," she began as he approached, frustrated that he wouldn't take a hint.

"No, I'm sorry." He smiled. "Your friend told me you've had a bad day. You sang beautifully… I sent this as a token of my appreciation, nothing more," he explained, raising the drink. "Why don't you enjoy it? It might make you feel better. Or I could buy you something else, if you'd prefer? Right before I return to my seat, of course."

If you enjoyed this sample then look for **Love Disrupted - Ardent Billionaire Romance Series, Book 1**.

Here is a preview of **another story** you may enjoy:

Love Anew: Lonely Billionaire Romance Series, Book 1

TRICIA REACHED for another blanket. "Are you cold?" she asked.

Rebecca's breath was raspy as she responded. As her lungs shut down due to ALS, or Amyotrophic Lateral Sclerosis, her ability to speak had started to decline. Muscle by muscle, ALS targeted the body and made it impossible for the individual to live a normal life. It had started a few years ago with Rebecca's legs. Now, her lung muscles were starting to freeze as well. Tricia winced as she thought about the future. If Rebecca chose to use machines to stay alive, her entire body would eventually stop working. At some point, her mind would remain functioning and she would be locked into her body.

Rebecca managed to squeeze out a feeble yes. Reaching over to the cupboard, Tricia removed a blanket and carefully tucked her in. Tricia had spent years training to be a nurse and really liked her job. Since she was an excellent nurse, she had caught the eye of the billionaire, John, at one of the couple's many trips to hospitals around the country. He had noticed the love and care she took with each patient. After a moment's hesitation, Tricia had allowed him to convince her to take care of his wife.

Pictures of Rebecca dotted the room. Since she was unable to leave, John had striven to make her room look like favorite memories of her life and activities. A young, healthy Rebecca smiled in each photo. In the few years she had been physically active, she had acquired awards for horseback riding, cooking and other projects. Now, though, this time of physical fitness had passed. Instead of dashing through the fields on her favorite horse, Rebecca spent her time in this room. She had taken her difficulties in stride and was truly brave in the face of all of these medical issues.

Finishing with the blanket, Rebecca started to say something. Leaning closer to hear her, Tricia finally pulled up a chair. "What do you need, Rebecca?" she queried.

Sighing, Rebecca whispered, "I need to talk to John. I have to tell him how I want to die."

Squeezing her hand, Tricia nodded. "Once I leave your room, I will go get him. Just in case he is not around, did you want me to give him a message?"

Rebecca tried to nod, but her head did not respond all the way. "Yes, I do. You need to tell him that I do not want any machines. He could keep me alive forever with a breathing tube, but I do not want to live a life where I am permanently locked into my body. And," she paused and struggled to take another breath. "I do not want him to stop enjoying life or waiting around for my eventual death. If God wants to take my soul now, we should not interfere."

Tricia nodded sadly. Most patients with ALS were more afraid of being stuck within their minds than actual death. She understood, but she could not imagine what life would be like without Rebecca's gentle soul. "I will tell him," she said.

Leaving the room, Tricia traversed the hallways of the mansion. John had built his fortune by buying and selling real estate properties. His initial money had arrived through an early investment in the dot com boom before the bubble burst. After seeing the dangers of the stock market, he had started to just buy and rent out properties. Even with the recent recession, he still made a profit. Instead of selling his properties or developing, he had continued to rent them out. In a decade or two, he had talked of selling and retiring. His plans had arrived before his wife had been diagnosed with ALS. Unwilling to speak of his life after her future death, Tricia had not asked about any change in his future plans.

The halls of the house were dotted with white oak doorways that led to a myriad of rooms. Plush white carpet softly surrounded Tricia's feet as she walked. She dreaded the conversation that was about to happen. Every day, she updated John about the status of his wife. Unfortunately, she seldom had good news to share. She nodded to John's secretary as she entered the office. Unlike most rich men, he used a male secretary. Before talking had become so difficult, Rebecca had explained that he tried to hire primarily males so that Rebecca would never worry about his fidelity. Since Tricia was intended to cater just to his wife, she had been allowed to work there despite her gender.

If you enjoyed this sample then look for **Love Anew: Lonely Billionaire Romance Series, Book 1**.

Here is a preview of **another story** you may enjoy:

"I WANT to know who the hell is responsible for this mess!" boomed Hendrick from the front of the boardroom.

Silence filled the room as all the top people in the company stared at Hendrick in awe. They knew he wasn't the kind of guy to be messed with. Considering the company had just been charged with federal and criminal charges for dumping industrial waste into the Arctic Ocean, they knew it was best to stay silent.

"I return from vacation to find the prosecutor in my office to tell me that a company that I built from the ground up to help humanity is being accused of filling the ocean with waste! Waste??" He screamed across the table, his face turning an angry red. Hendrick stopped for a moment to compose himself and looked at each person at the table, assessing their worth.

"Pray it was not one of you frontrunners that made the decision to handle the waste of the company in this manner. Now go, and I expect reports hourly about how we are making this right and where waste should be going from now on."

Everyone got up from the table quickly and filtered out of the room. Hendrick watched them all leave and turned to his right-hand man, Geoffrey, the CEO of the company.

"Tell me you didn't know."

A broad-shouldered man, Geoffrey held an imposing frame that fit well with the red beard that

made him appear like a Viking. He was incredibly loyal
and a great asset to the company.

"You have known me your whole life Hendrick, I'm
sure you know I had nothing to do with dumping waste
into the ocean. The person in charge of a decision like
that is one of your minions."

"How is it that the owner and CEO of a company
had no idea that his own company has been poisoning
the ocean?"

"Someone down the line obviously felt it would
save the company a lot of money."

Hendrick snorted, "Ya and no one would ever find
out that the Arctic Ocean was suddenly polluted? My
god they have vessel numbers and everything, it was
our guys to be sure, so how do I not know about it?"

"The prosecutors are doing their investigation and
so are we. I can guarantee that we will find out who is
responsible before anyone else does."

"I'm being prosecuted, Geoffrey! They think I knew
about this madness."

"Look you didn't know and they can't prove that you
did. You will have your day in court and they will
simply have to let it go. They can't pull evidence from
thin air so you're safe."

Hendrick went to the side table by the grand picture
window. He poured them both a glass of bourbon,
handing one to Geoffrey.

"I built this company because I believed in a vision and now our reputation is being smeared. All the while I'm off doing fundraisers and charity events while some asshole is destroying the ocean under my name."

If you enjoyed this sample then look for **Suspicion: Elusive Billionaire Romance Series, Book 1**.

Other Books by Shyla Starr

- Tenacious Billionaire BWWM Romance Series

- Elusive Billionaire Romance Series

- Lonely Billionaire Romance Series

- Ardent Billionaire Romance Series

- Fervent Billionaire BWWM Romance Series

- Audacious Billionaire BWWM Romance Series

Get the latest update on new releases from the author at:

https://shylastarr.com/newsletter/

About the Author - Shyla Starr

Shyla currently specializes in writing interracial romance stories and is a huge fan of the alpha male. Simply put, there just aren't enough stories about mixed couple romances, which is something she is aiming to fix.

Being a bookworm all her life, when Shyla discovered men she also realized how easy it was to fulfill her fantasies through her writing.

When not writing and fantasizing about men, Shyla enjoys dancing, reading and chilling with her friends.

Connect with Shyla Starr

I really appreciate you reading my book! Here are my social media coordinates:

Friend me on Facebook:
https://www.facebook.com/shylastarrauthor

Follow me on Twitter: https://twitter.com/shylstarr

Check me out on Goodreads:
https://www.goodreads.com/author/show/8436084.Shyla_Starr

Subscribe to my newsletter:
https://shylastarr.com/newsletter/

Visit my website: https://shylastarr.com/